In The Wake

by Grace Finley

Printed in the United States of America

ISBN (Kindle) 978-1-953781-03-1 ISBN (Paperback) 978-1-953781-04-8 ISBN (Hardcover) 978-1-953781-05-5

Finley Books
Phoenix, AZ

www.FinleyBooks.com

This is a work of fiction. Names, characters, business, events and incidents, aside from one, are the products of the author's imagination. The incident based upon an actual event has been fictionalized, as it occurs to a fictional character. The perpetrator's first name was not changed, but [spoiler] he was not beaten to a pulp, as he deserved, and as depicted in this book.

FINLEY BOOKS

PHOENIX, ARIZONA

for sherry,
a steadfast beacon in the most turbulent of seas

1

everything went great right up to the explosion

No matter what Will had witnessed during the day, she was always there.

No matter if it was all he could do but drop onto his bunk, his skin still coated in dried sweat and dust, he could feel the weight of her hand on his arm.

No matter what smell haunted the lackluster accommodations that day--the unpleasant cafeteria smells, the stagnant musk of unwashed humans, a backed up lavatory--every night, he was able to clear away all other senses, close his eyes, and she was there, smiling at him with her suppressed, lopsided grin.

Maggie.

Well, Maggie to the world. Reeves to him. He started calling her by her last name just after they met. He had been an active, but rather mellow eight year old, and she was six, wise beyond her years in many ways, painfully isolated and naive in others.

He laid back on the table, pictured Maggie the very first time he met her— wearing a sky blue raglan top under overalls and worn out dinosaur high top Converse. Her feet looked comically large, like they grew faster than the rest of her. Her hair was pulled back in a tightly weaved braid, while her bangs draped in her eyes.

She was sketching by a window at the Boys & Girls Club. He and his brother attended the after school program briefly while their mom was out of state taking care of their grandpa, who would die from pancreatic cancer by summer.

Maggie had glanced over her shoulder, sensing them behind her. Before her was an extraordinary sketch of a dog with an oversized tongue hanging from his upturned mouth.

Evan had recognized her from his grade and wanted to move along, but Will found himself staring into her eyes. They initially appeared to be brown, but as she gazed back at him, he noticed while the inner ring was a deep brown, the outer ring transitioned to emerald. He didn't usually pay much attention to the color of a person's eyes, but he was absolutely captivated by the vividness--and the sorrow in them.

Fourteen years later, he found himself lying in a modular medical center building, his left arm singed, the flesh screaming. For all he could tell, he had no broken bones. His desert fatigues were frayed on his arms and legs, the ragged edges still seeming to smoke, and his exposed skin had been hastily sliced, slowly seeping blood. He stared at one particular wound. Something was wedged there, something white and jagged, and it was preventing much blood from escaping.

He closed his eyes and tried to picture her.

She didn't smile much when he first met her. Somehow, even then, he knew this was not due to her being a serious or dull person. He found out shortly after meeting her that her dad had been killed two months prior. He found out from Evan, who decided at that point to cut him some slack about hanging out with her. "Still. She seems so--*boring*," he had reasoned.

Will had grinned in silence. Maggie chose to say little in front of most people so it was probably a common misconception. There was, in fact, very little that was boring about her, even then. The best way he could describe it was she just thought differently than anyone else. Her mind wasn't as constricted and flat as others her age.

She was passionate about reading, and despite being younger, was reading far beyond his own ability. She loved fantasy/sci-fi books, understood scientific theories, and had a passion for being outdoors.

His eyes flew open as a medical assistant gave his shoulder a shake. She clutched her chest reflexively then held her now blood soaked hand out as though to tell him to stay put.

Will exhaled and closed his eyes again.

Maggie's long limbs contributed to a clumsiness she could never quite overcome as she grew up and he found it incredibly endearing. It was comical how she had adapted to it over the years. It didn't bother her. She didn't even acknowledge if she tripped on a level surface since it was such a regular occurence. She would catch her foot on a rug or miss an entire step, get herself upright, and move on.

His brother was also unaware at that point of her wry sense of humor. It wasn't always obvious when she was jesting since she had such a deadpan delivery, which made it even more entertaining. If Evan was being rude, she could reply coolly and he would inevitably end the conversation with a confused eyeroll, or a "whatever."

Evan came around when he was older. Will remembered the first time he saw him wrap his arm around her, tugging her in with brotherly affection. They were leaving a baseball game and exited onto a dark city street. There were some rowdy gang members zeroing in on her and Will was caught in the back of the group. Evan maneuvered quickly to her, talking conspiratorially, putting his body between her and the men. Even after they passed the group, Evan had remained at her side, laughing with her.

In the medical modular, Will coughed forcefully, but it sounded muffled to him. His ears were clogged by blood, debris, or both and filtered noise as though he were underwater. The right ear registered a high pitched squeal like it was trying to regulate the pressure.

The air was thick with the odor of dust, raw flesh and blood. He couldn't stop his brain from intertwining the image of Maggie and flashes of his dead friend, literally blown apart by a roadside IED.

Ben's fiancée was busy planning their outdoor wedding on his family's ranch. The reception was going to be in a barn. She was obsessing about bouquets of wildflowers in mason jars for the centerpieces, strings of globe lights in the rafters, chalkboard signs to label tables and food. These were not things Ben or Will cared about normally, but after finding Ben looking through photos and magazines she had sent, Will had joined him. They had paged through magazines together in the dimly lit quarters, deciding that baby's breath was a decidedly creepy name for a flower, that it was a nice gesture for both families to sit together, that there were, indeed, substantial differences between shades of white.

Suddenly the memories were connected--Maggie and her long mink-like eyelashes blinking up at him--Ben catching his eye one last time, in terror, just before his half of the vehicle blew off.

Reeves, he thought, squeezing his eyes shut, summoning her image to override his most recent memories.

She taught herself to play guitar sometime around junior high, having acquired her dad's Cordoba from her grandparents' house. He could picture her strumming softly on the guitar, singing in a sweet, soulful, sometimes off-key voice. He loved the wincing face she made when she was pitchy.

He remembered watching her tuck the guitar away behind a panel she had carved out in the wall of her closet so her mom wouldn't find it, explaining this nonchalantly. In the wall she stored any possessions she said were irreplaceable. This included her dad's Bible, a surfboard, a ukelele camp craft Will had made her the year prior.

As she got older and her voice deepened, she either stopped going off-key, or he stopped hearing it if she did. He loved hearing her sing, seeing her fingers strumming gently on the guitar. Her favorites were Elvis, occasionally something unconventional like "The Rainbow Connection," which her dad used to sing to her.

He didn't flinch as a mask was placed over his nose, forcing a cool and slightly metallic air into his nostrils.

He had a strange fondness for the memory of his first argument with Maggie. It was the first time he felt like he was able to teach her something, rather than the other way around. They were pre-teens and he had been an "arrogant asshole," as he had put it. She had accepted his apology, but had dismissively used the phrase "It's okay" and dropped eye contact.

Her reaction troubled him. He had been firm in correcting her that it was not actually okay at all, that he should not have done it, and would not, repeat, *not* be doing it again. She had re-established eye contact, nodded, recoiling a bit subconsciously at his firmness. "Honestly, it's like you've never been apologized to before," he had said, half-laughing at her passive behavior. All at once, he realized she probably hadn't.

She maintained a defensive, guarded stance. There was a flicker of uneasiness in her eyes.

He frowned. "Your feelings *matter*, Reeves."

She stood silently, letting his words sink in.

He started to step forward, but she shook her head. She took a deep breath then in one fluid motion, closed the distance and kissed him on the cheek, wrapping her arms around his neck.

He had thought of joking about being a jerk more often to give her practice at receiving apologies, but as she buried her face in his shoulder, he could hear her pulling in her breath, trying not to cry. Her back shook as she slowly released the sobs she couldn't contain. His heart ached. She was so well-versed in being okay for everyone else, he had overlooked how much pain she carried everyday. He was as certain as he'd ever been about anything in his life that he would do just about anything to protect her.

It was in that moment, as the weight of this responsibility hit him at the age of fourteen, that he realized he was in love with her.

His memory flashed forward and he pictured her in the bay window seat at the apartment he shared with his brother during college. She had a fondness for the spot--come to think of it, she always had a fondness for seats by windows-- on airplanes, in classrooms--whenever she was required to spend time indoors. She much preferred being outside--the ocean, preferably. The marina. Sitting on the deck of the boat gazing out over the water. *My God*, he thought. *She looked so at peace on that boat.*

It was then he noticed something cold on his hand. He didn't remember the IV being placed, but based on the wavering of his thoughts, whatever was dripping into his arm was beckoning him to sleep.

He laid his head back. *The window seat*, he thought. Maggie spent quite a bit of time with her nose crammed in science textbooks, classic literature and contemporary fiction while sitting in that bay window. For as long as he'd known her, she read everything she could get her hands on.

It was a warm evening. She sat in the seat, the Edison street lamp giving her dark brown hair a reddish hue. She leaned into the wall with one of his old, flat bed pillows folded behind her, smiling covertly into her copy of *The Martian*. Her hair was pulled on top of her head in a haphazard bun. Her perpetually bruised legs were folded toward her so the book rested in her knees and her toes wiggled periodically as she read. He had been watching her for a short time before he noticed that she was wearing a weathered gray NASA shirt over a borrowed pair of his plaid boxers. He remembered wondering if she had dressed for the occasion of reading a book about space exploration or if it had been a coincidence, perhaps the last clean t-shirt.

She blindly reached for her coffee mug, something his brother had given to her as a gift. "This probably isn't coffee" was written on the side in a loopy cursive. The gift was a result of her routinely asking why they had acquired so many coffee mugs, rather than getting actual glassware since neither of them actually drank coffee. Most were giveaway prizes—for credit cards, travel websites, radio stations, eBay.

She sipped the contents gingerly. Based on the soft clinking of ice, he suspected a rum and Coke. At the time of the memory he was seated at the small kitchen table they had found at a garage sale. All the chairs were mismatched and he sat in the only padded chair behind his laptop screen, fingers poised over the keyboard. Perhaps prompted by something in the book, she glanced out the window and examined the night sky. Something seemed deeply gratifying to her as she settled deeper into the pillow and focused back on her book.

"What is it?" he asked.

Her eyes darted from him to the window and back to the book. "You'll think I'm silly," her soft voice said.

"I have a fondness for your particular brand of silliness. You know that."

She smiled lightly and explained: "*Well* it's just that it's my favorite kind of moon."

He crouched down in his chair to get a better look. "What kind is it?"

He anticipated a scientific name and explanation, but instead, she placed the open book pages down against her stomach and stared up at the moon. "You see how the middle is dipped into a 'u'?"

He couldn't actually see the moon from where he sat, but he nodded anyway.

"*Well* it kind of looks like the wide smile of the Cheshire Cat from *Alice in Wonderland*. You can almost see his eyes and ears. It's like the moon is being playful." She shrugged casually and returned to her book, bringing the mug to her lips for an extended sip.

This was his favorite memory of her, for it seemed to most accurately represent many of the aspects of her personality that most people didn't get to experience. It amazed him that her childlike wonder, her joy for the little things remained intact. Given her mother's handling of undesirable behaviors and traits, he would have thought her innocence would have been shamed out of her.

A nurse appeared suddenly at his side and said something he couldn't hear over the ringing in his ears, gently placing her hand on his shoulder. She removed his mask and placed it aside. The odors of the ward eagerly attacked his senses again. Despite the competing smells in the medical center, he noticed she smelled like peppermint. "You're going to be OK," she repeated in a steady voice. "The doctor is working with someone else then he'll be over. Is the morphine helping?"

He thought he should answer, but his brain seemed to have forgotten how to send a signal to his mouth to speak.

She pressed her flat palm to his cheek. Her skin was either very warm or his cheek was very cold. It reminded him of when his mother would check for a fever when he was young. "Hang in there," she said, and stepped across toward the curtained off area that appeared to be serving as the surgical suite.

Will took the opportunity to call up some of the other suspended images of Maggie he drifted to at times while stationed out in the desert. One was through a fogged hotel shower door in London the previous summer. She loved her long showers. She had been in there for fifteen minutes when he went to check on her. Her eyes were closed as she let the water splash against her face and drape down her torso. Her long legs glistened. He caught the glimmer of a diamond on her hand as she lathered her hair with shampoo, having just accepted his marriage proposal the day before. There was something marvelous in that moment. He remembered standing at the bathroom door watching, nearly dumbstruck at his good fortune to be with her, to have her want to marry him.

He thought of the fine detail images—the crease between her eyebrows when she was working something out in her head. She got the same look when she was trying to solve some impossible mathematical equation. He would often comment about how he could practically see the hamster wheel turning. He thought of how her right leg jutted out from under the bed covers as she slept, the small freckle cluster on her shoulder he felt compelled to kiss every time it was exposed.

He kept seeing Maggie smiling at him.

He saw her looking at him from the passenger seat with her hand out the window of his old pickup as they drove along the coast, her hair wavy and blowing wildly.

He saw her side eye him when he wouldn't stop staring at her during a formal military ball. He couldn't remember what she wore except it was red and long and she had her hair wrapped around her head in a braided crown--and she looked radiant.

He remembered her sleeping through a sizable earthquake that the news wouldn't shut up about for days, morning sun illuminating her peaceful face.

He saw her sitting on the restaurant patio overlooking the ocean sunset, her cheeks red from a slight sunburn and the daiquiri she stole sips of during a lively conversation with Katie.

The nurse returned with the doctor and they explained about needing to sedate him to remove shards of bone from his skin. He didn't suspect the bone was his own.

They injected a chilly substance that made his body feel like it had been absorbed into the exam table. His eyelids felt suddenly weighted.

He thought of his first and only childhood dog, Sammy, a beautiful Golden Retriever, and the day they had to put him to sleep. Will wondered if this is how he felt. Surely that vet office, with its framed cartoons was a preferable last sight than the antiquated medical center where he found himself.

He began dreaming, still able to very clearly smell the unpleasant odors of the medical building as his eyes transported him away.

Maggie was walking through a market, dressed comfortably in cutoff jeans, a relaxed shirt and sandals, her hair in a messy ponytail. She grinned at him from behind aviator sunglasses, but her face turned serious. That's when he noticed that the market was in a country where she had no business being; the country where he found himself. A swarm of figures started yelling at her, corralling her forcibly into a corner. One attacker seized hold of her hair and forced her face into the ground. The rest descended upon her. Will tried to push his way through them, but he was continuously thrown backwards. He heard her cry out as her fate became clear. He heard her scream as the first stone struck her skin, like a baseball into a catcher's mitt. More stones. The glare of the sunlight blinded him momentarily as he continued to press forward, and in that moment, he heard a cracking--no, a crushing--and she no longer screamed.

When his vision returned, the market, the attackers, and Maggie were all gone.

He found himself in his childhood home watching television. It was the night a thirteen year old Maggie showed up at his doorstep, her face streaked with tears. His mom had answered and, with her eyes lowered, ever polite, Maggie had asked if he was home. Will stood and started down the hall toward the front door, hearing her voice. She had taken off for him, crashing into his chest. She hadn't wanted to share the details with his parents listening, but he had witnessed what went on in her house. He imagined her mom and stepdad were having one of their regular screaming matches. They liked to use her as a pseudo referee, hurling insults and sharing too many details as a means to shock her and shame the other person. When he pulled her into his room to talk, she didn't want to share. She had spared him details before, but this was different. He had asked if they had hurt her and she had hesitated to answer, finally shaking her head after he clarified that he meant physically. Her hands were trembling and her eyes were frantic. He had never seen her so afraid.

His parents had been at a loss as to how to handle the situation, but when it became obvious any intervention on their part would result in a confrontation with her mother, Maggie insisted on going home alone. She tried to be reassuring that she would just go to her room when she got there, seeming to regret involving Will or his parents, who asked repeatedly if she had been hurt, if she was in danger. Maggie shook her head, suddenly resolved, and had told them she felt much better. Will could remember tugging her close, whispering in her ear to keep her window unlocked.

He snuck out after going to bed early and went to her house. There he camped out in her room, tucked in the open closet door so he would be hidden if anyone came inside, but close enough to protect her if things got out of hand.

This same girl did spontaneous cartwheels at the beach, had a fierce tickle spot under her left ribcage, and routinely made the most grotesque expressions whenever he tried to take her photo.

She was the daisy pushing up through the rubble, defying all logic that anything could grow under such conditions, let alone such a cheery looking flower.

Suddenly, her heavily shadowed childhood bedroom disappeared.

In their place was a cemetery. The day was cool and breezy and the many small American flags twisted a bit in the wind. He had been there before, helping to place the flags with Maggie on military holidays, including her birthday, which happened to be the 4th of July. He walked down a row of slightly aged, but clean stones and surveyed the lush trees outlining the edge of the property. The view of the grave markers with the ocean and horizon behind was breathtaking and haunting. A baby cried suddenly just to the right of him and he found a young woman with long dark hair comforting the baby girl. They were sitting on a large blanket and the woman was singing softly into the baby's ear, rocking, and stroking her back in small circles. He moved around in front of the pair and was horrified, but not surprised to find the young woman was

Maggie. The baby girl, dressed in a red sweater and jeans was her spitting image--dark hair, large striking eyes. As she took a deep breath and settled into her mom's chest, the shadow of a dimple revealed itself in her cheek, a trait she would have inherited from him. He wondered her name as he watched her reluctantly drift to sleep. Despite successfully lulling the baby, the expression on Maggie's face was anything but relaxed. It looked like it had been days since she herself had slept.

She started whispering the same words over and over. It required substantial effort to hear over the flapping of the large flag nearby. "You did this. You did this to us." Over and over. "You did this. You did this to us."

Please stop, he thought, unable to speak. I'm sorry. I didn't want to hurt you.

Suddenly she was silent, staring right at him from her place on the blanket.

I didn't want to hurt you, he thought with forceful desperation.

"You sure didn't try to protect me."

2
...so it goes

"Mercer, they gave you a chance to go home and you didn't take it?"

"I've got two months left."

"Oh OK, Boy Scout." Rogers slapped Will on the shoulder, not realizing how sore it still was, and moved up toward the cockpit of the KC-135. He was a solid guy with a kind face.

Will was actually an Eagle Scout, but he decided not to correct him.

"You should come back to fly with us on Christmas. We can cook a full ham dinner in that little convection oven."

"I'll have to check your Yelp rating."

"You can try to get some sleep--you have the place to yourself. I don't know about you, but I find the loud engines lulling."

"Good attribute in a pilot."

Rogers knocked on the metal wall. "We keep blankets in the cargo nets under the seats."

Will nodded.

"Any plans for your leave? You have that pretty fiancée?" Rogers prepped a cup of coffee in the tiny makeshift kitchen. "Want a cup?"

"No thanks. Yeah she's meeting me there."

"Kelly, was it?"

"Maggie." *Reeves*, he said silently.

"Tall?"

"That she is."

"Kind of has a girl next door look?"

"That would be her."

"Nice. Well enjoy the honeymoon phase. After the I do's, it's all baby fever and *Dancing with the Stars*."

"That's good to know."

"Not to mention the sex is purely procreative."

"Don't you have a plane to fly?"

"Eh these planes practically fly themselves," he said, casually sipping his coffee.

"Really?"

"No. Actually they're pretty old and my co-pilot routinely crashes the sim. I should get back up there. I think our auto-pilot is straight out of *Airplane*."

Will nodded appreciatively. "Thanks for the lift."

Rogers did a partial bow in response. "If you need someone to talk to, look me up. We'll get a beer." He paused and surveyed him knowingly. "Well--" he said, switching gears. "We know you have no choice when you fly, we really appreciate you joining us today. Snack service is self-serve and P.S. all that's left is turkey jerky. Don't ask."

Will peered around the cargo area. The sides were lined with empty metal seats, which was better than full ones as he had little desire for chitchat, yet a distraction would have been helpful. He saw the nets underneath that Rogers had mentioned, thinking he should get some sleep. The base doctor had provided some sleeping pills, which had mercifully allowed him dreamless sleep, but they made him feel foggy during the day, which was honestly tough to decipher from his new normal. He pulled out his duffel and found his tablet. Maggie had loaded digital versions of books she thought he would enjoy and shows he could watch, but everything brought thoughts to mind that inevitably circled back to watching his friend get blown apart.

He was comforted by the thought of seeing Maggie in Ramstein--she had suggested they visit some towns known for their Christmas festivals if he was feeling up to it, but for all she knew his leave wasn't anything out of the ordinary, just last minute. He was bandaged, but he had already laid the groundwork that it was due to some mishap on base. He hated lying to her, but he didn't want to talk about the truth and it seemed selfish to burden her with reason to worry more than she already was. He'd tell her about Ben. Just not right away.

Now he regretted inviting her at all.

He was finding it more and more difficult to see an accurate picture of her. He kept seeing Maggie sitting among graves--grieving and furious with him. Abandoned.

He told himself he signed up for the military before they were together. She signed up for this life, with him being deployed. Somehow it didn't make him feel any better.

———

Maggie paced along the train platform, both to stay warm and to stay alert. She had never been able to sleep on airplanes. With the last minute packing, a full day at work, two flight connections, and a train ride from Frankfurt, she hadn't slept in 34 hours.

She considered going on to a hotel after Will was 30 minutes late and wasn't answering his phone. After an hour, she was so exhausted, she found herself falling asleep standing up. She had finally decided it was best to head to the hotel and had located the elevator when her phone rang.

It was once she was in the warm interior of a taxi that Will's story and his voice felt--off. The plane had been required to make an unscheduled refueling and needed to return to the base in Afghanistan. He'd hopefully be in the following day. The whole thing seemed plausible, but it was his rigid tone that bothered her. His voice always seemed to have a relaxed, easy way about it with her, but he couldn't mask the tension that night, repeatedly clearing his throat.

Exhaustion overtook her thoughts and she could think of nothing but somehow breezing through the check-in process and collapsing onto what she hoped was a very soft bed.

She awoke after the hotel stopped serving breakfast, drenched in sweat for she had literally collapsed in bed still wearing her down jacket and fleece-lined boots. With the curtains drawn, she could pretend it was a bit earlier in the day. She wasn't even entirely sure what day of the week it was.

She pulled off layers of clothes, dropping them over the side of the bed until she was down to her tank top and boy short panties. She savored the chill of the sheets against her skin as she properly tucked herself in, ignoring Katie's voice in her head, warning about bed bugs.

After a few minutes, she dove into her clothes pile and retrieved her cell phone. There was a photo from Katie of her swollen ankles and an update that there was still no baby. Nothing from Will.

She rubbed roughly at her eyes and her two day old contact lenses, trying to calculate the time difference. Back home it was--3am?

Concluding that it didn't make much difference, she decided to take a shower before venturing out for food. If she had known what the coming days would bring, she would have savored those peaceful minutes under the hot stream of water a little longer. Even while squinting, sans contacts, trying to distinguish between shampoo and conditioner, she sensed something was wrong.

––––––––

He started off distant. Actually, to go chronologically, he started off lying. Maggie found out a few days in when Will's pilot friend ran into them at a restaurant and mentioned flying him in on Saturday. Not Sunday. Will tried explaining he must be confused by time zones. Then he shut down for the entirety of dessert, trying and failing to ease the tension with questions about school and work. He then topped off the four beers he had with dinner with three lowball glasses of something called a Drunk German and fell asleep immediately upon returning to the hotel room.

There was some normalcy when they went to the theater. He was chivalrous and affectionate and she was hopeful that it was a turning point. He even serenaded her in typical dramatic fashion, clutching at his chest to signify intensity, and showing off his four years of Italian. They barely made it back to the hotel room, as spontaneous kissing became increasingly passionate on the taxi ride through snow-covered streets lined with Christmas lights. The three story walk up proved especially exertive. Eventually he just scooped her up and attempted to jog the rest of the steps. Fortunately their room was right next to the stairs.

She had fallen asleep in his strong, gentle embrace. She woke having her arms crushed by his grip. He still seemed to be asleep and she considered bearing it until he let go, but then his face intensified, his jaw clenched, and he started throwing punches. His left fist caught her collarbone before she launched herself off the bed. He immediately stopped, his eyes suddenly registering the setting. He looked confused, staring at his clenched fists like he had never seen them before. Maggie had landed on her knees and watched him from an unintentionally cowered position, naked and crouched beside the pile of bed linens.

Her quick thoughts told her to be calm, support him, not make him feel worse, but her hands were shaking and she found it impossible to control the tears streaming from her eyes.

He moved toward her, enveloped her naked body. Her breathing was strained, the seething pain in her collarbone radiating into her chest. The warmth of him soothed her, but her breathing remained unsteady and her body was stiff. He gathered up the sheets and wrapped them around her shoulders.

In the darkness he wasn't able to see how red her collarbone had already become. By the next morning, it was black and blue and it was torture trying to lift that arm to wash her hair.

"What happened to your shoulder?" He asked, innocently concerned when she crossed the room from the bathroom to retrieve her clothes, the hotel spa robe sliding off her narrow shoulder. The look on her face answered his question. "I thought I just grabbed your arms?"

The use of the word "just" seemed to linger in the air as he took notice of where his hands rested. He shifted his palms and beneath he could see the dark outline of his fingers on her skin from the previous night.

"I'm fine, Will."

"This isn't fine," he said, angrily.

"Will?" She touched his cheek. "Please talk to me. I'm so glad to get to see you, but this wasn't a scheduled leave--" She extended her hand and touched his chest. "I can feel the pain radiating off of you. Something's happened."

He didn't intend to tell her, but he made eye contact and heard himself say: "Ben died."

In the silence that followed, her eyes welled with tears, but she patiently waited for more information.

"Roadside IED."

He could practically see the images flashing across her eye. Her breathing thickened and she dropped the shirt she had retrieved, her long bare arms suddenly wrapped around his neck. Her skin was warm in the cold hotel room.

In the end, he promised to see the base therapist for counseling, but he already dreaded it and wasn't entirely convinced he would follow through. She had stopped short of asking him about coming home and there was a moment when he knew what she wanted to ask. Desperately. It was followed by the moment he chose not to tell her that it was offered and he declined.

That moment, that decision, seemed to build a palpable barrier between them.

They tried to make something positive out of the time together. There were bits of it that almost felt like normal, but something always seemed to force the wedge again.

There was the female server who Will was a bit flirtatious with after several drinks.

Flirtatious is kind. He was obnoxious.

Actually, drinking a little too much was becoming habitual.

There was also the German lawyer they met at the concierge desk who was quite taken by Maggie, or "schönes Mädchen" as he called her. She surprised everyone with a paragraph length response in German. Will had been suspicious of the fact that he never knew she could speak the language, a fact he actually did know because occasionally she'd curse in German when she was really frustrated, something her grandfather also did to get around his wife's no cursing policy. The arguments just became more petty after that.

Will continued having violent fits in his sleep. Most of the time he was unaware of what was happening. She had managed to avoid his fists, darting out of bed at the first sign of unrest. One night, she had just settled back on the bed, having presumed it was over after 20 minutes of flailing, when he suddenly lunged on top of her, clasping her wrists tightly over her head. His eyes were open, but there was no recognition, only hollowness, and a savage determination.

Maggie wasn't sure what he would do next, but she didn't like the connection her brain was making with a memory she preferred to forget. She feared trying to push him away, both because she didn't know if she was strong enough, but also because she was afraid of his response in that state of mind.

"Will," she pleaded.

His face looked sinister.

"Will? I love you." She repeated herself several times, trying to establish eye contact. "Please, Will."

Mercifully, his face softened as he seemingly came to consciousness. He was Will again, but she feared his response now more than ever. He examined the grip he held on her wrists and released her. She was looking at him with love, but also with fear. He knew what memory had come to her mind. As he moved away, he shook his head, apologizing. "They should lock me up," he said.

She matched his motion and tried to grasp onto him. "No," she responded, trying to stifle her tears.

"You need to stay away from me."

"Will—"

"No," he said so firmly it startled her. "Stay away from me. Please. I can't— if I—" he couldn't bring himself to say it. He *had* hurt her. "I'm sorry. It's not enough, but I'm sorry."

"I'm fine. Please." She again tried to embrace him, only to be brushed away. He pushed himself off the bed and crossed to the bathroom.

"I could have *killed* you," he spat. "That is not 'fine'."

She resisted stating the obvious, that he hadn't, since it seemed like a weak response, and seconds earlier, she had feared he might. She expected to hear him taking out frustrations on some bathroom fixtures with the state he was in, but he emerged quietly a few minutes later. He walked straight over to her and kissed her on the forehead. "I'm sorry, Reeves."

She relaxed having him use his nickname for her. "Me, too."

"You're apologizing," he stated, seemingly unimpressed by that fact.

"Yes. I can only imagine what you're going through."

"Hurting you was unforgivable." He took a deep breath, his eyes glistening a bit. "There's no excusing it."

"I'm sorry about Ben. I'm sorry you had to see something like that happen to your friend."

His thoughts started to race, but he stopped them before the images became clear in his mind. He instead focused on Maggie standing before him looking so very tired. "I *love* you. You know that, don't you?"

"I do know that. And I love you." She stroked his arm. "Come *home*, Will. Please. We can go back together."

He sighed, tempted by the thought of walking with her through the airport, sitting on the airplane, having her lean her head on his shoulder, going home. He thought of the normalcy that would come with it--the familiar faces, a language he understood, palatable food. It was certainly preferable to military food, which had a tendency to taste gritty, like everything was coated in dust. "Can I hold you for a while? I won't fall asleep--" *And attack you* seemed to be the reasonable end thought of the sentence.

"Yes." She was relieved, seeing this as progress.

She had no intention to fall asleep, but she did. When she woke, the sky outside was gray and overcast. There would be no sunrise or sunset that day—the sky would simply get lighter and then dark again. She was laying on her side, her arm outstretched, but it grasped only bed sheets. "Will?"

The room was eerily quiet.

"Will?" she said louder, looking toward the open bathroom door.

It was then she noticed a sheet of hotel note paper on the bedside table. She squinted to see it then scrambled to sit upright.

"*I don't want to hurt you again. I hope someday you can forgive me. Please keep the ring. It'll help knowing you have it.*"

No name signed and there was nothing written on the back of the paper. She checked twice.

3
there is a reason

T en months later...

    Someone once told me worry doesn't prevent anything from happening so it's pointless to do it. Good advice really. Only my worry was seeded from the act of an ultrasound tech turning ashen and high-tailing it out of the room in search of a supervisor. She did this silently, very ninja-like. She was wearing ballet flats—perhaps those Italian Tieks things splattered all over promoted Pinterest posts, claiming to be comfortable. Cute? Yes. Ideal for running around a medical clinic all day? Not so much. But the fact that she was wearing completely impractical very expensive footwear was merely a distraction from the reality that had just wrapped itself around me in a stranglehold. *Was it just two months earlier I was looking at heartbeats?*

That was enough reason why they shouldn't have assigned me the recent technical college graduate. No offense to technical colleges--they help narrow the skills gap. I think they're undervalued. I only remark about the inexperience of recent grads, technical college or otherwise, in dealing with dire circumstances. They certainly haven't fine-tuned bedside manner when combined with said dire circumstances. If they were going to assign me a recent graduate, an excellent example of why they should properly train her on reading charts in their entirety, rather than just skimming. That thorough training would have prevented our awkward and awful introduction.

Actually, I should note here that to prep myself for this appointment, since I no longer had the amniotic sacs to make things easier to see, I was instructed to come in with a full bladder. Given that instruction, along with the nagging thought in the back of my mind (after some unsettling lab work results) telling me I had a whole lot to be scared about, not to mention that my respective role models growing up depended on large amounts of alcohol as a coping mechanism for all of life's stressors (from death to you know, Tuesdays), I figured a few splashes of rum in my Coca-Cola was as good as water at filling that bladder of mine. I did this in the parking lot, lacking the essential cognitive foresight that I would have some trouble getting home.

The rum made the long wait a notch less excruciating. I actually found some of the reading material amusing. It also made my weigh-in of 158 easier to take. I'm 5'11" so that's considered "healthy" mind you. 141 was my pre-pregnancy weight. I thought I could stand to lose a few pounds at that point, which is really ridiculous in hindsight. What's really troubling with the weigh-in was not dropping so much as an ounce since the last obstetrician appointment when everything was okay. Right on track. A teensy bit on the high side for the weight gain, but it was twins and I was spoon-fed a thousand and one excuses for why 158 was "a-okay." The assistant who retrieved me from the lobby 71 minutes after my appointment time didn't think it was so great. She kind of gulped when she announced it. The 5 foot 2 twig probably weighed 110 pounds sopping wet.

So, safely delivered to the ultrasound room by the anorexic prom queen, I hesitated to sit on the exam table. The paper crinkling would carry too many memories. My olfactory sensors were already identifying the thermal ultrasound printer, having recently been used. It wouldn't be used for me. Even if they did print photos, they wouldn't be plastered up on the fridge. Ultrasounds of internal organs get far fewer ooh's and aw's than babies.

I hadn't brought myself to remove the ultrasound photos of him lounging back like he was in a hammock and her with her hands over her eyes like she was looking at the ultrasound wand with binoculars. Despite my sister-in-law making a remark as she threw a couple baked zitis in the freezer about it being time to remove them, I just couldn't bring myself to do it. I also maintained she had no right to an opinion on the matter, *despite* her providing easy dinner solutions for our time of grief. I had signed paperwork to have them cremated, I arranged their cemetery placement, I donated bags of washed, but never worn newborn baby clothes. She melted cheese over boiled pasta. *Piss off, Jenna.*

Back in my own personal torture chamber for the day, I opted for a chair meant for family members eagerly watching the monitors and my body convulsed involuntarily from a sharp pain in my abdomen: the reason for the 71 minute wait, the weigh-in, the ultrasound, and the ninja-shoed ultrasound tech's truly awful introduction, which was about to take place:

She swept into the room, bringing in a rush of cold medical office air, the top half of her straight black hair tied back in a barrette. She had a giant diamond on her left hand. I don't normally notice these things, but she made a point of using her left hand to hold open the door, left hand clutching her white lab jacket collar, and she obsessively tossed her hair from blocking her employee badge with her—well, you see where I'm going with this. So, she walked in and exclaimed (her enthusiasm her first mistake):

"Maggie Callahan?" It was as though she was surprising a two-year-old with a snack.

I think I just stared at her. It was too much. I had only been a "Callahan" for two months. I almost felt like I had assumed the identity of a stranger, as though I simply had a new alias with a really tragic recent backstory.

"So, you're having twins! I'm so excited--you're my first set!" She waved her hands erratically in front of her eyes, fanning away melodramatic tears or something.

It was then my brain concluded: *Nope. I did live the really tragic recent backstory.* I could feel my heart being rung out again, twisted like a wet rag.

"Are you finding out genders?"

Oh, I forgot to mention that she had a hint of a New Orleans accent and the decibel of her accented voice cut through the air (and my ear drums) like a Cutco knife. There. I've gotten a potentially lucrative product endorsement out of the way and I can depict this encounter in much more accurate detail:

Again: "So, Mrs. Callahan, you're having twins! I'm so excited, you're the first set of twins I've had." (Or something like that.) Then she looked down at my stomach. My deflated, too-many-Krispy-Kremes looking stomach. She stupidly looked back at her notes. "*No*, there's *no way* you're having twins--"

All I could think of was: *Thank God I'm halfway drunk.*

If I were sober, I would have burst into tears. Okay, that's a dramatization, a lie even. I don't cry in front of people anymore. I really never did. I push those sad, dark feelings deep, deep down and pretend to be a functioning human being. Like a grown up.

Parental units taught me that one, too.

But I *was* halfway drunk, so rather than suffering in silence, I said: "Stop." I threw my left hand out to further demonstrate this. There was a ring there, but it looked like something pulled from one of those coin machines at Chuck-E-Cheese in comparison to hers. "Turn around, go back out in the hallway, pull up the Emergency Room notes from August 22nd and basically anything since. When you feel you have a more accurate grasp of who your patient is, you may come back. I waited over an hour already. I can wait a little longer." My hand fanned her back into the hallway.

She exited the room and I was left in the dark, the space illuminated only by under cabinet lighting and the glow of the ultrasound screen. When she returned a few minutes later, she delivered a rehearsed, but sincere apology and took her place on the padded stool, inviting me rather tenderly to sit on the exam chair.

"So we're looking to see if we can tell if your ovaries have returned to normal functioning and if there's anything else we should be concerned about. I understand you've had abdominal pain and some irregular lab work?"

The last part was accurate but not at all comforting and should have been omitted (as you'll remember, I cited the immature bedside manner previously). I rolled up my shirt and she squeezed warm ultrasound gel onto my stomach. It was too familiar a feeling and I turned my face away from the screen. There was no reason to look. There was nothing I wanted to see on that screen.

"Have you had a period since--?"

I shook my head.

She took her time looking things over, focusing for a long time on one area, measuring with the on screen tools. At one point she asked me if I was okay. She meant with the pressure she was applying, but she realized I might have taken it a different way and never asked again. My quivering lip may have tipped her off. Then she retracted the wand and got up.

"Just stay there. Don't wipe off the gel yet. I'll be right back."

If a member of the medical community, even a recent graduate, tells you they'll be right back and it's more like the length of an average lunch break, there may be some cause for concern, or a formal complaint letter. When a member of the medical community, even a recent graduate, tells you they'll be right back and before you have a chance to consider a magazine, they've returned with someone who outranks them, it'll scare the shit out of you. And it should because they're not getting a second opinion on your fantastic looking ovaries. They just want confirmation that their concerns are justified. It's likely they're also trying to recruit someone that outranks them to deliver the news.

This supervisor didn't work that way. She was thick-bodied with a blunt curtain of blond hair flat against her chin. She took her purple eye shadow seriously and had no patience for the newbies as she closed in on retirement. She was the veteran of the ultrasound technician team who threw her newbies to the sharks. And she *liked it.*

I sat up without being told to, but it seemed appropriate. I was the shark.

They were both silent so I read their name tags. The boss was Sue Gilchrist. I found focusing on how to pronounce her last name a welcome distraction.

I stared at the new grad's name badge in disbelief. I had just traumatized a girl whose professional name was Gabby Seaman. Rather, my likely medical prognosis had traumatized her and I just knocked her around a little beforehand. I tried to channel the sense of humor of a thirteen year old boy and cling to the idea of chatty sperm, but I didn't find it remotely funny, even after I was able to visualize them as a grownup animated short character even John Lasseter might produce.

She pointed to the blurred images on the screen. "There are two large masses on your ovary and fallopian tube. We don't know their nature, if they're benign tumors or—if they're benign or malignant." She said this quickly, like disclosures on a car commercial. "We'll send for official interpretation from the Radiologist and contact your physician so he or she can determine recommendations as soon as possible. Scheduling will call you, or you can try calling in tomorrow."

Then nothing. Gabby nodded, concluding the conversation, pleased with her delivery of the news, and essentially started cleaning up. She turned off the monitor, though I was certain I wasn't her last patient of the day. She put the ultrasound gel bottle back in the warmer. Boss lady was busy noting something in my chart, ignoring me.

Finally, I said: "So, it's okay that I wipe off the gel now then." And I did so without waiting for a response, pushed myself off the bed, grabbed my gold hobo handbag (a very "thoughtful"—see: expensive--gift I was guilt-tripped to use to please my mother in law of two months), and crashed out the door. It was a blur. The hallways were jarring—I don't actually know how I was able to navigate, but I found the waiting room. It was filled with pregnant women and advertisements for permanent birth control and vaginal reconstructive surgery-- and eyelash enhancement medication endorsed by Brooke Shields.

I swerved around a stroller filled with two of the most adorable faces I've seen in my whole damn life, my stomach still sticky from the gel, only to walk straight into a woman probably about as far along as I should have been, waddling to her appointment. I held the door for her, managing a polite expression as she remarked about "just wanting this to be over."

The sun was just starting to set.

The courtyard fountain was loud against my eardrums.

I took three solid breaths and called Nathan. While his ring-back tone played in my ear (some science fiction show theme song--*The X-Files*, perhaps), I removed my wallet and accessory bag from the metallic cowhide handbag and dropped the empty purse into the trash receptacle.

When he answered, I blurted out: "I want a divorce."

4
how nice--to feel nothing
and still be given credit for living

Did you ever catch lightning bugs in a mason jar growing up? I didn't, but the concept has always sort of bothered me. Here it's seen as a nostalgic activity, attributed to a particularly pleasant childhood, but it's sort of cruel capturing these little beings for the sake of your own amusement and, best case scenario, sending it back out into the world absolutely traumatized, cast off from the other lightning bugs for ranting about the giants that abducted him. Not to mention that the poor creature has probably sustained terrible neurological damage from hurling itself against solid glass repeatedly.

Beside the point.

I didn't grow up in a house with a healthy long-term relationship. In fact, the circumstances always seemed pretty dysfunctional--my mother was on the rebound after the end of her rebound marriage [that occurred a little too soon, seemed to be the consensus] after my dad died and she plucked Ray out of a marriage--so forgive my jaded outlook and the following metaphor: Marriage is like a pair of fireflies caught in a mason jar with a lid that you forgot to poke holes in. They still manage to flutter around for awhile, their butts aglow, but ultimately...well...lights out.

If that sounds cynical, it's because I am. I'm really, really good at it. Most people fail to pick up on my cynicism, or my sarcasm, or that I have much of a personality at all, since I more often than not keep my mouth shut. My thoughts and opinions aren't exactly welcome these days.

That's non-committal. They aren't welcome. This is evident by the looks of exhaustion I receive when I express one of them. I have some tolerance for this blatant disregard for my opinion, having been desensitized to it at a young age. My mother had a tendency to not just show disapproval for my opinion. She wouldn't just make me feel ashamed for the thought or action. A disapproval from my mother had the impact of a Category 5 hurricane on a trailer park: only rubble remained...and possibly a flamingo mailbox, wings still whirling.

My opinion about marriage wasn't always so bleak. Once it was hopeful and naive.

Not a flattering thing to be called "naive." This particular judgment was passed by the boy I would fall head over heels for when I was a young girl and several years after that, agree to marry.

But he's not the man I married.

Strange how true Will's assessment was back then since I often still imagine how easy and uncomplicated *our* marriage would have been. There would be challenges in our lives, but we would grace through the storm knowing that our love was impenetrable. [Insert dramatic sigh here.]

Naive, indeed. Idiotic, more like.

Going back to the fireflies thing? Full disclosure: Nobody caught me. I trapped myself. That's a regretful thing to have to admit. I was like one of those suicidal birds dive bombing into traffic. I had the whole damn sky and I set my sights on a six lane expressway.

Too many metaphors.

A very solid pair of pink lines is what drew a proposal from Nathan. We both had our own reasons why there would be no other resolution to the predicament than an official, licensed legal document. His reasons were noble-ish while mine were more or less motivated by depression.

I gave him far too much leeway on his remarks about "a woman's right to choose." I know that now. Back then I took it as evidence of his supportiveness, despite the fact that I would never choose abortion. Truly, it was not the first and certainly not the last red flag warning me about our incompatibility.

I started to show at 10 weeks, prompting a pregnancy test (after a tactless remark from a coworker and realizing that I had, in fact, missed two periods.) Since our one night stand--I should clarify here that I'm not the one night stand kind of person. I'm an introvert. I do not quickly trust or like people so it is highly out of the ordinary for me to get naked with a man I just met. So after getting naked *enough* with a man I just met, I had resolved to focusing on two things: Working and listening to Taylor Swift breakup songs. I limited crying and staring off into space to the latter. It was a focused, reasonably productive existence. It would get better, I told myself. I'd grieve and go on and do the things I had always wanted to do.

Soon after the pregnancy test, I had an awkward lunch with Nathan. We ended the lunch with the idea that we weren't going to let the pregnancy 'rush our relationship'. Truth be told, when he used that phrasing, I felt like vomiting. I had absolutely zero interest in a relationship with him. I got in my Jeep and I literally sat and stared at the steering wheel for twenty minutes processing this surreal new life I was living.

May I just say--people are so damn nosy when you're pregnant. They will ask and say just about anything. This is infinitely worse with twins. Did I use fertility treatments? Do twins run in either family? What position did we use? Did we use lubrication--was it sperm friendly? People started referring to him as my husband and upon being corrected, produced a horrifyingly sympathetic frown. It seemed even more devastating to them that we weren't planning to get married since it was twins.

There was also a bit of pressure from his parents. You'd think with a flume ride of a daughter, if you'll forgive the haunting mental image (She produced four children in three and a half years—no multiples), it would alleviate the pressure from their other children. Nope. We were having twins. Nathan was a twin. How amazing. What are the odds? They could see the photos flying up on the walls, coming out at social gatherings. They'd already started a false truth (see: lie) about how we had a whirlwind romance and eloped, but planned to have a big ceremony after the babies arrived. (Apparently news spread that my fluid retention was dreadful and my ring already didn't fit so my superficial need to look pretty was the reason for the delay. This had produced a lot of unsolicited tips and feedback from strangers to accept myself the way I am, it's a miracle what my body is doing, eat healthier, etc. Luckily I had sworn off social media since Tom started Myspace so I avoided a lot of this input. His sister was also expecting. There was talk of a double baby shower...me with my first pregnancy, her with her fifth. (If a baby shower for a second baby is a sprinkle, what the hell is a fifth one called?)

Then he encouraged me to reunite with my mother and her hostage of 13 years, Ray. I hadn't spoken to them in nearly three years, with the exception of running into my mother at Bed, Bath and Beyond. I had been picking up a wedding gift for a coworker--at the time I was getting my proverbial feet wet at a marine hospital as a Marine Biology researcher. The bride-to-be worked in public relations with her fiancée. As it turned out, her fiance was marketing a side relationship with his high school sweetheart, who crashed the rehearsal dinner. It didn't end well for anyone. The groom had unknowingly contracted a terribly uncomfortable, but mercifully treatable STD, which he was kind enough to have shared with his bride, who retaliated by knocking boots with their boss on her would-be wedding night. (Literally boots—she wanted a country look for the photos.) The *married* boss (and director of the hospital) ended up with a substantial alimony payment and child support payment, since their hookup resulted in a love child who looked like his clone.

I'm not sure who wound up with my gift, but I never saw it again--Or a thank you card.

I did get a baby shower invite, however.

I digress. Again. I was shopping. My mother was shopping--allegedly. The accidental run-in shouldn't have happened. She was not in her normal shopping territory and I had never known her to set foot in Bed, Bath and Beyond prior to this occasion. Then again, a lot can happen in three years. Whatever twisted karma brought us to the same store during the same strange 11am shopping hour, I was caught unarmed and off-guard. She spotted me looking at blenders. I was a sitting duck, about to be out $79 dollars minus coupon, plus tax.

I wouldn't have spent so long, but the item numbers weren't matching between the registry and the shelf label. A helpful associate had just resolved that it had to do with color. They registered for the stainless steel, but the store only carried black. Perhaps I would have been more seasoned in the idiosyncrasies of bridal registries had I gotten to that part of the wedding planning before I was dumped (see: abandoned) in a foreign country. This fact occurred to me as the sales associate checked inventory on the antiquated computer. I think we had a similar model back in elementary school when we'd play Oregon Trail on floppy disks. Even the memory of typhoid fever or, God forbid, dysentery, couldn't distract me from the fact that I'd just been emotionally destroyed just weeks earlier by the man who made me believe he loved me. Who *did* love me, I insisted silently. Except he wasn't responding to any efforts I had made to communicate with him--phone, emails, even two handwritten letters. This all produced a significant amount of anxiety in my poor masochistic brain.

Really though, the associate was quite helpful. He confirmed there was available inventory and that he could have it shipped to the store for free and accept my 20% off coupon. Still about $70 after tax, but mission accomplished. Since I always shop registries early, as to avoid the picked over list, the one week delivery time would ensure I would have it with weeks to spare. All in all, a fairly productive shopping experience.

I was tucking the receipt in my wallet when I felt a hand on my arm. You know those stories about animals caught in traps, how they'll chew off their own foot to get free? My first instinct, my first thought when I correctly identified that the hand belonged to my mother was: How crucial *is* this arm? I looked over my shoulder at her, once again sized up my arm and she removed her hand.

"*Hi,*" she gasped, as a question and approximately fourteen syllables. Her ever-changing hair was cropped short and haphazardly styled. The base was too dark for her and the highlights too copper. She must not have been in a good place with Ray--he preferred her hair blonde. Her green eyes were outlined by deep black mascara and liner. She looked more aged than she should have. I made a mental note to buy night eye cream.

"What's *wrong?*" she asked, with such a level of exaggeration I almost thought she was joking. You would have thought she had just seen me that morning. Like we talked every damn day and the reason for the disgusted look on my face couldn't possibly have anything to do with running into my mother, who I never intended to see again. Understandable position considering the last time I saw her she had smacked me across the face. We're talking about the very woman who also thought I was naïve--the one and only thing she and Will would ever agree on--if she had managed to tolerate him long enough to compare notes. This was the person who could make me burst into tears right in the middle of what I assumed fell into the vast "Beyond" category of products if she so much as mentioned his name. An "I told you so" would send me right over the damn edge. So I suppose the look on my face—I've never been good at disguising my emotions (though also not terribly effective at verbalizing them)—was a combination of disgust and a look of fear you might have if a terrorist materialized in front of you wearing a suicide vest. I'm not insane, so my initial thought was not to give her a damn hug.

My mind couldn't focus. All I knew was that I needed to distract my assailant long enough to escape out the automatic doors.

"Oh *no*. Did you hear about Will getting married?" She paused, pleased to have scooped this news, but she clasped her hand to her mouth for some sort of attempt at theatrics. "You know, he was *never* right for you."

I continued glaring at her. The associate handed me my debit card and I took it reflexively.

"Of course there was no telling you anything."

Snapshots of Will flashed before my eyes. I could see him chasing me across a field when I was six, remembering how I'd laughed with exhilaration, glancing over my shoulder as he closed the distance. I could see him holding my face in his hands, as a boy and later as a young man. He'd always seem to do that in more serious moments, never shying from serious conversations. I remembered how he'd sing to me—when I was sad, when he was being playful, or for no reason at all. Most of all, I remembered the look on his face when I entered a room. After so many years, he'd always stop to take notice and he'd always always always smile. I watched the images of him reel before my eyes and then vanish with a snap, the door on that part of my world slamming shut. *Must be how those Pevensie kids felt when they couldn't return to Narnia.*

"Lydia," I said through gritted teeth, tucking away the card in a side pocket. "You and I?" My index finger had hijacked my arm and was making a wagging motion like Babu from Seinfeld. "We don't speak."

She looked at me like I'd just offended her in the worst way imaginable. Which I had. The Bed, Bath & Beyond associate, who looked remarkably like Paul Rudd--was standing right there. He witnessed it (and was still fashioning an awkward smile, characteristic of good customer service). If it were just her and me, things would have been different. I would have been scolded like a child, shamed into apologizing. So rather than verbally beating me senseless about what an awful human being I was, she simply glared at me, turned and walked away from me (and Paul), stunned that I would dare embarrass her.

I was apologetic to Paul, hoping he'd judge me less harshly, but my head was spinning. Out of self-respect, I opted not to hide out in the store to be sure she had gone. On my walk out, I shakily called Katie after surveying the parking lot to head off enemy fire. Voicemail. Since I had shunned social media, my investigation capability was limited to Will's Facebook profile picture. It was enough. What I found was a photo of Will in a tux, his arms wrapped around a petite blonde bride.

"He doesn't even like blondes," I scowled. I had earned the attention of some employees on smoke break so I moved along, climbed into my Jeep.

Pressed for time, I drove back to work and parked. I didn't take a full breath the entire drive. All emotion seemed successfully repressed until I nearly hyperventilated as I nearly stepped on a sewer grate crossing the parking lot. The thought came to mind how Will's brother, Evan, had tried torturing me about alligators or deranged clowns living in them. Rather than join in the razzing, Will had swept me into his arms and carried me across the grate. He could have avoided the grate altogether and of course, once standing over it, he pretended his foot had been attacked, but oh how my heart had swelled. The memory took over my thoughts, leaving me standing in the middle of the employee parking lot staring at a sewer, stunned by my new reality--and then some asshole in a gigantic diesel engine pickup truck honked at me. The horn startled people who weren't in the middle of a psychotic break so you can only imagine how jarring it was to me.

So I wandered out of his way and started sobbing.

"I'm fine," I insisted as one of the IT guys came to help. "Go on with your day."

I had never officially met him, except for maybe directing him to a coworker's workstation for PC repairs, so my tone seemed to have confused him into thinking he'd offended me.

"Bad day?" He took a sip from his Subway cup casually. Too casually. I glared at him. He didn't wear sunglasses despite the piercing brightness of the sun. His sandy hair was coarse and thick and framed his pale eyes. His features were all quite pointed, but he had a kind face. He was wearing a blue long-sleeve button up shirt with a tie--I remember simply because the tie looked painfully outdated, like a teacher in an early 90s TGIF sitcom.

"Year."

"Bad *year*? The whole thing?"

I considered it. "Yeah. We're only 3 months in, but so far? There was only one year worse that I can recall."

"Maybe you're getting the bad stuff out of the way early."

"Well that's a cheery outlook--" I collected myself and my belongings, straightened up and started toward the entrance.

"Nathan. I sort of met you when you punched the vending machine last week."

So maybe we had a bit of a history. "You were supposed to pretend that didn't happen, Nathan. I thought we had an unspoken understanding." I still couldn't fully inhale, my airway constricted.

He laughed. "It deserved it. Trying to steal your white cheddar popcorn."

"Again, very observant." I glanced back toward the Jeep, wondering if I should just claim I got sick at lunch. "Believe it or not, I don't have emotional outbursts that often."

"No?"

I couldn't tell if he was trying to be funny. I tried to at least have the appearance of composure so he would perhaps leave me alone. "What is that on your tie? Stamps?" It was a diversion. I needed him to look away because at that moment my chest felt painfully constricted. I couldn't breathe properly. I had never known an anxiety attack before, but I was pretty sure it was the start of my first.

"No this was actually worn by Mulder in two episodes of *X-Files*."

I gulped against the pain. "Wow, two episodes. They must have had strong convictions about the style of the tie. Must have been very Mulder-esque." It was the ugliest tie I'd ever seen, with the exception of my staff white elephant gift exchange present--I had been absent, watching Will drink himself into a stupor more than likely--so the tie was that gift no one wanted. I couldn't say I blamed them given that it was Santa as a plumber. It was a very strange thing to find on my desk when I came back from Ramstein. Comically depressing.

"You're probably too young for that show."

"Well that makes you sound old." I focused on the horizon, slowed my intake of air.

"Older than you. What are you--23?"

"21. And you are?"

"Christ, *21?*"

"Not Christ. Maggie."

He seemed amused. "Alright *Maggie*. A few of us are going out for drinks tonight."

"No."

"Well that was direct."

He's married, I think my heart bellowed, clenching itself like a charley horse in my chest. I pictured Will gazing at me, smiling, loving me. Or so I thought. My chest writhed, swelling in its knotted form with the emotions from those moments. The love I had for him suddenly had nowhere to go and it felt like it would suffocate me.

"Call in sick," IT guy--Nathan--suggested.

"What?"

"You can't go back like this."

It was then I noticed how erratic my breathing had become.

"I'll drive you home."

"Don't you need to get back to work?" I said quickly, wanting to rid myself of spectators to my emotional collapse.

"I'll work from home a few hours later. Or tomorrow."

I couldn't bring him back to the boat I rented at the marina. It would intrude upon the last memories I had of Will there. My heart tightened. Nathan would probably also think I was more strange than he already did. He offered to take me "out on the town" for the afternoon instead. I reluctantly agreed.

"Out on the town" to an IT advisor involved arcade game playing and bowling, which, truth be told, actually was a fair distraction. The over-stimulation of noise and lights seemed to lure my senses and I was able to take out some aggression in a zombie apocalypse game.

"I am not a violent person," I declared after I earned a high score taking out a pack of zombie dogs with a satisfied "take that you undead mongrel bastards."

I may have said it in a British accent. There could have also been a profanity in there.

"I was going to compliment you on your precision." He raised his eyebrows. "Anything to not get on your bad side."

We had some drinks and were joined later by a few other IT guys, who all seemed to doubt that I was old enough to drink. The more they teased me, the more I felt like I belonged in some way and the less I wanted to be left alone to face my emotions. So I stayed. Despite a complicated history with alcohol, mainly emotionally damaging experiences, I drank more than I should have. The more I drank, the less I felt--or rather, the less I cared about what I felt. I buried the nagging thought that, if nothing else, my childhood should have provided enough cautionary tales not to drink in a vulnerable state of mind.

On the other hand, I started to understand why people turned to it to feel numb. I empathized with them. And oh how I wanted to feel numb. It occurred to me more than once to stop, to go home to my boat, face the tears and pain like a grownup, but as my new friends pointed out, I was barely an adult and as Will had said himself when we were a few years younger (when he thought my heart was too pure and he worried about people taking advantage), I was naive.

That night I resolved to do something that I decided was not at all naive. I succeeded. What I did was stupid and reckless and even in my drunken state, I was not naive to the fact that I was complacent in actions that embodied all I said I'd never be and never do.

Since I didn't want to be stuck at his place and I wasn't going to take him to the boat, I suggested an empty beach parking lot. I guided him to follow me into the backseat of his practical sedan, which led to a home pregnancy test formality, which led back to the IT guy with the ugly tie, which led to reuniting with my mother. Actually, after the sedan, it led to a very long, unadvised walk home to the boat along the coastal highway. By the time I reached the boat and realized I had walked the entire way barefoot, I was painfully but mercifully disoriented...and I did not care.

Truth be told, Nathan didn't know the full history with my mother. I knew that. I shouldn't have taken his advice, as it wasn't based on all the facts. But he kept at me. He said all parents make mistakes. They're human. We must forgive them. How can we expect our children to forgive us for all our mistakes if we don't forgive our own parents?

Now at that point, I knew Nathan about as well as I knew the guy who inexplicably got his mail at the post office at the same time as me every few days wearing bright red flip flops and always, always, always donning wet hair. But this "advice" Nathan was giving me had the distinct stench of parental influence. Their thinly veiled perception of me seemed to be that I was immature and lost and that my opinion was clouded and not to be trusted. They were displeased with the circumstances, but they felt they could perhaps mold me into an acceptable choice--eventually. They liked to compliment me on my appearance--

nothing specific, just saying that I was "so pretty," then they'd subconsciously squint a bit since I apparently wasn't living up to my potential there either.

So I called my parents—or rather, my mother and her husband. She had insisted that Ray was my father, or at least better than my actual father. That was enough for me to resent the pair of them, but there was more to it. There was something that shifted when the pair crossed paths when I was eight, after my mother kicked John to the curb and wrecked Ray's marriage. For one thing, their meeting introduced liquor into our kitchen pantry.

It was two days of dining torture. The first night was my parental figures. When we were making the plans on the phone, it was ten minutes of passive aggressive jousting with each other (which they claimed was "playful") before they finally told us to just decide on the restaurant. Actually, that was my mother. Ray had gotten annoyed with her and stopped contributing to the conversation. I had my head smothered with my pillow at that point so Nathan covered that I wasn't feeling well and chose Café Marco, a cutesy Italian place painted to look like you're sitting outside in Venice. You've seen the Venetian in Vegas? I hadn't at that point, but I did within the week. Kind of neat ambiance, right? Like that, but a much smaller scale with far less talented artists. Like a high school theatre production set. And no gondola, which *some* might say is an overpriced tourist trap anyway, but would have been my favorite thing about the hotel, had we gone on it. Too "spendy" said the Systems Analyst.

It was for the best. It would have been a masochistic, slow moving boat ride as I imagined Will there instead. He would have been all about it, probably stealing the stage from the gondolier and serenading me in Italian, a cheesy sentiment I would have lapped up happily.

"I knew it!" My mom said when she saw us, pointing immediately to my belly, which she touched repeatedly throughout the night. At one point, after calling me her 'precious girl' for the umpteenth time, and four times slipping and referring to the babies as her babies (not her grandbabies or her grandchildren— *her* babies), I lost it.

"I am 12 weeks along. *I* can't even feel them yet. You did not conceive these babies, you are not carrying these babies, and unless there has been some medical breakthrough, you're certainly not going to be birthing these babies so please back off."

Nathan, despite my biting words, did not skip a beat. Clearly he had been coached to play Dr. Phil, minus the southern accent. His exact words, to the best of my memory: "Let's all take a breath. I know family drama can be hard."

Ray and my mother were still out of sorts and wide-eyed from my remark. Actually, my mother was still out of sorts and wide-eyed from my remark. I thought I saw a smirk on Ray's face as he lowered his eyes to look at the bar menu. "There has to be a lot of anxiety built up from being apart, not to mention the added *hormones*." Nathan paused long enough for me to clench my hand into so tight of a fist that my knuckles cracked. "I just want the best for Maggie and our babies."

Then he just couldn't stop himself, captive audience and all: "She needs family around for support. We *all* do." And he kissed my cheek. Like a fucking Judas.

While I was fuming over my pile of fettuccini, which looked less and less appealing the more I stabbed at it with my fork, the sauce taking on a sticky, congealed quality, my mother? She was glowing. She beamed at Nathan. He was her dream come true.

I glanced over at Ray, who was frowning. He kept looking at his plate and across the restaurant like he didn't want to force eye contact with me. When we met them at the hostess stand and Nathan initiated an awkward hugging session, starting with my mother ("We're family after all!" he had chimed like a pandering politician), Ray had looked over at me in disbelief and disappointment. I was on the other side of the fence and had just crawled back through the sewer drains, emerged from behind the Rita Hayworth poster and locked myself back into prison.

Since I last saw him, Ray's light brown hair had thinned considerably and his shoulders were starting to curl forward. There were more lines around his light blue eyes. His large, pronounced nose and equally prominent chin always looked stern when he wasn't smiling. In the instances he did smile, which did not occur that night, he had a tendency to look like a caricature. He still looked like himself, but like an old building, environmental conditions having given him a weathered appearance.

His body was shrinking. I imagined that his legs were thinning out and his knees were getting a knobby quality. He was looking more like his own dad, but without the khaki jumpsuits. I distracted myself for a short time with the thought he might eventually start wearing such a jumpsuit, as his father had. My mother would really hate that.

That night would have been an opportune time to do some communicating, try to get Nathan to understand why things were so strained with my mother. But that would require talking about things I wasn't prepared to discuss. Not with a one-night stand I'd known 3 months.

Was I clear on this? We met in March. This was June. I didn't even speak to him after the one-night stand until mid-May.

Before we had taken to the back seat of his sedan, I remember thinking more than once: *Don't do this, Reeves. Put the drink down. Just go home. Just go to sleep.* It sounded like Will's voice in my head. I didn't really appreciate the intrusion. Nathan was attractive. Not my type, but attractive nonetheless. His pale eyes were especially kind in the bar lighting. His hair had a curl to it and I kept touching it randomly throughout the night. (He was overdue for a haircut so the curls never did make a reappearance.) I was genuinely impressed when he told me about swimming competitively in high school. (Something he hasn't done since.)

I could have lied. Since he had been so supportive of the idea of "choice," I could have taken that as his choice not to be involved. It was obviously his preference. I could have said I was having an abortion.

Could have.

I resigned pretty quickly to the fact that I couldn't stomach even saying those words out loud.

I *should have* sought out some really arrogant, asshole type if I was going to have a night of revengeful promiscuity. He would have ditched a pregnant one-night stand in a heartbeat (or he would have been well-stocked in condoms) and then I wouldn't have ended up at dinner with my parents. I would have been alone and pregnant (or not pregnant at all), but I could have coped even if I had ultimately ended up with a shaky hand holding a home pregnancy test in the marina bathroom with the perpetually wet tile floors. I would have figured it out. Rent was affordable, I had a well-paying job, great insurance...it would have worked somehow for awhile. Well, until the babies were waddling off the side of the boat into the marina…

But again, moot. The fact was I gravitated to the guy with impeccable manners, who had a good childhood and talked to one or both of his parents at least three times a day. Speaking from experience, this fact can and should be seen as a red flag.

Actually I should have gone with my alternative plan for the evening, which still involved consuming large amounts of alcohol (something I had concluded would be an isolated event), but alone, at home. The marina where I rented the sailboat was close to work and I actually really loved the experience of living on a boat.

I planned to pick up rum, a 2 liter of soda, and a thin crust pizza. Maybe sit up top and stare at the water and the sky before I got too tipsy, then retire down below to read or watch a Jane Austen movie on my laptop, to torture myself further.

Three months after the one night stand that should have never happened and I was gnawing the plastic, Made in China life out of a straw at the Japanese steakhouse (Nathan also chose) for night two: Dinner with my parents *and* his parents…and his very pregnant sister Jenna, husband (Mr. Jenna), 8 month old Jake, 21 month old Jax, and 33 month old Jasper, who had just discovered that if he projected enough force, the restaurant offered remarkably good acoustics for his screams and shrieks. I envied the chubby faced little bastard.

The first born, Jezebel Esther (yes, seriously), the "gifted" prodigy at 49 months old, was at gymnastics, prepping for the Olympics.

Appropriately, the name of the restaurant was Jigoku. Look it up. It means "Hell." I hadn't thought much about what Hell would look like, but I discovered that it has flaming cooking surfaces, a bar constructed around a fish tank filled with reef sharks, gigantic tropical floral arrangements (surprising to find foliage of any kind in Hell, let alone flowers), and occasionally there's a terrible out of sync rendition of "Happy Birthday" with an extra twist of adding "cha, cha, cha" between stanzas.

The narrative in the front cover of the menu said the restaurant was named for the owner's beloved cat. Channeling Will automatically--I found that due to his absence, I had been increasingly acting his part—I joked that the cat was probably served as the first meal so the name was to commemorate the significance, like how some restaurants save the first dollar. Recognizing I missed the mark (that would probably be a sketchy Chinese restaurant in a bad neighborhood) and it was in poor taste (pun intended), an obligatory uncomfortable smirk still would have been appreciated, at least from Nathan. I got nothing. Rather than letting the awkwardness go and moving on, I met the silence with an exaggerated meow as I continued to casually peruse my menu.

They also didn't find *that* amusing.

Hell served a fine meal, according to my dinner companions. I thought it was salty and under seasoned so I left a lot on my plate. My mom observed this and couldn't let it rest. She commented that I'd always been a picky eater. Just wait until I have two picky eaters of my own, she teased. That'll be justice. I chuckled at her as I sipped my water. *I wish this was rum.*

"Isn't that how you got pregnant?" She snipped at me.

I glanced to Nathan, whose face confirmed I did in fact say the rum bit out loud. His face also reflected a little shock and awe at my mother's retort. He realized pretty quickly that it didn't correlate with the horse shit story he was trying to feed his family and immediately did damage control. (Fun fact: Nathan lied to his family about how long we had known each other. Apparently we had been work friends longer than I'd actually been working at the marine hospital.)

I learned from the best how to drink my problems bigger, I wanted to say, but I found myself slinking back, making myself smaller.

Oh how quickly one slips into old habits.

They talked baby showers and registries during dessert, after the grill was cool and the chef had performed his last act, the flaming volcano. They talked about embarrassing baby shower games to play. They discussed the bizarre act of melting different candies in the diapers and make people guess the contents. They covered decorations, color schemes, themes. They talked about how they would word the invites since cough, cough, "they're not married." I was tuning out much of the insanity, hoping it was just a very drawn out, detailed nightmare. I pleaded silently that if I could just wake up I'd never touch alcohol again. Never, ever again. Would always insist on a condom, would always go for the bad boys who have a stash of them in their wallet, glove box, night table. Hell, I'll swear off sex altogether. Just let me wake up.

Important side note: The Systems Analyst had presumed I was on the pill and didn't worry much about STDs since I "didn't really seem like *that* kind of girl," while yours truly was so deliriously and irresponsibly intoxicated, I saw him fiddle around and retrieve something. I heard the crinkle of a plastic wrapper and wrongly assumed it was a condom. I was in the backseat of a practical sedan with multiple seat belt locking mechanisms digging into my back, the man above me, silhouetted by the yellow tinged street light, was essentially a stranger (and I was already pondering how to avoid him at work)— apparently I had enough occupying my poor drunken mind.

Spoiler: it was not, in fact, a condom, but a Lifesaver candy. Wild Cherry. Anyway.

Back to dinner in Hell.

"Oh your generation is so creative. I saw the art museum hosts showers, the zoo--Cadence is having *her* baby shower at a park."

I made eye contact with my mother for the second time all night and she raised her eyebrows at me.

"Did I tell you? She and Will are having a boy?" She mustered up some exaggerated enthusiasm, like she had adored him his whole life and he was like the son she never had. Which he was. Well, estranged son-in-law anyway. You'll recall I never intended to see her again.

Less than a year after he proposed to me and this is where we were: Both expecting children with someone we didn't know seven months earlier.

The moment froze there, our table frozen, the chaos of the restaurant swirling around me.

Then I vomited across the Teppanyaki grill.

The grill had mostly cooled at that point, but I thought I heard it sizzle as I fled the table.

My mother, helpful as she portrayed herself to be, found me in the restroom some time later. I had been hiding in there for at least twenty minutes, hoping everyone would leave and I could limit my interactions to the man I met three missing menstrual cycles earlier. He didn't know my favorite song or how I take my coffee, or if I drink coffee (nor would he allow me any amount of coffee even if the doctor said it was okay in moderation). He didn't know what my standby movie is for any number of emotional occasions. He didn't know that I sometimes wear the Mister Rogers style sweater with the leather elbow patches when I'm feeling sad or how I almost died when I was sixteen or why I keep a surfboard on display as home decor. He saw the boat once at his insistence—he found no redeeming qualities about it and, perhaps it was in my head, but he seemed more patronizing after that.

"Maggie?"

I considered pulling up my feet, but she'd come looking under stalls. Yeah, she's that person. She also knocks if you take too long. "I'll be right out."

"Nathan is wonderful. You did so well."

"I'll tell him." I went through half a roll of toilet paper wiping the tears from my eyes and as quietly as possible, blowing the snot from my nose.

"Don't give Will another thought."

I batted at the roll of toilet paper, tore off another section, rationing now.

"Meagan Olivia, did you hear me? Don't give Will another thought. You were never meant to be together. He wasn't right for you."

Please stop saying his name. The stall was starting to close in on me.

I thought of the lawyer in Jurassic Park, how the T-Rex picked him right off the porcelain throne and ripped him to pieces. I was feeling the same sort of anticipatory terror.

Please stop saying his name.

"And it worked out. You're with Nathan, who's fantastic; Will's with Cadence."

I narrowed my eyes at my gawdy gifted gold handbag, wondering if the strap was long enough for me to hang a grown woman.

"Oh they looked so in love."

"You saw them?" The words burst from my mouth. I couldn't believe Will would ever, in a thousand years, invite her to his wedding. Then again the wedding announcement with baby registry card was an unexpected punch to the gut I didn't expect he'd inflict either.

"No. You know Franny from work?"

No, I haven't talked to you in three years. Except for the day I got knocked up, that is.

I could see Will standing at the front of the aisle of St. Andrew's Church on Vista Avenue, where he had attended church growing up. Big heaping vases full of red roses mixed with stems of white orchids lined along the altar, Jesus hanging up on the cross made from rustic wood. Will would have worn an orchid boutonniere, the heavy utilization of orchids simply a psychological tactic of my mind to torture me since dendrodium orchids are my favorite flower and of course, Cadence would choose them as well. Because that's what really troubles me about the man I love marrying someone else--the floral selection.

Will would be wearing a classic James Bond tux accentuating his broad shoulders, dark hair styled just enough, but still slightly tousled, thick eyebrows, fresh shave, hands folded in front of him. When the doors at the back opened, did he cry? Did he smile?

No matter how my brain tried, it couldn't muster up an image of anyone but me in a white gown at the back of the church—lace sleeves, chiffon, long wavy hair delicately pulled off my face and gliding down the deep v-neck back.

He would be smiling.

He always smiled at me when I entered a room.

"Maggie? What are you doing in there? I said to take the phone." Her hand, adorned with a clunky charm bracelet from Brighton no doubt, reached up under the stall, waving her phone at me.

"Why am I taking the phone?"

"I told you. To show you the picture Franny sent me."

But I had already seen what she wanted me to see. Will in a tux, silver tie, big life of the party smile, cheek smashed against the face of a young blonde woman. The blonde had very heavy makeup and false eyelashes that made her eyes look huge, but she was probably very pretty without. She had long hair in a partial up-do, loose curls falling over her shoulders. Cadence. Cadence Mercer now. Cadence Mercer, wife to Will, mother-to-be of Will's son.

I felt like I was drowning, a familiar scenario. I cited my near-death experience? At a party Katie convinced me to attend, 16-year-old Jill Gibbs thought it would be funny to push me in the pool fully-clothed. Then she flipped on the automatic pool cover. She thought it was particularly hysterical when the cover walloped me in the head in the process of shooting across the surface. It was a few laughs too many when she discovered the controls weren't working to release the locked cover, as a human being was trapped underneath it and it only worked going in a straight line.

With perfect clarity, I could see Will pulling up in his old Ford pickup truck a few days later. We went to different high schools at that point after I had gotten a scholarship to a prep school downtown. I was walking out to the parking lot with Katie when he pulled up and dropped out of the driver side. He stepped right up to me, hands on either side of my face, like it was a completely natural thing he did all the time, despite us falling away from each other for some time. I had a bruised knot on my forehead, which he examined closely, pushing my bangs gently aside.

"I'm Katie," she had said, as this was the first time they'd met. It occurred to me it was actually the first time I'd been in conversational distance with him in over a year. She had a disbelieving expression on her face.

He glanced over at her, suddenly casual. "I'm Will. Nice to meet you." He even shook her hand. "I just wanted to check on you. Make sure you were alive and well."

"I'm alive. The rest is relative."

"That could have been really bad, Reeves." His voice was low, just above a whisper. He played a bit with my bangs, resituating them in probably really unflattering ways that appeared to be amusing him.

"Well I appreciate the fleeting interest in my well-being."

He snapped to attention then grinned, deciding to take my accurate observation as biting wit. His eyes floated to where Katie stood then back to me. "Do you want a ride home?"

I could feel how I felt then--cocooned in his presence, shielded from everything else around us, my skin tingling from my neck down to my toes.

"Maggie, these are your future in-laws, you can't just hide out in the bathroom because you're embarrassed."

My heart was racing. "I'm pregnant, I'm sure they'll understand."

"Oh, speaking of which, I noticed you ordered shrimp tonight."

"Observant."

"You might want to cut back. Mercury and all. Plus shrimp are disgusting creatures. Do you have that book *What to Expect When You're Expecting* yet? It's all in there. Things you probably never thought about. You don't want to slowly poison my grandbabies, do you?"

I wished the industrial toilet had enough power to swallow me with all the toilet paper I was stuffing in it. "Say goodnight to Ray for me."

"I'll apologize to Mr. and Mrs. Callahan on your behalf." She was fixing her lipstick. I could tell by the slurred way her words came out. "Such a strong name. Meagan *Callahan*."

"Good night."

It was just as I emerged from the stall that the restroom door flew back open. "Almost forgot my phone," she said, holding out her palm, drawn-in eyebrows raised.

I didn't realize that I had been staring at the picture. She appeared pleased by this fact.

I turned slowly to the mirror, raised my eyes to look at my reflection for once. My dark brown eyes, almond shaped and the spitting image of my dad's, were puffy and bloodshot, my cheeks blotchy. My lips looked inflamed, the corners downcast. The surge of hormones had caused skin discoloration, dark splotches that looked like smudged freckles. If not for my long hair, also a trait inherited from my dad, I wouldn't recognize myself. I teased at it, bringing the strands forward, to try to disguise my face. *Cousin It.*

I thought of Will that day so long ago, bracing my face in his hands. "Do you want a ride home?"

My mouth had curled up against my best efforts. " Well, as long as you're going that direction, I suppose I can save myself the public transportation experience."

He had stroked his fingers over my forehead, moving my hair off my face and examining the goose egg, which I knew had started to turn purple that morning. His forehead furrowed and he leaned forward, kissed it gingerly.

I looked up at him through the veil of bangs. He seemed pleased with my response.

I surveyed the interior of his truck as he rounded the back tailgate, talking briefly to Katie. It was tidy, his backpack seemingly stored on the floor of the backseat in preparation for me occupying the passenger side. There was a plethora of CDs stacked under the stereo, a to-go cup and water bottle in the console mounted beneath the dash, and his grandfather's dog tags from World War II hung from the rear view mirror. He was slightly winded when he joined me.

"I asked Katie if she wanted a ride--" He began, waving to her as she reached her two-door sporty hatchback. I can only imagine the look Katie had on her face--I was too busy watching Will in surreal disbelief as he checked his mirrors and glanced over his shoulder before pulling out into the parking lot traffic. Once on the main road, he sensed me staring. "What? Do I have something on my face? I grabbed lunch for the drive down." He brushed at his shirt, checked his face in the rearview.

"No. It's just weird to see you. Here. Anywhere, actually."

"How have you been?" he asked in mock formality. "Besides the assasination attempt."

"Other than that, things have been going well." My voice wavered a bit. "Just busy with school, studying for mid-terms."

"You're only taking 3 or 4 AP classes, I'm sure."

"5."

"You're joking."

I shook my head.

"Wait, did I say joking? I meant crazy."

"Well the key to overachieving is to remove the leisure time, like sleeping."

"No kidding." His eyes scanned over me. "You look good, Reeves."

I smiled tightly.

"I mean it. Good job growing up. Some really fumble it, but you, you stuck the landing."

I laughed uncomfortably. "I don't stick many landings. You know that."

"Hold on, let's see the knobby knees." At the red light, he examined my kneecaps, pulling back the hem of my uniform plaid skirt. "Yep, bruised as always." His eyes paused on the sight of my legs. "So smooth though. I don't think you were shaving the last time I took a close look." He ran his hand over my thigh.

My mouth fell open and I pulled forcefully at my skirt, batting his hand away. "You are so rude."

He smiled broadly and pressed on the accelerator. "You do look good though, Reeves."

"Thanks. I noticed you finally grew into your ears."

He chuckled.

"Have you figured out what you're doing after graduation?"

"Sure have. I'm joining the Army."

"You are?" My heart lurched, my eyes glancing to the dog tags on the rearview. His grandfather was in the Army, his uncles, his dad went the officer route… "Continuing the legacy?"

"I don't want that legacy pressure, but it's kind of in my blood, I guess. Also figure they'll pay for my school. Best to get out of college without a mountain of debt, right?"

"How does your mom feel about it?"

"Oh my mom is pissed. Blames my dad. She thinks he was too tough about my grades. He basically said I was on my own for paying for college."

"I'd bet he'd change his mind if you get your grades up.*

"I know and I'm working on it."

"Good. You've always been smarter than your grades reflect."

He peered across the cab at me, his eyes bright.

"From what I remember, you had a tendency to be a little lazy when it came to school."

He nods.

"Of course that was *way* back when I had leg hair."

A smile took over his face and he eyed my legs again. He reached out his right hand. "One more touch? They're so soft and smooth."

I allowed it, trying to keep a straight face, though my cheeks were hot. The last time we spent a lengthy amount of time together, we were riding bikes together and I was in a short-alls phase.

He retracted his hand slowly, focused on the road ahead. "You've got some long legs, Reeves." His eyebrows jumped. "I'll bet you have a lot of prep school boys eyeing those bad boys."

I rolled my eyes.

"You do."

I shook my head definitively. "No."

"Well what's a day in the life like?"

"Well my day is packed at school and then I have to catch the bus. Katie's been the only one I've gotten to hang out with since she lives closer to our side of town. I don't socialize too much with people from school. Mostly people Katie knows."

"Oh yeah?"

"Yeah, I'm going to Homecoming with this guy she's known since preschool."

"*Ahhhh.*" He stretches the word to a inquisitively awkward length. "Tell me about the young man."

I raised an eyebrow. "Young man? You're the same age."

"Oh, he's older than you."

"Everybody's older than me in my grade."

"That's right, you skipped 4th grade. So what's his name? What's he like?"

"His name is Chris. He's nice. Tall. He's involved in youth groups at his church. He plays hockey. He's in my AP English class."

He was regretfully impressed, like he almost wished I'd told him he was a felon. "Well you deserve someone nice."

"We're not shopping for rings, Will. He's a friend. Neither of us had dates," I say, shrugging. "Just worked out."

Will appeared somewhat satisfied by the explanation. "So, were you headed home or to your grandparents'?"

My heart sank. In an instant I could smell the leather-bound books, the fresh cut flowers, the crackling fire. I was quiet long enough for him to glance over at me a couple times as traffic allowed. "My grandparents' house was sold about a year and a half ago."

He frowned.

"My grandpa was diagnosed with a really aggressive, late stage cancer."

"I'm so sorry, I didn't know."

"He died a few weeks after they found it. My grandma really started to decline after he died--you know she had early Alzheimers--"

Will nodded.

"My aunt had her move in with her, but the transition was tough. She ended up in a nursing home memory unit. She seems to enjoy the activities--they do gardening and art and puzzles and things like that, but she doesn't know me anymore." The last time I had visited her, she thought it was 1980 and she was excited to vote for "that handsome actor" to be President.

Will took a firm hold of the wheel, his body tense suddenly. "I wish I had known, Reeves. I really wish--" He was abrupt braking at the next light. "He was such a cool person to talk to. He knew everything."

I sighed. "I haven't gotten used to it. I still find myself wanting to slip into my old routines, go over to their house, sit with him in the chairs by the fireplace."

"What happened to all those books? The tea sets?"

"Oh. Well, the tea sets went with my grandma, of course. I think the books got donated, which is a shame. I would have loved to have had some of them." I leaned my head back. "I did get his sweater."

"The one with the elbow patches?"

I smiled tightly. "It's silly I know, but I love it. It was washed and everything, but I swear I can still smell that room when I wear it."

"It's not silly," he said softly.

"I should have told you when it happened. He really liked you, Will."

He made the final turn and pulled up along the curb to my house. His eyes glistened a bit in the afternoon sun as I held his gaze. His mouth turned up on one end.

"Thank you for the ride," I said and in a moment of pure impulse, I slid across the bench seat and kissed his cheek.

***

"Is your stomach feeling better?" Nathan asked once we got back to his condo. It was a sterile looking place with a lot of windows, white walls, streamlined furnishings, and glass occasional tables. I was constantly leaving drink rings and was always fearful of breaking something. There were boxes everywhere because it was decided that it wasn't big enough for us and twins. I hadn't even moved my things in yet. I looked around and longed to be at my rented sailboat. Alone. Alone would be better. Alone, but 8 months earlier would have been even better.

Three months. Twins. House-hunting. Kind of a lot to take on with a man whose middle name I realized I didn't know when asked by a coworker who had taken on the challenge of naming the babies for us (something that didn't rhyme, but that still sounded like they fit together). And whose date of birth was still a little iffy in my mind. Was he born on the 15th or the 17th? Was he seven years older than me, or eight...or was it more? (I had to guess on the paperwork at my OB-GYN's office.)

I dropped to the couch. It was beige and felt like it had a millimeter of cushion over its frame so my landing was a bit painful. "No."

"Maybe it was the shrimp?"

I glared at him.

"Your mom was mentioning that seafood isn't the best during pregnancy--my mom said the same thing. They were talking about it while we were waiting for you."

"Can we not discuss food right now?"

"Oh. Right." He looked around awkwardly. "Are you tired?"

I didn't know much about him, but I did know that the man was serious about an early bedtime. "Not really."

"Do you mind if I head off to bed? I have an early meeting in the morning."

Thank God. What box has movies? "No, not at all."

He kissed me on the head and stumbled through saying "Love you."

Three months.

Once I heard the shower start, I grabbed Nathan's laptop (he wasn't satisfied with my virus protection and had quarantined it until he could upgrade it, as to prevent contamination with the rest of the home network), impatiently waited for it to come off hibernation. I did a quick search and found what I had been looking for. Will's profile photo was changed back to the one he used since he reluctantly joined the site at his brother's insistence. I took the photo. We were visiting Katie and her husband in Monterey. The picture was at a restaurant overlooking the ocean during his leave after his second tour--Will had enjoyed Happy Hour with Tim while I intended to support newly pregnant Katie with our virgin daiquiris. Will had taken the liberty of dumping a shot of rum in mine. We were all a little sunburned from going to the beach all day and not reapplying sunblock. Katie, all organic, gluten-free, dairy-free Katie, ate snow cones and snacked on Nacho Cheese Doritos, her latest craving while Tim and Will tried to teach me to surf. I finally popped up on what was to be my last attempt so we could still make our dinner reservation. I remember their cheers right before I face-planted.

In the photo, Will was showing off his beer bottle, which was a locally brewed ale of some kind, toasting the camera. His eyes, ordinarily a cool brown, were particularly glazed over, from the buzz and from the sun. His unmanageable hair, a shade darker than mine, flipped up in various directions.

He had made a joke out of taming his hair as we got ready for dinner, slicking it in two equal sections on either side of his head. He looked like a Congressman. To which I created an Alfalfa tail. Eventually I just scratched my fingers vigorously through his hair and that messy 'do was what he wore to dinner.

I remember looking at the photo when I first picked up the prints, thinking how happy he looked, his gaze fixed on me taking the photo, rather than the camera. I had a hard time believing I had a hand in that happiness. It had to have been some outside source—the beer, the locale, the friends—but the more I studied it, the more I felt a smile of my own creeping across my lips.

That's when he returned with a movie rental and a pint of gelato for us to share. He stopped short of the tattered bench seat in the boat, which served as the couch. He asked me what I was thinking about, to which I explained what my mind went through looking at the photo of him.

"You don't understand how happy you make me?" he asked, genuinely concerned. He crouched to the floor then plopped into a sitting position, releasing an exaggerated groan about being old. "Reeves, do you realize how much I love you?"

"Most of the time? Honestly, no. But I look at this photo and I see it. I feel it."

To which he had said: "Well at the risk of sounding egotistical, we need to blow that bad boy up to like billboard-size, frame it, and hang it on the wall. Make a keychain out of it. Put it on your mouse pad. So you never ever forget."

My heart exhaled, remembering those words, how they had flowed through me, warm and comforting.

I pulled my phone out of my pocket and dialed his number, blocking my number first. His phone rang. And rang. It was understandable. I let unknown numbers go to voicemail. Of course he would, too.

Then, he answered. Not too enthusiastic a hello, not a depressed hello. Not excited. Not sad. Not lonely, but not particularly happy either. "Hello?"

I panicked, slammed my phone shut. What did I have to say? I wasn't in a position to yell at him and what would that help? He was married. Baby on the way. He could just hang up on me. Why would he give me the time of day when he had a good life? *Too bad you're not dealing with things so well, Reeves, but I'm happy.*

I went out on the patio, pulled my knees up to my chest, stared at the stars. They weren't very bright with glow of the freeway so close. It would have been an idyllic time to cry, but my body didn't feel physically capable of doing so. I felt hollow. If I followed my instinct to go to the boat, I feared the repercussions. My mother would descend, Nathan's family would all descend on me. They would be worse. If possible, they would make me feel worse and I would potentially lose Nathan's support, which provided me with a layer of protection from their opinions. I would have no one on my side. I had Katie, but she was hundreds of miles away and was all too enthusiastic about having kids about the same age, regardless of the other circumstances.

At some point around 2 or 3 am, I found my way to Nathan's bed. I suppose the bed was technically mine, too, though I never knew myself to care for firm mattresses. He had made an effort to make me comfortable, buying a down alternative mattress topper, twin size for my side of the bed.

Here I was pining away for someone who didn't think I deserved a face-to-face break-up when I had a hard-working man who put up with my array of faults with such patience.

So your mother is living rent free in your head now, isn't that special?

I crawled into bed and rested my head on Nathan's outstretched arm. I nudged into him to try to wake him.

"Well hey there," he said, surprised and, I think, pleased to have me in such close proximity.

"Hey."

"What's on your mind?" he asked, groggily flopping his free arm over me.

"Nathan, do you *want* to marry me?"

"I'd be an idiot not to."

I was stumped by this response. Not one part of it made sense to me. I'd be less perplexed had he given the brutally honest answer.

"Are you warming to the idea?" He sounded more alert.

I shrugged.

"It doesn't have to be anything big."

"Can it be Vegas?"

"Vegas?"

This went against his traditional ways. His guest list would probably sound more like the population of a small town.

"I know it's a cliché, but it's a quick flight and it can serve as a getaway for us, too." *Plus the local courthouse would be an open invitation for guests.*

"Maggie, I don't want you to be stressed out with wedding plans. We can always have a big ceremony next year once the babies arrive."

I had purposely not thought too far ahead. Suddenly I saw us with twins: two cribs, double stroller, piles of bottles, tripping over toys. He would be the one up in the middle of night with me when the babies were fussy, if he wasn't the type to prioritize his own sleep, that is. He'd be the one in the delivery room trying to relax me, but what tactics would he try? Would they even work? He'd be the one to share memories of first solids, first Christmas, first day of school, first boyfriend or girlfriend. This would be the man sitting next to me at their school events, graduations, weddings.

What kind of father would he be? Would they look like him with his slim frame and pointed features? If we had a boy, would he have trouble growing facial hair down the road? Would they be three and wearing eyeglasses since their mom wore contacts most of the time and their dad wore glasses? Would they have a preference for glasses over contacts later because he wears them? Would they be laid back and a little clumsy like me or precise and orderly like him?

What kind of mother would I be, particularly when, according to my mother, our kids turned out to be little devils as payback for my childhood? Actually, regarding that remark, I remember being a pretty well-mannered child. I hushed my classmates in preschool when they were being noisy, for crying out loud. How bad could I have possibly been?

Would I be barreled over by my mother, by his family? Would my opinions be outnumbered and go unheard, like how I said we would create our own baby registry and my mother went ahead and started one (in between dining experiences)? Would I be like the girls in *The Giver,* sentenced to a life of reproduction, only to have each child essentially stripped away to be raised by someone else and be sent "Elsewhere" when I passed my prime reproductive years?

"It can be Vegas," he said, kissing me. "Vegas it is. I'll see if Pete will approve some PTO on such short notice."

His practicality failed to halt my psychological tailspin knowing I had really, really screwed up my life. In fact, it made the tailspin more jarring and nauseating. It could be worse--I was pregnant with twins, a blessing, and while I didn't know a lot about Nathan, he wasn't about to murder me and dump me in a river. He was a nice guy. Did I love him? No. I was pining for a married man who wanted nothing to do with me.

I was pining for a married man who wanted nothing to do with me.

Then why had he changed his profile picture from the one of him and Cadence to the one of just him, a photo I took that held so much significance and meaning?

To you.

It has significance and meaning *to you.*

Maybe he just likes how he looks.

5
shore thing

The day I was given my diagnosis did not start off well. It didn't end terribly well either I suppose.

It started off with me mistakenly being told to fast for my appointment. My appointment was at 1pm. I did nothing but plan what I was going to get for lunch on the drive home, distractions and the inner monologue my only two remaining coping mechanisms.

I had convinced Nathan to let me come to the appointment alone. It was a part of the negotiations of me not filing annulment papers. I had filled them out online and had just needed to download the proper printer driver that the court used in order to print the packet.

The deal we reached, after he convinced me that I was being impulsive to jump to an annulment because I was scared and that he loved me and wanted to be with me, was:

- Maggie does not file annulment or divorce papers.
- Maggie remains in recently closed residence. (He put an offer on a house his brother found without telling me before our elopement.)
- Nathan does not come to doctor's appointment for results.
- Nathan does not inform Maggie's mother about doctor's appointment.

- Should follow-up doctor's appointments be required, Maggie dictates who will know and who will attend.

In a short period of time, Nathan had become tolerant of my emotional shortcomings. After losing the babies and having to wait out "recovery" time in a house I hated, I threw myself into working. I often stayed after I was supposed to. When I wasn't working, I was sleeping. I never cried. I used monosyllabic responses. So I suppose hearing him out as he presented his counter to my announcing the dissolution of our marriage was a giant step for me.

It probably should have been a gigantic red flag that the man didn't take the out; escape from the crazy person who just couldn't seem to figure anything out. So rather than fleeing the entanglement of our Elvis witnessed vows (who went by the name Frank Whittenberg), he spoke about how we hadn't even given ourselves a chance to work. There was so much thrown at us. He joked about reuniting with my mother. *What a riot. Next we should peel off all your finger and toe nails.* "That also sounds like a grand idea, doesn't it?"

I laughed lightly out of sheer politeness. Then he made a jab at his own annoying habits and like most comedy based in truth, it was far more comical.

The conversation started to feel reminiscent, like we were friends. In spite of my inner sarcasm, we had become friends. He let me do whatever I had wanted with the nursery. [Although the rest of the house was stark, boring, and breakable so after we lost the babies and I couldn't bring myself to set foot in their room, it was back to feeling like a visitor in what was supposed to be my home.] He even called me in sick to a dinner with my parents in favor of sending me for a massage and meeting me for dinner after, just the two of us. Holding hands was mildly comforting and started to feel less foreign. Having him wrap his arms around me at night made me feel less alone.

So I agreed to give "us" a chance.

There was one additional provision of the agreement:

- Maggie gets whatever takeout she desires after fasting for said doctor's appointment.

I was joking when I insisted Nathan include it. I watched his eyes widen as he wrote it out in tiny neat letters, internalizing something.

I had chosen sushi. I had it all planned out. I would call in my order as I was walking out to the car. With the distance I would have to walk to reach the car and minimal traffic in the early afternoon, taking into account school zones and carpool lane restrictions, I would be sitting in our backyard struggling with chopsticks within 20 to 25 minutes of leaving my appointment. I could take a nap, possibly go for a swim in the community pool. There would be a window of time with no human interaction.

I scanned the menu on my phone as I sat in the waiting room. When they called my name, I was debating shrimp tempura and the customer favorite roll, which appeared to be double deep fried and drizzled with eel sauce. I would ask them to hold the smelt eggs because those little orange orbs only remind me of Nemo's mother and siblings being gobbled up by a barracuda.

I didn't know yet to take notice when they led me right past the scale, which is a sign of mercy in the medical community. If there's bad news to deliver, might as well spare the patient from having to take off shoes and feel guilt over meal choices. (Not to mention every single follow-up visit, every lab work visit, every infusion would require those checks.) The nurse didn't ask me any of the standard questions—"How are you today?", "Why are you here today?" She didn't even comment about the weather, which was actually quite pleasant. It would have been nice to remark about it. She just led me into the exam room, directed me to sit on the couch, which I did, like it was a regular annual exam and the most significant thing I would be inquiring about was perhaps a multivitamin or testing thyroid function (since I guess that's a thing women over 20 do regularly). She lingered at the door, looked back at me, exhaled. Then she was gone.

I do enjoy rainbow rolls, I remember thinking stupidly, glancing casually at the diplomas and certificates on the wall behind the exam table. USD. Johns Hopkins. A residency at Mayo Clinic. Clearly an under-achiever. *Rainbow rolls are healthier than the crunchy fried rolls.*

"Meagan, thanks for coming in."

Also, it's awkward to be thanked by a physician for an appointment. It's like telling a patient being discharged from the hospital to come back soon. Some customer service pleasantries simply don't cross industries very well.

Dr. Hennessy rolled her chair closer to the couch when I had failed to say a word for close to five minutes after she delivered the report.

The only thing I managed to utter in that time was: "I'm 22."

When I left, I was calm.

I clutched the information folder that also carried my treatment schedule in my hand, prepared prior to my appointment, as I called to place my food order.

I got to the Jeep, set the folder on the passenger seat (when you have a cancer diagnosis, they splurge on the color copies and expensive textured pamphlets and folders), put the key in the ignition and sat.

I sat there long enough to sincerely piss off a man in a Porshe Cayenne who had hoped to snag my parking spot.

I sat there long enough for clouds to roll in and darken the sky, then roll out again.

I sat there long enough to earn a glare from the sushi chef when I finally picked up my order. Apparently they had to scrap the original order since the hostess had combined the hot and cold rolls in one bag. If I had been there in 10-15 minutes, as I was supposed to be, it would have been fine. Because I arrived an hour and a half later than anticipated, the chef had to make a fresh order. I almost told them to forget it, I would pay, but I no longer wanted the food, but I thought that might be more offensive and awkward. So I apologized softly under my breath.

I was instructed to wait so I sat and stared at the waving cat on the hostess stand. It's supposed to be good luck, but to me it looks like a rejected Hello Kitty character. I glared at the happy little beast and wondered: *Why are you knocking?* The rhythm of the silent knocking did seem to go along well with the chant echoing in my head: *You have cancer. You have cancer. You have cancer.*

Aside from the knocking cat, the restaurant had a zen-like ambiance. One entire wall was bamboo, real bamboo as far as I could tell. The floors were glossy concrete. The wall behind the sushi chefs looked like stone, the restaurant name bold against the gray in a contemporary handwritten font. The name looked incomplete, like it was missing an adjective. Nice Day. Sunny Day. Fucked up day.

Nathan finally texted me. "*R u still at doc?*"

I hate text-talk, by the way. I feel like it is making the human population incrementally less intelligent. "*No.*"

"*?*"

Does he really expect me to dive into my diagnosis via text? I rolled my eyes. I knew I should call him, but I didn't want to so I responded with "*T2A.*" I wondered what Google search would do with that search term. It would probably return some electronics component or something sold by a third-party seller on Amazon that would take 3 months to arrive.

It's cancer. Stage 2 ovarian cancer. T2A describes a cancer that has spread or attached to the uterus and/or fallopian tubes.

He didn't get it. How could he? I didn't clarify further. Instead, I texted that I needed to be alone, which he returned with several more question mark texts and three follow-up phone calls before I turned off my phone. Katie had wanted to come along with me to the appointment, but was on her planned vacation at my insistence. There was no signal at her family's cabin, which was optimal if anyone started to call her repeatedly, but inconvenient to those who desperately needed to talk to her best friend.

Since Nathan was in meetings, I braved going to the house. I spent all of 90 seconds there, paranoid Nathan would show up any minute and stop me. I grabbed my passport and the ultrasound printouts (though I didn't know why).

I knew there was no way I could stay there.

I had big plans for what I could do--fly somewhere exotic, be adventurous, deny the hell out of reality. I was on the coastal highway when three inescapable facts consumed my thoughts:

1) I had an aggressive form of cancer.

2) I had just buried two babies.

3) I had absolutely no one to talk to about 1 or 2. Not about the disaster that was my life without considering the cancer. Not about the fact that attempts

had been made to comfort me with 5-year survival statistics. 85%. 85% chance of living 5 more years if additional testing didn't present any other surprises.

I had stared blankly at Dr. Hennessy when she went through the statistics, frowned probably, and said weakly: "I'd be 27."

She had dropped her optimistic eyebrows, moved to the couch beside me and embraced me. She wasn't well-practiced at the act, that was obvious, but I appreciated the sentiment.

After the brief stop at the house, I went to the boat. It was the only place I could go. Despite being ridiculed for the living arrangement, it was home, more so than anywhere else I'd lived. There I stayed, tucked in the cool sheets in the cozy alcove bed reading until my swollen eyes mercifully couldn't stay open any longer.

The next morning, I woke a bit disoriented in the silence. I climbed out of the cabin, finding a sunrise and the hum of the regular morning commute close by.

I had sailed just far enough from the dock and anchored there so I wouldn't have any visitors. My confused neighbor waved to me from the dock, some fifty yards away. I looked over my shoulder at the horizon beyond the bow, yawning, then back across the dock to the nearby highway.

It was one of the quickest decisions I had ever made. I drifted the boat back to the dock, secured the cabin then swung my way through the rails onto the dock. I made a very surreal shopping excursion for groceries then returned to the boat named *Shore Thing* and set sail for the next 10 days.

When I think of that time, it's one of my favorite segments of my life. I remember the open ocean. The wind in my unmanageably long dark hair. I remember wearing a bikini I had in my clothes collection for about 5 years that I had never had the courage to wear before. I didn't care how I looked. There wasn't a mirror on the boat. I made good use of groceries, but I also fished for dinner. I played the ukulele sitting on the bench seats surrounding the helm. At night I'd sit on the bow, resting against the cabin windows staring up at the sky and all its constellations. I read at least a book a day. When I got warm, I'd leap into the cold Pacific. I thought about life, but in more of a reflective, mindful sense. With fondness. Focused on the moment at hand. I changed tasks to keep my mind from wandering to uncomfortable topics. That seemed to be the trick-- distraction.

No distractions could save me from running out of groceries. I would have come back after a week had I not convinced myself that living on fish and water was a feasible option. I had to face reality and I had a slew of doctor appointments that had been set. Plus I needed to get back to work. I had been making such headway on getting a research grant approved prior to going out on leave—I longed getting back to it.

I actually pulled into the marina feeling quite motivated--and grimey. I opted to take a shower in the marina facilities, where I got a look at myself for the first time in a week and a half. Besides being about 20 shades darker than my usual skin tone, I looked--content. I also looked a bit fitter. My hair was untamed. It look a solid 15 minutes to brush it out. I couldn't help but notice that my mouth seemed to be naturally upturned, ready to face the challenges ahead.

That changed when I got to the house. I drove there visualizing myself getting lost in my job, even the menial tasks. Loving every bit of it, even the data analysis, impressing the powers that be, who incidentally liked me quite a bit anyway. I didn't think about all that was involved with treatment. I hadn't thought of losing my hair or becoming weak and having to rely on someone for daily care.

I was planning to file those papers once and for all.

Nathan quickly brought me down to reality.

I stopped short of telling him that I still wanted to get a divorce, if annulment wasn't an option. I was too busy getting hit by the tsunami of information he had prepared for me, while I was off doing my "thrillseeker thing," as he called it. Each time he hinted a jab at my behavior, I nearly told him off, but he was strategic and followed up with a fact that reminded me how young and irresponsible I was and just how much I needed him. It was eerily familiar. Effective.

During our "conversation," we were in the kitchen. My arriving "home," which he had taken the liberty of decorating to his liking, coincided with him returning from Whole Grain, Crunchy Snobbery Foods Market, so he was unpacking groceries. Not just unpacking—*smelling* each melon, squeezing each piece of fruit to make sure that it was the same texture as at the store, divvying up everything into their separate stay-fresh containers. If it weren't for the fact that I lived with him and his quirks annoyed the hell out of me, I would have been taking notes on how he managed to get strawberries to last for two weeks without turning to mush and fuzz. But I did live with him so therefore when he was annoying me I found his abundance of knowledge on everything from fruit to computer components to aboriginal cultures to be insufferable. Like Frasier Crane, but with less fondness for wine. Unfortunately. Wine probably would have loosened him up a little.

Where was I?

Yes, I was discussing with my husband of 3.5 months, acquaintance of 8.5, plus the one-night stand, that at twenty-two years old, I had ovarian cancer. And he was sniffing his fruit for quality assurance.

Finally he took his nose away from the cantaloupe and crossed the kitchen to grab a binder I had never seen before. I took the opportunity to take a deep breath. In doing so, I noticed the air smelled overwhelmingly like toilet bowl cleaner. The odor turned out to be an "ocean breeze" room deodorizer plug-in. The longer I stood there, the more uneasy I felt. The smell sparked memories of a rather horrible morning I woke up smelling like the bar soap version by no action of my own. The scene of the messy bedroom flashed in my head from the night prior--the lights were on and glared in my eyes. Darkness. Flash of my body flailing in an eerily ragdoll fashion. That son of a bitch Jerry. Darkness. Flash to struggling, fighting, being pushed down. Merciful darkness again.

"Maggie." Nathan was staring at me, suddenly very close, reassuringly stroking my arm. "We'll get through this."

The loneliness of that memory made me fearful of being on my own again--Nathan would protect me, love me, be with me. And so I nodded. I looked at the fresh groceries sprawled across the counter with a new appreciation. Healthy foods. Foods to help me fight the cancer.

He came out with this plan for me from the newly retrieved binder (he likes bulleted lists):

- I would quit my job, or at the very least, take an extended leave if they were agreeable and focus on just getting well. I hated this item the most, but I nodded along because everything he was saying made perfect, logical sense.

- His independent contractor insurance was decent. High deductible and the yearly out of pocket max was substantial, but at least it covered most cancer treatments, even experimental.

- We would eat nothing that wasn't organic and nothing that had ever been frozen, canned, seen the inside of a factory that also handles nuts, or that was delivered, either through a window, in a takeout bag, or in a vehicle marked with a big sign on its roof.

- We would travel to the main hubs of premier healthcare for second opinions—Minnesota, Maryland, if we were not satisfied with my care. There was a college in Colorado currently doing a research study he was inquiring about.

- My cell phone would need to be upgraded, despite not qualifying for the discount yet, so I could keep in contact with unlimited everything.

- We would do brunch every Sunday with our parents. I should spend at least an evening or two—or daytime even since I wouldn't be working—with my mother. Because I would really need her. His mother would also love to spend time with me. And it would be positive for me to bond with his sister. And make other friends due to the fact that I wasn't "very social".

I had an out of body experience--and a terrible headache--by the time he hit the point about our parents so I excused myself to go to bed. I climbed right in, not bothering to brush my teeth or wash my face or put on lotion. No one had given me instruction to do any of those things, after all, and clearly I needed guidance for all aspects of life or I'd make a disaster of it.

6
distress signals

Five months later...

When I was little, there were few things I feared more than my mother's sneeze. Perhaps I was traumatized whilst in the womb. Another possibility is that the force and decibel reminded me of how she sounded when she yelled. Both had a constricted, shrill quality.

This is what I'm thinking about in Chemo. I'm also trying to psychoanalyze my seven year old self who often heard yelling and screaming in her head. Not even intelligible words, just words garbled together in an off-key, nails on the chalkboard kind of pitch. I don't remember ever telling anyone. Actually I remember knowing even back then that telling my mother would be more trouble than it was worth. I suspect it was echoing what my mind heard at night when I was sleeping. Eventually the yelling in my head stopped, coincidentally around the age that she had decided I was old enough to hear quite a bit of yelling while fully awake.

My internal self-help session is interrupted when Dennis drops the f-bomb, breaking the silence. It's no emergency, not medical at least, but I do see his Excel spreadsheets up on his screen.

Chemo is like an institution-mandated social event/study hall with a group of misfit strangers. They could make a movie of it, like a spin of *Breakfast Club*.

I had been assured repeatedly that the hospital was aiming to make the experience more private, that the designs were going to committees, that it was in the 5 year plan. It was meant as an apology for the lack of privacy in their current facilities, and to deter complaints, I assume. The hospital seemed a bit too fixated on 5 year plans. I resisted the urge several times to share that my 5 year plan was to not die.

Chemo takes place in one large room lined with windows that let in a slightly too optimistic amount of daylight. The room is filled with five maroon recliners, each with its own IV telescoping pole attached to the wooden armrest. Two beds are situated in the corner with the luxury of privacy curtains for patients too weak to sit for the entire session. In my particular group, for four designated hours, five people of varying ages are positioned toward each other, trying to come up with something to talk about other than their stage of cancer.

If you don't like your session companions, well, it's like a really long flight trapped in the center seat when you have to pee. Oh and peeing before you start a session is absolutely essential. I once had to roll the IV pole into the bathroom with me and was terrified the whole time of accidentally pulling out the line and being sprayed by radioactive substance, which in my head, would melt the skin from the bone. Logic be damned.

Fortunately for me, I've decided to like everyone in the group. I find it easier to offer patience to those who are going through the same hell as me. *Most other people can kiss my alabaster ass.*

Walt is the elder of the group in that he's the oldest and has been in chemo the longest. Age spots line the smooth ebony skin of his cheekbones and his muted brown eyes have specks of copper. He has the warm wisdom you'd expect of a grandpa. I look at him and can imagine him a bit younger before his legs became so weak, with grandchildren on both knees listening intently to his stories. He's an amazing story teller. His voice is calming, his words paint amazing scenes, and he's lived a really fascinating life. His stories kept me sane early on and are, without a doubt, the only draw I have to come to chemo...besides the not-wanting-to-die 5 year plan.

He was an English Lit professor with an exceptional talent for the saxophone. He married his high school sweetheart whom he wrote letters to every day he was deployed during the Korean War. He has six children, four boys, two girls, and fifteen grandchildren. I believe wholeheartedly that he should provide the voice for audio books. If I believed in social media, I would totally promote him to family and friends on some obnoxious crowd-funding site.

He's had prostate cancer, testicular cancer, and most recently, bone cancer. He says the bright side is that he doesn't have to attach an unfortunate body part to the name of his cancer this time around, although saying "bone" leads to more questions, whereas people tended to end the questioning when he had testicular.

Dennis is in his mid-50s and swears a lot. Despite the weakening effects of treatments, he's maintained much of his muscle tone, which he shows off under tight-fitting shirts. His gray hair is cropped short, which helps to disguise the bald spots. He has a really kind, albeit passive wife, who tolerates his hostility with a vague smile on her face. He worked construction all his life and now runs his own business, a position that allows him to be absent much of the time. During treatments, he can be counted on to provide additional mood lighting from the glow of his laptop as he does the accounting for the business, which evidently (based on the swearing) could be doing better. He has twin sons, both in the police academy.

He was diagnosed with aggressive stage 4 lung cancer three months ago.

Gayle is in her mid-sixties and promiscuous as Britney Spears, circa 2003. If you're too young to get that reference, look at any current so-called "feminist" pop singer. Poor Britney was tame compared to these girls with buzzed haircuts and strap ons grinding up on their backup dancers.

What the hell is wrong with pop culture anyway? Serious question. Cool is now overtly and grotesquely sexual? But you need to judge me for my mind. But you also need to find me attractive no matter what. But you are not to sexualize me.

Anyway.

Gayle.

She has big hair, black and heavily teased--A wig that suits her personality. Her skin is leathery from years of tanning. Clinique probably maintains itself as a public trading asset with the monthly contribution of her purchases alone. Everything is an extreme with her—either the best or the worst, gorgeous or hideous, wonderful or awful. She calls everyone "sweetie." She's endearing in her own way. She is twice divorced, still madly in love with a man who cheated on her when her kids were teenagers.

Breast cancer, detected early.

Lenny is in his mid-thirties, tall and lanky, former Navy, who still maintains a thick head of short black hair. He has a chiseled jawline that has become more prominent with each session and not in the way you want to see. His eyes are disarmingly blue. He's definitely the strong, silent type, politely keeping to himself. He has a sweet wife and an adorable curly haired daughter with down syndrome.

Blood cancer. Stage Two.

I'm typically situated between Walt and Lenny. Walt is filling in his crosswords book, a pair of thick reading glasses positioned at the base of his nose. He's chosen a subtle plaid button down shirt, the sleeves cuffed up to just below his elbows. Lenny has his earbuds in and his Kindle Fire in his hand, effectively deterring anyone from conversing with him.

Nurse Trish finishes adjusting the line on my left arm and I regret forgetting my extra pillow in the car before Nathan left for a few hours of work, my body already stiff and dreading the next four hours. She places her hand reassuringly on my back and tells me to let her know if I need anything. She then moves over to check on Lenny's drip. I settle into my chair, putting up the foot rest. The vinyl already feels sweaty against my skin, despite the chilly hospital air. I stagger the stack of magazines, books and movies. Nothing is the same anymore. Magazines that feature celebrities that once offered cheap entertainment value during pedicures make me resentful of their seemingly easy lives. They don't have to deal with cancer and if they do, they have buckets of cash. They would have chemo in the privacy of their own home. Yes, same drugs, same side effects, but they could also afford the medical marijuana. The good stuff.

I move on to book options. I've always been picky about books—if the first few pages didn't jump out and grab my attention they'd be shelved. Now, it's even worse. I don't have time for boring books. 5-year-plan and all. I once got halfway through a paperback (this was after a particularly bad experience at a mandated Sunday brunch with my mother) and didn't like the direction the author was taking (it was too sickeningly sweet and fairytale like for my taste) so I tossed it in the kitchen trash with some used coffee grinds. Then I felt guilty because it seemed disrespectful to destroy a person's life work. I was unsuccessful in retrieving it from the garbage due to some dripping egg shells that made me nauseous.

But in my defense, I was in a delicate emotional state and the protagonist was too damn happy.

Movies also contain references I never noticed before and am probably far too sensitive to at this point.

I finally decide on *Pirates of the Caribbean*, which I find sufficiently emotional neutral, and insert the disc into Nathan's spare computer, dumping the remaining objectionable materials into my backpack. As I slip on headphones, I notice the disapproving stare of Lenny. I must seem so disheveled. By comparison, he is so orderly and efficient. I imagine that he has a method for everything he does. It probably frustrates him that the process of chemo takes so long, that it has to be one drip at a time. He goes back to whatever he's reading and I return to my hand-me-down computer, feeling only a slight sting as I disappoint yet another person in my life.

I open an Internet window and follow Nathan's instructions to connect the WiFi. I find the bookmark for a dog rescue, where I've been following the Adoptables page. Nathan wouldn't go for a puppy. Not even with the justification that I'm home so much and I could really use the company. Actually, a perfectly trained adult dog would be a stretch, given his intolerance for dirt. I click the Favorites menu and find the other folders—Travel: Hawaii, Key West, Italy, Nepal, Japan, Maldives; To Do: Ice Skating lessons, Bungee jumping, Adoption tips for cancer survivors, Doctorate program, Organic gardening for beginners, Cooking 101, Horseback riding lessons. I close the menu and switch back to the movie. Bucket lists are supposed to be inspiring, but these days I find them depressing. It's as unrealistic as making a lottery list to me at this point, but in case you're wondering: Beach house in some remote part of Hawaii, dog, some travel.

Unwisely, I allow myself the thought I usually push to the back of my mind, particularly unwise because I'm stuck in this chair for four hours:

It's depressing because you will never get to do those things.

"Sweetie, that's a pretty scarf."

It takes me a second to realize Gayle is talking to me. I instinctively lift the soft knitted fabric between my fingers. "Thanks, I'll be sure to let my sister-in-law know. She makes them."

"Oh really? Does she have a business?"

"Yeah. She started an Etsy shop after she got pregnant so that she could stay at home." *And become a baby-making machine.*

"A what-shop?"

"Etsy. It's an online thing. Crafts, jewelry, clothes, personalized things."

"So she just makes scarves?"

"Scarves, blankets, and she sells her organizational tools."

"Organizational tools?"

"Yeah, she has these to-do lists, family organizers, budget spreadsheets. She sells the digital files."

"And her tools are better than those you can get for free?"

There's a rush of validation in the form of a smile that I try to suppress. "Her fonts are pretty."

Gayle seems to understand. "So, if I may ask—sweetie, what is your cup size?" At first I think she's referring to my water bottle, but the numbers had worn off.

"Oh for Christ's sake, really?" Dennis says, throwing his newspaper in his lap. At first I think it's about work, but then he twists his head around to us. "You're asking the poor girl about her bra size *here*?"

"Well, as you know, I recently lost my breasts and in considering replacements, I just want to make the right decision about size." She sits up a little straighter and cups her hands in front of where her breasts used to be. "Mine have always been very—voluptuous." She waits until she has the attention of everyone, including Walt. His reading glasses give the illusion that he's really intrigued by her statement. "But I can't help admiring the understated appeal of the smaller breast." She motions to me and everyone's eyes follow.

I pull the sides of my zip up hoodie over my chest, feel my cheeks reddening.

"They're not that small," Walt says benignly and goes back to his crossword.

"I agree," Gayle says. "They're not too big or too small. Arguably, you have a perfect pair of boobs, Sweetie--they'd probably be a bit firmer even if you weren't so underweight. How old are you now, dear?"

"22."

There's a long pause and I tighten my arms.

"That said, I'm not understated or subtle or perfect like our friend Maggie. So what would suit *me*?"

"Double Ds." Walt.

"Have you seen Pamela Anderson?" Dennis.

"Somewhere between Hooters girl and one of those Howard Stern guests whose boobs look like beach balls." Me.

There's a collective shift of attention.

"I have trouble sleeping at night."

Everyone's trying to suppress laughter, but mercifully seem to be losing interest. I drop my arms to my sides, fumble with the DVD menu.

"So can I touch them?"

"Can you—what?"

"So I know what consistency to go with? I had old lady boobs, fabulous in their prime, but as they are no longer with us, may they rest in peace, they're no help. I want a youthful feel. They should soften a bit over time, too."

Dennis shakes his head and hides behind his newspaper. "I feel porn has given me unrealistic expectations for this situation."

"Nurse Trish, how is the afternoon group?" I ask, as she returns with pitchers of milk and ice water.

"Is it more or less likely that the poor girl will be sexually harassed?" Dennis clarifies.

"Who's harassing you?"

Walt clears his throat, pointing toward Gayle impatiently.

Trish chuckles awkwardly. "I don't know. They can get pretty frisky." She sets a cup of water on my tray. I start the movie and thankfully Gayle releases me from our awkward exchange, though I sense her literally sizing me up a few times throughout the session.

Nathan gets impatient waiting for food at counter service restaurants so he had found hospital waits intolerable. He had made the effort to sit beside me through my first chemo treatment. Ultimately he wouldn't stop fidgeting and after I resisted the urge to beat him with a rolled up magazine, I pointed out that I'm just sitting for four hours. The nurses have me covered. He can work or run errands or something. *I'm not going to play with the sharp scissors or color all over the walls.*

The whole process becomes routine after a while. I know what to expect. My first go at treatment was 3 weeks on, 3 weeks off times six and there was no difference in the scans. Now it's 3 weekly treatments with six cycles planned, so 18 weeks. I'm in round six, one week in.

Thursday night through Sunday night are pretty awful. If I manage to brush my teeth, I consider it a victory.

I start to feel pretty decent on Sunday evening and while everyone hates Mondays, I love them--and not just because it's Nathan's "gamer night" so he spends all afternoon and evening wearing a headset and trash-talking teenagers. I feel recharged. By Monday evening I'm dreading the start of the next treatment.

After Nurse Trish gives me the clear, I pull my backpack over my shoulder and give a friendly wave to the rest of the group.

Typically I'd go straight home, but Dr. Hennessy is leaving for vacation and wanted to fit me in beforehand. I'd be flattered in a sick, needy way if it weren't for the fact that I'm absolutely terrified of what she's about to tell me. Her office actually called Nurse Trish to tell me I'd been added on for the appointment.

"Hey Babe," Nathan says, just after I remembered that he was in meetings all day.

"Hey, I'm sorry. I completely forgot that you're busy today. I just--"

"*Babe*? Don't apologize. You're more important than any meeting."

I sink into one of the chairs by the elevator. Calling me "Babe" has been a recent development. I haven't quite figured out the significance, but I've observed that it's usually when coworkers are in the room.

"Are you okay? You sound out of breath."

"Fine. Long hallway."

"I got your text. So you should be ready by 2-2:15?"

"Yeah, but I know you're busy. I can wait if you need to work later. I brought a book."

He laughs for no apparent reason. "No I'll be there. We can pick you up a smoothie or coffee or something on the way home since I know your throat gets so dry, then we can have whatever you want for dinner, okay?"

I'm silent long enough that he throws out another "Babe?"

We get it, you're a hero husband.

"Okay."

"Did everything go alright this morning?"

"The usual. Dennis swore a lot, Walt finished the New York Times Crossword unassisted, Gayle asked to touch my boobs."

The teenage guy at the elevator picked up on what I said and his grin fell only slightly when he saw me. Meanwhile there was a rustling on the other end of the line.

"That sounds good--so 2?"

My shoulders slump. "Yeah, 2."

He tells me he loves me and says he'll see me soon.

I feel weaker than I usually do after treatment, not as sure-footed as I approach the third floor check-in desk and a woman I don't recognize. "I have an appointment with Dr. Hennessy. Meagan Callahan."

"Could you spell that?"

I do, squeezing my eyes to try to eliminate the flashes I'm suddenly seeing in my vision.

"What time is your appointment?" She looks up at my knit beanie with what appears to be (given my limited vision) a judgmental glare. Surely she's familiar with the idea of cancer patients wearing hats, but there's something more shallow to the squint of her eye, like I've committed a crime of fashion. Wrong color or fabric or something.

"She just told me to come straight from downstairs; she was going to fit me in."

"Dr. Hennessy's schedule is *very* full. I'll check on this, but in the meantime I'll have you complete this form." She hands me a clipboard with a multi-page, highly-detailed, grid format, new patient form. It's a staggering number of questions without having double vision. I'm sure I've completed it at least 4 times.

"I know you're just doing your job, but I'm definitely not a new patient."

"Ma'am, *everyone* has to fill that out. It was recently revised."

She doesn't understand. Not my obsessive blinking or my white-knuckle grip on the granite counter has tipped her off that maybe she should ease up and perhaps get a nurse. I take the clipboard and begrudgingly turn to find a chair.

"Maggie, I'll take you back."

I turn to find the blurry, but familiar face of Heather, with her fiery red hair wrapping her head in a braid, stepping behind the check-in Nazi. She disappears behind the partition and opens the door leading to the exam rooms.

It's one thing to be known at your doctor's office, it's another to be prioritized over other cancer patients. She immediately takes the clipboard and discards it on the counter with a loud clatter.

We stop at the scale—119. 15 pounds into the "underweight" category, 25 pounds less than I weighed at my high school graduation. 39 pounds less than that stupid ultrasound weigh in. I am the incredible shrinking woman—or the shrinking woman, at least. She also takes my blood pressure and temperature. She usually chimes these off out if they're in normal range, but she's gone silent.

The only fortunate thing is not being asked to change into a gown, though in the 14 seconds it takes Dr. Hennessy to enter the room once Heather leaves, it occurs to me that perhaps this also isn't such a good thing.

Dr. Hennessy flip flops between intense, like an evangelical motivational speaker, and kind of a sedated attentiveness a lot. I appreciate her awkwardness. At least it's authentic.

She enters the room with an expression on her face that I can't quite decipher, shakes my hand strangely, one hand on my opposite shoulder.

"Thank you for coming in right after treatment. I know it can be a draining process."

"Usually Tuesdays are okay, but today it seems to be affecting me more," I tell the two of her I see in front of me. "My vision is really off."

Her lack of alarm for this onset of symptoms and subtle nodding tells me that her news directly coincides with these new symptoms and was to be expected. "Maggie, as you know, we had you complete some testing last week. Typically we'll wait until the end of the treatment cycle, but I wanted to be sure that if we needed to change things that we could before I leave for vacation. I'll be checking in, but I won't have phone coverage in much of the areas. The good news is that your chest x-ray was clear."

Oh shit.

She takes a breath. "Unfortunately, it appears the cancer has spread into the uterus. Before it was looking like it could be just limited to the outer parts, but--" She stops herself from over-explaining. "It's now imperative that we operate again."

Not *my* uterus. *The* uterus. "To remove—"

"Everything, pretty much. It's going to be the best chance we have to stop the cancer from going anywhere else. The chemo just doesn't seem to be working in this case."

See? You will never have children. "When?"

"As soon as possible. The germ cells collected last time were very active. The sooner we can get rid of them the better."

I sit, trying to absorb what I've been told, but it barely penetrates the surface of my brain. I'm numb. All I can muster is: "Okay."

"I've spoken with Dr. Wheeler. He can schedule you for Thursday."

"Wow, that's fast," I say, sounding more impressed with their ability to accommodate a patient last minute than alarmed that schedules were rearranged because my situation is that serious.

"The sooner, the better. With this surgery, you'll be out of commission for several weeks at least. We'll do more testing before we consider sending you back for treatment. This takes precedence over treatment at this point."

"I just had--"

She nods quickly. "I'm so sorry--there was a miscommunication. By the time it got sorted out, you were already in the middle of treatment. It won't impact anything."

Except I'll feel like shit for the surgery.

"I can take care of any FMLA or disability paperwork for work. Are you still working for—Scripps was it?"

I nod. At this point, I check in fairly regularly. By "fairly regularly" I mean I'm pretty sure they still have at least a fleeting interest in fish. I'm far less certain they're holding a place for me.

She clears her throat, glances subconsciously at my head. It looks like she wants to ask me a question, but she holds back. "I'll be away for three weeks, but I have access to records and will check in with you post-op. We'll schedule you for a follow-up with me on the—" She runs her slender finger across her desk calendar casually, like scheduling a manicure. "I'm back the evening of the 23rd. How's the 24th? You prefer mornings I know so--9?"

Fan-fucking-tastic, doc. It's a date.

She looks up suddenly.

"I'm sorry. The inner voice has a potty mouth sometimes."

I step into the elevator and one thought keeps nagging at me: *I should have just let Gayle touch my boobs.* The next time I see her—if I see her—she may have already had the surgery. I try to push that guilt away as ridiculous, but people don't bring me their problems anymore (and I refuse to deal with my own, as persistent as they are) so therefore I have fewer viable distractions.

When the elevator opens to the lobby, the sound of the grand piano, which turns out to be playing itself, swells around me and the bright mid-day sun floods the tile floor. My breathing is shallow, constricted. My thoughts are taunting, like my very own bully in my head. *You won't have children.* Pause. *Yeah, but even if you could, it's not like you're going to live very much longer. It'd be selfish to have kids.*

I shake my head to try to dislodge the thoughts, focus on the present. Observe the good things. The blue sky. The prompt elevator. The ghost piano playing contemporary favorites--is that the song from *Twilight?*

You're going to die.

I close my eyes, take a deep breath. I let the stinging of tears in my eyes dry before I proceed, deciding to focus on something else.

Dr. Hennessy was so efficient with my appointment that I have more than an hour before Nathan is to pick me up. If I called, he'd come sooner, but I don't. He's busy at work. I can't have another "babe" conversation. It won't kill me to wait an hour. All I would do at home is sleep and watch sitcom reruns. That is my 5-year-plan: Sleep, watch every fan favorite sitcom series, don't die.

So I don't call him. Instead, I find my way to the cafeteria, my vision still not 100%. I don't know why I go there. I'm not hungry. The clanking of silverware and dishes hurts my ears. The sight of patients looking weak in their robes and slippers, dragging around IV drips depresses me. The slumped exhaustion of family members sitting at tables reminds me that I'm a burden. But still, I go.

I decide to get a soda because I read somewhere that the stuff's powerful enough to eat away at engine sludge and figure it's worth a shot to eat away at my "active" germ cells. And hey, it revived an entire alien family from dehydration and certain death in *Mac and Me.*

Once I fill the cup, I feel guilty because I've also been told it's poison and probably causes cancer. This causes me to feel like I'm making an honest enough effort to be healthy so I get a salad, too. Then I see they have a special display of mini bundt cakes so I get a chocolate one. Because I have cancer and I will never have children.

I'm in line, thumbing through my wallet for cash, my fingers unsteady, when someone bumps my tray, nudging it forward on the counter. I frown, deciding not to look up. It must be some poor patient with muscle spasms. I pull out my debit card because I don't feel much like fumbling with loose change when my hands are shaking.

"Are you together?" The cashier asks. I shake my head, glare out the side of my vision. Whoever it is is wearing a navy polo shirt, and is tanner than I expected. He clears his throat purposefully as I'm paying. I take my debit card, smile politely to the cashier and move to the counter where they keep the plastic utensils and condiments. It's then I notice that the "salad" I've assembled consists of nothing more than lettuce. I consider discarding the plate since I have no plans to eat it or anything else anyway.

A tray appears right next to mine, filled with a far more nutritious selection of grilled chicken, brown rice and vegetables, bottled water, carton of milk and an apple. It looks like it belongs on a poster in a grade school nurse's office. I feel the presence of the tray's owner, alarmingly close.

Now I'm annoyed. I whip my head around to see who exactly doesn't understand the concept of personal space.

My entire body freezes. My last breath is still caught up in my throat. Everything is at a standstill.

"Hey Reeves."

I'm lost in a state of bewilderment as I feel my arm wind back and my palm make impact with Will's cheekbone.

7
all that never was

His facial hair is thicker, his normal stubble plus two or three days. He has a fresh tan that still has a slightly reddish hue. The area on his cheek where my palm made contact is a slightly darker shade of red, while my hand will likely need to be x-rayed. Before the impact of the slap could reach the people in the outlying tables of the cafeteria, I was trying to shake out the pain. He wasn't angry—a little surprised, perhaps.

He reached for my hand and I was too distracted by the contrast of cold hospital air to his body heat to withdraw. It didn't occur to me to speak. I was lost in watching him examine my hand so tenderly. When he noticed it trembling, he reconsidered his actions and suggested we find a table, carrying both of our trays.

"You know, I'm surprised they offer some of the foods they do here. It's a hospital, aren't they supposed to be promoting good health?" Will says once we've sat down, not directing his comment toward my food specifically, but I can't help but be self-conscious. He looks at my tray and seems regretful. "Well. I think the plate of plain romaine more than balances out the cake."

I exhale deeply, determined to be better at being casual than him, out of spite mainly. "You know, I'm grateful I didn't get the double bacon cheeseburger, Judgy McJudgerson."

"I'd actually prefer it. it appears you need the calories." He smirks slightly, getting a taste of our usual banter, then frowns. "I'll bet it's itchy?"

"What?" I say stupidly, then realize I'm fidgeting with my damn hat again. "Yeah a bit."

Glancing again at his plate, I can't take feeling so exposed with my poor nutritional choices anymore. At least the soda is disguised in a Styrofoam cup, probably also oozing poison. I remove the bundt cake in its little plastic case and slide it into my bag.

He raises one thick eyebrow set over one half of his kind eyes. They're very round and pronounced in the sockets. Kind eyes. "What? You're not going to share?"

"That was to be the highlight of my day and I won't be able to enjoy it in front of you."

"I didn't think you liked sweets."

"I don't. Just stealing coping mechanisms from *Eat Your Feelings Away Weekly.*"

"Is that a weekly publication now?"

"If you're interested, I have a postcard with a discount code." I try to keep a straight face.

"So you're really not going to share?" He pretends to act hurt.

I eye him, unconvinced, but put the cake back on my tray and open the top, primarily with my left hand, which is challenging. "Your cheek really did a number on my hand," I mutter. "It's the only reason I believe you're not a figment of my imagination." The lid finally releases. "Or a hologram."

He gives me his dimpled smile as he presents me with a fork and I'm sixteen again, rendered speechless by his charm.

I can see my backyard back then--small and green with the smallest pool ever built. I returned from my school's Homecoming dance to an empty house. My date had been incredibly nice, but I had admittedly bumbled the "goodnight." In fact, you'd think someone had yelled "fire." I did manage a thank you and I didn't get my dress caught in the car door so that's something.

I changed into pajamas and retired to one of the patio loungers, where I had gotten caught up in Vonnegut's *Slaughterhouse Five*. Will appeared at the side gate and strolled over to me, like it was a regular occurrence. Granted, he knew his way around my house. He spent plenty of time there when we were kids, mainly without my mother being aware, which was easy once she started traveling more frequently with Ray.

Will and I were best friends up until I received a scholarship to go to a private prep school in 8th grade and our schedules never seemed to align. He also went through a really severe bout of obnoxious, arrogant puberty for about three or four years. He had made that unexpected visit to pick me up at school a few days earlier so his appearance should have been anticipated. Unfortunately, I knew very little about this older Will except that the last time I saw him, I impulsively kissed his cheek.

I couldn't help but feel nervous surges through my arms as he came closer.

"You're doing schoolwork on a Saturday night?"

I must have looked confused.

He motioned to the book as he pulled a chair up right next to me.

"It was recommended reading."

He had a focused and amused look on his face. That's the best I can describe it. No one ever exhibited such curiosity about me. "Hi Reeves," he said with a smile.

"What's on your mind, Will?"

"How was the dance?"

I assessed his question. When he had picked me up at school a few days earlier, concerned after my near drowning, he had seemed tense about the fact that I had a date to the dance. "Were you staking out my house, Mercer?"

"You're avoiding the question." Something vulnerable flickered in his eye.

"Well, I'm home reading. *Alone.*" The emphasis on the last word had a very obvious impact on his tension.

"You're *not* alone."

And apparently his confidence, too. "No. I guess not."

"We don't spend time together anymore, Reeves."

"No. I guess not."

"We should change that--spend lots and lots of time together."

I smiled apprehensively.

"It that OK with you?" he asked softly, learning toward me, placing his hand on my chin to draw me closer.

"Yes." My voice was barely a whisper.

Our eyes locked in an ease that only comes from knowing each other as childhood friends. I knew he was a deliberate person. There was intention behind his actions and words--always. Before I had a chance to figure out what that was, he kissed me.

It was sweet and delicate and I remember watching his face move away again, a funny little satisfied smile on his face.

In a much less intimate setting, I slice off a delicate piece of cake, draw it to my lips. I can smell the sugar and I want nothing to do with it and the chocolate it rode in on, but I force it down, drop the fork.

"Really? That's all you're going to take? Anorexics eat more." He seems to want to swallow the words back up. Because I look like I could be one. Surely he's heard from someone that I'm sick. Of course, one look at me with my bony shoulders and sunken eyes, and it's sort of a given. No one chooses to look this way except teenage girls with body image issues in after school specials.

My fingers are playing once again with the hem of the beanie. I let my hand fall back to my lap, my shoulders slumped forward. "Sorry, today's been a little rough." I recognize that I've just apologized to him, but my brain has decided it has other ways to torture me. *How the hell does my body deal with no reproductive organs? Do they just seal up those connections? Does that bypass menopause? Will I wind up with a mustache and sounding like the daughter—what's her face—Dorothy— in Golden Girls at the age of 24?* "If I live that long."

Moments pass when he just stares at me, a pained expression on his face. In a series of rushed movements, he takes my plate and slides it next to his own, dividing his chicken and placing it atop my salad.

I frown. "What's going on there with the chicken?"

He presents me with my made over lunch. "You need protein."

"That's *your* food."

He opens the milk carton, takes a swig and sets it next to my tray. "And milk. Calcium. Vitamin D. Good stuff. No added Omega 3's or DHA, but you're smart enough."

I must zone out with the sureality of the moment because he taps my plate to get me to eat, his face turning serious. So I eat, as instructed, for a solid few minutes.

Will's jaw is clenched tight. He is purposely trying not to watch me too closely, but the effect is that he seems distrustful of everyone and everything in the cafeteria, like any one of them might be carrying a grenade.

After I make my way through half of the salad and chicken and the entire carton of milk, which has my shrinking stomach at about maximum capacity, I push my tray slightly away.

I'm trying to figure out what to say when he speaks, his eyes lowered. "I didn't know if I'd ever get to talk to you again—I've wanted to. So much."

My heart feels like it's on fire. I stare across the table at him, trying to keep my expression neutral. I surprise myself by admitting: "I didn't think you wanted to talk to me again."

It looks like I've shot him, his eyebrows tensed, his kind eyes glistening in the sunlight pouring in through the windows. "For what it's worth? I'm sorry." He shakes his head. "That doesn't cover it. It sounds pathet--it's *not* enough, I know that, but Reeves?" He waits for me to meet his gaze. "I'm *sorry*."

My impulse is to say 'Me, too," but I find I can't speak. There is an authenticity to Will's apology, his eyes regretful and unbearably sad.

He swallows hard, taking in our surroundings. His eyes settle on an old couple having lunch. They have to be at least ninety. Neither has a wheelchair or cane and they look to be in good spirits. The wife is wearing a great deal of blush and pearls. She probably applied too much perfume. The husband is dressed like he's going golfing and has combed his hair neatly. This is probably a part of their routine. They have doctor appointments once a week or once a month, probably for hearing aids or for physical therapy. They probably make a date out of it. Then they go home. They've probably had 70 years together. At least.

I start to hate them. Not because I wish ill upon them, but out of pure self-pity. I am twenty-two-years-old and I may not make it to twenty-five. I will never have children, let alone grandchildren. I will never get to retire. I won't even get the chance to start a real career. I will live out my days being bossed around and spoken down to. I will not experience getting dressed up in pearls to go visit the doctor, who I secretly (and perhaps, depending on my mental state, not so secretly) have a crush on. I will not get 10, 20, 30, 50, 70 years of marriage. Not an "if," a certainty. I will never have those things.

"Let's go for a walk, Reeves." There's an urgency in his voice, in his eyes.

He's already grabbing my backpack, which looks small against the muscle of his tanned bicep, and he helps me stand. It's as I catch the breeze of the cold hospital air against my damp face that I realize I'm crying.

He leads me outside by the meditation fountain, surrounded by every color of rosebush, sets down my bag and wraps me in his arms.

8
blissful unconsciousness became foggy awareness which transitioned into painful reality

Nathan does not take the news well. I can see his mind reeling as soon as I tell him. He's on his phone battling beta level voice recognition technology to do a web search before we can manage to get halfway home. It takes all my willpower not to burst into tears the second time his phone presents her findings for "canker" on the web and he yells "*cancer*" at it over the hum of the road noise.

He didn't ask who was hugging me when he pulled up to the curb. Will had gently rubbed my back, motioning to Nathan in his Audi when he pulled up and I had looked over at that car and the reality it carried and all I wanted to do was hold tighter to Will. You know the moment when parents drop their 5-year-old off to school on the first day and the poor kid is so desperate not to go, like they're being sold to a labor camp? I was the 5-year-old. I was terrified to detach from Will's arms, afraid I'd never feel them again. I was terrified of cancer. For the first time, it really hit me that I could die. That if I wasn't in the favorable survival statistics, I would die soon. And I was so disappointed in how my life had turned out, how it would end. How incomplete it felt.

Will whispered something to me I didn't quite hear and took a step back, clearing the path for Nathan, who got out of the car and, like the teacher on the first day, reached for my elbow, calmly but apprehensively led me away. I looked over my shoulder at Will through the blur of tears. He had his hands in his pockets, his jaw was clenched shut and I could see his nose slowly flaring as he breathed.

The first time I saw him cry was after his grandfather's funeral when he was eleven. He cried for Ben in Ramstein. In 16 years, this was only the third time I had seen him cry.

Nathan said something about my "friend" with a hint of a jealous tone, but I ignored him and he moved on to my news, which he had to receive through hiccups of air as I tried to recover from crying.

He has seen me at my weakest physical moments. He has seen me in disbelief. He has seen me angry. He has seen me exhausted. He has seen me in denial. *Oh Lord, the denial.*

He has never seen me cry before. Even when the babies died, I cried when no one was around.

When we get to the house I tell him I'm going to take a bath. He agrees that it's a good plan and tells me he'll make me a grilled cheese, since I must be starving, and a strawberry smoothie. His arrogant tone has gone, replaced by insecurity.

I reach the bathroom and close the door, quickly turn on the faucet in the garden tub. I need the white noise. In addition to clattering around in the kitchen looking for the griddle—no, actually, he was probably rearranging the pans since I was the last one to do dishes and I don't always respect the cabinet labels. I'm surprised there isn't yet a tape outline of each of the pans and gadgets in the drawers and cabinets. If they all went missing, it would have the appearance of a massive kitchenware crime scene, the thought of which entertained my brain quite a bit.

So the entire time Nathan was rectifying the displaced pan fiasco, he was more than likely on the phone with his mom, the retired emergency room nurse for advice, and probably already had the laptop fired up. I find conversations with her exhausting. She pulls out her medical knowledge and questions everything I'm advised of in my appointments. She has a tendency of sharing medical horror stories at inopportune times, as well. "It was just a routine appendectomy and boom, embolism. Dead at 30." All the stories seemed to be the same: Healthy. Disaster or medical mishap. Dead. 'So horrible.'

At the beginning I think my in-laws were caught up in the twins news and were kind to me and forgiving of flaws. Then they looked at me like a fixer upper, just needing some basic polishing up and I could be a good fit. Now that my health issues have intensified, I think they fail to see much return potential. They also blame me for the babies, for both being conceived and for being dead now. They disapprove of Nathan's decision to stay with me. If I were a house, they would have torched the place months ago and collected the insurance payout.

You can imagine the undertone at those family gatherings.

The light through the window is overcast. The weather has turned from the sunny day it had been this morning during treatment to an eerie gray. It seemed weeks ago that I was sitting in the recliner between Walt and Lenny.

Chemo offers all sorts of days. There are the restless days. There are days you just stare. Days you hate everyone. Days you feel so sick, are in so much pain, you just grit your teeth and shut your eyes. There was the one day that Gayle brought in brownies—*special* brownies—and we had ourselves four hours (and beyond) of church giggles. Of course a hospital administrator happened to stop by that day and put a stop to special brownies, but I'm convinced that experience bonded our group.

Today I did not see coming.

I should have given them a better goodbye. *Maybe I can still visit them on Thursday before my surgery.* No, Nathan will not want to make extra stops. Mom will probably be there.

I pull off my clothes--sweatpants, a tank and a hoodie--and stand in front of the mirror. I have a fresh bruise on my left arm from bumping into the door frame this morning. I've always bruised so easily and it's only gotten worse. There are several on my arms and legs that I can't account for. My ribs show. They're pronounced and ugly. I wonder what my stomach will look like after they remove my uterus.

I run my finger along the existing scar over my bikini line, which looks more like the work of Dr. Frankenstein than a highly-acclaimed surgeon. That initial surgery didn't exactly set a great tone for treatment. He has since had his license taken away for performing surgery while intoxicated. I was assured that the hospital was not aware if he was drunk during mine specifically. Nathan had sworn to sue just as he had sworn to travel for second opinions if we were unhappy with my medical care.

It's a different doctor this time. He'll cut through the same scar. I try not to think of what that would feel like if I were awake, cutting through scar tissue. Dr. Hennessy suggested he might end up doing a mini tummy tuck to help repair the damage from the last surgery, but added that I don't need it. Oddly, complimentary plastic surgery did little to brighten my outlook of the impending surgery.

For Gayle's sake, I take notice of my breasts, give them a good look over from the front and side, shrug then I turn to my bath, ease myself into the steaming water. My right hand is achy so I rely heavily on my left.

I dip my head, slick my invisible hair back and settle into the inflatable pillow. I attempt to float on my back, feel the luxury of weightlessness, but the tub is too short or I'm too long.

With my foot, I turn the water to cool, let the contrast of temperatures lap around me and think of the cool waters in Maui. Katie's family had invited me to join them one summer. Snorkeling off Ka'anapali Beach, we had some spectacular encounters with sea turtles just off the black rocks. The sun was hot on my back, but the water was so cool and refreshing. I felt free in those vast blue waters.

I picture the pool, where Katie and I spent a lot of our days. I try to see the details, imagine myself there, but the image is interrupted by another memory-- the pool at the resort where Katie got married. It lacked the ukulele music and white sand beaches, but the lush landscaping offered an oasis from the chaos of the wedding. From life. I still had a few hours until rehearsal and Katie was swept away to a spa experience with her mom. She offered to have me join them, but I told her I was more than happy hanging out poolside. I woke from a brief snooze on my mesh-bottom raft with two thoughts: One, I should apply more sunblock. Two, someone is watching me. I was right about both.

I tipped myself off the raft and noticed my skin had taken on a red hue that usually took several hours and a shower to come to the surface. It would not look good in photos. I dropped myself into the chilly and heavily chlorinated water, still feeling the weight of eyes upon me. I adjusted my bathing suit, my eyes scanning the line of lounge chairs surrounding the pool. I was about to dismiss the thought that I was being watched when I saw him. He was sitting on the edge of the pool in American flag board shorts, a red t-shirt, dark sunglasses, and was holding a plastic drink cup. He suppressed a smile.

I narrowed my eyes suspiciously as I approached him. I hadn't seen him since he had deployed 7 months earlier. Before that, it had been several months since we had even spoken, since we went from everything to nothing in the span of my high school graduation ceremony.

I had worn a ridiculously bold dress to graduation and had felt more confident than I had my entire life. (Prior to his declaration.) Not even my mother's sulking presence could derail my mood. At an after graduation party at Katie's house, Will's demeanor was entirely different. He was tense, but resolved. He said he needed to get out in the world and date was for his sake and also for mine. It would be good for us.

I couldn't quite figure out why he was using the term 'us' so much in a breakup.

Standing out in the driveway at what seemed like the close of the "conversation," I started to absorb what was going on. At some point earlier in the evening, he had wrapped his jacket around me. Its presence after what he had just said felt wrong, surreal. I said nothing, pulled the jacket off and chucked it at his face, glaring at him.

He looked surprised, catching the jacket only after it smacked him in the face.

"Reeves, maybe I didn't explain things well."

I considered my exit options, glancing down at my heels. I'd break an ankle for sure if I tried to walk home and I didn't have a phone to call a cab.

"It's too far to walk."

I looked up through a veil of hair that had come loose from my updo and moved toward his truck cab. I knew he kept his trail sneakers in the back seat. Evan gave him a lot of hassle for the alleged smell, which I had never noticed. I dangled myself over the bench seat until my fingertips found the laces.

"I'll give you a ride, Reeves," he said as I sat down on the driver's side to put them on.

I untied the red straps of my heels and chucked them one by one at his feet.

"You can't walk. It's not safe."

At that point, I was standing next to the driver's door of his truck. I'm not sure what made me think I could or should try to kick that 3000 pound solid metal beast of a truck, but I kicked that sturdy old truck with all my might--and fell backwards awkwardly, skinning my right hip and hand on the pavement. The surge of pain was at best, a distraction.

I managed to stand, narrowing my eyes when he offered his hand.

"Reeves, please let me drive you home."

I glanced at the long winding street that I would have to take to even reach the main road in town. My eyes scanned the familiar street lights, strip mall signs. Home was miles away and I could feel the burning of skinned flesh exposed to the night air. It would be unbearable to sleep on that side for weeks. It seemed my ankle was sprained and felt unsteady and sore. I looked toward the house. I imagined walking through the doors looking the way I did--disheveled, sobbing, wearing comically large shoes with far too cheerful a dress.

No. I would not be going into that house.

"Come on," he beckoned, reaching for the door handle. He tugged a few times, about to joke about me breaking it, but accurately read the expression on my face, and opened the door without trouble. I climbed inside, scooting to the far side of the bench seat. I normally sat in the middle next to him. "Reeves, you're important to me. You're the most important person in the world to me."

I frowned, gazing across the cab at him.

"I think this is something we really need to do."

Something we really need to do.

When we ran into each other literally hours before he deployed, I was angry with him, not just because he had broken my heart, but for something he wouldn't know about for some time after. I was angry and hurt, and justified in wanting to shut him out, but as I watched him walk away through the front windows of the coffee shop, the dangers flashed before me. I couldn't let the way we ended things to be the last memory he had of me, and vice versa. There was too much history. In an instant, I had forgiven him.

I abandoned the espresso machine and my lineup of orders and jogged after him. I threw myself at him with so much force it knocked the wind out of him. I had taken a half step back, studied his face, thinner than I had ever seen it, but smiling in that familiar way, and I kissed him.

"Hi Reeves," poolside Will said. There was something in how he said my name, or last name rather, the way it rolled off his tongue slowly, the way I was the only one he referred to by last name. Something particularly intimate about it.

"Hi Mercer," I said, attempting the same tone and exaggeration and failing terribly.

"*Maggie?*" The pool, the trees, and Will are gone. I wake to Nathan yanking me to a sitting position in the tub. I must have been submerged because I find myself gulping for air. When I've gotten my bearings, he steps backward, eyeing the displaced bubbles.

Evidently he likes my breasts as well—or at least they've distracted him enough to diffuse his concern about water damage. He breathes a sigh of relief as he shuts off the faucet. Or annoyance, I can't tell. Nathan doesn't yell in general. It seems he's adopted the philosophy that you can't be mad at your wife if she has cancer. But I do make him mad so his face is in a persistent state of restraint. He drops a towel to the floor to soak up the water that overflowed the ledge of the tub.

"Your sandwich got wet," he says apologetically, putting it back on its plate.

"Thank you for making it."

"We need some groceries. I was going to run to the store if you're okay here. You know, as long as you promise not to flood the house?"

I nod, painfully disappointed to be in my own reality again.

"Maybe don't fill it so high?"

"Good idea."

"Do you feel—okay?"

I'm not going to die while you're out. "Yeah." It occurs to me he might mean mentally okay, which is perhaps justified concern.

He gathers the soaked towel and rings it out in the sink. "Enjoy your bath," he says as he kisses me. I don't care for his breath, but then again, the nausea might be kicking in.

As the door closes behind him, I hear my thoughts escape my lips involuntarily: "You don't deserve him." I'm not sure who my brain meant.

I lay back in the tub, watching my chest rise and fall. I can't be thinking of Will. There are too many emotional landmines there, too many gaping wounds. At age 17, it was jarring and heartbreaking to be caught in the wake of Will Mercer. It consumed me. At nearly 23, I feel like treading through those emotions from last year again would drown me. It was comforting seeing him. Perhaps it's best to leave it at that.

You'll probably never see him again.

Tears start filling my eyes at the thought. I use the dexterity of my toes to unplug the drain. It's as I stare at my distorted reflection in the faucet that I piece together the words Will whispered to me standing outside the hospital. I sit up straighter:

"You're not alone."

————

Nathan insisted I call my mother and Ray to tell them about the surgery. Invite them along like it's a damn ballet recital.

I really sound pathetic, don't I? He *insisted*? Nathan told me that they'd want to know, to be there.

I regretted it immediately. As per usual, I ended up comforting them, reassuring them that I'll be okay. By "them," I mean my mother, although Ray has seemed increasingly concerned about my prognosis. When I tell them: I'm not dying... I'm also thinking: but I kind of wish I was.

Also per usual, they have found something to fight about. Evidently they got to the hospital early and had breakfast in the cafeteria. My mother didn't feel like eating, but Ray insisted. She was offended by the use of powdered eggs. Evidently there had been a study she heard about on *Dateline* or *The View* or hell, maybe *Maury* that said powdered eggs were said to be connected with the development of cancer in lab rats. That it's as potent as artificial sweeteners.

Nathan's sitting next to me and reaches for my hand. He squeezes it to get my attention and he mouths the words: "I'm sorry."

I roll my eyes, feel the sting of tears pushing their way out. I hate him for this and I hate his insincere, half-hearted apology, but I can't hate him. Because his wife has cancer and will never give him children. Because he didn't sign up for this. Because he's stuck it out far longer than he should have.

Hearing my name called to lead me to a surgery that terrifies me should freeze my muscles, glue me to the upholstered waiting room chair. But it doesn't. In fact, I jump up, relieved. You'd think I just got called back for a spa day. I even greet the nurse with probably too enthusiastic a hello.

My entourage follows quickly behind, but are stopped by the surgical nurse. I must give him a look that says "Please, dear God, make them wait here. I don't need my mother's shrill complaints about cafeteria powdered eggs echo in my head as my uterus is ripped from my body." Something transmits telepathically, or I've stepped into hospital territory that has gloriously insightful visitor rules, because he takes a strong position that only Nathan can come back with me.

As I turn to say goodbye, my relief turns to disgust in myself because the pair of them, despite just being at each other's throats look absolutely devastated. If I do die during surgery, their last memory of me, the last thing I would have left them with is resentment about their presence.

You know, being on death watch is really high pressure.

I hug them simultaneously, but the tender state of my body makes this really painful. It doesn't help that my mother has a hold on me like she's trying to literally squeeze the life out of me.

I turn on my heel and all I can think is: *Well that's going to leave a mark.*

The Anesthesiologist is both a dreaded and welcome sight. In her hands is my ticket to a temporary hiatus from reality, but also a sleep from which I may never wake. I'm terrified of never waking up, but the thought of waking up to this life is--disappointing.

Now that would be an interesting movie trailer: *"It was just a routine surgery, but this summer, Maggie Callahan will find herself going to sleep a sad, lonely young woman surrounded by overbearing relatives and waking up—a sad, lonely young woman on a beach, drinking cocktails out of a pineapple..."* The deep voice narrating the trailer in my head clears his throat, and adds: *"No Whole Foods, no robot appointment reminder calls, no—mother."*

I get stuck trying to come up with a movie title and that levels me enough in reality watching the team prep the surgical room. Someone mistakenly turns on the spotlight and it practically blinds me. I squeeze my eyes shut. And then the bully is there again to keep me company, like the spotlight awoke her from slumber. My thoughts begin reeling:

This is my life. This is all I get to live. I will never get to have a family of my own. I will never live by the beach. I will never travel to Italy, visit the museums and pretend to like wine on a tour of vineyards. I will never hike through temples and shrines in Japan, stay in a traditional ryokan or brave the public onsens. I will never go for another sunrise hike. I will never drive with my window down along the coast again. I will never have another birthday. I will never taste movie popcorn again. I will never take another sip of ice cold water. I will never see the sky again, appreciate seeing the clouds drift by.

I open my eyes as someone sits by my head. The Anesthesiologist is so young she looks like she should be babysitting, but she has very pretty blue eyes.

They are further framed by a navy surgical mask. Everyone has masks and my God are there a lot of people in here for a routine surgery.

"Residents," she explains, when she catches me looking over her shoulder at a pair of nervous looking people in full surgical gown gear, safety glasses and masks.

"They're not in charge of anything vital?"

"Standing."

"They passed that competency?"

She smiles, her eyes squeezing in the tell-tale way. "I was told you're a bit of a hoot."

"I'm a hoot?" I pump my fist lightly. "Wait, that's not like an insult now, right? I'm not up to speed on the urban dictionary."

"It's a compliment."

There's a clattering as one of the residents bumps into a storage cabinet. I glance in his direction, then look up at Dr. Kessler.

"We're going to take good care of you today. We'll get you dozing here and then move you over to surgery."

I nod, focus on breathing

Nathan appears in the corner of my vision as I start to feel the analgesic hit my bloodstream. I motion loosely toward the Anesthesiologist. "Dr. Kessler is putting me on the high octane," I whisper loudly.

He doesn't respond as he seems to be occupied by a member of the medical staff.

I sigh, blinking slowly. When I open my eyes again, I notice that there is an entire ceiling tile sized backlit image of a rainbow over a green hillside. "Where be the leprechauns?"

Dr. Kessler checks my vitals, makes an adjustment on the machine before moving in closer, following my gaze. "At the end of the rainbow of course," she says in an impressive Irish accent.

I giggle lightly and feel my body sink into the mattress. I re-open my eyes once without remembering that I had closed them, and then I drift into nothingness.

Ocean waves follow nothingness...and then, a voice.

"You look amazing, Reeves."

The use of my maiden name startles me. I hear myself say: "Well thank you, Mercer, but I fear your eyes doth deceive you." My eyes fly open and I'm not in the surgical prep area. Above me is a sea of stars in a blanket of black sky. A cool, humid breeze lifts my hair slightly off my shoulders as I walk next to Will. I'm wearing a long flowing navy dress I recognize from Katie's rehearsal dinner, which limits contact with my sunburned skin, but the cool night sends chills through me. He wears a white button down with khaki shorts and brown leather sandals. We walk close enough so that our arms repeatedly touch. "I look like a cooked lobster. You, however, look like you fell out of resort stock images."

He grins widely. "God I missed you," he says, squeezing my hand gently, continuing to lead us through the winding path down to the dark beach. I can hear the waves ahead, but I'm distracted by his hand holding mine and the heat of his body so close.

The evening breeze whirls around us, tickling my arms, making the hair stand on end. We leave our shoes by the path, continuing barefoot. I have always adored the feel of sand between my toes. I even like how it sticks to my skin long after I've left the beach.

The rumble of the waves is quiet, but steady. We walk, hand in hand, to the edge of the sea and let the chilly water swallow our ankles. The moment is continuously building, like how the water seems to climb higher with each wave. There is nothing else in the world. The only thing that exists is that stretch of beach, the nearly full moon overhead and the two of us.

"Now about what you said at dinner—" I began, surprising myself with my directness.

"Yes?"

"Don't you find it curious that you said you think you might marry me someday, but we've never gone on an *official* date? I mean, we did previously spend 'lots and lots of time together.'"

"That's true. We did. As for the lack of an *official* date--it's an unfortunate fact I plan to resolve."

"Is that what you came here to accomplish?"

"Ah. You want to know my intentions."

"I make a point of not speculating given your unpredictable history."

His eyebrows jumped, enjoying this familiar banter. "Well I'm really glad you asked." He paused. Gulped. "Don't give me that look. I am. I see the doubt in your eyes—actually I think it might be the champagne? And *you*, under the drinking age."

"I had sparkling cider."

"So just doubt then." His fingers tenderly stroked my cheek. His eyes had his trademarked relaxed focus. "What did I want to accomplish by crashing your best friend's wedding?"

"As I understand it, you were invited as a means of ambush," I whispered, starting to lose any sense of our surroundings.

He momentarily stopped stroking my face. "Would you like my answer, feisty pants?"

I craved him being so close. I barely let out a 'yes' and his hand slid to frame my face, guiding me to look into his eyes.

"I came here to accomplish nothing short of telling you, and knowing without a doubt you understand, that I love you. Have always. Will always. Love you."

I moved against him, drawn to him like how the currents are pulled by the moon, and he kissed my lips, my cheeks, my chin, my neck. Oh I loved him kissing my neck.

I breathed his name as he lowered me to the sand...

And then I wake, chilled. I can practically feel his hand encasing mine, the heat spreading up my arm, but my palm is pale and empty. The polyester blanket they have tucked around me is doing little to keep out the cold of the hospital. I'm confused and disappointed.

I'm supposed to be on a beach. How easy it seems to go back there. Live there in that moment. Or in the minutes that followed—when Security took mercy on us after spotlighting us with flashlight beams and we jogged up the pathways, down the quiet corridors, to my room, tangled in each other's arms.

The pain of a sunburn seems sweetly forgiving compared to the ache of the muscles in my lower abdomen I feel now. They seem to be in a state of flexion I can't release.

I find a familiar friend positioned in the form of a morphine drip in my left hand. I press repeatedly until the machine beeps in protest that I've met my limit. Nathan appears then, slipping his phone in his pocket. My mother and Ray are right behind him.

"Well there's our girl."

I reflexively roll my eyes then try to cover by slowly closing them. The light's too bright, but I seem to be the only one bothered by it.

"You did great," Mom says, stroking my forehead. I can't help but cringe every time the woman touches me.

I didn't do anything.

"Hi Maggie, Dr. Wheeler. I introduced myself before surgery, but I know you were pretty groggy." I see gray hair. Glasses. Harry Potter style glasses. And a nose. He definitely has a nose.

If the morphine weren't flowing through me, I'd probably be embarrassed or paranoid that there's something implied in the word "groggy," that I did or said something humiliating, but I simply smile, the hospital bed suddenly feeling like a thick summer cloud. "Thank you for the morphine, it was very thoughtful of you. Or was that Dr. Kessler?"

"Yes, well, you're going to experience quite a bit of discomfort from the surgery, but that will get you over the initial hump."

"That's okay, just bottle up some of this and I'll manage just fine."

He's not interested in this suggestion. In fact, he seems a little annoyed so I put on my most serious morphine-influenced face. The accompanying voice is low and mocking.

"'So--how did it go?'" The words sound bizarre as I throw in a movie reference he won't understand, but I try to keep a straight face so he knows I respect him as a professional. What results is suppressed snorts. "Iago," I clarify, citing the parrot from *Aladdin*.

"Can she overdose on the morphine?" That's my mom.

"No, it's set up with a maximum dose it'll dispense every five minutes."

"Tick tock. Tick tock." Me.

"We can see about lowering the dose a bit though."

"No," I whimper, getting the attention of everyone in the room. "Let me be morphine drunk. Please? It hurts. " I giggle. I think the "morphine drunk" part is clever, but I seem to be exhausting the room's occupants.

"You're prescribing her something strong for the pain for when we go home, right?" Mom again. It's not lost on me that she just implied that she's staying with us. Nathan and I exchange a look.

"I'd rather be set on fire than have you in the guest room."

Nathan actually chuckles, in spite of his proper ways, and this endears him to me just a bit more than when he pre-dialed their number for me last night.

I turn to Dr. Wheeler. "So how did the removal of my uterus go? Did you get all of it? Because *coincidentally* I was one uterus away from my goal weight."

Nathan is suddenly serious.

Dr. Wheeler decides to forgo the formal reading of the chart because his patient is morphine drunk and protocol is lost on her. He sets his laptop on the table at the foot of the bed with a sigh.

"Sorry, I joke as a defense mechanism. Plus my goal weight would be if I gain 15-20 pounds, for the record. I don't have an eating disorder, just a disease eating away all my fat stores. Please go on." I eye the clock behind his head. About three minutes until I can get another surge of morphine.

"We found the cancer had spread beyond the already removed ovary and fallopian tube and quickly, even since your last scans."

Just over 2 and a half minutes.

"However—"

One word is enough to snap me from my fixation on the clock. However? There isn't supposed to be a "however." However carries hope. This is a mistake. I've misheard him.

"We discovered the cells had spread to the outside of the uterus, as opposed to the inside, as well as to the abdomen and pelvis. There are very few cells affected in the left ovary and fallopian tube that we could see. So with your husband's approval—" I follow his hand motioning to Nathan, who doesn't seem quite sure about his apparent decision, and my eyes don't leave the side of his head. "We left the remaining ovary and fallopian tube, as well as the uterus, and concentrated on getting as much tumor out of the abdomen and pelvis as possible."

Still with my eyes glued on Nathan, I ask about the cancer cells in my remaining ovary, tube, and uterus. I picture the skewed anatomy of my reproductive organs.

"Dr. Hennessy will likely recommend a chemotherapy done through the abdomen to more aggressively target those cells. The hope is that it'll be enough to take out the cells and allow you the ability to have children since he had expressed that's a priority for the two of you."

Nathan finally makes eye contact and immediately regrets the hopeful smile on his face.

I turn back to my salt and pepper fox of a doctor (if only he had some form of a sense of humor) and exhale heavily. "So if you had removed everything as planned, I might not have to have this intense chemo?"

He's a bit flabbergasted. "Well—it's hard to know for sure. Obviously if we had taken everything, it likely would have included all of those active cells."

"Oh it's just one more treatment—tough it out." Mom.

"It's a bit more than that," Dr. Wheeler corrects. His approach with me softens. "Three times a week for probably six weeks or so and go from there."

"See? It's like a month. You'll be fine."

It's involuntary, but I sort of snarl in her direction.

"I know it's a whirlwind of emotions, Maggie. I think it would be good to get you settled into your room for the night, get some dinner and some rest. I'll check in with you later."

I nod. "Thank you." It's not enough. Here he thought he was performing a miracle for me, allowing me the ability to still have kids potentially--heck, he probably saw a human interest article for their organization's publication coming out after I had a "miracle baby"--and yet I'm unappreciative. My brain isn't processing the idea of having children and what I feel about this; it's just very tired at the thought of having more chemo. I was struggling before, but was somewhat comforted by the idea that the chemo piece might be over for the time being.

"We're going to get some coffee while they get you relocated, okay?" Ray says. He pats my hand then reaches for the arm of my protesting mother who obviously does not *want* to get coffee.

But she loses the non verbal fight, comes to my side and kisses my forehead. I flinch away again. She's had a haircut recently. I didn't notice earlier, unless she had it during surgery. She sighs deeply, blotting away tears. "Precious girl."

I gurgle in response, seemingly unable to form words anymore. She moves to Nathan, sighs again and embraces him, rubs his back as they hug. She whispers something to him about not worrying about setting up the guest room for her—she'll manage.

It's all very melodramatic and self-sacrificing. It's a wonder a spotlight from the heavens doesn't shine down upon her.

And they go.

Nathan seems to be preparing himself for what I'm about to say, but rather than speaking, I glance to the wall clock, hit my morphine drip five times, turn my head to face the opposite curtain, and close my eyes.

9
for it's there that I belong

One of my best childhood memories was going to the beach in the early morning hours with my dad. He liked to get up before the sun and I caught onto this quickly. It was his time to take a run, to work on a car, sit and sip his coffee.

One morning he found me pulling his designated mug out of the cabinet, milk and sugar containers already on the counter. After a few weekends of this, of me happily sitting down to munch on cereal while he drank his coffee, then seeing him off, I woke one Saturday to find him up before me, dressed in swim trunks, a Beach Boys concert shirt, and sandals at the garage door.

I tilted my head to the side, unsure of what to make of this. He motioned for me to follow him and whispered, "Go change into your swimsuit."

I remember climbing into the nearly restored 1960 Cadillac convertible, the red paint glossy even before dawn, a couple of surfboards sticking out of the back seat. I quickly buckled myself in and eagerly observed my surroundings as he pulled out onto the road. He smiled at me out the corner of his eye and turned on the radio, found a familiar Elvis song. The wind whipped my hair around as we reached the Pacific Coast Highway.

We had the beach to ourselves, the only exception being a surfer offshore, who was taking advantage of some intense waves as a storm started to brew in the distance. Dad grabbed one of the longboards, which looked tall even next to his 6 foot 4 frame, and I followed him down to the water. And he gave me my first surf lesson.

The sunrise was subtle that morning, but we were still in the water at my insistence long after it poked through the clouds. He finally coaxed me into getting some breakfast. We ate at a breakfast dive, the restaurant name, *Sunny Side Up Cafe*, stenciled onto the painted brick exterior. The interior was exposed red brick with road signs scattered on the walls. He had me order first, telling me to order whatever my heart desired. I hesitated a moment before listing my order: a Belgian waffle with strawberries, whipped cream, and chocolate chips, a side of sausage patties, a vanilla milkshake with colored sprinkles and a big glass of ice water. He nodded in approval, handed over his menu, and said "I'll have the same."

His dark, coarse hair was messy and still had some remnants of sand. He stretched his neck, gazing out the front windows toward the ocean across the way. "That was fun this morning, kid."

I beamed at him, swinging my legs beneath the table. "Do you think we could teach JoJo to surf?"

He considered this. "Well, she *does* like to swim."

If I had my way, the day would have continued on with us returning to the beach, but the winds were picking up and the storm that had been brewing throughout the morning was fast approaching. So we went home.

Mom shooed me off to have a shower before the lightning started, saying something about getting electrocuted by the lightning bolt, and I obediently moved up the stairs. I stopped halfway up, turned around and told my dad "thank you for the best day ever."

I had the strongest desire to run down the stairs and throw my arms around him, but my mom's glare was burning the side of my head so I continued on obediently.

I will forever regret not hugging him.

When I turned the shower off, I heard the door slam downstairs, my mother yelling. I ran to my room to see my dad drive off in his regular work car, far less glamorous than the Cadillac parked in the detached garage. When she came back inside, the rain coming down in sheets, she slammed the door behind her.

I asked her where he was going and she told me he had to run an errand. Her demeanor changed to nonchalant, which only thinly veiled her resentment.

I waited up for him, not understanding what could take so long. I kept myself occupied in my room, rearranging my stuffed animals, giving them surf lessons, putting sunglasses and hats on poor JoJo, our Golden Retriever, who always stayed close to my side when my dad wasn't home. The rain didn't let up. The scene outside my window of peeling eucalyptus trees slowly slipped from a grey cast to blue to black.

Mom put me to bed early, but I stayed up and flipped through books, resting my head on JoJo's back. She perked up at the sound of a car in the driveway, but when we both scrambled to the window, it wasn't my dad walking up the front steps. The state trooper glanced up at me just as my mother answered the front door. It was in his brief pause when my presence seemed to take him by surprise that I felt an emptiness I didn't quite understand for the first time.

It was after dad's funeral that I noticed his Cadillac was gone. I had already claimed the longboard out of the back, hid it behind my dresser and a pile of stuffed animals, sensing even at the age of six that none of his possessions were safe. When I asked my mom what happened to the car, she told me he was driving that car when he had the accident. It was destroyed, she said dismissively. I tried to convince myself to be okay with the lie. *There's no practical reason to keep the car when food needs to be put on the table.*

She told me JoJo was better off with another family. She said I wasn't responsible enough to take care of a dog and cited the two mornings I had left for school without feeding her.

She sold the house. *Too much work,* she said. *You don't appreciate all the space anyway.*

She married a man she didn't love.

*****

Nathan shifts into Park, probably wanting to have some sort of resolution to our argument this morning, but I already have my door flung open. I muster up strength in my legs to keep myself steady as I stand, close the door behind me.

The argument started shortly after he found me sitting in the shower at 2:47am. I know the time because he checked his phone and he used the time frequently to support his position on my mental shortcomings. I think he was just angry the sound of the water woke him from his precious slumber. I didn't tell him that I soaked through pads again, though I had changed them right before bed. The couch cushion was flipped. I'd attempt to clean the blood off with hydrogen peroxide later. The bleeding was supposed to have stopped by now, an impact of the surgery. Best they could explain, it was hormonal.

The argument took an intermission when I told him I was tired and settled back into my now-regular place on the couch.

The argument continued as he made coffee, though I had opted for giving him the silent treatment rather than respond to his occasional scoff, evidence of his new fondness for melodrama.

I take a deep breath as he rolls off in his impeccably tidy dark gray Audi sedan. I don't belong in a car like that, or rather, I have never imagined being with a man who drives such a car.

Suddenly I feel guilty for slamming the car door, for being admittedly immature throughout the course of our argument, for being so unyielding with him. He's doing the best he can, the best he knows how. *I was a one-night stand for him, too.*

My new chemo schedule is three days per week. Monday, Wednesday, Friday. Still mornings, but there's a different staff. Different patients. These are more severe cases and higher doses of medications are used so the side effects are much stronger. There is little chatter. No one asks to touch my boobs.

I'm two weeks into this new arrangement, eight weeks post-op and I admittedly don't have the best attitude. The leader of the hippie support group, which I was bullied into attending at a pseudo-intervention where Nathan, my mother, his parents, fertile sister and husband implied that I was on the verge of a mental collapse, said a good attitude is the best medicine. I habitually added the fortune cookie phrase "in bed' to the end of her sentences. It helped to entertain me for the 90 minute meeting.

The treatment aftermaths are brutal. My IV is connected through a catheter port in my abdomen, efficiently inserted during my surgery that granted penance to my uterus. The "front lines defense," as Dr. Hennessy phrased it, comes with a price. I'm exhausted all the time. While the original treatment protocol eventually drained me, I had a period of reprieve after treatment when I felt fairly decent. Normal. Not anymore. I can barely make my way down the corridor for treatments and the return trip is worse, but I do, because the alternative is someone bringing me. Nathan needs to work, all our friends (see: his friends) are afraid of me or need to work, my only friend lives in Monterey, my mother-in-law is a know-it-all, my sister-in-law was placed on bed rest immediately after becoming pregnant with baby #6. (Baby #4 was born a month after I met Jenna', Baby #5 was born 9 months after that. Joel & Jacqueline. You'll recall she liked "J" names. I have a theory she has her eye on her own TLC series.) I think the presence of either my mother or stepfather and their commentary would counteract whatever good the treatment is doing.

Or I'd hang myself by my IV tubing, if it would hold...and if someone would assist me in climbing on my chair, weak legs and all.

So I slowly make my way down the corridor that's actually rather picturesque. There's a courtyard along the entire length of the hallway filled with a koi pond and thick foliage, very solid, but uncomfortable looking benches. The opposite wall features a rotating art gallery switched out quarterly. This quarter is an artist who paints so realistically it looks like a photograph, coastal scenes mainly.

I check in at the desk with Nurse Jenkins—no first name, she's all business. Late-forties, short spiky hair dyed that unnatural shade of deep maroon meant to be red. Sometimes I arrive a couple minutes late if I've had an unfortunate bout of nausea--the restroom in the corridor is surprisingly nice--or I got out of breath and had to sit on the walk down. There is always a bench. I suspect the designers actually did walk in the shoes of a patient to set it up so functionally.

Jenkins doesn't judge my tardiness; she's merciful that way and gets me seated and hands me a blanket. They have no control over the air conditioning and most days, it rivals the arctic. Once she's connected to the picc line, she'll retrieve a couple of magazines and leave them on my table. I've stopped bringing my backpack. I found I could no longer lift it after my first treatment and I refuse to be wheeled in by a volunteer.

I thank her sincerely, cover myself with the blanket, and see that she's left me *In Touch* and *Entertainment Weekly*. I'm less choosy these days. I'll leaf through both, my eyes glazing over the pictures, not really taking in any of the gossip. The celebrity kids all seem to be growing up rather quickly. For two treatments, I simply stared off into space for the four hours. It was on my 4th visit that she started offering me magazines. So I stare at the glossy pages instead of the walls and she seems to feel more at ease.

Perhaps the intervention was merited, but I still resent it. *In bed.*

I'm hyper-aware of the beanie that I'm wearing today. It's terribly itchy acrylic and I try to scratch firmly through the material, but it's not helping. It's making me restless.

When I first began treatment, I had constantly checked for loose strands, paranoid that I would lose my hair at an inopportune time. At a family dinner. At the movies. Somewhere public.

It happened the week before Valentine's Day. It was private, but it didn't matter. I had been up all night going back and forth from the bed to the bathroom. I hadn't noticed it happening. After throwing up green bile, which doesn't raise the alarms anymore—it's just an indicator that my stomach is below empty--I went to the sink to wash out my mouth. I splashed cold water against my face to counteract the sweating. My hands instinctively went to pull back my hair and I found wisps of hair at best. My trail to and from the bathroom was lined with my hair. Clump here. Clump there. Big knot of it on my pillow.

I left the hair and went into the kitchen, sat at the table and stared. I've gotten brilliant at staring, considering I've had such a short period of time, relatively speaking, to fine tune my skill. Nathan had woken and found the hair and filled in the blanks. He didn't say anything when he came up behind me. He just briefly placed a hand on my shoulder. Made coffee. Waited a *solid* 10 minutes before utilizing the broom and handheld dustbuster.

With the new treatment, Nathan is still attentive, but there's an edge to his behavior and his voice is less sympathetic. Something shifted with the surgery. There seemed to be more riding on the surgery than my health. His attitude had become more desperate prior--he was trying too hard. When it became clear that I did not approve of his decision to preserve the potential of having children in exchange for this hell, he first tried to convince me of his position on the issue. Then he stopped trying to convince me and guilted me instead. Then he stopped doing either. Now it's just the elephant in the room. I didn't think I'd voluntarily give up my chance for biological children, but I just can't see knowingly passing cancer-prone genes on to children. We disagree on that point, too. We don't agree about much these days. Every day when the smell of toast fills the house and wakes me from a sloth-like sleep on the couch, it surprises me that he's still there.

Every day, I want to say: *Just go already.*

But then I realize I'm not directing the statement at him and I resolve to make pleasant conversation in the kitchen, ask him about the multi-factor authentication security system he's working on. He talks about security tokens, hard and soft, things I know much more about these days.

If it's a treatment day, I get myself dressed. If it's not a treatment day, I stand upright as long as my body allows, or until he makes the suggestion I sit back on the couch. And I do—until he leaves. Then I collapse into it, sleep until I hear the garage door open around 6 and try to look like I've done more than sleep on the couch all day.

I rest my forehead in my hand, let my fingers feel the bizarre smoothness of my scalp under my hat, the ridges of my skull as I make my own decision about which celebrity wore a dress best. I really couldn't give two tiny rat asses.

I sense a couple of my fellow patients watching me so I pull the hat back down, try to ignore them, today being one of the days I wish the hospital would finish construction so I can have my own private chemo "suite."

It's then that my heart starts racing. Not because of the itching or the poison being injected into my body, but because of the man Nurse Jenkins now leads into the treatment room. Because I recognize him—his strong face, his broad shoulders, his dimple that's only prominent now because he's wincing as he walks.

One word pulses through my brain: *No.*

10
when everything was beautiful and nothing hurt

O ur first "official" date happened the Tuesday after Katie's wedding. I emphasize the word "official" because Will air-quoted it several times leading up to it and a couple of times during the actual date.

"You know, it doesn't bother me that we didn't have dates in high school," I offered. "I was just giving you a hard time."

"You deserve to be courted, Reeves."

"Oh. I'm being courted?"

"Yes," he said with a grin.

"How does one behave when being courted? Do I need to curtsy? Because that's a hazard."

"You don't need to do anything other than be yourself."

I watched the 21 year old version of him across the cab of his truck as we sat at the red light. He actually looked nervous, sitting a little more upright behind the wheel than usual. He made the turn into the parking lot, where he second-guessed his choice of space twice before deciding on the spot that would get me a whole ten feet closer to the door. I slid across the bench seat to address his nervousness; I had to throw my hand out to catch his arm before he could slide out.

"Will," I began, fully intending to have a followup statement, but he turned and pulled me into a kiss, his warm hand resting on my cheek, and I lost my sense of anything else.

He had to be the one to break the kiss. "I don't want to screw this up."

I kept my eyes closed in hopes that the kiss was merely at intermission, but I started to feel ridiculous. When I opened my eyes, I found him looking at me intently. The backs of his fingers ran delicately along my cheek, giving me goosebumps.

"I *respect* you." His words were matter of fact and determined.

I nearly laughed out loud, but just crooked an eyebrow instead. "That's-- good?"

"I mean it and you should know that."

"That you respect me."

He nodded. "I'm bound to mess up and do something stupid again."

"*OK*. Comforting."

"I care about you more than anything or anyone in the world."

I smiled patiently.

"I know I screwed things up before."

I shrugged and nodded at the same time. "Yeah, you kind of did. Screw things up."

"What can I do to show you how much I love you?"

"Well that's easy."

He waited expectantly.

"I like *cars*...and gaudy, expensive jewelry." I purposefully bugged out my eyes, getting very expressive with my hands.

"Weirdo, you like neither of those things." He smiled to himself, slid out of the cab. When he opened my door, a rush of cool air whirled around me. I took my time, enjoying him standing there in his white button down shirt, khaki pants, and suntan--waiting for me.

"Will," I began, sliding out of the truck. "You know I'm a simple girl."

"Untrue. You are an incredibly complex young woman--with simple tastes."

I wrinkled my nose. "Just love me, Will. I don't care about anything else."

He moved in close, bumped our foreheads together. "I do love you," he whispered.

He had chosen an outdoor restaurant set in the middle of a courtyard filled with huge trees and lit up by strings of globe lights. I kept finding myself gazing around, taking in the serene ambiance and smiling, not able to recall a time I felt more at peace.

"I'm really nervous," Will confessed, after we had placed our order. He was fidgety, centering the mason jar candle on the table, finding the glass warmer than he expected.

"It doesn't show at all."

"Really?" He picked up on something in my expression. "I was going to say-- I thought you were more observant, Reeves."

"Why are you so nervous? It's just me."

He sat a little more confidently, perking an eyebrow. "I'd prefer if you didn't refer to yourself as 'just' anything. You answered your own question."

"I make you nervous?"

"*You* make me calm. What I feel for you makes me nervous."

I frowned.

"Let me put it this way--if you won the lottery, you might be a little nervous holding the winning ticket."

Chills ran up my spine. "*Well*," I began, taking a sip of water and leaning forward, conspiratorially. "You could laminate the ticket. Or do they have rules about that because it might impact them being able to validate it?"

"Reeves."

"I mean once it's laminated, that's it. There's no undoing that." I gave the idea some intentionally long thought. "Not even with those no-heat, self-laminating sheets. It splits the paper if you try to undo it."

"Reeves."

"But then you have to consider if you even truly *want* to win the lottery. There are all those stories about it actually being rather detrimental to a person's life. Friends, family, would all treat you differently. They might be resentful. You might wonder if some people are only in your life because you have money." I sat up straighter, really getting into the scenario. "I mean, you buy everything you want, do everything you want...then what? Some people just blow right through millions. I don't get that. In my lottery fantasy, I sock away at least a few million to invest so theoretically I'll at least have the interest to live on if things go awry."

"Well you're practical like that."

"But really, if you can get everything you want, *then what*? Sometimes not having something and just fantasizing about having something is better than actually having it." I had hit upon something that resonated with me. My words had slowed dramatically as it all started to sink in. Perhaps fantasizing about being with me was better than actually being with me. Maybe he would tire quickly of my little silly rants. I glanced around at the pretty little setting, the cobblestone courtyard, the big trees, the soft globe lights, and suddenly felt like it was all an illusion that would disappear in an instant.

"Reeves." His hand rested on mine. He had managed to relocate the mason jar candle undetected. I stared at the contrast of our skin, noticing my chest rising and falling with a little more force than normal. Meanwhile, he looked suddenly relaxed.

"That escalated quickly," I breathed.

He furrowed his eyebrows. "How did you do that?" he whispered.

"Do what?"

"You took on all the anxiety I was feeling. I could almost see it transfer over to you."

I took a few deep breaths, trying to exhale out the panic literally pulsing through my body. "Is that what that was? Holy Toledo, that was worse than an encounter with a Dementor."

"I didn't know you were into wizard movies."

"What movies?" I winked slightly, shook out my shoulders and with them, I hoped, the bad feelings I'd just manifested from thin air. "You know how I feel about film adaptations."

He waited for me to return to as neutral an expression as I could manage. "Better?"

"I'm fine. How are you?"

"I feel great. You cured me."

I frowned, then shrugged. "OK, good deal."

"Do you remember when we first met?"

I nodded, but took a few moments to take some deep breaths. "After school care." *Two months after my dad died.* My mom had returned to a full-time work schedule. We were just unpacking from our sudden move from the only house I'd ever known. I tried to be as normal as possible for her. Actually I pretended to be better than normal. I was chatty and helpful and I never complained. Because she needed that.

"And do you remember when I came over to your house for the first time? What I said to you?"

My mom yelled at me for something stupid, not knowing he was there since she had just arrived home. I was just coming out of the hallway bathroom on my way back to my room when she barreled around the corner, grabbed me by the arm. I had gathered that I had left one of my bedroom blankets on the couch by the presence of it wadded up in her hand, shaking in my face. She said the house was a disaster area and that I was spoiled and ungrateful, shoving the blanket at me and storming away. When I returned to my bedroom, closing the door quietly behind me, he was watching me. I remember apologizing for her, giving him an opening to leave. I suggested the window, as to avoid a confrontation. He shook his head, stepped to me, placed his hand on my arm, and said: *You don't have to pretend everything's OK. Not with me. Just be you.*

Thirteen years later, I nodded, stood as confidently as I could manage in heels. He stood reflexively, uncertain what I was doing as I approached, leaving little night air between us. His eyes were locked into mine. I focused on his other facial features--his freshly shaved tan cheeks and the small area he managed to miss, his thick eyebrows, the subtle worry line between them, the dent halfway down his nose, which he broke playing field hockey, the scar on his square chin from a fall rock climbing, his pronounced dimple, his upturned lips. I rested the tips of my fingers on his cheeks and kissed him.

"I have your salads," the waiter offered, putting them at each of our places.

I gazed into Will's warm eyes--and my heel tipped into one of the gaps between the paver stones. The sudden jolt apparently caused a funny expression on my face. Will caught me, but struggled to contain his laughter. Once I was fully upright, my cheeks tight with embarrassment, I rolled my eyes and scolded myself: "A little too 'you,' Reeves."

As we took our seats, Will was smiling broadly. "Not possible."

*   *   *

Nurse Jenkins is leading Will to the curtained off beds when there's recognition in his eyes. She seems unconvinced when he motions to the vacant chair beside me, but he redirects his feet and she has no choice but to follow.

There's silence in the room as she situates him in the chair. Marjorie, seventy-three, is asleep and quietly snoring two chairs to my left. I haven't gotten to know my new social mates very well. I believe she has colon cancer. And dementia. Sam, who sits next to her is in his sixties. He was once a professional golfer. Now he scowls at a muted game on his tablet. Bone cancer of the spine. And Walt immediately to my left. He moved with me to the new group, but the new treatment regimen has taken its toll. He always has a stash of emebags next to him. (An emebag is the medical community's answer to the airsick bag only plastic and blue with a measurement tool on the side, as to track output.) He still attempts his crosswords, but most days, half is still blank by the time they unhook his IV. I wish he would discontinue chemo, have more good days, but then I can't think of coming here without him. At the end of every session, he places his hand lovingly on my shoulder and says something along the lines of "See you next time, kiddo."

I'm trying not to stare as Jenkins sets up Will's IV. She retrieves him a blanket, which stays folded on the tray after she's walked back to the nurse's station.

He turns his chin toward me and raises his eyes. Still disarming even with his eyebrows not nearly as thick as they once had been. Still clear and bright, despite the potency of the medications I see they're giving him.

His hair is gone. I remember his buzzed head before deployment was extremely short, but at this point, there's no trace he ever had hair to begin with.

His skin is lighter, a far cry from the suntan I'm used to him having. His veins seem to rest just below the surface of his skin. Is this the same man I saw a couple months ago? I realize I never asked him why he was at the hospital. He had let me soak through his shirt with my tears as I told him about my impending surgery, but I hadn't bothered to ask why he was there. I didn't even get his phone number. Not that I didn't have it. I just didn't think I had a right to call it. So I didn't.

I don't know what to say. I feel my nose start to burn at the same time my suddenly tear-streaked cheeks are chilled by the hospital air.

And then his hand, surprisingly warm despite his weak appearance, is holding mine. He leans toward his arm rest, pulls our hands to his lips and kisses my fingers.

He rests our hands back on the vinyl and eases back into his chair, breathes deeply. So I do the same. My shoulders, perpetually tense and pulled upwards relax. The racing thoughts quiet.

We must look peaceful because Jenkins is in a panic when she wakes us. She watches us both open our eyes, the noon light in the room unbearable. She looks confused and embarrassed as she catches her breath. "Sorry."

Do many patients drop dead in the middle of a session?

She's taken back. "There was one--not one of mine--"

"I didn't mean to say that," I say, confused.

"I'm sorry. It was stupid of me to react that way. Ridiculous," she says, rubbing her face. "I need to sleep more at night." Jenkins clamps the line on my port, wraps the tubing, and begins the disposal process. My name and ID tag are removed from the bag marked with a hazard sticker.

"I'm sorry, that was rude of me, what I said," I say.

"I thought it was slightly funny--in a really morbid sort of way," Will says, his voice surprisingly crisp. He gets Nurse Jenkins' attention, motioning lightly to me. "She's usually much funnier," he adds in a whisper.

Nurse Jenkins has an awestruck smile on her face. "Is that right? This girl here?"

"Don't let the scowl fool you. I'm actually hilarious under normal circumstances," I say boldly.

Will sighs. "Well, let's not go too far, Reeves. Most of what makes you funny is unintentional."

I settle back into my chair then realize there isn't a clinical reason for me to be there. Will still has about a half hour to go and I can't bring myself to stand up and walk away.

I haven't texted Nathan yet so I do. I lie. I tell him they got started late. He texts back that he was probably going to be late anyway...and that he loves me. That's the followup text. An afterthought.

I feel guilt rising in my chest, along with something else I haven't felt in years.

I've been trying to sort my thoughts about what to say and while I question if I have the courage, I realize I need to say it. My eyes drift over to the empty chairs, Jenkins back on her stool. Otherwise, it's just us.

"Testicular. Stage one. Extremely curable I'm told." He answers the question that oddly didn't occur to me.

"Oh. Good." I frown. "Not 'good.'"

"I know what you meant. I look like hell, don't I?"

"Guess that makes two of us."

"Yeah I wasn't going to say anything, but since you brought it up."

I laugh louder than I expect. A honk. This brings a familiar look of amusement to his face.

"I should have called you after your surgery. I wanted to."

"It's fine," I let my voice trail off, then mutter: "God, I do say that phrase a lot."

"I couldn't seem to catch you awake when you were still in the hospital."

"Honestly I kind of thought that run in with you was a figment of my imagination--I haven't been in the best frame of mind—" I pause, my brain slow to comprehend what he has just said. "You came to see me."

"About time I show up for something," he says, seemingly to scold himself.

"You show up. A *lot*. Randomly. Sort of stalker-like, actually."

His expression lightens.

"When?"

"It was the night after your surgery, after your *visitors* left. You were pretty heavily medicated."

I picture myself with my mouth hanging open, drool draining down my cheek. "That's right. I was morphine drunk. I swear even sleeping, my hand muscles would contract to keep it flowing on schedule."

The corner of his lips curls up. "That explains it."

"You had surgery, too?"

"Yep," he says. "Two weeks after you. Hey, want to hear a bad pickup line?"

I widen my eyes. "*That's* what this place is missing. You know, it really has started to bother me how infrequently I'm hit on while I'm here."

This doesn't deter him. He actually sits up straighter, leans close to me. "Most guys don't have the balls to talk to you. *I* only need one." He raises his eyebrows expectantly.

"You're right. That was a bad pickup line."

"I have another. A joke, not a pickup line." He already looks amused. "So this guy goes in for surgery after finding out he has testicular cancer. He comes out of it and the doctor says, I've got good news and bad news. Guy says what's the bad news? Doc says we removed the wrong testicle so now you don't have any. Guy says what's the good news? Doc says--you probably won't get prostate cancer."

"I see we both have the same coping mechanism." I frown. "So they decided chemo over radiation?"

"I was told radiation might have worse side effects."

"So you opted for the homeopathic route. Good decision."

He stares at me, saying nothing, then: "Alright, that was fair sarcasm."

The sudden appearance of a figure between us startles me. "Sorry to break this up. Bag's empty." Jenkins starts the same ritual she did with me. Disconnect, clamp, tubing, patient ID label. We're silent as she works. "I don't want to kick you guys out, but the Space & Planning Design Committee is coming through in a few minutes."

***

"Can we sit?" Will asks as we reach the main corridor, motioning to the garden.

I start to object, as it feels too intimate a setting, but the hall's about to be swarmed by administrative personnel. I feel far too disheveled to face people looking polished and accomplished in business suits.

We sit on the bench by the waterfall and the koi fish and I'm struck with nostalgia and pain. Because it reminds me of the gardens at the hotel where Katie got married and where he told me he loved me for the first time.

"Do you remember the night at the beach?" I ask after a few minutes.

He nods. A younger Will would joke that it's not *all* he remembers, but he's read the situation correctly to not make an innuendo. Or he just doesn't feel well enough. I already feel the medicine clouding my thoughts. "Wait--night at the beach at Katie's wedding or night at the beach when we went camping?"

I can practically hear the crackle of our fire and have to jar myself to the present. "Katie's wedding. Though camping is a really great memory."

He nods again.

"When I had surgery, I was really scared. As you *know*."

He waits for me to continue.

"I had nightmares leading up to the surgery. Really horrible nightmares actually." Instantly, I can see the operating room in the dream, hear the doctor telling me that it was important I was awake for it, that they didn't use anesthetic for this time of surgery, and then I felt every cut, every organ being removed. "When they were putting me under, I started to feel calm because all of a sudden, I was on that beach with you. Standing, walking--not the sandy part."

The fact that he's keeping eye contact starts to blur my thoughts.

"The sandy part is also--but--"

"I know what part you mean, Reeves," he says softly.

"That memory has gotten me through some very rough times--And if it weren't for you, I wouldn't have that memory. So no matter what happened after that--"

His breathing is more constricted.

"Thank you. For giving me so many happy memories."

He sighs, shaking his head. It takes him a few moments of glancing around at our surroundings to respond. "Oh Reeves. You've got it wrong."

I'm dumbfounded. *Is he being mean*? No. The tears in his eyes tell me otherwise.

"I should be thanking you--for—*caring* about a dope like me."

It pains me that he self-edited. "You're not a dope."

"Too kind a word?"

"*Way* too kind."

He swallows hard. "I'm sorry."

"Really, it's--." *Dammit. There I go again.* But it's not fine. "It's in the past. It's-- I mean, you were going through a lot. It is what it is."

"*Reeves.*" His voice is firm, meant to grab my attention, which it does, but his eyes are gentle. "It wasn't okay. Ramstein? Nothing about it was okay. I was wrong to leave you. I stupidly thought I was protecting you."

I say nothing, staring at the ground.

"I did the opposite. I abandoned you."

I try to swallow, take some deep breaths.

"I *never* doubted my love for you. Not for a second. You need to know that."

My inner monologue, which I expect to be whimpering out follow-up questions, demanding answers, clarification, is silent. Evidently, validation is enough for her.

"Ditto," I manage, catching his eye for a brief moment. I lean back into the bench, finding his arm behind me, and I exhale, looking away. There isn't a point really. I can feel the tears flowing down my cheeks.

I don't say a word as he curls his hand around my shoulder.

11
contrast

Will met me at Heathrow the week after I turned 21. We had "officially" been a couple for 2 years, but he had been deployed for 6 months and I was ridiculously excited to spend 3 weeks trekking around Europe with him for his leave.

Excited is an understatement. I purposely sat as far to the front of the plane as possible without having to pay a premium so I could barrel off the plane to get to the front of the line at customs to meet him sooner. The woman checking my passport watched in amusement as I weaved through the miraculously light line--mainly a test of my ability to navigate the dividers and collided with the podium as I presented my passport.

"In a hurry, Miss?"

In one long exhale, I explained the circumstances, then spent the next minute trying to catch my breath.

She scanned my empty passport book, compared my somber photo with the exuberant face before her and smiled tightly. "Anything to declare? Fruits, pets, plants?"

I shook my head.

"Enjoy yourself."

I took my passport, gulping at the surrealty of the moment, and followed her directions--past the baggage reclaim toward the "Nothing to Declare" channel. She advised me that customs should be a breeze and that my "love" should be waiting just on the other side. I paused for just a moment, my heart in my throat, my stomach in knots, the moment building with each step. I didn't know what I would do when I saw him. I didn't consider that I would feel the need to charge the corridor until I found myself running, my bag flopping against my back as I weaved around people in wheelchairs and families with unruly children, needing to cross that Customs threshold and find him in the crowd.

He turned out to be immediately outside the threshold, waiting for me to (calmly) emerge so he could (calmly) sneak up behind me and surprise me. Of course, I didn't realize this and I was halfway across the corridor, twirling on my heel, frantically searching the faces for him.

My cell phone started buzzing in my pocket. I could hear the airport noise through the phone.

"You're going to hurt yourself, Crazy Head. Did you caffeinate on the plane ride?"

I froze, eyeing my surroundings. "Caffeine is bad for jet lag."

"Rotate 90 degrees to your left."

Quarter of a circle. Check.

"Take 5-7 medium length steps forward." He counted them out, getting only to 5, since I was taking abnormally long strides. "Stop. Wait for the soccer team to pass. Stay right where you are. I'll see you in a second."

The lime green uniforms slowly filed toward ground transportation, dragging rolling duffel bags of the same color behind them and I could catch flashes of a tall, broad shouldered man, wearing a simple charcoal gray t-shirt, dark wash jeans. He was holding a bouquet of dendrobium orchids, my favorite.

As soon as I saw those gentle brown eyes I knew so well, that smile, I bolted toward him, but he raised his thick eyebrow at me and held up his palm. My shoe squeaked to a stop five feet short of crashing into him. I had originally grabbed my standard flip-flops then decided open toes were probably not practical for air travel or rainy London so I opted instead for my worn-in black

Converse sneakers. Because despite popular belief, I've found that the best things in life, the things that seem most genuine and true to who I am, I love as much now as I did when I was six. Back then it was a pair of dinosaur high-top Converse, reading endless amounts of books, writing stories about magical horses, and my classmate's older brother, the same brother who was looking at me like I was the only person in the International terminal.

Turns out I was a very wise six-year-old.

He closed the distance between us. His skin was very tan and looked a size small for his muscles. Never having been one to be drawn to physical characteristics—beauty is on the inside and all that—I surprised myself by eyeing that fine specimen of a man like he was on display in a store window--and with absolutely zero sense of subtlety.

"Eyes up top."

I fluttered my eyelashes innocently and I made a feeble effort not to look. *Damn.*

He shook his head, clearly flattered. "Reeves, I've known you most of my life. Honestly, I don't remember much before you--"

Sweet Baby Jesus, do they have a personal trainer at the base?

"Do you have thoughts you'd like to share with the whole class?"

"I'm sorry." I took a step forward and he stopped me short again.

"I have a speech prepared."

I frowned impatiently.

"You don't think I want to sweep you up in my arms right now?"

I exhaled, wrinkling my forehead in desperation.

"Fine I'll paraphrase, but it'll be like the movie version of your favorite novel."

That got me. I smiled. "I'm listening."

He gave the impression he was mentally editing his notes, standing there outside Customs. I'm pretty sure he was doing it on purpose to see my tortured facial expression because when he started again, his words were smooth and unwavering.

"I love you--Meagan Olivia Reeves." He paused. "*Reeves.*"

The sound of him using his nickname for me enveloped me in an invisible blanket.

"There are three things I know I need to live: Air, water—four things I know I need to live," he corrected, grinning. "Air, water, food, and you. If I don't have you, then the first three things don't matter.

"I don't deserve you. I know that. *You* haven't wised up yet to know that, but honestly that's not my fault. You've had like 15 years," he said quickly, smiling. "I've *always* loved you, but one day I looked at you. I had seen you a thousand times, but suddenly it was different. I looked at you and saw my future wife.

"Whether it's walking on the beach...or relaxing in a coffee shop reading a book...or sitting in a hospital room hearing our baby's first cry, it's your hand I want to be holding."

And he hit one knee. "Please be my wife?"

I stood there for either 2.5 seconds or 2.5 minutes with a dumb, awestruck, dazed, deliriously happy smile on my face.

He squinted one eye. "Going to need a response, Reeves," he whispered.

I nodded repeatedly.

"Preferably verbal."

"Yes," I breathed, my eyes, my nose burning as tears started to pour from my eyes.

He held his hand to his ear. "Yes what?"

"Yes, *please?*"

He chuckled.

"Yes, I'll be your wife," I said louder.

"It's *so* noisy--" he said, hand cupped around his ear, forehead furrowed.

"Yes, I'll marry you!" I yelled for all of Heathrow to hear, which they did. It wasn't a sudden swelling of applause, but there was some confused clapping and cheering. Perhaps the yelling threw them off. A comment called from the bar about getting naked distracted me enough so that it took me by surprise when Will rushed forward and swept me up in his arms.

———

2 years later...

I have spent the afternoon and evening in a perpetual state of disbelief and surreality. If not for Nathan ensuring I had food and water before he left for a work dinner, I probably would have gone without. I'm like a Labrador like that. Scratch that. I have no hair so I'm like that weird breed of dog covered in creepy Yoda skin and pointy ears. Chinese Crested? Mexican Hairless? Take your pick.

It was too much to expect my inner voice to stay silent and give me a peaceful night. Instead, she's picking at old wounds. Evidently the earlier validation just stunned her temporarily.

Something doesn't add up.

I try calling Katie, but she texts me mid-ring to say she's giving the kids baths and she'll try calling after. She texts again to make sure everything's okay.

I don't know how to respond. It's not okay, but I reply: *I'm medically stable. Mentally? Not so much. Please don't intervene me.*

I put down the phone, start pacing again. I peek into the styrofoam takeout container and find a huge piece of salmon atop mashed potatoes and asparagus. I immediately close it, concluding I'm too preoccupied to eat, but then the aroma fully reaches my nose and I snatch the box and a fork, settle into the couch. I really must be careful--it really annoys Nathan when I eat on the couch and he did treat me to my favorite dinner. Plus I already flipped the cushions.

Why my favorite dinner? He's never felt compelled to before and his latest research says that carbs needed to be investigated for their role in causing cancer. It's not a special occasion. Is he feeling guilty? Is this his form of flowers? What was the work function tonight?

I shove a forkful of buttery salmon into my mouth and realize I don't care. *Will.*

Will said he loved me, but did that stop after he dumped me in Germany?

If it didn't, why did he get married so soon afterward? *He knocked her up.*

I suddenly feel nauseous.

Did he mean to run into me at the hospital? Was it all a really twisted coincidence?

"*Sorry bedtime took longer than expected. Baby's sleeping on me,*" Katie texts later. "*You okay?*"

"*No.*"

"*What is it?*"

"*Will.*"

The phone shows her typing, but she appears to be struggling with her response. "*What about him?*"

"*He's in my chemo group.*"

"*Oh my God. That's a weird coincidence.*"

It strikes me as odd that she doesn't seem surprised he'd be in chemo. "*Did you know he has cancer?*"

There's once again a delayed, indecisive response, then: "*Someone tagged him online--his aunt or something--asking for prayers for him.*"

"*You're friends online? Since when?*"

"*Everyone I ever met is on there. Except you.*"

I frown. "*Mark Z has too much of a Not Quite Human vibe.*"

"*How does he seem? He had to be surprised to see you.*"

"*I ran into him before my surgery.*"

"*??*"

I do as brief of a recap as I can while providing all pertinent information. "*He really seemed weak today, Katie. 8 weeks ago, he looked healthy.*"

"*That's cancer treatment though, Hon.*"

"*But I look fabulous(??)*"

"*You're a beauty.*"

"*I look like Gollum and you know it.*"

"*I don't know who that is.*"

I send her a photo I found online.

"*Well I haven't seen you lately.*"

"*Ouch?*"

"*Did you two talk much?*"

"*Not much.*" Telling her we held hands for the entire treatment session perhaps doesn't paint me in the best light, out of context. Or in. "*He told me he loved me.*" Much better.

"*What???!!!*"

"*BEFORE. He said he was sorry for breaking things off the way he did. That he didn't mean to hurt me. That he loved me BACK THEN.*"

"*Anything else?*"

I know my best friend. "*What do you know, Katie?*"

There is a painfully long response delay. Long enough for me to watch half a rerun of *24*. "*Nothing. It just seems like you two might have more to talk about.*"

"*Do you talk to him?*"

"*Every once in awhile.*"

"*You never told me that.*"

Delay.

"*I put the baby to bed. Calling now.*" The phone rings.

"You know, you have some nerve interrupting Jack Bauer."

"So what was it like? Seeing him?"

I mute the television. "A little bizarre. How the hell did we both end up with cancer...and in our reproductive organs? Seriously? "

"Yeah that's weird. Testicular is very treatable though."

Ovarian? Less so. "I guess it's good he had a kid already. God just decided I didn't have much to contribute genetically to the human race."

Silence.

"Katie, I'm just pointing out the practical side notes. It's okay, I'm funny now. Did I tell you my Anesthesiologist told me she heard I was a hoot?"

"How did it feel? Talking to him?"

"The truth?" I turn off the television, take my to-go box to the trash can. "Like being home."

I hear her sigh sympathetically.

"But not *this* home." I look around at my stark surroundings lit up by the faux crystal chandelier. "I shouldn't feel that way though. I was living on a boat before. The house didn't do anything wrong."

"You loved living on that boat."

"I really did. I loved the creaky boards and how it swayed me to sleep every night. I even loved the fishy stink."

"Is the boat a metaphor?"

"I'm not sure. If it is, I'm much more capable of deep thought than I give myself credit. And I think I just insulted myself. And Nathan. And fish, come to think of it."

"You're nothing but thought. *Focus*."

I sigh. "It was strange, Katie. I have to keep reminding myself that he's married."

She clears her throat.

"Because the way he looked at me?"

"Yeah?"

"It's like nothing changed. It was like before that Christmas in Ramstein."

I hear her strain to pick something up.

"I don't know how I'm going to deal with meeting his wife, if I do. I can't even think of that."

"Or him meeting Nathan?"

Oh. I try to imagine standing beside Nathan, Will standing beside Cadence--

"That would be--"

"Bizarre."

"Yeah. I mean, I'm so glad to see him again, not under these circumstances mind you--but then again?"

"Yes?"

"It's sort of torture. It's not 'sort of,' it is. It's torture. He was sitting right there and I just wanted to--"

"Wanted to what?"

"*Be with him*. Not *with* him--" *Liar.* "but with him. But after treatment, he went his way, I went mine--"

"Did someone pick him up?"

"I don't know. I left first."

"Huh."

"I mean, we were together before. We were engaged. We loved each other our whole lives basically. But now? There have to be boundaries. After everything, we're what? Acquaintances?"

"It's weird, I agree. But maybe--" she seems to be choosing her words carefully. "Maybe God is bringing you together for a reason?"

"We're both married. If there's a biblical story like this, I doubt it ended well."

She laughs appreciatively. "It sounds like you've forgiven him though?"

I consider this, but before I've had a chance to respond:

"I'm so sorry, Mags. Baby's crying and the husband is out of town. Can you call me tomorrow? I want to talk more, but she's cutting 3 teeth right now."

"No, no, you go. Give her a kiss for me."

"Love you."

I return to the couch and set the phone on the coffee table. I eye the laptop, which is unknowingly tormenting me from the seat of the occasional chair. *"Don't do it, Reeves,"* I say aloud. "It won't do you any good." I sit in silence for a solid twenty seconds before practically lunging for it.

First stop: his public profile. Same photo from Monterey. Cover photo is a silhouette of a dog in a beach sunrise. It looks to be a very large dog. He didn't have a dog before. I scroll the page. Any profile details are hidden. In his friends list are several familiar faces, including his parents, extended family, some military friends, Katie with her two adorable kiddos, oddly Evan's profile photo features a miniature carbon copy of himself with floppy blonde curls.

All at once, it hits me how much I miss Evan, how I lost a would-be brother. I wish I had kept contact with him when he moved away. After the lease ran out and he took that job up north, I knew it would be up to me to keep the lines of communication open. I didn't. Then it didn't seem appropriate to check in with him after Will ended things. Here Evan had been like a brother to me and now I didn't even know he had a baby. If things had been different, this angelic looking boy would have been my nephew. Evan wouldn't have just felt like family--he would have actually been family.

It wasn't just the loss of the man I had thought I would grow old with, it was the loss of everything I had become so accustomed to--having a brother, having future in-laws who adored me and made me feel like I always belonged with them. It all disappeared.

The note he left me in the hotel was just the start. I stayed in Ramstein. I stayed at the hotel, conspicuously planting myself in the lobby when I couldn't stand sitting in the room any longer just in case he came by but ran short on courage to come up to the room. When that was fruitless and I suspected the concierge was starting to keep a closer watch on me, I went to the base.

The Security officer, a young soldier with a soft chestnut complexion and kind, dark eyes, stepped into a tiny office to call to verify my eligibility to be on base. His voice carried into the entrance at first, but after waiting in silence, he turned away from the window, speaking too quietly into the phone receiver for me to hear. He returned to the desk, uncertain of himself and his words.

"It's tough to get a hold of people sometimes. He--uh--might have flown out already. I--uh--talked to my superior and he's gonna check. You can leave your information--if you want."

"Do you go by Jackson?" I asked, eyes glancing to his name patch.

"These days, yeah. Still getting used to it. It's Darryl."

"Darryl," I repeated, trying to keep my voice from breaking. "I'm Maggie." I thought to add that Will called me Reeves, but decided better of it. It served no purpose but to make me cry.

"Nice to meet you, Maggie."

I smiled briefly. "He didn't want to see me, did he, Darryl?"

He hesitated. "Ma'am?"

"Listen, Darryl," I whispered. "Could you do me a favor?" I pulled the cushion cut engagement ring off my finger and placed it on the counter, frowning at it. "I know it's not your job, but could you see he gets that?"

"Ma'am--"

"Maggie."

"Maggie. You should keep that." He slid it toward me, searched around for a tissue, I think. He finally came up with a handkerchief instead. "It's clean. I promise."

I blotted at my eyes with the cloth, but it was no use. "Thank you." I motioned my eyes to the ring on the counter. "Please, Darryl? Be sure he gets it?"

He lifted it tenderly between his fingers, slid it in his chest pocket, securing the button. "As soon as my shift is over."

So that was him on the phone. I nodded at nothing in particular. "Is a girl supposed to return a handkerchief?"

"You hang onto it, Maggie." He straightened his posture, his expression regretful.

The return trip was a bit of a blur. I retrieved my suitcase from the hotel. There was the short cab ride back to the train. The driver kept trying to make conversation, asking about America and all the dancing and singing competitions. He eventually let me be and turned on a German translated version of *Harry Potter and the Half-Blood Prince*.

The train ride was cold due to the heating system being broken in some compartments. Since I was already seated with my bag stowed, I didn't feel much like switching, plus the cold left me in a car entirely to myself. I claimed a window seat for both flights of my trip home. I didn't watch movies or read books. I just sat with my head leaning against the side of the plane, staring out at the clouds, the night sky, the rising sun. I took a cab from the airport to the marina just before lunch time when the sun was high and unforgivingly bright. I placed my suitcase in the cabin, returned to the bow and with my arm wrapped around the rail, stared out at the horizon. I ended up laying across the cabin windows until after sunset when my stomach became downright insistent I eat.

I didn't. I couldn't bring myself to even consider crossing the street to the strip mall and picking something up. It seemed too big a feat. *Tomorrow,* I told myself. *Tomorrow I will take on simple tasks like eating.* I walked unsteadily down into the cabin, secured the door. I nudged my suitcase out of my way, took a long gulp of water from an open bottle in the fridge, crossed to the bed, and crawled under the covers. It took a painfully long time for me to fall asleep.

———

When I arrive to Chemo on Wednesday, I'm running on no sleep and a half-piece of toast.

I'm late arriving and Will's already set up. His face brightens when he sees me, but immediately fades as he reads my expression. I look away. Jenkins is on auto-pilot to take me to my chair and seems quite chipper about it, but I stop her, ask quietly for one of the beds instead.

This gets the attention of everyone to some extent except Marjorie, who's asleep.

"Not feeling well today, sweetie?" Jenkins asks.

Will's persistent eyes capture my attention against my best efforts. I've tried not to alter my facial expression, which I hope is vague, neutral, but I know it's not. I know my eyes are puffy and shadowed from crying and lack of sleep. I know my face gets a ghostly gray shade when I haven't slept or haven't eaten enough. He'll see my clenched jaw, my trembling hands. I snap away. "Not really."

"Okay, we can get you set up over here." She leads me into the curtained off area, but keeps the curtain open to the rest of the room. "Now, just remember you'll probably feel dizzier than normal from lying down."

I settle into the bed as she sets me up and as the cool liquid begins to find its way to my abdomen, she turns to leave. She's four steps away from the bed and I call out to her, asking that she close the curtain.

"Oh, I thought you might want it open so you can still socialize a bit?"

I shake my head and she closes the curtains, her mood far more solemn than just a couple minutes earlier. I shut my eyes, try to force sleep, which shouldn't be too difficult. I'm exhausted. If only my mind would shut the hell up.

My phone vibrates on the bed next to my hip.

"*Talk to me?*" Will. I recognize the phone number, but I hadn't programmed him into this phone.

So he didn't somehow lose my number. He's been totally capable of calling me this entire time. I glare at the screen, at the familiar number and absorb the surrealty of having it appear on my phone after all this time. I glance at the curtain, picture

134

the man sitting on just the other side of it. First I see the Will I know best--strong, muscular. *You took everything from me. All the good, all the happiness, you took it all. You said you'd never hurt me, you said you loved me.* I see Darryl looking at me with such pity. I remember the embarrassment, the hurt, the overwhelming feeling of isolation that overtook me as I turned to leave the base. I remember the sorrow I felt getting on that train to go home, how the sound of the doors closing, the train trudging away from the station brought forth a hiccup of sobs. He said he never doubted he loved me, but within weeks, he was impregnating someone else.

Then the image comes forward of Will now--weak and regretful, as much the charmer as he ever was. I think of him wrapping his arms around me, holding me, how he still has the power to make me feel absolutely protected from the world.

He's still my Will. How unforgivably cruel.

He made his choice--and I wasn't it.

I read and re-read his message: *"Talk to me?"* A question mark so he doesn't sound forceful. Desperation? No. He has a life, a wife, a son. He may have cancer now, but it's highly treatable. He'll be able to put this all behind him, have more kids, a full life.

And I'll have my five year plan. Or--I won't.

I type a few words, then several sentences, a long, emotional stream of consciousness. Then I delete it all and instead, simply say: *"No."*

There's a long silence and I can almost hear the weight of a simple two-letter word slamming into his chest. I can feel his sadness filling up the room, flooding the floor.

I intended to inflict pain, but I'd be lying if I said it made me feel better to do it. I may have plunged the dagger into his heart, but I feel the same blade piercing into mine.

Across the curtained off area is a waiting room chair. Next to the waiting room chair is a trash can, half in/half out of the curtain territory. This is where I spontaneously chuck my cell phone. It smacks the plastic side and settles, with a rumble, into the bottom. I turn on my side that doesn't host a surgically-implanted port and close my eyes.

Jenkins finally wakes me after everyone else has left. My phone has returned to my side. "The screen is alright. Those can be expensive to replace. I figured you might need it."

My eyes strain to see the lineup of maroon recliners to see if there are any occupants.

"He left a few minutes ago. Will. I think he was waiting for you to wake up."

I nod, jaw clenched tight again. "OK."

"You're all set, my dear," she says and puts her hand on my shoulder.

"There you are," Nathan says, tossing back the curtain. "I've been texting you for an hour."

Jenkins doesn't seem to appreciate his tone.

I dangle my legs off the side of the bed, slip on my flip flops, and stand. "Sorry, I fell asleep."

"You sleep more than anyone I've ever met."

Jenkins looks up from pulling off the linens. If looks could kill, Nathan would be incinerated.

"I just wanted to make sure I got you home. My flight's at 3."

"All set," I say, but I'm not okay. It feels like my knee caps and any steadying force in my legs has been surgically removed. Two steps out of the double doors and my body folds. My wrists break my fall and fortunately it doesn't seem that I've broken them, but they hurt quite a bit.

Jenkins races to my side, where Nathan is asking me what happened, cell phone poised in his hand. "It's probably from laying down for so long," Jenkins says. "Are you alright, sweetheart?"

I'm not, but I nod.

Nathan looks nervous, not just for me, but for the time issue.

"Administration would want me to have you checked out. Did you hit your head?"

"No."

"Let's get you a wheelchair," Nathan suggests. "It'll be faster."

"I'm okay," I say and allow them to help me to my feet.

"A wheelchair might be a good idea," Jenkins suggests.

"She's stubborn sometimes," Nathan explains. "Come on, let's get a wheelchair, Maggie."

"No, I'm *fine*," I growl, fighting tears. "If you're in that much of a hurry--why did you--" I stop short. "I'm sorry--I'm fine--I'll walk." I'm avoiding looking around too much, but I see him. In the far reaches of my peripheral vision, Will is just coming inside from the meditation garden, door propped open against his shoulder.

Nathan tucks away his cell phone finally and takes my arm. "I have some time. I'm carrying on anyway and I have PreCheck."

I feel steady again, if only out of stubbornness and spite, and I raise my eyes to meet Will's gaze. I consciously try to look angry. Honestly, it's hard to feel angry when he looks so weak, when I feel a thrill just having him so close. I can feel the indecisiveness of my facial expression. I turn toward the parking lot, hoping the cold hospital air dries my eyes on the walk out.

Despite the time crunch, Nathan pulls into a drive thru and gets me a strawberry slushie and a medium tater tot. It was the combination that seemed to sit well enough during the bouts of nausea I get after treatments. Something with the sugar content, starch, and grease. I'm honestly not sure there's a single strawberry involved in the creation of the drink. At first he would lecture me about healthier choices. Not anymore.

When we get to the house, he carries in my giant cup and paper bag, sets it up on the side table next to the couch, along with all required remote controls to operate every piece of electronic equipment in the living room.

I trail behind him, glance around the dimly lit house. The cleaning lady came by this morning. There are fresh vacuum streaks in the carpet, the kitchen looks staged for an open house. It's just missing a plate of cookies and real estate flyers. "Humans live here?"

"She does good work."

He finishes setting up my area. He places the house phone on the table, above the napkin that holds the paper cylinder of tater tots--perfectly parallel to be exact. "You're a good man, Nathan. Thank you for picking me up."

"I think I remembered everything. Oh—" He disappears and returns with a bucket. I get the impression that his primary intention is to protect the off-white carpet. "Just in case."

"You better get going in case you hit traffic."

"Enjoy your birthday, OK? Don't do anything I wouldn't do."

"Well that doesn't leave me many options." The words have flowed out before I realize I've spoken them.

He nods, takes another glance around. He's still not satisfied with the state of things, but he kisses my cheek and leaves.

I sigh, stare at the tater tots and shrug, take my seat. He's covered my area of the couch with a blanket, though he's failed to retrieve one for me to actually use for its intended purpose.

The silence within the squeaky clean walls is deafening. I turn on the television to fill the void, throw a tater tot in my mouth. "So it goes."

12
all this happened, more or less

On my ninth birthday, my mom and Ray had a big fight. Not terribly shocking, but still disheartening, especially so early in their budding relationship. I woke up hoping for a day of reprieve, hoping I'd find smiling faces in the kitchen when I emerged. I should clarify—I did meet smiling faces once they realized I was standing there. My mother was spitting words at him about his coworker, how she was certain he was having an affair. It went something like: "I hope you wear protection for Maggie's sake. So she doesn't lose her mom to an STD you brought home from that common office slu— there she is! Happy birthday, precious girl—"

I stood there, uncertain of what I just heard. What it meant. I had no idea what an STD was, never mind a "slu—", which my nine-year-old filter decided was "slaw." I went around saying the word for a week, trying to sort out how to use it properly, confusing my teacher by arguing that it was, in fact, a type of person. This obsession also severely irked my mother, who finally yelled at me to stop saying it. I still have trouble ordering the side dish without feeling a phantom death grip on my upper arm.

The rest of the day was spent with them attempting to put on a happy face (one between the two of them didn't seem too much to ask, but it was), which generally meant my mother doting on me in her classic over-the-top way while blatantly snubbing Ray. It was difficult to take her sugar sweet affection as being anything but passive aggressive vengeance when it was quickly followed by a death glare to my stepfather. Meanwhile Ray rolled his eyes a lot, didn't look me in the eyes once as he watched a baseball game on television and developed a lot of nervous tics to fill silences, like clearing his throat.

There was something that happened during these arguments, when my mother staked her claim on me. Any other time, Ray would be fond of me, explain documentaries he liked to watch on television, talk about the World Wars. I craved a fatherly figure so the subject matter didn't matter much. I was a captivated audience. A pat on the back or a rustle of my hair from him was invigorating. Truth be told, it meant more to me when I had his approval than my mother's, despite Ray having absolutely zero parenting instincts whatsoever. Still, he was impressed by my ability to absorb information, and he thought I was clever, so I was validated and rewarded with his attention. During these arguments, however, I was expendable. He seemed heartlessly unaffected by my mother blocking him from spending time, or even conversing with me. I didn't mean enough to him for him to challenge her.

I never liked having my birthday fall on the 4th of July. It meant no matter what, I'd have to spend more time at home than I would on a regular weekday. My saving grace on my ninth birthday was Will and his mom, who had asked if she could please take us, meaning just Will and me, to a local amusement park and then onto a BBQ. My mother forgot she had reluctantly agreed to it after my persistent pleading until they pulled into the driveway and I went barreling out the front door.

My seventeenth birthday fell on a Friday and I met Katie for lunch. I had a feeling we should have gone somewhere else. I figured it was because the bagel place was always packed and my subconscious was avoiding a long wait in line. The thought had just crossed my mind, after I had decided to get macaroni salad as my accompaniment to my sandwich, whether Will might be in town for the weekend. And then I got my answer. Waiting for his order at the end of the counter stood the soon-to-be college sophomore in a white Henley, cargo shorts, and flip flops. My heart had just skipped a beat when an exotic looking co-ed who had probably never tasted macaroni salad in her life (my selected side dish) put her arm around his waist and he slid his hand in the back pocket of her jeans.

"Have you talked to Will lately?" Katie asked, unaware of his presence as she retrieved her debit card from her wallet.

She was excited when she heard we had spoken since graduation —she had been shocked and confused by his assessment, saying repeatedly how it didn't make any sense at all. There was a light in her eyes when I told her we had spoken, not only because she knew how I felt about him, but also because it would be all-too convenient for us to double-date with her and her high school boyfriend Dean. (They broke up 3 weeks after my birthday.)

"Have you talked to Will lately?" She repeated, looking up at me. Clearly I had already seeped into awkwardness. "Are you okay?"

"Maybe we should go somewhere else?"

"I kind of wanted a coffee."

"Katie—" My voice was filled with desperation.

"Of course we can, it's your birthday."

Then there was the matter of weaving through the line that snaked around tables and out the door. I made a point not to look back as I maneuvered around people, who offered glares and raised eyebrows. I keep thinking Will might spot me and run after me, explain away the incident as something else entirely, a misunderstanding.

After a disappointing lunch at a burger place, I spent a few hours wandering around Barnes & Noble, refusing to go home as Katie did her afternoon shift. I enjoyed the quiet, the instrumental soundtrack, and the fact most people maintained respectful physical distances from each other. I spent my time sitting sideways in an armchair reading *Pride and Prejudice*.

We decided to go to a movie, with plans to go to an evening barbecue and fireworks show. Dean met us at the theater and Katie was telling him about a customer who had tried to return obviously used books as we waited at Concessions. I was pondering getting my very own butter drenched bag of popcorn.

"Um, Mags?" Katie said. She motioned to my right and I watched as Will approached me, that lopsided smile plastered on his face, his eyes dreamily focused on me.

I shifted my weight, wondering if he saw me staring at the snack menu, if he was judging my fondness for salty, calorie laden foods.

Katie immediately directed Dean's attention forward, awaiting their turn. This gave Will the opportunity to address me directly. "Hi Reeves," he said.

"Hi Mercer," I replied flatly.

"Would the birthday girl care to share a popcorn?"

"You're joining us?"

"Your BFF invited me, thought it would be fun." He took a step back, picking up on something in my facial expression. "Unless you've forbidden fun. You are the birthday girl; what you say goes."

I couldn't think of how to respond. We weren't dating anymore, not since his strange "not girlfriend material" assessment, so I didn't seem to have a right to be upset about his bagel shop date. I thought of all the times I had thought of him kissing me again and then I thought of the curvaceous co-ed and I just felt--foolish. "I'm not comfortable with that level of control over the emotions of others." *You are though.*

Seemingly cued by my thoughts and not my biting words, he reached for my hand, made effortless eye contact. "Is this new?" he asked, lifting the starfish pendant around my neck in his free hand. I thought for sure my thumping heart would be visible through my chest.

It was our turn at Concessions, but he was still examining my necklace. The prompting of the cashier for our order triggered him to release the pendant and step forward.

I visibly gulped. I know because Katie gave me a knowing grin as she grabbed a fistful of napkins.

Only she didn't know.

The quintessential pimple-faced movie theater employee talked us into the large popcorn bag with free refill. I handed over my souvenir cup for a refill and Will bought one for "future movie outings," eyeing me as he said it. He took the liberty of sipping from my cup first even though he was having the same thing, explaining that he was thirsty. He handed it to me, smiling. "It's extra fizzy. Try it." He waited for me to take a sip before removing the cup from my face.

"So Maggie, how are you just now 17 and you already graduated?" Dean asked.

"Because she's a brainiac," Katie replied.

"She skipped first grade," Will added. "She was doing multiplication and division when everyone else was still learning to count."

"Math isn't even her best subject," Katie added.

"Is that true?" Dean asked, impressed.

My cheeks were starting to burn.

Will nodded enthusiastically beside me. "That's how she got a full scholarship to the fancy high school."

Katie pulled Dean into conversation about the barbecue plans for the evening and mercifully that seemed to close the conversation.

"You don't like being in the spotlight," Will observed.

"Not really, how could you tell?"

He leaned in close to my ear and whispered: "I know you."

"Maybe not as well as you think," I challenged, raising an eyebrow.

"Well then. I guess we need to spend more time together—so I can learn."

"I thought that's what we were doing before," I blurted out.

He smirked, lowering his gaze. "You've got goosebumps, Reeves."

"It's cold in here."

He immediately let go of my hand and wrapped his arms around me, rubbed his hands in circles on my back.

"Where's your jacket to give her? What kind of gentleman are you?" Dean remarked.

"I never claimed to be a gentleman."

"Then what are you?" I asked.

"I'm Will," he said, smiling cooly. "And to answer your question, Dean, they're packed away for the summer I'm afraid. Only Knobby Knees here gets cold when it's 84 degrees outside."

"Are you going to hold her like that the whole movie?" Dean teased.

"If she's OK with it, I will."

I waited for the "but" and found silence instead--actually he was standing firm on his response. I found myself smiling against my better judgment, cheek pressed into his warm shirt, forgetting briefly why I meant to be keeping a distance from him.

The cashier held out our giant popcorn and Will was forced to release me to claim it. He repositioned the bag into the nook of his right elbow to be able to carry his drink cup and still hold my hand. It looked a bit comical...and endearing...since it took a couple attempts for him to appear secure with it.

The souvenir cups weren't exactly insulated so my hand holding it was freezing, but my other, the one he had to release to make adjustments, felt colder. When he reached for it again, his eyes brightened, and I felt the heat immediately in my hand, spreading throughout my body. There was nothing behind his gaze to alert me that he was being insincere with me. The girl at the bagel shop seemed like an illusion now. The Will I saw that afternoon seemed like a stranger. The Will standing before me was the Will I knew.

Still, my mind persistently doubted what was true. The scenario at the bagel place was more realistic. It was just how things were supposed to be according to the world I lived in—Will with a very attractive girl in fashionable clothes (specifically a shirt with designer holes in the shoulders, as to show attractive girl's attractive deep beige shoulders, and low-rise jeans to show off her tiny waist and round, taut backside) and me? I glanced down at my broken-in jeans, frayed at the feet, black v-neck shirt (which I noticed had some dog fur from the Labrador named Charley outside Barnes & Noble stuck to it), and flip flops.

I should have asked him about the girl. Directly. Instead, I heard myself attempt to casually ask him about her in a roundabout, cowardly sort of way: "So are you seeing anyone, College Boy?"

"No one serious." *Translation: Yes.*

I frowned and wondered if I was included in that category.

"So why a starfish?" he asked as we followed Katie and Dean into the theater.

"Well there's a story I've always liked."

"You do read a lot. Do tell."

"It's more of a fable. It's about how hundreds of starfish were washed upon the shore during a storm."

He didn't look sure if he had heard it, but his eyebrows pressed me to continue.

I lowered my voice. Previews hadn't started yet, but the theater was full. "So the story says that this man sees a little girl--some versions say it's a boy, but my grandpa liked to say it was a little girl--" I could smell the old book bindings, the leather high back armchairs, feel the weight of his elbow patch sweater on my shoulders. Will was captivated as we shuffled into our row. "She's running up and down the beach picking up the starfish and tossing them back in the water." We fumbled with the popcorn as we took our seats. It was a long enough pause that I questioned continuing the story.

"So then what?" Will whispered, leaning in close.

"The man asks her why she's doing that, that there are too many, she'll never be able to save them all, that it won't make a difference. At first it deflates her, but then she picks up another starfish, tosses it back in the ocean and she calls back to him as she picks up another: 'It makes a difference to this one.' Soon he started joining in, along with some other people who had been watching, and they saved all the starfish on the beach."

"I like that story." He smiled thoughtfully. "They can regrow legs, you know."

I nodded.

"Of course you know that." His smile broadened as he reached over to examine the charm again. "They're fighters--starfish." He placed the charm gently back on my chest and in one motion, swept the hair from my eyes, letting his fingers rest on my cheek.

I allowed perhaps a twenty second pause to savor the feeling of his hand on my cheek. "So--not seeing anyone serious."

His face turned severe. "Well *you* look a little stern right now."

"I ask because while you seem particularly interested in me right now, you also seemed pretty interested in the backside of the girl you had lunch with today."

Katie and Dean peered over, having heard my whispers.

The previews started and the lights dimmed and he was still looking at me. No, not looking, gazin intently, trying to read my expression.

I took a sip of my drink, trying to look confident, though my hand suddenly shook with nerves.

"May I talk to you outside, please?" He asked softly.

I glared at him.

"Please."

"Only because you used proper grammar—and because I probably need more napkins."

He handed the popcorn bag to Dean rather abruptly and then followed me back down the row to the corridor. We weren't even out to the main hallway when he grabbed my hand and pulled me briskly toward him. I thought he was going to kiss me and I was admittedly disappointed when he didn't, despite being angry with him. I found myself stubbornly intolerant to the mixed signals, but fearful of never feeling the exhilaration I felt of being close to him again.

"I'm an idiot. We've just been on a couple of dates. It's not serious. I'm so sorry you had to see that."

I raised an eyebrow, unconvinced. Since we were still in the theater and the preview was for a loud action movie, I motioned to the lobby and he followed. He seemed to expect me to speak once we arrived there. "Go on," I said, nodding.

"Oh--" he stuttered.

My heart ached terribly. "So--you had a lunch date, your hand seemed rather familiar with her butt cheek and she seemed very comfortable having your hand on said butt cheek."

His eyes had widened and winced a little as I spoke. He shook his head. "I'm such an asshole."

I ignored his remark. "One can easily conclude that if she's going to let a guy openly grope her butt cheek in a bagel shop, she's likely letting him do a whole lot more privately--"

He looked pale.

"Right?" He saw the moment my veil of anger fell away. He saw the exact moment I broke. I looked away as the tears started to stream from my eyes. Just as I saw him inch forward, I continued: "Never mind the fact that all of whatever happened took place while you were planning to meet up with me--*for my birthday*. Not that that should really matter since you so kindly informed me that you have no interest in me romantically—except that literally everything you do sends the opposite message."

"Maggie."

So not Reeves now. "*Will.*"

"I'm trying to not make my dad's mistakes. I don't care about her, I—"

My heart rose in my chest anticipating he might say he loved me.

"—I want to be with you, but—"

I released my bated breath. "But you wanted to be sure there wasn't something better out there than me."

He frowned. "There is nothing in the world better than you." The words flowed out quickly, matter-of-factly and seemed to surprise even him.

My heart inflated in my chest.

His voice was calm and methodical when he continued. "I thought if we allowed ourselves to explore the world, date, that--" He had a pained expression as he tried to articulate borrowed thoughts. "I thought I needed to learn to walk before I run."

I narrowed my eyes.

"What I mean is that if I don't go through, at least the motions, of dating, I'm going to end up hurting you more in the long run."

I had never seen him less comfortable speaking and yet he continued.

"So I have to focus on girls who are more so girlfriend material--"

"What? So you don't have an affair in 20 years?"

The color drained from his cheeks.

"You are not your father. Just like I'm not my mother. I will not make her mistakes. I'll make my own for sure, but I won't make hers."

He nodded, finding clarity in what I said.

"What you did was not like what your dad did at all." I took a breath. "Your dad didn't set out to cheat on your mom. Not to my knowledge anyway."

"He said it just sort of happened."

"He loved your mom."

"They had their share of problems, but he did."

I could remember how Will's dad had smiled over at me when I was waiting for Will to get something from his room before we went out for the day at the beach. His dad said how seeing us together reminded him of how he and his wife were at that age. For a moment, I saw Will in his smile and nose, Evan in his eyes and blond curls. "I take it he suggested you sow some wild oats or whatever?"

Will seemed relieved, like I was starting to understand. "Yes, exactly."

"He forgot what he told me then."

The relief in his face faded.

"He told me once he knew at 15 she was the love of his life. He said the mistake he made was to forget that. He forgot how much she meant to him." I felt my lip quiver as I spoke. I wanted to stop. I knew what I was about to say would destroy him. I knew the extent of the damage I would cause. My voice wavered as I spoke. "You said you did this to protect me from the same pain your mom went through."

"Yes." He looked regretfully into my eyes, saw the tears streaming from them.

"Tell me Will, do I look protected?" I found myself staring at a movie display featuring an animatronic yeti. "Your dad didn't set out to hurt your mom, Will. It wasn't a calculated move. What *you* did was."

At first, it seems as though he's going to say something profound, but he stops himself, lowers his eyes. "I'm sorry, Reeves." And he walked away.

***

I decide to go to the community pool. I don't think I could venture much further, even though I want to desperately. Somewhere with an expansive horizon and lots and lots of water.

The pool is abandoned during the week so there's little chance of frightening too many people with my Skeletor body and GI Jane head. I slip into my swimsuit, which I bought optimistically too small and is now three sizes too big. I throw a maxi dress over it with flip flops, tug on a worn out Cubs baseball cap, grab a beach towel from the laundry room, slip on my sunglasses and cross the street, my keys jingling in my hand.

Once I'm in the pool, I really have no idea what to do with myself. The water is like bath water, not refreshing like I'd hoped and I have little interest in swimming laps.

The medication this morning is a turbulent combination. I know better. I don't have a handle on my thoughts and they are not at all productive. I feel like a spectator in my brain. For example, I can very easily identify suicidal ideation in its infancy stage, a likely side effect of one of the meds in my pharmaceutical cocktail.

Think of something good.
The sunshine.
Bright light.
Streetlight glaring in my eyes.
A window.
A bed next to a window.
A streetlight glaring in my eyes as I laid on a bed next to a window.
Not laid. Flailed. Fought.
Jerry's manic smile.
I couldn't scream. My eyes kept finding darkness.
The streetlight. Fighting him.
My wrists bound. Desperate. Trapped. No longer able to fight.
Darkness again.

I wade across the pool. I want to push this memory out of my head. I stare at my hands, my wrists, remembering how they hurt for days after. How I couldn't escape the smell of ocean breeze bar soap. How I can still smell it now if I allow my brain too much leeway.

Rebounding from Will has led to the most horrific moments in my life, I realize. Most recently, the one-night-stand and terrifying drunk walk down the Pacific Coast Highway, delivering the babies at 23 weeks...and, well, I've told you the rest. I learned nothing from my emotional spiral after my seventeenth birthday or Jerry, a coworker I should have never trusted.

You never learn, Maggie. For such a smart girl, you sure do dumb things.

That would be my mother's voice dropping truth bombs in my head.

"The drugs have made me delirious," I think I say out loud.

Delirious or not, I've been preoccupied enough not to have noticed that a truck has parked in our driveway. Older, black. Unless I'm hallucinating, which is quite possible, I know that truck. *The cancer's gone to my brain, it's the only explanation. I'll be dead in a week. Two weeks tops.*

Will is returning to his truck, having given up at the front door. Just before he climbs inside, he stops, turns his head and spots me. Just like that. I haven't moved. Only the baseball cap is even visible.

He crosses the street at a jog and makes his way to the gate, also wearing a baseball cap, weathered, featuring an American flag.

"I can try to pick the lock, but my skills are rusty," he says, after attempting to open the gate, finding it deadbolted.

I look straight at him through my sunglasses. Nothing is registering very efficiently in my brain. When what he said does, I manage an "Oh," and move toward the shallow end stairs, grip the metal railing tightly, finding the stairs to be a bit of a gravitational challenge. At last, I emerge from the pool and retrieve my keys from my chair.

When I get to the gate, his sunglasses are propped up on his head and there's a serious look of concern in his eyes, which intensifies when I fumble with the keys. "Here," he says, reaching over the top of the gate and taking them from my hand. He quickly unlocks the gate, but has to gently guide me away from the gate so he can open it. "I think you should sit down," he says once he's at my side.

"I think you're right. Don't worry about me though."

"Why do you say that?"

"Worry doesn't stop bad things from happening." He lowers me to the lounge chair and sits next to me. I find myself slumping into his chest, which is a relief because my head feels foggy and I have a chill from the dry air on my damp skin. "*You* told me that."

"You seem—"

"Off." I attempt to sit back up, but fall back into him again, my limbs heavy. "I'm not drunk. That's how I wound up in Suburbia, but I don't drink anymore. I know better now," I say. "Besides, I'm a happy drunk, not a suicidal drunk." I frown. "I'm not suicidal. My brain just thinks it is right now. I'm not though. Not really."

He feels my forehead. "Did you eat today?"

I lean into his hand. "Toast very early this morning. Heavy butter." He removes his hand, still supporting me. "I don't drink anymore, *however*, I decided this week to finally take one of the pain pills they prescribed for me."

His shoulders drop, a little relieved to have an explanation for my behavior. He rubs my shoulder, and holds me a bit tighter.

"Nothing more than they recommended. Of course I've always been a lightweight. For drinking and for medications. I should have known better. I definitely shouldn't have taken the second—or third pill. In my defense, it says 2-4 pills PRN. That comes from the Latin 'pro re nata' you know."

He exhales deeply. "You're a Jeopardy contestant in the making."

"Medical jargon for 1000, Alex." I let my hand hover too long in the air. "For the record, four is within the prescribed range."

"Christ, you took four? Are you sure you're not trying to kill yourself, Reeves?"

"I love when you call me that."

"Good to know."

"Did I say that out loud?"

"You did."

"Oh. I have to use the inner voice a lot these days."

"That's regrettable." He breathes heavily, letting me rest against him.

"To address your question: no, I don't want to kill myself. I was trying to dull my pain."

"OK well then it was semi appropriate to take them."

"No it wasn't. *Emotional* pain," I clarify. "I probably shouldn't have said that."

"Lucky for you I'm not a doctor or cop."

"Will you please duct tape my mouth though? Who knows what I'll say."

"Indeed." He gathers up my belongings with his left hand, still holding me with his right. "Oh and I will absolutely *not* duct tape your mouth. For one thing, it'll look like I'm kidnapping you."

"Good point." I manage to keep myself from pleading with him to do just that, to steal me away from this strange existence.

"Plus I happen to enjoy when your censor is on the fritz."

"I think it's busted at this point."

"Even better." He slips my shoes on my feet. "Let's get you out of the sun. You need food."

"I totally sympathize with Gollum now. I'm trying to keep it together and my brain is trying to drive me mad."

"Leave it to you to make a movie reference," he says under his breath, shaking his head. "Actually, is that a literary reference? I'm not sure how Gollum was depicted in the books."

"I'm having a mental collapse here, try to take it seriously, Mercer. And *Lord of the Rings* was required reading in high school."

"I do remember the Cliff Notes vaguely."

"Of course you do," I mutter.

"Let's get you inside."

"Oh I'm not taking you in the house. Forget it. We're both far too messy and everything in there is breakable or white."

"Well I'm getting you out of the sun and I'm getting you food. I don't care where. We can go to my place."

"*I can meet the whole fam.* Oh that'll be swell." I start sliding to the bottom of the chair so I can stand.

He has to catch me when I get to a full upright standing position and my legs buckle.

"I can't go there, Will. Jack Bauer hasn't even endured that sort of torture. And let's face it, the man has endured *a lot*."

He doesn't want to argue anymore with this version of me. "Come on."

"No, we can just come back to the Off White Wonderland. Nathan won't be back for weeks anyway."

"Why's that?"

"Work. Hey, do you remember the dog? The Benji dog?" We're basically hugging at this point.

"Yes I remember. The stray you took care of. Listen, I'm going to carry you."

"I'm going to be carried?"

"Yes," he says and hoists me in his arms with only a slight loss of balance, however, the change of barometric pressure causes me to become painfully dizzy. I slam my eyes shut.

"I seem to have poor connection with my legs. They're still there?"

"Both here and accounted for."

He takes care crossing the street and soon I hear the familiar groan of the passenger side door.

"My mom was so angry at me for the dog."

"Why?"

"I told her what happened and she told me if I hadn't broken the rules the dog wouldn't be dead. That I was selfish. She told me I wouldn't get any sympathy from her because I made her look like a bad mother."

He shakes his head. "That sounds like something she'd say."

Keeping my eyes closed seems to be assisting the medication with muting any sense of verbal inhibition. "She said I loved your mom more than her, that she couldn't do anything right. When I tried to tell her she was a good mom, which at the time I may have believed, she called me ungrateful. She said I wasn't her daughter and that I meant nothing to her and clearly I had a new mother. That I wasn't her daughter." I pause. "I said that already."

The inside of his truck is cool, the air conditioning blowing steadily in my face.

"You never told me all that."

"You saw enough of her to get the gist." It's then I open my eyes and I'm met with the familiar setting of the truck he's had since he first learned to drive. It's tidy, but smells a bit like lumber. There is a stainless steel water bottle in his cup holder, a gray fleece hoodie in the middle of the bench seat. Being that it's the middle of summer, I wonder if he experiences varying temperatures like I do--one moment sweating, the next freezing cold. A patient itinerary is tucked in the passenger sun visor.

"I always did like this truck," I remark, finding the dent in the dash from moving some random furniture in the cab. I run my hand over the spot affectionately, then sit back.

His forehead is furrowed in thought.

"Your mind is doing a number on you, too, it seems."

He shakes his head, but not out of anger. "Yeah." Once I'm situated, he tucks my things in the second row, closes my door. Before I know it, we're in reverse, then pulling out onto Vista Avenue.

"I don't know why I told you that. About the dog."

"You know it wasn't your fault, right?"

I think of the moment Will's neighbor scared the dog away and the car came screeching around the corner.

He's silent making his turns, using his blinker, hands at 10 and 2. He uses textbook driving techniques when he's upset.

I think of how I lunged into the street after the dog. I feel the arms around me; see the arms around me, yanking me back. I always assumed it was Will's dad who pulled me back, but as I try to visualize the moment, I realize they weren't a man's hands around me. Will's dad had wiped the tears from my eyes with his thick fingers, but it wasn't a man's body that shielded me from the street, wasn't a man's arms holding me against his side, shielding me from the scene on the street, wasn't a man's hand stroking my back.

"It was you."

"Leave your seat belt alone," he says, oddly authoritative. "What was me?"

I didn't fully realize I'd undone it. "I thought it was your dad who pulled me back from getting hit by the car that day, but it wasn't. It was you."

He swallows. "What sounds good to eat?"

"Curly fries. Was it you?"

"That was a long time ago. What's got you thinking about it anyway?"

"I was thinking this morning about how I really want a dog. You saved my life."

He's quiet again, his body still tense, but his movement is less rigid as he makes a left hand turn into a drive thru.

"That's inconvenient."

"What is?"

"I'm trying to be angry with you, Will. *Really* trying." *I'm even summoning accounts of the bagel shop girl.* "The truth is I've never been angry with you. Even when I should have been. I've never even been angry with you for what happened between us."

"You haven't?"

"Not even a little bit," I say quietly, shaking my head. "Just very very sad."

"May I take your order?" the speaker asks. It has to ask again because Will is still processing what I've just said.

He spills out a scroll of a lunch order. While we wait at the window, his voice is soft. "Where would you like to eat? There's a park nearby, but with the heat I think you should probably be inside, rehydrating. We can go to my house or yours. Whatever you want." He raises an eyebrow at me.

I resist the urge to make a joke. "The Beige Bungalow then."

He nods. "You do enjoy alliteration."

"I do enjoy it, but it doesn't work. Two stories aren't bungalows."

He stares through the windshield. "Off-White Wonderland it is."

"I feel 'Wonderland' is misleading. It sets unrealistic expectations."

On the drive, we're both quiet. I lean my head against the window and close my eyes because I'm dizzy. I try to focus my mind on one thing, other than the memories that have been haunting me all morning. I use a meditation technique

I was taught in support group, using a positive memory to bring about positive feelings in the present. So I think of driving with my dad through deserted back roads. He controlled the pedals, I steered. I remember holding onto the leather wrapped steering wheel of his classic Cadillac feeling so empowered. Really, he had a hand ready to grab the bottom of the wheel, if necessary, but to me, I felt like I could do anything.

Will says my name and I reflexively roll myself out my door, getting caught up in the seat belt on my exit. Before I know which way the front door is, he hoists me into his arms. Again. It must be a strain in his weakened state, but he doesn't let on.

He carries me into the living room, glances around, decides the only feasible place is the blanketed area on the couch. Still holding me, he tugs the tucked edges of the blanket from the cushion, places me directly on the cushion with increasing care. He drapes the blanket across my bare legs, up my skinny torso. "Please don't try to get up until you eat something. It would be ideal if it wasn't just grease, but it'll have to do. Plates?"

"Cabinet next to the fridge."

He moves quickly to the kitchen. "Huh. I always put glasses there." As he makes his way back to the living room, he takes in his surroundings. He pays particular attention to the wet bar and its glass shelves lined with frames of people he doesn't know and the official wedding portrait taken against a backdrop of lighted tulle. "It's a nice house."

He hates it.

He slides food in front of me on the coffee table. Most of the food makes my stomach turn, but he's satisfied enough, if not a bit amused when I start dipping my curly fries in a milkshake.

"I need to get healthier," I say once my head starts to feel more level, the starch doing its job admirably.

"Me, too. It's amazing how quickly muscles break down."

"If the zombie apocalypse happens, I don't stand a chance anymore."

That brings a little grin to his face.

"At one point, I was borderline athletic."

"I remember. Minus the 'borderline.'"

"I wish I could feel that strong again."

He hesitates, then offers: "I'll exercise with you, if you want."

Responding to my silence, he continues: "Some easy stuff to start. It would probably be good for both of us."

"Might need to work on my balance before doing anything too strenuous," I say. "Last week, I took a turn around the kitchen island too fast and I wound up on the floor like the Life Alert lady." I smirk at him, flail my hands in the air for effect.

"Hilarious. The food is helping, I think."

"In the category of ancient memories that popped up in my head under the influence of narcotics--Do you remember the school's end of the year rolling rink trip?"

His eyes narrow.

"I blame the pain meds, but a girl never forgets her first slow skate." I smile. I can feel it take over my face.

"As I recall that was your first *and last* skate."

I fell in the bathroom whilst still on skates shortly after. "It was, which heightens its importance. I loved that song."

"MC Hammer *was* underrated."

"Not that one."

"Ah, the Brian Adams power ballad."

I sigh reminiscently. "You serenaded me with the same song when I was 16. You meant it to be silly, but it's one of my most favorite memories. Inconveniently. You occupy the majority of my happy memories, Will." I dip another fry and lean back in the cushions as I savor it along with the memory.

"You too, Reeves."

I stop chewing, gaze across the couch at him. It doesn't make sense. He saved my life, saved me from public humiliation, professed his love publicly on more than one occasion. The rest of the story, the sudden isolated oversight of my feelings seems like a poorly cut puzzle piece that will never ever fit. I finish chewing and watch him sort through the feast on the coffee table. "I don't know how I'm supposed to be angry with you. Because given what happened, I think I'm supposed to be quite angry with you."

He takes a deep breath, his eyebrows furrowed again.

"It doesn't make sense, Will," I say, forced to speak to his cheek. His jaw is clenched.

"I don't know if this is the best time to talk," he manages to say, his voice practically a whisper.

I have to hear it. I need him to be blunt, need the truth, need something to make sense. "Tell me." My eyelids are also getting really difficult to hold open, thanks to the codeine and the food. "How did you end up married to someone else? I don't understand how I could have been so wrong." My words trail off as my eyes drift closed.

When I wake, my head is resting on a bed pillow that wasn't there earlier and I'm tucked into the beige couch. Only my drink cup remains on the table.

Will is gone.

13
live another sol

The act of parking a car is ordinarily not a huge feat. Consider then that you haven't been able or otherwise permitted to do so for an extended period of time. Like a year. Then you might grasp how it feels as I shift into Park in Lot G at the hospital, having driven myself to my first medical appointment since being given my diagnosis [and fleeing land for 10 days].

There is a designated lot for cancer patients, but those are occupied this morning by a conspicuous number of cars driven by individuals who don't look particularly ill. I pull into the first space I can find, cheerfully put up the sunshade, gather up my belongings, which are neatly organized on the passenger seat. I slip the canvas tote bag painted with a handprint elephant, a gift from my Godson Trevor, on my shoulder, lock my Jeep, and head inside. I'm not used to this route, usually dropped off at the front, but I take notice of all the details I usually miss--the thick trees raining warm colored leaves all across the concrete, the sky transitioning from early morning orange to blue. I usually only see the inside of the hospital windows, but from here I see how they reflect the scene outside and I appreciate their presence. No thick fog this morning, but there is a cool breeze and I have a peekaboo view of the coast. It's actually prime real estate. I don't desire to have a reason to experience it for myself, but I'm sure the views from the higher floors are pretty extraordinary.

I take the side entrance, which is closest to treatment and start down the familiar corridor. Over the weekend they've lined it with nature photographs. I make a mental note to look closer at them on my way back since I'll probably be moving a little slower and I'm already a bit late.

Jenkins smiles at me as I approach the check-in desk. "Feeling better today?"

"I got to drive this morning," I say enthusiastically, then see the uncertain grin on her face. "I sound like a fifteen year old with a learner's permit, don't I?"

"A little, but I'm happy for you, sweetie." She motions toward my normal seat. Will is already seated in the next recliner and is watching me in suppressed amusement.

I glare at him, which just increases the curve of his smile. I take my seat, place my bag on the table and wait for Jenkins. "Shut up, Mercer."

"Morning, kiddo," Walt murmurs, glancing up over his reading glasses.

"Morning, Walt. How's the crossword?"

"Daunting, but the challenge will not--" He searches the puzzle and points to one of the clues. "'thwart' my attempt."

"I have faith in you, Walt."

"We missed you on Friday." He dips toward me and whispers loudly: "*Especially* new guy."

"Is that right?"

Will is acting distracted by Jenkins.

"How was your birthday?" Walt asks.

I sigh. "Well I spent a lot of time outside, had some good food, and there were fireworks, per the norm. It was good--" I pinch my face--the word sounds foreign. "Yeah, it *was* good actually--thanks for asking."

Jenkins finishes hooking up the line and I tug my shirt to cover my stomach, as well as my hip bone, which is obnoxiously protruding through my skin. She pulls the blanket from the back pocket of the recliner and places it on my lap. "Born on the 4th of July," she says, amused. "How many candles on that birthday cake?"

"No birthday cake."

"What?" she exclaims. "You have to have a birthday cake."

"I had a chocolate souffle. With one sparkle candle. The other 22 wouldn't have fit."

She seems satisfied by this information. "You look like you got some sun."

I watch her move to check on Walt, knowing Will is now watching me. He waits for me to look at him to say hello.

I turn and try to keep a straight face, try to look firm, if not nonchalant.

"I figured I'd read today," he says, smiling lightly, then looks back down at the book he's reading. He frowns at the page, slowly lifting the book so the cover is visible. Trying to get my reaction. Same old Will.

I dig into my tote, find my sudoku, a pen and my latest re-read, and settle into my seat. I open the spiral bound sudoku, setting the novel on the table. It's a different cover than his and my version is lovingly worn, but I see when he notices the title. "'Recommended reading?'" I say facetiously, focusing on my first puzzle.

He leans toward me, but clearly finds the gap between our chairs does not offer the closeness he's looking for. I lean his direction, extending my neck toward him, the puzzle blurring in my vision. I anticipate a witty retort. His voice is soft and low: "'If I am going to spend eternity visiting this moment and that--'"

I smile. He's read it before. Based on his page marker, he's not far enough to know that quote.

"'I'm grateful that so many of those moments are nice.'" The words are deliberate, seemingly reflective and intended to deliver a message.

I lean back into my seat. "Nobody likes a show-off, Mercer."

Walt looks over at the pair of us, forehead furrowed in concentration. He seems undecided about saying something, his eyes slowly gliding from Will to me. He gives me a wink, clears his throat and goes back to his crossword.

"I'm surprised it's not the *Lord of the Rings* Cliff Notes," I observe. "Wasn't that your favorite?"

"I prefer the on-screen chemistry of Frodo and Sam, actually."

I smirk.

"It was a tough journey and I might be a sentimental fool, but I think those crazy kids are going to make it," he says with mock sentiment, even sniffling a bit.

I stare at him, having dropped my expression, breathing intently.

He steals a glance at me expectantly.

Finally I release an airy laugh, my shoulders shaking. It takes me several moments to recover and I find a tear in the corner of my eye.

He smiles broadly.

Walt glances over his newspaper and Nurse Jenkins, who was getting a bottle of water for Marjorie, looks over in amazement. "You know, kiddo, I don't think I've ever heard you laugh."

"I laughed just last week I think."

"*That* was a laugh? I thought there was a sea lion in the building," Will says, flipping through the pages until he finds where he left off.

I glare at him.

"It seems you've been out of practice," Nurse Jenkins says, smiling toward him appreciatively.

I slump my shoulders and sit back in my chair, still grinning in spite of my embarrassment.

"It's a good laugh, Reeves," Will says, thoughtfully.

"A *great* laugh," Walt corrects. "Smile, too."

Walt is looking at me in his wise, knowing way. I wait for him to break the gaze with a gentle blink of his eyes as he returns to his crossword.

* * *

"What are you doing the rest of the day?" Will asks after Jenkins finishes with him and has gone back to her lunch at the desk. I'm her last patient until the 1pm session.

"Well it's my first treatment day without a chauffeur. *Endless* possibilities."

"Knowing you, you have an itinerary."

"Knowing me? OK, smarty pants, what am I doing?"

He sighs. "I would say that you have two options in mind for lunch. One healthy, one not so much. You're more likely to want to choose the latter because your poor deprived stomach has been grumbling for the past hour, but your good sense will compromise and you'll just get a larger portion of Option A. High in protein and omega-whatevers, low in carbs, and will likely contain seaweed."

"*Okay?*"

"If you're not working right now, which in itself is probably driving you crazy, I can't imagine you going to the Off-White Wonderland if you have the option to be outside. Even if you are tired."

"Okay?"

He smiles. "I can wait, walk you out."

"You're not answering."

He glances up at the bag, then pulls up my shirt by the port to see how much is left in the tube. "Almost done."

I'm absolutely flabbergasted by this act, but I shouldn't be. It's very in character for him to challenge my personal bubble.

His hand's retreat is delayed, his fingers resting on the taut skin surrounding the port. He suddenly jolts to attention. "So why the freedom today? Your--*husband*--is out of town--"

My stomach wrenches. "Wow, that word sounds strange coming from you," I say, though I didn't intend to.

"It did. Kind of left a poor taste in my mouth actually." He's not really joking, but he plays it off like he is, contorting his face.

I raise an eyebrow. "Not fair, Mercer."

"You're right. I have no right to say anything like that." He's entirely serious.

"Yes, Nathan is out of town for training for awhile."

"No substitute chauffeur?"

"I expertly maneuvered around that arrangement."

"So where's the training?"

"Silicon Valley." Nathan wasn't amused when I made a joke about it so I sound a little uncertain.

He nods. "Beverly Hills? That's not too far."

My jaw drops.

"It's a joke, Reeves. I know where it is."

"No, it's not that." *At least he didn't try to explain the joke further with hand gestures over his chest.* I shake my head. "Never mind."

"So is there a chance that you'll move up there?"

"He's not a permanent fixture," I say, but quickly clarify: "He's an independent contractor so he's training staff for a company there."

"Too bad it's not during a break from treatment. You could have visited Katie." He sounds convincingly neutral.

I nod, distracted as I try to remember when her due date is.

"Let's not have any falls today," Jenkins says, pulling up my shirt to reach the port almost as casually as Will had.

"I'll spot her."

"We can get a wheelchair, you know," Jenkins says.

The memory flashes before my eyes in an instant, carrying all the emotions with it--being forced to ride in a wheelchair out to the front circle driveway empty-handed, having just authorized the cremation of my tiny babies with so shaky a signature I would have been better off just putting an "X". As I waited for Nathan, a new mother was wheeled next to me, cradling a heavily swaddled baby girl with a giant lace bow on her head. A cart filled with balloons, gift bags, and impractically large stuffed animals followed her. Her husband was more efficient than Nathan, even made a joke intended for my amusement about something so little having so much stuff as he filled the back of their SUV with the suitcase, duffle, diaper bag and gifts. By the time Nathan pulled up, they had both climbed into the back seat to conquer buckling the tiny infant in together.

"What do you think? I'm an excellent wheelchair driver." Jenkins rubs my upper arm.

"I'll manage," I say, a little curtly.

"Stubborn girl, this one," Jenkins says to Will. She doesn't seem to notice my tone.

I expect Will to agree in his joking manner, but he doesn't say anything, his eyes are focused on me.

"All set. You're both back Wednesday, I think."

Will nods. "Same place, same time."

As she walks away, I glare at him.

"Get out of my head, Will Mercer."

He frowns, still concentrating on something.

I push myself to stand, gather my bag on my shoulder.

He smiles faintly at the toddler artwork. "Is this a Louis Vuitton bag?"

"From the Summer Collection," I say, steadying myself.

"Good to go?"

I stretch my back, stand up straighter.

"Oh don't do that," he says, giving a pained expression.

"Don't do what?"

"You're even thinner when you stretch like that." He grimaces.

I seize the opportunity to torture him a little. "You should see my back. It's like Skeletor. Here, have a look."

"I'll take your word for it, Weirdo," he says.

The sky is overcast as we move into the corridor.

"Don't worry. This looks like it'll clear," he says, assessing the sky.

"I'm not worried."

He steps ahead and opens the door for me. "So I have a quick meeting to go to, but if you do want some company, I can meet up with you around 2:30."

"Oh you think you're *so* smart," I say. "Where is it you think I'm going?"

He smiles broadly. "Where'd you park?"

"Your Magic 8 Ball didn't tell you that?"

"I got here before you."

"Two over, I think." I start to feel a little winded. Perhaps my plans are a little too ambitious. I picture the ocean, the marina, grasping the sides of the paddleboard for the first time in a year and a half. Perhaps standing is out of the question. Kneeling would be better.

"You kept the Jeep," he observes.

"Garage life has been dull, I'm afraid."

"Guess you'll have to make up for lost time." He pats the hood, seemingly satisfied that he got me to my destination without allowing a fall. "2:30?"

"Will, do you just want me to tell you where I'll be?"

"So you *want* me to join you. *Excellent* because I'm looking forward to it."

"It just seems like a waste of time to have you go to the wrong place." I dangle the words out there like bait on a hook.

"Have a little confidence in me."

"Maybe I'll just go to the house. I do so enjoy the afternoon television lineup," I pretend to ponder.

"You're testing to see if I'd be disappointed if you cancelled your plans. I would be, Reeves. And you hate most television. It's all court shows and soap operas this time of day anyway."

I straighten my posture. "I mean it, Will. Get out of my head."

He chuckles. "See you at 2:30." He slips on his mirrored aviator sunglasses with a confident smile. "Please get some food."

*****

Just before 2, I'm walking the length of the dock to throw away my lunch containers. The chemo port was achy on my stomach so I've switched into my bikini, which is more forgiving than my usual underwear. I've covered up my sickly little body with a pair of elastic waist shorts and the softest gray pocket t-shirt ever made. I found my Cubs hat and I'm suddenly feeling like I'm on vacation and not a couple hours out of a grueling chemo treatment. The place is quiet besides the lapping water and my Bluetooth speaker playing Sister Hazel.

Walking back to *Shore Thing*, I find myself singing along to the music, tapping my foot to the refrain. I climb aboard and retrieve my paddleboard and paddle from the cabin, lean them against the helm. The cabin needs a thorough cleaning. I'm considering what type of new bed linens I should buy when I hear a knock on the side of the boat.

"Permission to come aboard?"

I climb up top. "You're either a stalker or I have a leaker."

"Or I know how much you love it out here," Will says, motioning to the bamboo and lime green board leaning against the dock post. "I rented what they called an 'all-arounder.'"

"The beauty of only having one confidante is it's easy to figure out where leaks are coming from."

"Don't be angry with her."

"She knows my whole life history. I can't train up a new best friend now. I don't have the energy."

"I know your life history."

You're also married. "And I know yours." I pull myself up to the dock, hands on my hip bones.

"Yeah, I'm not sure if you know how to pull off anger."

"I hit you, didn't I?"

"And nearly broke your hand. Did you have it x-rayed?"

"I did. Hairline. I had to wear a hand brace for 4 weeks."

He winces. "Sorry." He reaches for my arms, rotating them and examining the bruises from my fall last Wednesday. He touches one delicately.

"Evidently being angry with you does not agree with me."

"It would appear not."

I squint up at him. With his sizable sunglasses, narrowed jaw and baseball cap, he looks a bit like he did in high school. "I wonder if Katie's more so *your* confidante these days, actually."

"Why do you say that?"

"Because she is avoidant and uncharacteristically vague when it comes to any questions about you." I hand him my board distrustfully.

"Oh—happy belated birthday," he says, holding out a small rectangular box wrapped in teal paper with a wave pattern on it.

The paper is thick and he's been generous with the tape, but I manage to rip it off and slowly open the box. Inside is a wood guitar pick engraved with a starfish. It has one shortened limb, seemingly in the process of regenerating. I stare at it for probably too long. "Thank you," I say with a small smile, securing the lid and placing the box on the deck seating. I think to hug him, but decide against it. Too intimate. "I love it."

I'm about to burst into tears because of a guitar pick.

He smiles knowingly. "Shall we?"

"Do you have your Speedo on under there?" I motion to his cargo shorts as I climb back onto the boat and secure the cabin.

"The zebra print one. It's my favorite."

I can't help but grin, shake my head. As I wait for him to change clothes, I sit on the picnic bench taking in the sights of the marina, breathing deeply. There is a steady breeze, the various flags displayed around the marina entrance flapping wildly. I notice the California state flag is upside down, more likely a political reference to the disdain several boat owners have for the governor than a simple error.

"Those are above average marina restroom facilities," Will says, stepping across the grass divide to where I sit. He's chosen simple navy board shorts and a white t-shirt with a graphic I can't make out on the right chest. "It wasn't always that nice."

"They remodeled last year, the stall doors no longer look like they were built for hobbits."

"Do you come out here much?"

"There's been a concern about me over exerting myself." I lower my feet to the ground and shrug. "Ready?"

"I am. It's like riding a bike, right?"

"I never had good balance and it's only gotten worse so try not to show me up too much." I wade into the cold water, instructing him about placement of the board. He has a determined look about him.

"Alright, going to need your guidance here, Reeves. If you'll recall, we were rained out when you planned on teaching me."

I do recall. I can very clearly remember his arms around me as we laid on the lofted bed, gazing through the windows at the stars above. He had two weeks leave during his second deployment and we were determined to make the most of it. We walked across the street in the morning and had fresh croissants and coffee. We had planned to paddleboard that day, but found a solid sheet of rain blocked our path back to the marina when we left the bakery. We ran together, laughing. By the time we crashed back onto that bed, we had discarded our drenched clothes.

"No popping up, right?" he offers.

I nod. "Right. You'll want to forget your surfer instincts. It needs to be a slow and controlled movement or you'll be in the water," I say once we're both tensely balancing on our respective boards. "Try paddling a bit to settle in. Get your center of gravity."

I can tell Will would be able to stand up anytime, but he's waiting for me to stand first.

"It really is pretty here," he says casually, to distract me from my jittery legs I think. "I can see why you decided to live out here."

"It's kind of like camping on the water."

"I remember when you told me, I couldn't believe it. The other guys really thought it was something."

"Something good or something crazy?"

"Something good. I don't think many of them had encountered such a low-maintenance girl. You probably single-handedly ruined the expectations of a half dozen or so young soldiers."

"Funny, I had someone include it on a list of my 'reckless' and 'impulsive' behaviors." My legs are aching, but I stand, holding the paddle in front of me. "My mother was particularly proud of having coming up with the phrasing 'reckless recluse.'" I close my eyes and slow my breathing, try not to overthink my balance corrections. "The alliteration stung a little."

"You've got this, Reeves."

Slowly I lower the paddle into the water, do a few strokes before opening my eyes again. "The counselor was a little less keen on the wording. It wasn't 'constructive,' she said."

"And you?"

"I told her that if I'm going to be labeled as something, positive or negative, I want to have earned it, but avoiding one person does not a recluse make." Out the corner of my eye, I see he's up on his board.

My mother had fired back that in that case she didn't think she should be labeled as my enemy. I had wanted so badly to respond matter-of-factly with "No you've earned it," but I had cowered and she had smirked victoriously.

"When was *this* group therapy session?"

"They had an intervention for me on Thanksgiving. They baited me with football, pigs in blankets, and green bean casserole, which I felt was a really unfair tactic."

"An *intervention?*"

"It was a common perception that I was losing my mind. You disappear for almost two weeks on a sailboat and everyone thinks you're nuts."

He shakes his head, glaring at the water. "Who's 'everyone'?"

"Well you know my family's representatives. Then the in-laws."

"So they scheduled an intervention on Thanksgiving."

"They did." I remember them glossing over talking about my dead babies, referencing me having been pregnant, but that I wasn't anymore, like it was a bout of indigestion.

"And I thought Evan burning off his eyebrows deep frying a turkey made for a bad Thanksgiving."

My foot slides about two inches, but that's enough to throw off my balance. I catch sight of the waving flags in the distance, noting that California had been flipped upright, and then I land in the most awkward of positions, legs straddling the board, the top of the board bonking me on the head before settling back flat in the water.

There's a splash in the water, but by the time Will reaches me, I'm lost in hysterical laughter, laying forward on the board, practically hugging it. My laughter echoes against it, muffled slightly. "Well at least I didn't split my shorts. That would have been worse."

He peers toward my backside. "Yes, they appear to be intact."

"Did you just check out my butt, Will?"

"No, a butt implies the presence of fat deposits. There is only bone, skin and denim back here. I hope you had a substantial lunch."

I shake my head and reposition myself into a sitting position on the board while he swims over to retrieve his rental.

"Besides being a show off stand-up paddleboarder, what are you doing these days, Will?"

"I micromanage other people's projects mainly."

"'Send in the micromanagers!'"

He laughs. "Exactly. Though you realize you're quoting an animated film now."

"Dammit. I've been seduced by cheap entertainment." I get my balance and make my first full paddling motion. "'*First try!*'" I exclaim, my voice intentionally deep and raspy. "Sorry. Trevor's favorite." *Well, in December it was his favorite.*

"Alright, Batman. Where are we going?"

"Up to the pier and back?"

He nods.

"So what's your official job title?"

"Civil engineer. Well, 'Civil Engineering Specialist I.'"

"What kinds of projects?"

"Mainly buildings. I evaluate the materials, safety and longevity of using those materials, I look at how realistic the budget is. Right now they're having me draw up my own plan and budget proposal. Kind of a trial."

"What for?"

"Restoring a section in Gaslamp Quarter."

I wobble a bit as I try to stand, but recover. "That sounds like it would be interesting--well not necessarily to me, but you've always been a bit of a history geek."

It's remarkable the ease he has sliding onto his board and returning to a standing position. "It is. I'm working on building up my own business though."

"What kind of business?"

"Architecture--residential, landscape, renovations mainly--Granted my boss would be me and I can *kind of* be an asshole--"

"You know, no job is without its drawbacks. Well, you've been busy. Must be challenging with a little one at home."

He's quiet.

I've tread into unchartered conversational waters and we both seem uneasy about it.

"What about you, Reeves?"

"My days of leisure will soon be behind me."

"'Days of leisure' being chemo."

"Most cancer patients still have to work, or do something productive. I don't have so much as a houseplant to take care of."

"Something tells me you didn't give up school or work without a fight."

Nope. But I still gave it up easier than I should have. "I finished my undergrad, but I gave up my spot in the doctoral program. I'm applying to do the one year masters program. A doctorate seems like a lot to take on."

"Five years?"

"Yeah. Required yearly research, papers, presentations--"

"You know you are completely capable of doing all that blindfolded, right?"

I glance over my shoulder at him.

"Well you are."

I turn back around, exhale.

"Is Nathan on board with you going back to school?"

No. "He knows it's important to me." I can hear my throat tighten as I speak.

"Would you prefer we not talk about Nathan?"

Yes. I shrug. "Talking about spouses seems like an essential conversation I would rather procrastinate having. It's surreal to even be speaking with you and considering there wasn't tremendous closure from us, it's a little much for my brain."

"As long as he's good to you." His board has slid up to be directly parallel to mine.

I drop my chin, look at him over the top of my sunglasses. "He's a good person."

He gives an almost imperceptible nod. "Okay."

I consider reciprocating with a question about his wife, but the image of her makes me unbearably self-conscious. I don't want her to exist, let alone find out she teaches ballet, likes kale, and is just generally--*stop it, Reeves*. I swallow hard and I'm quiet as we paddle along the line of boats. The water is suddenly so still that it perfectly reflects a mirror image of the white boats with blue sails and the cloud-filled sky overhead. I love how the board seems to split the water.

"This setting suits you, Reeves."

I gaze out to the horizon. There's something about this view. I can see how people used to think that Earth was flat. The place where the contrasting shades of blue meet does look like the edge of the world, like you could sail to it and fall into nothingness. I've chased that horizon, longing for peace, an escape from feeling so much.

Something inside begins to hurt. "So have you had many projects for your business?" I ask, clearing my throat.

"A few. Some just to get photos for the portfolio and website. All friends and family guilted into it, but they got everything at cost so win/win."

"What were the projects?"

"I did a few backyards, a daycare, a vet clinic, a rooftop garden, Evan's yard, my yard. My *house*, actually."

"So you really haven't been busy at all."

"Nope," he answers with a smile.

Cadence must be very supportive. How nice for you. "What's Evan's story? I thought he wanted to be a bachelor until at least 40?"

"He's a different guy these days. He fell head over heels, had a whirlwind romance, wedding."

I'm suddenly nostalgic for old Evan. I don't know how to interact with new Evan. "Must be some girl."

"Yeah, she's a sweetheart."

"What's she like?"

"Bubbly without being obnoxious, a lot more down to earth than one might expect, and really health and fitness conscious."

"Good for him."

"He seems pretty happy."

"You'll have to show me pictures sometime--of your work I mean." *Seeing all I've missed in Evan's life would be a punch to the gut.*

"I could show you the *actual* work. It's not finished, but I think you'd like what I've done at my house."

I vaguely remember turning down an invitation to his house last Thursday. My heart tightens. "I'd like to see it, Will--"

"I suspect a 'but'."

"We already established I am without a butt."

He grins. "For the time being."

"A few more lunches like I had, a few thousand squats and I'll have one of those booties the rap stars sing about." Over my shoulder I see that he's amused. "This part can be tricky," I say, gliding up to the dock. I slowly turn and plop my backbone on the dock, managing to not knock myself in the head with the board. "I'd like to do more, but I'm getting a little dizzy."

He copies my motions, but seems to make a smoother transition than what I managed. "Thanks for inviting me today."

"Technically I didn't."

"But you wanted to."

"Stop it."

He peers over his shoulder toward *Shore Thing*. "I'm glad you kept the boat."

My heart inflates at the validation.

"Seems like you should just try to buy that boat at this point rather than renting it."

"Katie didn't tell you?"

"Tell me what?"

"She wasn't sold on the idea either. As it turned out, Frank, the previous owner, needed to liquidate some assets."

He looks back to the boat, then back to me, furrowing his forehead. "You *did* buy it?"

"Yes."

He nods, impressed I think. "What kind of boat is it?"

"88 Catalina 30 foot."

"That means nothing to me."

"She's not a classic by any means, but she's sturdy and I honestly didn't want to part with her. We've been through a lot together."

"Is Nathan a boat guy?"

I exhale, my heart deflating again. "No. He was raised by a family that values climate control."

"He does something with computers?"

Prying. "I.T. Cybersecurity."

"Good field to be in."

"Yep."

"So how did you meet?"

"He worked as a contractor for Scripps."

"Ah." He says shortly, connecting a dot it seems.

Katie didn't tell you that either?

"You're such an outdoor person, I wondered--"

How I wound up with an indoor person who cannot cope with sand? "He's a good guy. You'd like him."

He grunts.

"Or you'd hate him?" I frown, then concede: "Actually the two of you would probably be totally incompatible."

"Describe him in three words."

"Smart. Responsible. Meticulous."

"Describe yourself in three words."

"Rageful Reckless Recluse."

"Reeves, we already established you are incapable of anger."

"Correction--anger toward *you*."

"Try harder."

"On my description or my anger?"

We made eye contact through the side of my sunglasses.

"*Okay*--Bookworm. Introverted. Analytical."

He's narrowing his eyes at me.

"What?"

"So you're focused on one dimension of your personality."

"You gave me three words to work with."

"Still."

"Okay, describe *yourself* in three words."

"Outdoorsy. Laid-back. Friendly."

"Me?"

"Adventurous. Introspective. Resilient."

Not naive anymore? "Adventurous. Introspective. Resilient," I repeat. *AIR?*

"Your turn for me."

"Yours were good. I concur."

"Oh come on."

"Creative. Charming. Chivalrous. Sorry, I'm still stuck on alliteration."

"I sound like a catch," he says in a deep voice, raising one sparse eyebrow.

I shake my head, fold over and laugh away from him.

"What? It looks weird doesn't it?" He rubs at his eyebrows. "Grow stupid hair follicles, *grow*."

"They're still quite expressive. It was just how you said that."

"Oh gosh, don't add 'conceded.' I just said I sound like a catch, not that I am one. You know that better than anyone."

"You had a conceited streak in junior high, but you got over it faster than most." I lean in close to his ear and add: "And you *are* a catch, Will. Or I wouldn't have been so upset that you dumped me. Twice, was it?" I quickly stand up, grab my board and paddle. "I need to use the recently remodeled restroom facilities. Walk with me?"

He stands. "Yeah, I should probably get going." We walk together, a breeze tossing our shirts around a bit. I cling to my hat.

"So was Nathan on board with the boat purchase?"

He thought I was nuts. "Pun intended I assume?"

"Maybe."

"Well, it wasn't his money and he didn't want to give me too hard a time given all that was going on." *Plus he probably sensed it was a trigger point for me to file divorce papers--and that would not have played well with his charade to downplay the reality that our marriage stemmed from a one night stand.*

"I didn't realize you had a trust fund."

"The money my dad would have gotten from his parents. Not a fortune, but a fair amount. Locked away until I'm 25 so I don't do anything impulsive with the money--like buy a boat. I'm allowed to withdraw money for medical and educational expenses prior to then, so that's helpful." Reading his confusion, I continue. "My aunt spotted me the money for the boat and remodel. She said my dad would wholeheartedly approve of the project."

He smiles respectfully, knowing the remark would have been a comfort to me. "Remodel?"

"You recall the burgundy and green color scheme?"

"It's not the Christmas boat anymore?" He looks hurt.

"Not for long."

"When did you start *that* project?"

"Friday."

He nodded slowly, pondering this. "Do you want to show me what you're planning, or are you waiting for a big reveal?"

"Oh it's a mess inside. I demoed the kitchen over the weekend." I look affectionately over the 30 foot boat--the reflection off the windows, the deep blue sails. I lay my paddleboard and paddle on the edge of the dock by the entrance.

"It's a very pretty boat."

"I like her."

We walk in silence until the end of the dock.

"You should look at buying one--" I say, tapping the edge of the rental paddle board. "I know it doesn't have the excitement of surfing, but you seem to be a natural."

"It's more zen than surfing. I might have to look into it." His dimple deepens. "Get some rest." He steps closer, wraps his free arm around me. I have to keep myself from nestling in too much. The awkwardness of the baseball cap helps.

"Have a good night, Will," I say, kissing his cheek, more so out of nervousness, and to conclude the hug. *He's married. You can be friends, no more.* I turn and walk quickly toward the restrooms.

"Get home safe, Reeves."

I twist around at the waist, grinning, and throw my arms out to the sides. "I *am* home." It's a quick glance before I'm facing forward again, slightly dizzied by the motion, but he's smiling at me in that familiar way.

14
the worst moments in life are heralded by small observations

The double door isn't even an inch open when I smell perfume.

There's actually a written rule for staff treating chemo patients, that they not smoke, wear perfumes or scented lotions or anything else of the sort. It's only polite. We're hacking up our stomachs most of the time anyway, it's only polite not to induce it with a urea blend of synthetic fruit or flowers.

"Um, sweetie. You have a visitor today," Jenkins says as I approach.

"I do? Who?"

"It's your mother. I'm sorry, but I had to ask her to scrub off her fragrance in the restroom."

"I hope you had a power sander on hand."

"I'm not sure how long she was planning to stay?"

Just long enough to drain me of my will to live.

Jenkins does a spit take with her coffee.

"No censor. Sorry."

"You can ask her to go at any time and she has to. Or I can put a time limit?"

"You have Security on speed dial, right?"

"Do you think she might need to be escorted out?"

"Oh, *there's* my precious girl. I thought I'd come visit you."

All I can do is nod. "I see that."

"You don't call your mother very much. You know I like to hear from you every day."

There she is, dolled up and then scaled back as to not make her cancer-stricken daughter feel too bad. "I didn't even think to *not* wear perfume," she says, presenting her still damp arms.

She hugs me. Tightly. I might throw up, not just because I'm repulsed or that I can still catch a whiff of the gardenia something or another she was wearing, but because of the sheer force to my abdomen. My stomach is hollow at the moment and green bile would be a real pain to get out of her white silk shirt and white cropped pants. Her gold and pearl necklace digs into my chest. "Mom, they don't like visitors during the treatments because we're in such close proximity to each other."

"A mother can't want to know what her daughter goes through? You spend so much time here. I haven't seen you in weeks."

Someone asked what's it like and she didn't know. "Mom, I usually just sleep through it." *I've had 47 sessions before this. Now you want to have a bring your overbearing mother to chemo day?*

"Well I'll stay for awhile and then I'll come back when you're done and I can take you out to lunch and maybe we can do some shopping. I know you probably don't have a chance to go out much." She glances at my outfit-- drawstring pants, a soft t-shirt, hoodie, and flip flops. The flip flops aren't practical, my feet are cold already, but I had marveled at the tan I had acquired and took the time to paint my toenails.

Jenkins is glaring. "We tend to discourage visitors because we find it's disruptive to the other patients." Translation: You are disruptive and I don't like you.

"My daughter has cancer," she says conclusively like it ends the debate. You can't give me a ticket, my daughter has cancer. Let me barge ahead in line, my daughter has cancer. The customer is always right, but me even more so. Because my daughter has cancer.

"Yes, I know."

"She needs her *mother*."

"Mom, I usually fall asleep right away." Out the corner of my eye I can see Will's vacant chair. We flipped appointment times due to a meeting he had scheduled.

"Then I will stay until you do."

"Well let's get you set up then," Jenkins says, raising an eyebrow at my mother.

I knew I liked her.

As soon as we start to cross to the chairs, Mom briskly starts rubbing at her arms. "Do they have to keep it so cold in here?"

"We don't have access to adjust the temperature," Jenkins says.

"But it's absolutely *freezing*."

"I have my hoodie and they give us blankets," I conclude and Jenkins sets one in my lap. She offers one to my mom, but she turns her nose up.

"How often are they washed?"

Yearly whether they need it or not.

Jenkins snorts as she goes right to attaching the line.

"Wait, already?" Her shrill outburst echoes around the room. Marjorie stirs in her sleep.

"You have to keep your voice down."

She does the motion for a zipper across her lips, but clearly she thinks I'm being dramatic.

"Yes, during my surgery they installed a port in my stomach. That way it's a lot quicker to do treatment."

"So they don't have to stick you? That's easy."

Walt grunts.

"Is it just me or is this other chair really close? If someone else is going to be occupying it, it's really confining. I couldn't sit like this for--how long?" She gets up and takes the liberty of putting a foot and a half between my chair and Will's chair. I suddenly wonder if the other groups space our chairs and Jenkins pulls them together before we come in.

I look up at the wall clock. 8:39. Will will be here by 8:45 since he had an early meeting, though realistically, with his pattern, he'll be here within 60 seconds. He doesn't mind waiting for Jenkins to finish up with me and his definition of on-time is typically at least 5-10 minutes early.

My mother gets up to examine the bags. "All of that goes into her?"

"Well this one is the medicine, these are fluids," Jenkins says, patiently.

Right on schedule. I can't help but smile when I see him swing through the doors in his mirrored aviator sunglasses. I can't see his eyes, but I can tell the exact second he recognizes who's questioning the placement of my bags. Her voice is garbled chatter like adults in the *Peanuts* cartoons in the back of my head. If I was annoyed with her before, I'm downright furious that I can't immediately provide commentary on his sunglasses. At least call him Maverick or ask him if he has "the need for speed."

Then a hand is on my shoulder.

"You're all set, sweetheart." Jenkins. "Come on in, Handsome. Take a seat."

He follows her instruction and has decided to stay anonymous behind his sunglasses.

My mom is left standing, but is too preoccupied with the bags, running her fingertips across them like they're window curtains, that she's failed to give him any acknowledgment. "What does it feel like?"

"The fluids are cold. It's like being really hydrated." I try not to think of the medication as it brings up visuals of singeing flesh.

Jenkins rolls a stool over to her before starting with Will. The height adjustment is broken—this is well-known--and it's stuck at the lowest setting, which is about as high as a child's chair. Still, the woman tries to make do. Those cropped pants look insanely uncomfortable at this point. She tucks herself close to me, sort of gives an annoyed glance toward Will's chair, still too close for her. "Ah. So when Nathan gets back and you're done with treatment, I was thinking we'd do a nice dinner out to celebrate." She fidgets a bit. "He must be very busy. His number is still the same, right?"

He actually listened when I asked him to let her go to voicemail. "Yep, still the same."

"Must be bad reception there."

"Probably a lot of interference. Technology capital of the country and all."

Jenkins side eyes me.

"Such a wonderful man, *Nathan*. You did so well."

Walt clears his throat, shuffles his newspaper.

"I've come by the house a few times. You must not have heard the doorbell?"

"Sound sleeper."

She doesn't believe me, but she readjusts on her stool. "So you've been driving yourself? Is that a good idea?"

"Walking seemed too strenuous."

Walt glances over at me, a very slight smirk.

She waves her hands around. "*I've* offered, but Ms. *Independent* over here won't have it." I don't know who she's talking to. "Just think, a couple more treatments and you'll be cancer-free. I just know it."

Shushing her does nothing.

"Then you can move on with your life, have a big vow renewal since your wedding—well, it wasn't really a wedding was it?"

"It was more than I wanted."

She waves me off. "I just *adore* Nathan."

"I know you do."

"He's wonderful. He's been *so* good to you."

I clear my throat.

"You know once when you two used to have us around for Sunday brunch, he told me I was his favorite mother-in-law. Such a jokester."

"Yes, a real king of comedy. Mom--"

I catch a flicker of a smile on Will's face.

"So you'll have a *big* wedding."

I exhale.

"Then, just think," she says, getting really enthusiastic with her hands. "Then you can have *babies*...Oh I can't wait to shop for maternity clothes with you. With what happened last year, maybe it'll be different this time around and you'll want my support."

I stare blankly at her as she takes in my appearance. Out the corner of my eye I see Will's jaw tensing.

"You know, *I* would have insisted on you having the extra screening for complications that you refused to have. The amnio and whatever else they do?"

The needle was over three inches long. There was a small, but very real risk of causing a miscarriage.

"The pregnancy wasn't healthy so the babies probably weren't either. That's what they say."

They were healthy babies. If not for me, they'd be alive. "The placenta detached." She knows this.

"That's what I'm saying. If you knew it wasn't a healthy pregnancy, you could have dealt with things then."

Walt seems to be adjusting his newspaper a lot.

"You know, I can get you some nice quality wigs," she whispers, like it's the most offensive thing she's said, "to last until your hair grows in a bit. There are some darling short cuts these days—what are they called? Pixel cuts?" She reaches out, but doesn't seem keen on touching my beanie.

"Pixie," I practically spit the ridiculous word, my eyes burning with tears.

I see a jolt of movement coming from Will's direction.

"Yes, that's it. My treat. You'll look just darling with your short hair and pregnant belly."

We have at least two excellent marksmen in this room. Someone shoot her with a tranq gun.

My heart feels restricted, my lungs tightening.

"You'll *have* to have portraits done. I wish I had some photos of you from your last pregnancy. Of course I guess there's no reason, really, for maternity portraits from *that* pregnancy."

Nothing. I feel nothing. I drop my eyes to the floor and stare, praying for it to be over.

"You know, I mourn for my little grandbabies every day."

I hear Will start to make an effort to get out of his chair, but Jenkins is protesting, probably fearing he'll pull the lines in his port. I do the only thing that comes to mind: I snap my eyes shut and slump my head to the side.

There's still a moment of stirring and then quiet.

"Is that normal?" I hear my mother ask.

I raise the volume on my breathing, make it slow and rhythmic, just shy of snoring.

Jenkins is at my side. "What happened?"

"She was just sitting there, we were having a lovely conversation, and she fell asleep. Passed out right in front of me."

Jenkins checks my breathing and pulse. "Yeah it can. Most patients are advised to take something to relax them prior to treatment if they have anxiety, but she's never had a problem. She's had one fainting spell early on, but she seems--fine."

"She *fainted?*"

"It can be a side effect of the chemo drug."

"Does she usually stay asleep the whole time? I don't want to leave and have her wake up right afterward."

I let out a snore.

"No, she's slept through entire sessions before, hasn't she, Will?"

Oh shit. There's silence.

"*Will?*" Jenkins prompts again.

I have to look. I peek through my right eye at *Top Gun* Will. His jaw is solidly tense, but he is still managing to look composed, like he could be sleeping behind his sunglasses. And then he takes off the aviator frames, coolly, in one fluid movement, and cocks his head to the side as he speaks. "Yes, Maggie usually sleeps through sessions."

I close my eye again, my heart thumping wildly against the walls of my chest.

There's an awkward rattling of the broken metal stool.

Then Jenkins jumps in: "I'll let her know to give you a call if she's feeling well enough for lunch. Most patients just like to go home."

There isn't another word from my mother and the next thing I hear is Will's chair groaning as it's slid across the floor. His hand—it's his right because of the positioning on my cheek—rests against my skin, his thumb is stroking my cheekbone.

I open my eyes, gaze over at him, get lost in the warmness of his eyes, the dark outer ring, the smooth chocolate color, seeking out the darker splashes that are only visible at this proximity.

He continues to stroke my cheek and the tears stream silently from my eyes.

I want to climb onto his recliner, fall into his arms, melt into him, let him shield me from the world, but a sinking feeling overtakes me. Reality singes my veins, my heart. His presence seems cruel, his touch torture. *He's not yours,* I tell myself silently. That thought pierces something deep in my chest and makes it difficult to breathe. *He chose someone else. You don't mean as much to him as you think you do.*

I sit up, avoiding the looks of the other patients, move away from his outstretched hand, position myself over the opposite arm rest.

"Reeves," he whispers, his eyes beckoning me closer.

"They would be about eight months old now, if I had reached their due date," I say in a near whisper. I can't let my mind wander too much to seeing my babies, visualizing them crawling, smiling, their sweet faces sound asleep.

Walt turns his chin toward me.

"I got past the first trimester. Almost no morning sickness. I felt them kick. She always had a really strong heartbeat—170s and 180s. He was the calm one. Nathan had just felt them for the first time." I actually remember feeling happy then. Nathan and I had really bonded in prenatal classes, doing our registry (he was utterly confused by breast pumps, much to my reluctant amusement). "I was 23 weeks when they were born."

Will has a pained expression, helplessly distanced--from me, from the experience I'm describing.

"He lived three minutes. She lived five. By the time they brought them to me, they were gone." *The blankets holding them seemed to weigh more than they did.* "Nathan was in a meeting." I swallow hard, the memory of the day filling my mind. Throughout the pregnancy, I had been overwhelmed by the presence of people telling me what to do. When it came down to that moment, it was me alone sitting in that painfully quiet room, holding my lifeless babies, listening to the unfortunate timing of the music box lullaby playing through the overhead speaker announcing a birth. I shake the memory away, wipe the tears roughly from my eyes. "He had forgotten his cell phone in the car. I called his office and the receptionist didn't want to interrupt." I release a prolonged breath. "He got there an hour after they were born. By that point they had already taken them away. He didn't want to see them."

Will's forehead furrows, a flash of anger appearing before he neutralizes his expression.

I shrug. "Maybe it was different since he got there later, but--"

"You hold your babies," he says through gritted teeth, his voice breaking, looking toward me longingly.

His statement eases something in me and I exhale, my breathing more steady. "I had to come back for an ultrasound a few weeks later because I was having pain. That's when they found the tumor. They think it had something to do with the placenta detaching and causing me to go into labor." I frown, my calmness fading. "They were healthy. *If*--they would have been born healthy if not for--" I shake my head fiercely, squeeze my eyes shut.

"It wasn't your fault," Walt says solidly. He waits for me to look at him and raises his eyebrows. "It was *not* your fault."

The room is silent as I let his words reverberate in my brain. "They were beautiful," I manage, choking on my suppressed sobs.

"Did you name them?" Walt asks, exhaling deeply.

I take several deep breaths. "Charlotte and Noah."

"Good names," he murmurs.

Will nods in agreement, but seems especially restricted in his chair.

My session takes longer than Will's. We had planned to get lunch together and I had passively wondered if that plan had changed, if he would simply leave, or make an excuse. As he prepares to leave, I wonder this again. I don't flinch when he leans in to kiss my temple, expecting he might offer a farewell and that would be that. *See you next session, Reeves.* The Will that abandoned me in a foreign country, didn't call or write, and married someone else not three months later would do something like that. The Will I danced with under the globe lights at Katie's wedding would never dream of it. The Will who held my face in his hands, his eyes relaxed and enamored--the thought would never--

I sit tensely as he squeezes my chilled hand, his skin warm and inviting. He leans in well within the perimeter of my personal bubble and tells me he's going to pull his truck around so I won't need to walk as far. He says this in a whisper for only me to hear, like a secret.

I feel a rush of desperate relief. Despite knowing I could blame him for how things turned out, I don't want to. I need him, even if it will inevitably lead to more pain. As I watch him walk away, I allow the thought that I would risk ending a marriage and putting a child through the disorder and pain of a broken home (something I always associated with the likes of my mother), just so I could feel his arms around me again.

I hate myself for it.

"He's obviously in love with you," Walt says once he leaves.

I readjust in my recliner, moving back toward the center of the chair. "I'm married, Walt," I say dismissively, trying to sound casual, though my immediate attentiveness to his remark probably didn't align well. "And as you heard, 'Nathan is *wonderful.*'"

"You love this husband of yours?"

I'm silent. I can't lie to him.

"Does he look at you the way that boy looks at you?"

"How does he look at me, Walt?" I say, suddenly very tired.

He sighs. "Before I got diagnosed this time around, I took care of my youngest grandson a couple days a week. James. His favorite thing to do was go to the playground. We went there every day I had him, but every morning he'd still ask if we were going. We walked the same route to the park and every single time when we reached the baseball field where we could see the playground, he'd stop, just for a second. His eyes would widen and he'd get this look of pure joy and say "*Wow*," like it was the greatest thing he had ever seen. Like he was seeing it for the very first time.

"That's how that young man looks at you. Every. Single. Day."

"Walt."

"Life is short, Kid. No matter what you do, whether you stay with your husband or leave him, whether you run off with the love of your life or stay with the guy who you feel obligated to because you blame yourself for what happened to those little babies, at least one of you is going to get hurt."

"It's complicated."

"No it's not." His eyes look crisp, but wise. "Maggie, I will tell you the same thing I'd tell my own kids--and grandkids, for that matter, since I feel you're my honorary granddaughter. I'm old enough. Put aside what anyone else thinks or might say. Put aside the fears, of hurting anyone, or being hurt. Forget guilt. You'll feel it either way. What do you want for your life?"

I imagine being cancer-free. Sitting at the beach, wind in my hair, feet dug into the warm sand. Someone is holding my hand. I don't need to look up to see who it is, I just stare at his fingers, how the contrast of his tan skin against my naturally fair skin offset each other.

I think to tell him Will is married, but it doesn't seem to align with Walt's read on the situation and while his advice would undoubtedly be useful, I don't feel like I could say the words out loud so instead I nod slightly toward my empty tissue box.

"Now I'm a church-going man. I'm all for making a marriage work, but if that's your intention, let me give you some advice." He leans forward, places a hand on my knee. "I've been told I can't eat red meat. I love a good steak, but I don't eat them. I also don't put a big juicy Porterhouse on the table next to a dry, under seasoned chicken breast. I would call that torture."

He nods to Jenkins as he stands, and she returns to my side.

"No offense to that husband of yours," he adds, putting on his newsboy hat.

***

"Your chariot," Will pronounces as I slowly make my way outside. He opens the passenger door for me.

Once on the road, a strange feeling starts to overtake me, expectant, like I'm about to embark on a journey down an unfamiliar path. "I'm sorry about my mom."

"You're apologizing to me?"

"Yes."

"For her."

"Is that weird?"

"'Weird' isn't the right word."

"What is?"

"Infuriating." He shakes his head. "*Her*, not you."

I suppose I'm used to being on the defensive on the subject of my mother, being questioned whether perhaps I exaggerated some details, there are two sides to every story, etcetera, etcetera. Not with Will. *He remembers. Of course he remembers.*

It was Katie's wedding day, the day after he found me at the pool, the day after our walk to the beach. I was sitting with him at the poolside restaurant having breakfast. I remember I was laughing, my cheeks tensed in a wide, blissful smile when my mother walked up. To say she was displeased to see us together would be like saying a hurricane is just a little storm.

"Are you up to eating?" present day Will asks.

"Actually yes."

He takes a quick turn onto the freeway. "Good, I've got the place. Feeling carnivorous?"

"I don't eat meat."

He glanced across at my withering frame. "You don't say."

"What'd you have in mind?"

"Burgers."

My hollow stomach wants burgers more than anything it has ever wanted before. "I always did enjoy your indulgent side."

"It's all about balance."

I can't help but contrast this attitude to Nathan with his hardline granola mentality. The thought of plant-based burgers makes me crinkle my nose in disgust. "Do they have good fries at this burger place?"

"*So* good. They make them fresh."

"Excellent."

"I don't know. Anything more and you might move up a weight class. We can't have you breaking back into triple digits."

"Cancer is a terribly effective weight loss program."

"I know you're never supposed to ask a lady her weight, but--Reeves, you're so thin."

"I know. Last time I got on the scale at the hospital, I was 108."

"Shit." He waves his hand. "I'm sorry, but *108*? And you're how tall?"

"5'11". Healthy weight range is 136-170-something. I think I've lost more weight since then though."

"Yeah, you could use some over-indulgence daily."

"Even the boobs gave up their fat stores."

"That's tragic."

I grin. "I didn't mean to say that out loud."

The burger place is a red food truck at a beach park. Will expertly orders an enormous amount of food without a glance at the intense chalkboard menu and passes cash through the window before I've taken in the starters.

"I'll pay you back," I offer as he slides a red orange smoothie in my direction.

"That is the healthiest thing they serve," he explains, ignoring my comment.

I plunge in my straw and take a sip. "Wow. That's disgusting."

Both Will and the food truck chef give me a disbelieving look.

"I'm kidding. It's delicious. It's like a sherbert shake. This is healthy?"

"Real fruit," Will says with a smirk.

With three styrofoam containers in hand, Will leads the way toward the sound of crashing waves. He looks much more prepared for an impromptu beach trip than I do, as he's wearing long cargo shorts, a Hanalei surf t-shirt, and Reef sandals. I catch myself watching his calves as he walks. They don't have the muscle definition they once did, but I feel guilt rise up--*Someone else's calves to admire, Reeves*--and focus on his t-shirt instead. He circles around the opposite side of a picnic table and I sit across from him.

"So are you ready for the best burger of your life?"

"Bring on the beef."

"Oh beef is just the starting point."

I unwrap the colossally stacked burger. Of the layers, there are all the classic toppings plus avocado slices.

He signals for me to try it first.

As I chomp into it, cheese sauces oozes out of the center. This complicates my attempt to eat semi-gracefully. I release an involuntary "Oh my God--"

"Right?"

"Bacon?" I'm attempting to cover my stuffed mouth with the burger itself. It requires both hands.

"Bacon."

I'm still devouring my first bite when he pops open the container between us to reveal the most decadent potato preparation I've ever seen. Wedged and fried and coated in the same cheese sauce currently causing my taste buds to do backflips, topped with bacon pieces and a glop of guacamole.

I swallow hard, drop my shoulders. "It's so pretty I could cry."

He grins.

I take another big bite and savor the juices, the crispness of the bun. "Will, I have a question."

He hesitates as he pokes into the fries with a fork. "Okay."

"It's something that's bothered me for a long time." I chomp down on a fry then wipe my face with a napkin. "When you said I wasn't girlfriend material, did it have anything to do with what a messy eater I am?" I'm pretty sure my exposed chin and probably my nose are coated in cheese sauce.

He smiles, relieved I think. "Funny you should mention, but *actually* I find your ability to, despite your best efforts, spill something on yourself at most meals kind of endearing. It won't be quite as cute when you're 96, but--"

We sit in silence, except for appreciative sounds about our food. "Will?" I hesitate, but continue anyway. "This is strictly for survey purposes, but what *did* make you love me?" I had asked Nathan the same question at one point. He told me I was a good person and "pretty" smart.

He thinks a moment, then says: "Nothing."

"Wow." My mouth is full so my words are garbled. "Tough day. I'm glad I have binge worthy food to comfort me during this difficult time."

"Oh stop it, Drama Queen."

Still with food in my mouth: "I'm *so* not a drama queen."

"You're right, you really aren't."

I grab a fistful of napkins and wipe my face, laughing a bit at the sheer volume of the grease and sauce.

"*Nothing* makes you love someone. It's the sum of who they are."

Will can make himself sound like such an old soul. It always catches me off guard.

"If their weirdness is compatible with your weirdness," I say clumsily.

"Weirdness compatibility is a must."

I nod.

"I told you before that it was instant."

"When you were eight?"

"Yes."

"That's friendship though, right? I meant when it changed to *love*."

"I loved you when I was eight. You're asking for when it turned--*romantic*?"

"Yes."

"I knew it was *romantic* love one night when I was standing outside your house."

"That needs context."

"It was my senior year."

"Before or after my near death experience when you stalked me at school? "

"Before."

"Interesting. We hadn't seen each other for a while. What were you doing outside my house?"

He looks away. "I was dropping off a date. She happened to live across the street from you."

"You couldn't date outside my neighborhood?" I ask, shaking my head. "Casey?"

"Yeah, I think that was her name."

"It was Sara, Don Juan."

There's a smile on his face as he continues: "Well, after dropping off Sara from the homecoming dance—"

His homecoming dance took place two weekends prior to my school so this stalking occasion was a week before the near-drowning.

"I was just about to get back in my car when I heard music, which turned out to be coming from your house. Your room."

I can feel my cheeks getting hot. Ray had taken my mother on an out of state business trip, during which they had gotten intoxicated and she had disappeared for 12 hours.

"You were dancing around your room in this wildly--uninhibited way."

"Oh to have that kind of energy," I say with a sigh. "*That* made you fall in love with me?"

"I told you. Nothing *makes* you fall in love. It's just an example of compatible weirdness."

"Your weirdness for not remembering your Homecoming date, Cassie?"

"*Cassie*--that's it. See, in front of most people, it's like you were trying to go through life unseen. We had been best friends and I had seen this side of you before, but we were so young then. It was just different. I missed you and was drawn to you in a way I didn't totally understand."

"So then you waited until an attempt was made on my life to approach me?"

He seems to be working out how to put his thoughts into words. I wonder if his wife thinks his eyes are as gentle as I do, if she sees the boyish charm in his lopsided smile, if she realizes how soulful he is. "I shouldn't have asked about it. It was inappropriate. I just—sometimes I feel—" *like I'm not worthy of being loved at all.* "like you weren't real. Like what I thought you felt wasn't real."

"Is that after spending any length of time with your mother?"

I chuckle appreciatively, having taken another bite.

"That woman could have Tony Robbins ready to jump off a building." He sets down the remainder of his burger.

"Be honest. How bad was the dancing?"

He ignores the question. "Working up the courage to speak to you after so long apart—was a challenge. So yes, the pool incident served as a welcome conversation starter."

I nod. "Who knew it would be my terrible dancing that won you over."

"I saw you that night being unapologetically the girl I loved and that was it for me. I needed to be near you."

"Until you didn't. Until you stopped loving me."

His face has turned serious. "I didn't stop. Reeves, I'd be married to you right now if it hadn't been for--"

I frown. "Been for what?"

For what seems like minutes, he fixes his eyes on the ocean, gritting his teeth, clearly having an inner conflict.

Hadn't been for breaking things off with me via hotel notepad? Hadn't been for knocking up Cadence? "What am I missing?"

He coughs oddly to himself, turning his eyes toward me, but otherwise facing forward as he says: "What made you reunite with your mother?"

"I don't want to talk about my mother."

He nods slowly. "I don't want to talk about her either, but you said you were done with her after the morning of Katie's wedding. What changed?"

"Why does it matter?" I feel sheepish.

"It just does."

I shrug. "Nathan made me call her."

My answer surprises him and he visibly veers off his mental track. "He *made* you? Since when do you take orders?"

I feel small. I shouldn't have phrased it that way, but he's being more forceful than I'm used to. "Will. Stop."

"After everything you went through with her, you let someone who barely knew you order you to call her, have a relationship with her?"

I stand up. "So it's an awful thing for a daughter to have a relationship with her mother?"

He cocks his eyebrow at me.

"OK, that left a bad taste in my mouth." I shrug. "I had no intention to reunite with her. I regret doing so. I had a run in with her once before that and I honestly wanted to chew off my own arm just to get away from her."

He stares at me intently, seemingly to send a telepathic message.

I ball up my trash, tuck it in one of the styrofoam containers. "You have a whole lot of nerve to question my life after you were the one who derailed it." My face must reflect that I didn't fully intend to let that arrow fly and I certainly didn't mean to practically spit the words at him.

"You found a little anger there."

"Don't patronize me."

"No. I'm glad. You should be angry with me."

I shake my head, sit back down so I don't have to look at him directly. "I can't be mad at you."

"Why?"

I glare at him.

"Because I have cancer?"

The word strikes deep in my chest. I hear myself say "no" before I've even thought it.

His face furrows, wanting to understand, but I turn away because saying the words I'm thinking will serve no one, least of all me. He softens his voice. "I'm just curious why you suddenly allowed a woman you despise to run your life."

I shrug, defeated. "If we're being honest, that responsibility has been split between several parties and she has not been the controlling shareholder."

"I know you're being funny, but that just makes me sad. Where was the girl who stands up for herself? Where was the confident, stubborn, willful girl you were--and are?"

I hear my thoughts escaping my mouth reflexively: "I don't know, maybe I left her in Germany like you did." I slide out of the bench and stomp across the empty lot toward the beach access. "Sorry I can't compete with your *perfect* life," I mutter under my breath, thinking he's out of earshot. "Is that enough anger for you?"

"Who says my life is perfect?" He's caught up with me quicker than I expected.

I don't answer, trudge on through the sand.

"Do you want to look me in the face right now and tell me my life is perfect? I can assure you that it isn't. Far from it."

"It was a stupid thing to say. I'm sorry."

"I might consider believing you if you'd stop running away from me."

"I'm not—" I say, whipping around and flinging myself unintentionally into his chest. I take a step back.

"She makes you miserable, Reeves." His arms are around me. The whirling temporarily disorients me so I allow myself to linger in his embrace.

It's just as I realize that this embrace will end and I have no entitlements to others like it that I hear myself say: "Well so do you." I circle away from him to put some distance between us.

"I make you miserable?" His voice is rigid and sad.

Yes--No.

I feel the words burning the back of my throat. "You left me, Will." I close my eyes so in the absence of other input, I continue: "You were going through a whole hell of a lot--I understood that. Even then. What mattered most to me was that you came home. That you were safe. I told God just to bring you home safe, that I would be OK if we weren't together, as long as you were safe."

"But?"

The sound of his voice makes me open my eyes and turn to look at him. "But I was *waiting* for you. It devastated me when you were going through all you were and you pushed me away, but in the back of my mind, I thought you'd come home--to *me*. I just can't accept what happened after that. I know I made that deal with God, but I didn't think He'd actually hold me to it. I wanted you home--*with me*."

He raises his eyebrows, which have grown in considerably fast and thick. "It's not what you think--" He pauses, visibly regroups. "It wasn't how it--how it appeared."

I start wandering away, working up courage. Or rage. Or stirring them together like some chemical experiment.

"Reeves?"

"*It wasn't how it appeared?*" My shouting the words has taken him off guard. I lower my voice, as I've also attracted the attention of the food truck cook clearing up for the day. "Well it appeared that you dumped me on a German hotel notepad. It appeared that you moved on with your life. It *appeared* that while you were getting ready to welcome *your* baby into the world I was burying mine. That's how it 'appeared.'" I'm making a lot of air quotes. I drop my hands to my sides.

He takes a step toward me and I take a step back, glare at him.

"I don't want to talk about the babies again," I say quickly.

He nods. "You do not deserve any of the bad things that have happened to you. You didn't do anything wrong."

I stare at him, disbelieving.

"Reeves--"

"You know," I interject, "I expect some really horrible days with cancer. I even expect that it could kill me."

He cringes.

"My mother? I expect her to be overbearing and manipulative. But *you*? I wasn't prepared for what you did. And now you're speaking to me in code? 'It's not what it appeared? What is that?" I eexhale deeply, exhausted. I suddenly want to sleep for a very long time.

"I don't want to hurt you any more than you have been."

I turn and walk slowly toward him. "I'm tired, Will. I'm trying to put myself back together. I'm trying to survive the past year and a half. That's where I'm at-- simply surviving would be a win." I shrug, move toward the picnic table and take a seat on the dining top facing the seaside horizon. "Up until recently, it was the only thing on my 5-year-plan."

He sits down next to me.

"I feel more like myself since you came around again," I conclude.

"Me too."

"I just can't process you being married with a kid. I can't stand the thoughts that I've had about it. I'm not a cheater. I'm not a homewrecker. I tend to associate those things with my mother."

He stares out at the waves.

"I'm sorry. That's not fair of me. I will make my peace with the way things are. I have to."

"*Well,*" he begins, his optimism building. "Let's just go with that--"

"What? Me being a cheater and homewrecker?"

He's suppressing a smile. "No, I agree. It's not you. But maybe we don't need to take on everything at once. Think of me as just Will. I'm not married and I don't have a kid."

"No, it's not fair to you."

"Reeves, I'm just Will."

I chuckle to myself. "I would prefer if you wouldn't refer yourself as 'just' anything," I say, echoing something he once said to me. I smile tightly, feeling a constriction in my chest.

"You know what I mean."

"Who am I to say that anyway?" I exhale. "*I'm* married." *Technically. A marriage witnessed by a fake Elvis, half-heartedly supported by in-laws who hate me, fully-supported by a woman who has Nathan's ear at every turn, and to a man who I suspect has been having an affair with a hippie vegan computer analyst who I've decided does not shave her armpit hair.*

I sense Will staring at me. He looks both surprised and maybe slightly satisfied.

"I used the inner voice that time didn't I?"

"You did, but I really wish you hadn't."

"God, what does Cadence even think of me?" I pause. I've never considered that. I've never managed to speak her name. "Don't tell me." *She probably doesn't know a thing about you.* I wipe aggressively at my eyes.

If only there was a parallel universe. I see myself sitting closer to him, him wrapping his arm around me, kissing me. *Stop it, Maggie. You have to stop thinking this way. Appreciate this for what it is. Stop fantasizing. Stop pining.*

We sit in silence until the sun starts to set, our hands nearly touching. He nods toward the scene before us. "Have you gotten to use your birthday present?"

"I have."

"What was that song you played all the time? The Elvis one?"

"*Love Me Tender.*" *My dad used to sing it to me.* I smile. At first my voice is quiet, barely audible over the crashing waves. I sing the first couple verses then I hear him singing softly along.

My heart swells in a familiar way. He has serenaded me so many times. It's one of my favorite things he does, even above funny accents. Tears well in my eyes.

It's just as he overlaps our pinky fingers that I push myself off the bench and start walking back to his truck.

"They're ending my treatments early," I say, a little too abruptly, a little too sternly. My voice is tight. "Today was the last one." *Well it will be.* The thought of being done with chemo is strange, like hearing a favorite song in a different language.

"Why?"

"Dr. Hennessy thinks it's best to give me a break from chemo." *She didn't think I should be having this chemo anyway.*

He catches up with me. "How long?"

I shrug. "I don't know. We'll see how it goes. I'll have scans in late September or so. At least it'll give me the chance to go spend some time with Katie."

"You're going up to Monterey?"

Your informant didn't tell you? "Baby number three is on the way." *I missed out with Savannah and I feel like I'm losing my friendship with Katie.*

"It'll be nice to spend some time with all of them," he says.

"I can help with the kids when the baby arrives." I clear my throat.

"When do you leave?"

"Tomorrow." I'm honestly not sure I'll be able to find a flight. *Maybe I'll drive. Maybe I'll take the boat.*

The thought is crossing his mind to ask me why I didn't tell him sooner--I can tell in the furrow of his eyebrows. He decides against it.

He walks ahead of me, seemingly to get my door for me, but stops for an excruciatingly long time, blocking me from reaching the truck. "*Reeves.*" He takes a deep breath, building to something, then as he exhales, opens the passenger door. "I won't see you before I leave for Italy."

I climb in, smile politely. "The whole family is going this time?"

"Yeah, well Evan's only coming out for a week. Leigh is due with their second in October so she can't go."

"Your parents are enjoying retirement there?"

"They are." He closes the door, rests his arm on the open window. "Three months?"

I nod, but I find it difficult to look him in the eye. "Three months."

Seeming to sense the awkwardness building again, he pats the side of the truck and heads over to the driver side. I don't watch him and think instead of him jogging around the front of the truck when we first dated; the enthusiastic, slightly mischievous grin as he bounced inside, his dimple particularly prominent as he peered over at me. I'd rather cement that image in my memory. When I think of riding in this truck with him, I want to see that charming, albeit sometimes immature, Will--not this tense, divided, somber version. *I'd prefer thinking of him when he was mine.*

I look out my open window as he starts the engine, and I take a deep breath. *I have to let you go now.*

15
it's the simple things in life

Two months later...

Katie gathers some spare pillows from the closet and dumps them on the floor. Trevor eagerly flings himself into them, arms spread wide to the sides. "Who wants to watch a movie?"

Savannah, a genetic carbon copy of Katie, with her doe eyes and round nose, crawls over to the pillows and climbs up on the one beside her brother.

"That'll keep them occupied for a while," Katie says, crossing her fingers for me to see. She lays back down in her bed, supporting her belly as she slides in.

"I could have done that, Katie. You need to stay in bed."

She waved me off. "We need to send the Husband our dinner order. He'll be leaving the office soon."

She wiggles close to me and we browse the menu she's chosen together. Then something catches my eye—Savannah has repositioned and is now snuggled against her brother. And just to add to the torture, the adorable little bastard puts his arm around her.

My heart aches sharply.

"What is it?" Katie asks, turning abruptly, probably thinking she'd catch them tearing feathers out of the pillows. They look up at her, alarmed. "Oh you're okay." They turn back to their movie and Katie turns back to me.

"They're so adorable, Katie. Seriously."

"Yeah, it's moments like this that make the difficult moments a little easier. They say."

"The difficult moment that was like 90 seconds ago when they were screaming at each other?"

"Exactly. Just wait. You'll see." She gets enamored in the menu, not realizing what she's said.

I feel hollow.

"That was stupid. I'm sorry. But you will someday. I know it. Adoption? Plus you can borrow my kids anytime."

I keep staring off across the room, not really at the kids, though it probably looks that way. Everything's blurred. "Adoption agencies aren't quick to place children with parents with a history of cancer." I shrug.

"That was another stupid thing to say." She frowns. "*Fuck.*"

My vision refocuses on the pair of kids wide-eyed on the mountain of pillows. On cue, Savannah repeats: "Yuck!"

"Was that her first word?" I ask, not quite sure when babies start saying legitimate words.

To which Trevor corrects: "No, Sav. Mommy said—"

"Okay!" Katie and I say at the same time. Katie takes over. "That's not a nice word Mommy said and I didn't mean to. I'm really sorry. Mommy will try not to say it again, but I don't want either of you to say it either, okay?"

They both stare at her, pondering.

"Can we have macaroni and cheese?" Trevor asks, craning his neck to see around her.

"Absolutely," Katie concludes and scrolls to the kids menu. "There better be mac and cheese on that goddamn menu. I think we're out."

"There is. There's even one with *truffles*--that sounds kid-friendly." I scan the menu prices, past the point of sticker shock. I don't mention it to Katie, but I see that Savannah is whispering "uck" repeatedly to herself.

We place our order without discussion of anything else, each vaguely watching the animated movie.

"There have to be adoption agencies that specialize in cancer survivors," she finally says, her voice rushed. "Ask Tim—surely he would know or be able to find out if it's even legal to reject someone because of having had cancer." She decides it's a form of discrimination and I'm not sure how that thought and her rant about the woman who sued McDonald's for her coffee being too hot were connected, but the two statements fly out of her mouth right on top of each other. She gets to the possibility of surrogacy and as soon as she mulls over the logistics of that—donor egg, or perhaps a complete donor embryo—finds it to be the most viable option, she clings to it, tries to force feed it to me like bad-tasting medicine. "Couples doing IVF end up with too many embryos! Surely letting them grow and be born is better than—what do they do with them?"

"Donate them to science? There's probably a nondescript warehouse with creepy fetus incubators or artificial wombs, like some dystopian sci-fi thriller."

"That's terrible."

"Actually that *is* terrible," I concede. "I have a really twisted mind sometimes."

"What does Nathan think? About adoption? Surrogacy?"

I want to disappear. "You know, I'm doing so much better focusing on not basing my life's value on my ability to have children and my best friend is making it sound like it's a fundamental requirement in life. I adore you, Katie, I adore your children. I'm a little jealous of you for having them and a wonderful, ginger husband, who I have to mention because he's been an amazing caregiver--and he's probably standing terrified outside the door--"

Katie whips her head toward the door, but Tim doesn't appear.

"Or not. I thought I heard something." I soften my tone. "My life will never look like your life. I'm trying to be OK with that."

"I'm sorry," she says regretfully, her eyes filled with tears.

It's a perfect time for said ginger husband to walk in with dinner.

"Oh Christ, was the ASPCA commercial on again?"

She waves her hand at him, sitting up. "I'm so sorry, Maggie."

"Mommy said bad word," Trevor reports, not turning from the screen.

Tim shrugs. "I'm not sure that's worth crying over. Which one? Let's see, she really likes to say--"

"Tim!" we both yell.

"I don't know what to say," Katie says.

"Katie, I don't want you walking on eggshells with me. Chances are you're going to be unintentionally insensitive even if I didn't have cancer so I'd rather you just be yourself."

"Fair enough."

It's a peaceful scene as we situate ourselves and start to eat.

"*Now*, I have kept my mouth shut about--"

Tim very loudly clears his throat.

"Tim, she should know."

He glares at her. "Kate, I'm sure it's frowned upon to duct tape your pregnant wife's mouth shut, but I'm really tempted right now."

I swallow my bite. "Pretty sure it's frowned upon to duct tape anyone's mouth shut, pregnant or otherwise."

He toasts me with his cup.

"You're the legal expert though."

He shakes his head firmly at her.

She sighs, resigns to eating her dinner.

"Now I'm curious," I bait.

Tim groans as Katie sits bolt upright. "Katie, no."

"Tim, my water just broke."

*****

The day started off with Trevor smacking me across my face. I sat straight up in bed, almost knocking him to the floor. "What the—"

"George."

"No, Mags."

"No, George." He points toward the television.

I squint. "As in Curious?"

"Yes. George. Now."

"OK, fine. Where do you keep George?" I ask, pushing myself up off the bed. "You're really impolite in the mornings, by the way."

He gets up excitedly, runs to the living room. I follow behind him and he's already located the movie and is shoving it in the DVD player. The rest of the place is quiet and very dark. "Aunt Maggie, sit. Here."

"Aunt Maggie needs coffee."

"Sit here," he orders, sternly, pointing to the couch cushion next to him. Then he gets this angelic little smile on his face. "Please."

I sit, lean back into the couch.

"Thank you."

"You're welcome, young dictator."

As the advertisement for the latest season on PBS plays out, I glance around for a clock. Based on the sun, it's hard to tell. "It's 4:18, Buddy."

Trevor finds the remote and points insistently to the menu button. I oblige and the movie starts. He climbs up on the couch, squeezing between my hip and the couch cushions, snuggles against my side, but makes sure he can see the flat-screen.

"Hey Trevor? I love you."

He rolls over and rests his chin on my chest. He stays there, studying me. Then he sits up a little, leans in and plants a kiss on my lips.

I bury my nose in his sandy blonde hair when he settles back into my side, hug my arm around him.

When I wake, the sun is much more alert in the sky. Trevor and Savannah are playing quietly on the floor with her My Little Pony dolls.

Savannah's tightly woven blonde curls bounce as she plays, fall into her eyes so she has to continuously sweep them off her face. There's a delicate, very proper quality to how she does this, her fingers bent backwards as she sweeps, her face pulled tight, her full lips pursed. She falls back onto the blanket, watching as Trevor gallops the ponies over her head, rolls over and gallops them across the floor. He tucks them one by one in a line under the coffee table, a makeshift barn, having her kiss each one before he does. When the ponies are all tucked in, he gets to his feet, starts twirling. Round and round…and right into the armchair, which wins the fight unfairly, and Trevor is left dizzily sitting on the carpet. It's after the second time I realize he's doing it to make his sister laugh. She is in hysterics, giggling, her curly hair toppled into her eyes.

Once he jumps to his feet again, he runs into the bedroom and calls for his mom.

"She'll be home later today, Trev. Remember? Your baby sister comes home today."

"No baby!" he suddenly screams, throwing the pony he was holding across the room.

"Oh no, poor pony!" I say dramatically, rushing to retrieve it, lovingly check for injuries.

He runs over, concerned. "Oh no! I sorry, I sorry--" His R's are like W's.

"I think she's OK. Just a little scared I think."

"It OK," he coos, taking the purple pony with balloons on its hindquarters tenderly in his hands. "I sorry."

I glance over to Savannah. "I'm not really sure about this Montessori floor bed thing," I say to no one in particular, crossing the room to scoop her up. "Because *you* could have gotten in a whole lot of trouble while Auntie Mags was snoring on the couch."

Trevor laughs. "You not snore."

"Oh, that's a relief." I make a silly face at Savannah and she tenses up her face and body, breaking into giggles, intensified by any variance of my facial expression.

I always thought of myself having a daughter. I've imagined she would look like I did as a child—tall, mainly legs, dark hair, big brown eyes, enthusiastic smile that wrinkled her nose--but she'd be comfortable with her appearance, not how I was. She'd be kind to animals, but not as sensitive as I've been at times. She'd love science. She'd subtly stand out in the crowd, but given a second look, everyone would see the remarkably unique girl she was. She'd know her mom loved her.

"So today we're going to the aquarium. Why don't I change your diaper and then I'll make a special breakfast?" I sniff in the general vicinity of her diaper. "Dear sweet baby Jesus, child, what have they been feeding you?"

Trevor finds this extremely funny so I perform another sniff test just to confirm.

"Can we have waffles?"

I pretend to ponder his suggestion. "Waffles I can do. I'll make waffles, you change your sister's diaper."

He giggles, pulling up his nose in disgust. "Yeah, that's a no."

***

When you really think about what new baby smell *is*, it's a bit bizarre—I have pushed the thoughts away enough obviously, because I can't get enough of Baby Izzy's fuzzy head, and I find the sheer daintiness of her tiny toes, fingers, facial features fascinating. It worked well for me then that of all the attempts to soothe her in the 5 weeks since she was born, lying on my chest was the only known solution. She seemed drawn to my heartbeat, laying her ear flat on my chest.

I find myself rubbing her back in rhythmic circles, something very calming in the act, soaking in this last morning of having a tiny infant to snuggle.

Katie appears at the doorway to the nursery, her spiral curls pulled on top of her head, face still puffy with water retention, yawning widely. "Do you want me to take over?" she mouths.

I shake my head, breathe in deeply.

She nods, yawning again, pointing in the general direction of the kitchen, silently saying: "I'm going to make some coffee."

Tim is thirty seconds behind her and lingers in the doorway, already dressed in his business suit with silver printed tie, smiling kindly. "Aww, my baby and second wife look so sweet together."

"Thank you, Tim. For everything."

His eyebrows jump and he crosses the nursery, leans down and kisses Isabelle's forehead. Then he does the same to me. "I love you, Maggie O."

16
life is amazingly tenacious

I have to say--I handled Will's deployment a bit better than I expected.

I think it helped that I put myself in a state of denial that Will could conceivably die at any moment. Perhaps I decided after our goodbye at the base that I wouldn't give into that much of a breakdown again. We had breakfast that morning with his family before heading to the base. I was strong in front of them. I kissed him, hugged him tightly. I had ridden in his parents' SUV and held it together for the commute in. The ride back to their house is what did me in. His mother was devastated, blubbering on about safety concerns since he would be stationed at a different base than the first time and his dad tried reassuring her by telling her it was what he signed up for. It went on like this for 84 minutes due to an insane amount of traffic. Evan sat beside me in the backseat. He patted my leg and silently urged me not to listen. After it was clear the bickering was the audio of choice for the long drive home, he put his arm up on the seat behind me, tugged my opposite shoulder so I fell toward him, and kissed the top of my head. I spent the ride reeling through the images of the other soldiers saying goodbye to their families. I wondered how many would never see them again.

When I got in my Jeep at their house, I pulled a street away and sobbed. It all hit me: he could die. He might never come back or he could be seriously injured. He could lose a limb.

He could die.

I lived alone after being unofficial roommates with Evan and Will. Evan had taken a job up in Carmel and Will had helped move me into my new place the week before. The new place happened to be my beloved sailboat.

Having an abundance of life experience in which I was required to self-soothe, I knew giving myself tasks was my best bet to keep myself sanely distracted and a productive member of society. Still. Will was a huge presence in my world. It didn't get easier. It was like having a sinkhole appear in the middle of your commute. You learn to navigate around it.

"What time is it there?" I said as soon as I picked up the phone. I had found anything Caller ID registered as "Out of Area" as being Will.

"Well hello to you, too," he said, chuckling lightly. "Wife-to-be."

I grinned widely. "Hi future husband. What time is it there?"

"4:30."

"AM? You should probably be sleeping."

"What are you doing?"

At that moment I was deciding between varieties of ice cream I shouldn't have been buying. *"Gettin' nekkid."*

He laughed. "Is that right? Shall we video chat?"

I eyed the obese man buying a party tub of sherbert. "No, you called during too responsible of an hour. I'm at the grocery store and my phone lacks all those fancy features the kids are using these days."

"Then you probably shouldn't get naked. Unless that's a thing now."

"No, things are decidedly unchanged. How's the desert?"

"Hot."

"How are you calling me? I thought they were restricting cell phones."

"Sat phone. There are a few floating around. We've had no personal internet at all, just in case you've emailed me naked photos."

"Yes I would have thought you'd have responded to those by now. The red stilettos seemed a bit much, but they really accented the American flag bikini I started off wearing. Truth be told, I kind of felt like I was in a Lenny Kravitz music video."

"*That* I'd like to see."

"How is it there?"

"I don't want to talk about here. I'm picturing you in that flag bikini. You should get one--patriotic colors look amazing on you. I've been meaning to tell you."

"I'll keep that in mind next time I buy clothes."

"Where did this Lenny Kravitz music video photo shoot take place?"

"Well the bikini part was on the beach. No shoes there. I did some rather graceful cartwheels on the shore and then did some dance poses in the waves. I've gotten much more acrobatic in the three months since I saw you."

"Is that right?"

"Oh yes. Oh and then the naked part was in a World War II airplane hanger. Absolutely incredible aircraft--there was a whole line of the Curtiss P-36s? Or is it P-40? I can never keep those straight. The Kittyhawk?"

"P-40."

"I felt a little strange lying naked across the wing, leaning against the prop, but it felt like my patriotic duty, my way to support the military, you know?"

"Oh thank you, Reeves, for your attention to fantasy detail."

I smiled, keeping my eyes downcast in case anyone was judging me.

"How are you?" His voice sounded tired suddenly.

"I miss you."

"Well that's a given. I can be a likable guy, but that's not what I asked."

"Busy. Working. I'm a finalist for a research grant—would be big."

"That's awesome. Congratulations."

"Between that, grocery shopping, nude but artistic rock video photo shoots—and laundry, I keep pretty busy."

"Don't forget the Latin lover."

"*Hugo*," I say with exaggerated longing. "He's on tour. He should be here next weekend. Oh that's right! I'll have to put in some late nights next week so my weekend is free. He's teaching me Spanish, but I'm afraid it's limited to phrases to use--how do you say--*a puerta cerrada.*"

"Do I want to know what that means?"

"Behind closed doors," I whispered into the phone with my best fake accent.

"I know I started it, but this conversation has taken a turn. Let's go back to the photo shoot. Was it chilly?"

I circled around to the deli, eyeing the sushi trays. "Unseasonably so. And no one had a blanket or jacket to offer."

"Thoughtless bastards."

"Are you still working out like a villain in a Batman movie?"

"Joker, the Riddler, & Baine--thanks."

"Wrong franchise. Which one has a really buff, really hot villain?"

"Why am I the villain?"

"Mmm, you're right. Captain America. You're like a dark-haired version of Captain America."

"Maybe for the next photoshoot, go full Wonder Woman."

"Ah, you like the patriotic look then."

"I'm a soldier, Knobby Knees."

"Oh, they photoshopped the knobbiness out of my knees."

"That's not right. I insist on authentic knobbiness."

"So what's going on with you, Cap?"

"Same as usual."

"Have you watched any movies at night? Read any good books?"

"I've gotten through a couple Cussler books."

"What's on the menu for breakfast?"

"Slop with a side of eggs. So slop with slop."

"I think Alton Brown had that last week."

"How's the boat?"

"*Love* the boat."

"I'll have you know the guys here are highly impressed that a girl can be that low maintenance."

"Well it makes up for some of my shortcomings."

"What shortcomings?"

"Living on a boat is not impressive like, say, being on the other side of the world fighting terrorists."

He grunted.

"That's what I get? A grunt? Tell me something."

"I love watching you playing guitar."

I smiled.

"You in those librarian glasses, a bun, and a loose t-shirt reading on the window seat."

"I love the boat, but I do miss that window seat."

"You making faces at yourself in the mirror while you get ready in the morning.

"When you'd suddenly snort in your sleep and wake yourself up."

I had stopped in the bulk food section, as it was the least occupied. "Oh gosh, that's mortifying. You witnessed me doing that?"

"Nonsense. And yes I've witnessed it. It's adorable. I do fear your snoring in your later years though."

"By then the medical community should have a cure--like LASIK for vision."

"See? Then it's even more precious. I wish I could snuggle in with you tonight and be awoken by your surprisingly boisterous snort."

"Speaking of bothersome snoring, I picked up some nasal strips and I think Mr. and Mrs. Smallenlarge are getting a divorce."

"Do I know these people?"

"The couple on the boxes. They started off doing the photos together, sleeping blissfully with their his and her sized nasal strips. Then I saw an ad in some magazine where she is really annoyed with him, glaring at him while he was sleeping. The box I picked up today? He's all by himself. Oddly enough, for both sizes. He still seems to be sleeping soundly, but still."

There's a silence on the other end of the line.

"I miss you, Reeves." There was a pause when I thought I could hear him smile. He sighed deeply. "Well I'm sure you'd like to leave the grocery store at some point and Parker has dibs on the phone next."

"Hi, Magnolia," I heard Parker say, his southern accent as thick as ever.

"Just wanted to hear your voice."

I froze in the middle of the aisle, suddenly feeling very lonely and regretful I'd spent so much of the conversation talking about models on a nasal strip box.

"I love you."

"I love you more," I said sadly.

"Not possible."

***

"Do you know how long it's been since your caller ID showed up on my phone?"

My heart is thumping heavily in my chest at the sound of his voice on the other end of my phone, my pulse racing. "I'm very curious about my current ringtone setting. It's the *Imperial March*, isn't it? Maybe the wicked witch theme from *Wizard of Oz*?"

"Would you be amused if I said the screaming goat?"

I laugh. "Maybe. *Am* I the screaming goat?"

"No."

"So I don't want to call out of the blue to ask you for something, but there's a selfish reason for the call."

"Do tell." His voice is playful, intrigued.

"Are you in the middle of something right now?"

"I am having an impromptu wet t-shirt contest—" There are a number of voices in the background. There's a distinctly female laugh, then a child's squeal.

"Is that right?"

"Well, muddy t-shirt at least and I'm the only contestant. A pipe burst in my backyard. I'm pretty sure I've got this competition in the bag though."

"I would assume so. Well done you." I'm momentarily distracted by the mental image. "I can let you get back to that. You're probably busy--"

"Reeves?"

I sigh. "I don't feel right, my vision is spotty, I'm dizzy..."

"You're in town? Where are you?"

"Airport." I exhale deeply, find an empty seat in the nearest gate. "I can grab a cab, or whatever that service the kids are using these days. There haven't been recent murders."

"I'm coming."

"I'm probably just dehydrated."

"Are you OK until I get there? There shouldn't be traffic." His voice is muffled and then I hear water turn on. He must be in his bathroom.

"I just sat down. I still have to pass through that hellishly long Security corridor, but it's not too far. Although, I could just live here at Gate--OK, I can't read a gigantic number. I'm sorry. I was planning on coming over anyway, but--"

I listen to the splatter of water, the brisk scrubbing I imagine is happening on the other end of the line. "Hold on—"

The water stops and I can tell by the echo of my voice that I'm on speaker. "Okay, I just have to throw on some clothes and I'll be on my way."

I don't know what his bathroom looks like so I'm visualizing a scene from memory--standing in the hotel shower in London and turning around to find him walking toward me, shedding his clothes, stepping under the water with me. I remember placing a hand on each of his thick arms, a size too small for the muscles he'd built while he had been away, taking in the sight of his smooth chest, his strong jaw, his familiar, kind eyes.

"Reeves? Are you still there?" There are some rushed movements and then he's switched back from speaker mode.

I shake myself back into awareness, eyeing travelers sweeping by. "Yeah."

"Thought I lost you."

"No, my brain was caught up in something for a moment." My phone buzzes. "I'm below 10% battery."

"OK, save your battery, just in case. I'll be there as quickly as I can."

I sit back and watch the people passing by. It's a perfect illustration for how I feel--others moving hundreds of miles per hour through life while I sit dazed and confused.

I remember the staggering steps of old castles in Europe we toured when I visited Will in London, how we raced each other to the tops, occasionally doing a Rocky Balboa celebration once we reached it. Now I stare down the hundred yard corridor and it looks far too daunting a task.

Fifteen minutes later and I'm sitting on a bench outside watching the cars driving by--too quickly for the liking of my vision. A businessman has just lit his second cigarette just feet away. The air is thick with nicotine, exhaust fumes, and a cloud of cold recirculated air, carried out the automatic doors.

As the old black pickup pulls up, a familiar ease flows through me.

It happens suddenly. I stand: a mistake. I reach for my suitcase handle: utter stupidity. Fortunately Will is quick getting out of the truck and as I stumble forward off the curb, he catches me.

His hands are bracing my shoulders, firmly but gently.

"I don't want to alarm you--" I begin.

"What's happening?" he asks, his voice directly before me.

"I can't see."

74 minutes in the Emergency Room waiting area and my vision has returned, with the exception of some continued flashes. Because I didn't come in with a bullet wound, I wasn't prioritized. Since I described the state of my vision as "spotty," triage speculates (after laying eyes on me for 3 entire seconds) I had probably stood up too fast. They also suggest I get something to eat. When Will questions if that's advised if they'll be taking lab work, they agree. It's the type of encounter with medical personnel that makes people opt for diagnosing and treating themselves based on Google search rather than seeking medical treatment.

While I could see, when they told us to take a seat, my dizziness had become so severe that I could hardly negotiate the waiting room even with Will to guide me.

Lying down made things far worse. I attempted to stay sitting upright on my side of the double chair bench, struck suddenly by the surreality of being in an emergency room level situation and relying on Will, who a few months earlier, I had resolved I would never see again. I finally settle into his chest. It's more comforting than I had anticipated and I find myself burrowing gently, pleased when this results in him wrapping his arms around me.

"You mentioned you were going to come to my house?" He asks.

"I was."

"I didn't know you had my address."

"Katie."

"Ah."

"You had company?"

"Evan's family. They were just stopping in. They were visiting his in-laws in La Jolla with the new baby."

"I didn't think the baby was due yet?"

"She arrived a little early, but she's doing well. *Ramona.*"

"As in Quimby?"

"Pardon?"

"You probably didn't read the Ramona book series?"

"No."

"Oh. Great character. She's doing well?"

"Yeah, she's a little thing--only a week and a half old--but good appetite."

"Good. Cadence is doing well, too?"

His body tenses beneath me. "Yes."

"She seems really nice."

"You met?"

"We bumped into each other at the jellyfish exhibit at the Monterey Aquarium. I don't think she knew who I was. I didn't realize who she was until I heard her on the phone with Evan." I swallow hard. "Cadence is Evan's wife."

"Yes." His breathing is heavier.

"You called her 'Leigh.'"

"She goes by her middle name outside of work."

I nod. "You're 'not married' and you 'don't have a kid.'" *He says nothing without a reason,* I remind myself.

"Correct."

"You're 'just Will.'"

"Yes." He clears his throat. I've shifted to be tucked beneath his chin and I indulgently nestle into his chest, place a hand on his forearm.

"You asked me why I reunited with my mother," I say quietly, taking a deep breath before continuing. "Nathan had me call her once we got together, but I ran into her before that."

He's following along easily, his body starting to relax.

"She told me you sent a wedding announcement to her house." I pause to listen to his heart beat through the walls of his chest, feel his breath on my ear. "It never made sense. It seemed--cruel. And despite you breaking up with me via hotel notepad and years before that by telling me I wasn't 'girlfriend material,' you're not cruel." I smirk, turning up my chin so he knows I'm trying to somehow make light of the circumstances.

"Now I thought I resolved the whole 'girlfriend material' remark," he says, his voice teasing, peering down at me. There's a moment that he instinctively strokes my shoulder but then seems to think better of it.

"Uh. Yeah. Over a year after the remark that turned my 17 year old world upside down. Thanks for the follow-up."

"You're impossible, Reeves. Do you know that?" He whispers, breathing into my beanie.

"When did you find out?"

"That you're impossible? I think I've always known on some level."

I exhale fully.

"I got back Stateside in February, but I had gone into a trauma rehab program. No phones, no computers. They reluctantly approved me to go to Evan's wedding, provided I didn't drink. I went back right after the reception." I could see the photo of him smiling widely with Cadence--successfully pulling off a lighthearted, life of the party smile, like only he could. "It was nice—horses, open air. The Rehab center, not the wedding. I was paired with a retired police horse named Indy."

"Good name."

"I was there for a few months then came home in June. At that point, I sort of relapsed."

"When you found out I was pregnant."

"I should have called you when I left Ramstein. When they let us invite family to visit. I just--I wanted to apologize and make things right, but I wanted to be sure my mind was ready. Not with you, but with--"

I nod.

"I managed to stay out of trouble until July then I had to call Tim for something. It all came out then."

"What did you call him about?"

"A legal issue. It doesn't matter. It had to do with the anger thing."

I frown up at him.

"Bar fight."

"William Harrison."

His face carries no boyish regret, like I would expect. Instead, he looks serious. This makes it difficult to even attempt to lecture him.

"Did you start the fight?"

"Yes."

In Ramstein, I saw bits of anger bubbling to the surface, but even with the influence of several hard shots of liquor, he seemed to still be conscientious of what he was doing, saying. It's why he looked regretful after being a bit of an ass. It's difficult for me to believe he would pick a bar fight randomly. "Did you win it?" I say this somewhat gently, in case he didn't.

"Yes."

I frown. "I can't see you picking a bar fight, Will. Did the guy deserve it or was it something dumb?"

He lets out a breath. "He deserved it," he says quietly, kissing the top of my head, committing to stroking my arm now.

Strange how the same man capable of getting into a bar fight can make me feel so comforted and calm. "So Tim helped you?"

"He did."

"Wait, wait, wait--it was *Tim*—" I try sitting up and am instantly dizzy. "Zoinks Scoobs, that's a lot of spots in my vision."

He smiles, holding me steady. "Scooby Doo? Really?"

"Trevor," I reply. I keep my eyes closed, waiting for the dizziness to subside. "So you mean to tell me that Tim and Katie--they've known since—why wouldn't they tell me?"

"I asked them not to tell you. Katie didn't know for awhile after that."

I force my eyes open, focus on his face, blinking a few times. "Okay. Why wouldn't *you* tell me?" I keep myself upright to support my wanting to look firm.

"You won't like my answer."

"Obviously."

"Well there were a few things--"

"Excuses."

"Fine. Excuses. First, it wasn't right for me to impose on your life when you were trying to make things work with Nathan."

"OK, that's fair."

"I also knew you reunited with your mom and if I had come around, even to support you--"

I squint, both from thinking of the scenario and because of the fluorescent lighting.

He offers his arms again and I settle back into his chest.

"It would have all come out and I thought it would destroy your relationship with her."

"Oh it certainly would have--A tragedy."

"I didn't know."

I glare up at him.

"Alright I knew odds were she hadn't changed, but I hoped, for your sake it was better. I thought maybe with me out of the picture, things were better with her."

"But you found out about the babies."

"Tim told me when the babies were born."

I'm grateful he didn't hesitate in his words. Most people trip over themselves trying to describe what happened without humanizing them, unable to accept that they were, in fact, born alive and died.

"I came to see you."

There's a long silence as I take in this information. "I was escaping from reality quite a bit then, but I would have remembered that."

"You were just being discharged. I thought they'd keep you longer--I was planning to come up to your room."

"Yeah they didn't waste any time. One night, out the door." I consider what he's said. "When I was discharged--"

"I was walking in from the parking lot. You were waiting out front in a wheelchair." That look again. *His words always have purpose.*

"You were there." I frown.

"What?"

"Never mind." I shake my head, my eyes filling a bit with tears. I hope he can't feel them through his shirt. *I felt so alone. More than ever in my life and you were there. You let me be alone.* I try to imagine what it would have been like to have Will appear before me.

"I wanted to go to you. I should have gone to you."

"Nathan took forever getting the car." *Complimentary valet wasn't an option, pressure to tip and all.*

"I walked past him. I didn't realize it at the time."

"Did he look upset?" I always did wonder how he dealt with the loss.

"I thought he was hyperventilating. I helped him to a bench, had him put his head between his knees."

"Of course you did."

"He was having a difficult time."

"Robots do tend to struggle with the sensation of human emotions."

"Is that right?" He peers down at me.

I wince. "That was--the inner voice. She has unresolved hostility."

"Anger's bubbling up a little easier for you these days?"

"I only struggle being angry with you," I grumble.

"He didn't act upset in front of you?"

"He went on like they were nothing. 'They're not even real humans at that point' he said. It seemed to make it easier for him to think of them as being less than human." I take a breath. "I grew them inside me. I felt them kick. I held them. He didn't even look at them." Tears are streaming from my eyes as my voice constricts.

"Maybe he thought he was being strong for you," he offers, "But that was a shit for brains thing to say."

I laugh awkwardly through the tears. *If only you knew.*

I remember that day in July when I finally worked up the courage to go into their bedroom. I expected a vibrant aqua and lime color scheme, black and white beach photography prints. I had planned to have my dad's longboard mounted on the wall, but hadn't gotten around to finding someone handy enough to accomplish the task. I had prepared myself for what I would feel seeing that room, but when I opened the door, I found Nathan had cleared it out, repainted it to match the rest of the house and repurposed it as office storage. 'It's still legal for women to get abortions at that point' was what he thrust at me as justification for the presence of old computer parts housed in the closet that used to hold their newborn clothes. Almost a year was past the statute of limitations to mourn for 'fetuses.'

"I'm sorry if that's disrespectful--he's still your--"

I shake my head. *Tell him.*

"What?"

The thoughts reeling in my head refuse to come out so instead I hear myself say: "You're right. It was an awful thing to say."

"It's not what you needed."

"I needed *you.*" The words come out before I know I've thought them. They sound angry and desperate. He tightens his arms around me and I dig myself into his chest, squeeze his arm a little too tightly.

"I should have gone to you," he whispers.

I can't speak so I nod. Repeatedly.

His heartbeat seems particularly heavy, echoing against the walls of his chest. "I'm sorry."

"*You wanted to be with me.*"

"Yes."

"You loved me."

He pauses long enough for me to wonder if he heard me. "That implies I stopped at some point."

I feel him breathing, hear more clearly the weight of his voice, even though he's almost whispering.

"Whatever feelings you think I have? Multiple it by a thousand. Without you it was like someone turned off the sun."

It's a hell of a time for them to decide to finally call my name.

"I have excellent timing for sweeping declarations," he says, unsure of himself as he helps me to my feet. He takes hold of my hand and guides me back toward triage. He sweeps his arm around my back to further steady me.

"Are you OK to walk? We have--" The nurse begins.

I sense him waving her off. *In my head again, Mercer? As usual?*

She takes me straight to the blood pressure cuff. It's extremely low. I know because she takes it three times. She then has me backtrack to the scale. 117. She resets the scale, has me step on again. 117. She jots it down. "How tall are you?"

"5'11."

"You're doing better with the new diet," Will says, steadying me as I step down.

"That's like supermodel weight," I observe, amused.

The nurse glares at me enroute to the room. "You're dieting?"

I can see her already trying to remember the extension for Social Work. "No. I'm reverse dieting. I was at 108 from the chemo."

Thankfully this seems to appease her. "I was going to say--"

The moment they get me into a scratchy, faded hospital gown (one of the ties is also broken), a phlebotomist is there to draw my blood. One bizarre and inconclusive eye exam later and they've abandoned us in the semi-private triage room to await my blood results. Will waits with me, sitting uncomfortably stiffin the chair next to the hospital bed. I have felt his tension rise with each additional test being performed.

I feel a momentary surge of anxiety thinking that at any moment Nathan or my mother could come charging in to take control of the situation and try to dismiss Will, but the concern passes. Neither knows I'm here. Neither knows a lot about me these days. Also, at this point, I'd be more than willing and able to tell either to go to Hell in one colorful way or another.

I sigh, look around at my fuzzy surroundings. "We spend too much time in hospitals." I close my eyes and lay back on the paper covered pillow.

"I agree."

"117 pounds of bone, water, skin and atrophied muscles. So sad."

"We could start up with some workouts again. Strength training would probably be best for you as long as you up your calories. Carb load."

I open one eye. His face is filled with concern. "'Life is amazingly tenacious', Will."

"Thank God for that," he says, his forehead furrowed.

An uneasy cough catches my attention and the moment dissipates into the sterilized air. An athletic looking woman with light brown hair tied up casually with a clip, wearing dark blue scrubs under a lab coat appears before us. She introduces herself as Julie, a physical therapist. I assume she's in the wrong room, but she's so kind and caring, I don't interrupt to tell her. Her voice is high and youthful and she raises her voice at the end of most of her sentences so she sounds more inquisitive than she probably intends. Eventually I catch on to the fact that she's in the right place, but apparently they called for a consult from her prior to the doctor giving me my results. She reads my confusion and ultimately gives me my results herself.

I'm anemic. Severely. They plan to prescribe something, but they also have provided dietary instructions for me. I have a minimum weight gain calorie count of 2800 calories to be tapered as I approach normal weight. They are also concerned that my chemotherapy treatments affected my equilibrium. We've relaxed enough, thanks to Julie's calming bedside manner, that Will jokes about my balance and coordination always being a little off. As she makes a few notes, she remarks about what a cute couple we are. We exchange a quick look, but neither corrects her.

She doesn't think it's the best idea to try the techniques for this today, but she will have an outpatient appointment set up for me in two days. She offers what I assume is her lunch hour. Now it's a matter of waiting for discharge paperwork.

"How are you feeling?" he asks, leaning forward from his seat on a rolling stool. I try to picture what he sees. My cheekbones, which have always been pronounced now add to the hollow look of my face and the dark circles under my eyes. The freckles on my nose and arms have faded considerably. My once small shoulders are now frail, my chest deflated and my ribs poking against the skin.

"Better."

He seems to become hyper-aware that he was staring and sits up a little straighter, makes a point of looking me in the eye.

"I hate my body being this weak."

He smiles, genuinely, his eyes with a slight twinkle to them, though that might be a flash in my vision. "We'll bulk you up, Reeves."

I smirk at the familiarity of the name, how only he refers to me by last name. I scratch at my beanie, which starts a chain reaction. "Gosh, could they make these things with a material that doesn't itch?"

His eyes widen. "You have hair."

My hand flies up to my exposed hairline. "Oh it's all sorts of crazy," I explain. "It's decided to be curly now."

When I lost my hair, it seemed socially expected to cover the offensive sight of my head. Nathan muscled his way through sightings without the hat, though I got the feeling it was like how people can hold their breath if there's a foul smell, but they'd prefer if they didn't have to.

I think to pull the hat back down into proper positioning, but stop short.

Will watches my fingers gripping the hem of the acrylic fabric without any perceptible change in his expression. He just waits silently. I pull off the hat, feel the chilly hospital air cling to the warmth it's left on my scalp. He reaches his hand out, first resting his fingers on my cheek, then slides them up the side of my face to where my hair is probably poking out in all directions, complete with fuzzy patches and multiple cowlicks. His eyes are focused, but I can see the strain in them and in the crease on his forehead. Then he smiles. "You're beautiful, Reeves."

I want to make a joke, but the words don't come. *Not the time, Reeves. Not the time.*

"Well Maggie, you're a free woman. I have your discharge papers," Nurse Shauna, a heavy set woman with curly dark hair and a pretty, cheerful face announces, pulling the privacy curtain back. It's evident that she startled us--Will drops his hand from my cheek and I sit a little straighter. She glances at my hair. "You know, I've wondered about doing super short hair, but I haven't been brave enough. How do you like it?"

"Getting used to it," I say, hesitantly, watching Will take my hand in his.

She moves on with explaining what my instructions are. I hardly hear a word, as I'm focused on the feel of Will's hand holding mine. She kindly lectures Will that he is to take good care of me.

"Let's get you changed out of that lovely smock. I'll let Hubby help you if you need it. You can use the shared restroom in there. Just lock the other door or you could get a visitor from the other room."

I'm wobbly as I stand and they both are quick to assist.

"Try taking deep breaths. That's a big help when dealing with dizziness." She strokes my back as I follow her instruction and start walking with less issue. "Is that a little better?"

"Yep. I think I've got it." I move toward the restroom. "'Hubby' can wait out here."

"I'll get you a bottle of water for the road," she offers. "You'll want to stay hydrated."

"Are you sure you don't need help in there?" Will asks once she's out of the room. He smirks and I see a flash of him at seventeen, flirtatious, immature and exceedingly confident. Even his bushy, arched eyebrows have made a triumphant return. It's really something--one smile from him and I forget all the things that make me self-conscious. It wasn't what made me fall for him, but it has always been highly addictive.

He hasn't yet broken his gaze and now I see the subtle dent of a dimple intensify on his left cheek.

"Still a flirt," I mumble, trying to suppress a smile unsuccessfully. I nearly bump into the door jam. "Pulled out the dimple--*so* not fair."

I hear him quietly laugh as I close the door.

I tug on my soft heather grey v-neck tee, meant to be form fitting, but is far from it these days, and distressed jeans, slip on my flip flops.

Shauna is suddenly close to the door: "Are you doing okay in there?"

"I'm fine, thanks." I automatically slide my hat on, then stop and look at myself in the harsh bathroom lighting. After making a number of very unattractive faces at myself, I pull the slouchy hat off, grimace, try to tame the cowlicks, then give up entirely. I leave the bathroom without looking at my reflection again.

"How did the two of you meet?" Shauna asks him as I make my entrance. Will twists the cap from the water bottle she's given him and steps forward to hand it to me, his expression reassuring.

"Oh we met in the waiting room," he says casually. "It was a really long wait. But it was an instant connection."

She believes him for a split second, but he must have purposely given himself away. "He's funny isn't he?"

"Hilarious," I say, sipping some water.

"We met in elementary school."

"Really? Elementary school?" This seems to have taken her by surprise more than we just met an hour ago.

"Yep. I met her when I was eight. Life was never the same again."

She clasps at her chest. "That's amazing."

Hearing it stated like that puts our relationship into perspective in terms of percentage of my life. Puts him into perspective.

"Well let's get you on your way home," she says.

He extends his arm, reading the expression on my face. I take his hand.

As we wait for his truck at the valet station, I can imagine him turning and kissing me. He doesn't. Instead he opens the passenger door for me and helps me inside. He walks quickly around the front of the truck, passing a tip almost imperceptibly to the valet, his face focused as he climbs behind the wheel.

Once he's pulled onto the main road, he takes my hand and rests our hands on the small section of seat between us. Still he says nothing. He takes a turn onto a side street that I'm not familiar with and I sense is not enroute to the freeway. He pulls along the curb in front of a park, stops the truck and hops out. My eyes follow him as he retraces his steps to my door, opens it, and offers his hand.

I scan the neighborhood--it has the appearance of being potentially historic with a spacious park on the corner, sopping wet from a rainstorm that hit while we were in the hospital.

Once out on the curb, he places his hands on either side of my face and kisses me, softly at first, then more intensely as to match my response. Without conscious intent to do so, I find myself with my back against the cab of his truck, arms wrapped around his neck. I'm breathless as our lips part.

He studies my face, my eyes, and his smile broadens. "I'll wait for you."

I must look confused. *Nathan. He thinks I'm still with Nathan.*

He strokes my face with the tips of his fingers. "I probably shouldn't have done that yet. I just couldn't *not* kiss you."

I find I've leaned forward anticipating more, but I try to inconspicuously lower my heels. I feel a primal urge to lunge forward.

"I'm not all that sorry, if I'm being honest," he whispers.

My breathing is shallow. "Will?" I picture the boat, the newly finished cabin, the work completed in my absence. I picture him laying me down on the cozy bed, climbing under the sloped ceiling, his dark eyes following me as I slide up to the pillows, the boat swaying a bit more than usual. "Please come home with me?"

His smile is audible.

***

Will found himself stirred awake by the rocking of the boat. An engine murmured nearby, likely the reason for the sudden current. He checked his watch. 4am. Probably a fishing trip, he decided.

The full moon illuminated Maggie's face. As free and untamed as she had been hours earlier, she still seemed to have found a tense sleep, her forehead furrowed, her shoulder pulled to her ear. Goosebumps rose on the pale skin of her back. He pulled the blankets high up to her neck.

He hoped it was just the cold that had given her the appearance of being uneasy.

Just as he began to dread trekking to the marina restrooms, he remembered that in the remodel, she had mentioned putting in a legitimate bathroom. He slid down the length of the bed, being careful not to bump his head and started across to the door that used to serve as a closet. He navigated the cabin with just the moonlight, not wanting to wake her by turning on overhead lights.

When he emerged, his vision having adjusted to the lighting, he took in the familiar, but remodeled setting. What had once been dark wood paneled, was painted white. Most of the wood surfaces that had been warped, were either sanded and treated or replaced. The floor was smooth on his feet. He peered around the small cabin, about the size of an airstream trailer, and pictured the maroon fabrics, the one wall covered with a smoked mirror. Before her impromptu flight to Germany, she had sent him a photo of her small Christmas tree by that mirror. She hadn't realized she had photobombed her own picture. She had been wearing a pair of plaid boxer shorts and his Cubs shirt, her hair pulled into a wild knot on top of her head. He had enjoyed this glimpse of her in the life she lived while he was away and that it still included him.

In place of the mirrored wall was a collection of framed sketches. Her sketches. He recognized the one of her childhood dog she had been working on the day they met. She had always been talented at drawing, but the later sketches were absolutely remarkable. He saw her dad from the perspective of the passenger seat as he smiled over an old leather wrapped steering wheel. His hair was medium length and wavy, his face crinkled in a smile. He saw her grandpa, a half wreath of hair on his otherwise bald head, reading in a high back armchair. He saw her grandma with one long side braid, picking flowers in a garden, wearing a distant Mona Lisa smile. There was Katie grinning down at her pregnant belly, her curly blonde hair untamed and falling in her face. Dylan was the next sketch, an angelic, but mischievous grin on his face. His hair fell back from his head as though he was spinning. The next he gathered was Savannah. It was a portrait of a sweet little girl with big blue eyes and big loopy blonde curls playing with horse dolls.

Then he came to a face he recognized as his own. It was the night at the restaurant in Monterey. The detail of the drawing was incredible, like she had looked at his expression under a magnifying glass. *"You don't have any idea how much I love you? How happy you make me?"*

"Most of the time? No. But I look at this photo and I see it. I feel it."

He remembered jokingly suggesting making a billboard size of the photo to display, so she'd see it and never forget. What she had done seemed to exceed that. To draw with such granular detail, he knew she had scrutinized everything about it.

Will moved back toward the bed nook as Maggie stirred awake. Uncertainty had just registered on her face as she took in the empty sheets beside her.

"Reeves," he whispered.

She rested her head back on the pillow, smiling lightly as he crawled in beside her. "I thought maybe--" She had thought of Ramstein. He knew that. He hated that she had thought of Ramstein.

He shook his head and beckoned her into his arms. "I'm with you."

17
the rainbow connection

I do not anticipate a good report.

I don't consider myself a terribly superstitious person, but I don't interpret my mother showing up in the waiting room as a particularly good omen. Can't say the woman's stupid. It's kind of like how toddlers will misbehave in public, where most parents scale back their punishments for fear of judgment. She knows I can't readily unleash on her--too many people. There's also a baby sleeping in a car seat by the fish tank. I don't want to stir him from sleep. There's something about a baby's cry that pierces deep into my soul. I wish I could say it's simply because I don't want a baby to feel distraught or alone, but it's more selfish than that. A part of me dies every time I hear a baby cry. It reminds me that my babies never got the chance to even do that.

Anyway.

She walked straight up to me in a white cashmere sweater, pearls, periwinkle pencil skirt and decided the best approach would be to tell me she knew I didn't have anyone to come with me since Nathan's time in Silicon Valley was extended through the end of the year. Evidently there had been a conversation that had taken place with Nathan for her to have this information. That I anticipated. What I failed to anticipate was that evidently Nathan still had access to my patient portal, and therefore, my itinerary and shared *that* information. That was not planned, and that was, I presumed, a result of her obsessively calling him.

She didn't mention Will as she forced me into a hug, or as she took her seat. Not one word. It seemed, by her eerily calm demeanor, that she hadn't seen him drop me off up front before going to park the truck. Hospital construction had pushed parking to the overflow lot across the street.

She had interpreted my silence as passive acceptance of her presence and had taken the liberty of getting herself some reading material. She sat with her back to the window and began flipping through a magazine. In reality, my silence was due to a severe bout of nausea that had overtaken my thoughts. The hug and her perfume did not help me feel remotely better. I had sat back down, wobbly and uncertain I would retain consciousness.

Will spotted me sitting by the window as he was walking up to the building entrance, returning from parking his truck. His eyes lit up a little in that moment. His lips curled up on both sides as if by automation. *I see it, Walt.*

I regretfully put up my hand, signaling him to stay back. I try to look reassuring and apologetic.

I can sense him assessing the situation, assessing me, his face suddenly serious. He looks at the back of my mother's head, then nods supportively. He turns away, his body rigid as he walks, his hands clenched. He stands with his cheek to me, his chest rising and falling heavily with each breath. On guard.

I lean back in my seat, my poor posture both a habit and a reflection of my state of mind. I try to muster some inner strength, nausea be damned. I find my eyes continuously drifting to the window.

"What are you looking at?" She asks, bored with her magazine.

My throat suddenly feels like wet sandpaper. I start coughing and can't stop.

"Where is your appointment exactly?"

I had stopped just inside of the front entrance. Given my low endurance and continued dizziness, I had planned to wait for Will to walk with me. I don't tell her this—mainly because I'm still coughing.

She's concerned about my sickly state, but she's steadfast in that she tries to keep her composure, continues thumbing through *Reader's Digest* at the same consistent pace. I imagine the weight of Will's hand on my back, stroking reassuringly and I try to steady my breathing, ignore the scratchy tickle in my throat.

As expected, she's oblivious to possible causes of my coughing other than it must be my intention to embarrass her. As a result, she thinks it's a total overreaction when she suggests clearing my throat inconspicuously might ease my cough and I stand up and walk away.

She finds me standing at the window overlooking the surrounding trees and parking lot, watching Will, daring her to see him. He's positioned himself on a concrete bench under a tree. He's wearing a layered gray shirt with the sleeves pushed up to just below his elbows, jeans, sandals, sunglasses, and his cell phone in front of him. For the briefest of moments, I indulge in the fact that he's there for me.

Guilt slithers its way up my spine and in one breath, I've never felt more alone. *He's going to hate you for lying to him.*

My back pocket buzzes.

"*I love you.*"

I stare at the concise words, glance up to see him place his phone beside him, lean forward and prop his chin up against his fists.

"Isn't your appointment at 10?" Mom says, coming up beside me. She touches my hair cautiously, like it might bite her. "Do you not like the wigs I bought for you? I think they'd make you feel more comfortable, wouldn't they?"

My hand snaps up over hers automatically, removes it from my head. "Would that make me look more presentable?"

She takes a step back, holds her hand to her cheek as though I've slapped her. "I don't need this attitude right now, you know. It's been a very tough few weeks. I'm leaving Ray." She is successfully projecting a facial expression someone might have if they were devastated and about to burst into tears.

"*Again?*" She's moved out three times that I know of.

She starts pacing a bit, like a bad actor in a high school drama production. "I tried. I tried so hard to make it work. You have no idea what I've been through."

I freeze. "I'm sure it's been awful." *Not working, driving a brand new car, traveling to exotic destinations...* I find myself missing Ray a bit.

"I wanted to leave him *years* ago. I was finally going to and then we got your call, that you were getting married."

I cringe at the inaccuracy.

"I just wanted everything to be *perfect* for you."

A chuckle spontaneously emits from my throat. Then more laughter quickly follows.

"What is the *matter* with you? You're laughing?"

"I am." *She wanted to make everything perfect for me.* I picture my mother as Russell Crowe in *Gladiator* demanding "Are you not *grateful*?" More suppressed laughing. "I really am." I'm having trouble gaining enough vocal momentum to produce words. "It's just absurd. This total lack--" I snort. "--lack of awareness." I cover my mouth. "Have you always been like this?"

"Meagan Olivia--"

"*Oh*, but what last name to use?" I mock, still laughing. "You made me change from Reeves to Hurst, I switched back to Reeves, then Callahan. 'Sooo strong, Meagan *Callahan*.'"

"You are acting like a mental patient."

"Thank you for your evaluation, Dr. It Takes One to Know One." I giggle. "Oh I just insulted myself and I don't even care." I gasp dramatically. "But is she still even *with* Nathan, you may ask?"

She looks stunned. "Are you?"

I stop, glare at her. I want it to sting. "You know I thought I had this figured out years ago, but what you said just made something click for me. So thank you."

"*What?*"

"It is not my job to make you happy." I swallow hard. "You have acted like the child in this relationship since I was six." I can see her taking the chunky picture frame in her hands, glaring at the photograph of me sitting on the hood of his Cadillac with him leaning beside me, both enjoying popsicles fresh from the ice cream truck. She had scoffed at it. *Still putting him up on a pedestal even though he missed most of your childhood and couldn't be bothered to participate in your life when he was here.* "I had to comfort *you* after dad died. I had to make sure you didn't feel worse. That wasn't my job. It was *my* job to be a little girl. It was your job to let me be a little girl."

"Oh I'm sure you'll be a *perfect* mother, right?" There is nothing but contempt on her face.

"No. I probably won't be a mother at all." My voice is low and surprisingly restrained.

"Oh don't be dramatic."

"You know, you are the last person I want next to me when I hear whatever news I'm going to hear today. Good or bad. The *last* person." I point at her definitively, the way she's done to me to make me feel small. It's not satisfying like I expected.

She shakes her head, starts to walk away then stops short, finding ammunition in that leather handbag of hers. "You've never been happy. Nothing is good enough for you. Ray even said so. He thought I spoiled you. I gave you *everything*." She waves her hand, dismissing an imaginary object. The object, in my mind, and with those biting words, was a gauntlet. I watched it drop heavily to the floor, breathing heavily, trying to determine if I would accept the implied challenge. "No, nothing is good enough, but go ahead and blame me for everything. I'm a horrible mother."

I decide against bending symbolically to pick up the gauntlet, already dizzy from the exertion of simply standing. I raise my eyes to meet hers. Her eyeliner is too thick and has an aging effect. Her green eyes glare at me, judging me, disgusted by me. I take another breath. "You thought he'd leave his family and run away with you."

Her eye flickers almost imperceptibly.

"He turned you down. He didn't want you." The nausea has subdued me. I feel calm, sedate.

"You don't know what you're talking about, *little girl*," she says through gritted teeth.

"But I do. You were probably hoping I'd forget, right? You might not even remember the night I found out. That was a lot of bourbon you and Ray went through." *The night I ran to Will's house. The look from his parents.* "He was my best friend and you went after his dad."

It looks like I've shot her, the color is draining from her cheeks.

In context, it makes sense. Why she never liked Will. How unglued she became that morning when she saw us sharing breakfast; how she smacked me across the face. "Now, I have to wonder if you did that because you really *liked* him, or if it was some sick twisted jealousy thing."

For what seems like minutes, we stand there staring each other down. My back is to the parking lot so I don't know if Will is about to make an appearance. This would be new information to him. *I didn't think that through.*

"I've been meaning to ask what company you used for that wedding announcement. The quality was really excellent." I pause, wait for the realization to hit. The smallest widening of her green eyes tells me she does. *"What kind of mother tortures her child with things she conjured up?* Torturing them with something true would have been bad enough, but to make it up? That's pathological. That's some scary shit." I cough hard, my body's weak state failing me. When I pull my hand back, there's a small amount of blood. I quickly wipe it off on the hip of my jeans.

She shakes her head, scowls at me. "You're not my daughter."

The familiar phrase halts all movement. I take a very purposeful breath then slowly lock eyes with her again. I smile tightly. "And I didn't think I'd get any good news today."

And I leave her standing there.

When I reach the waiting room upstairs, Nurse Heather is standing at the door, having just called my name. I silently follow her down the hallway. She weighs me. 120. Still at least 10 pounds underweight. She puts the blood pressure cuff on me and I'm not surprised when she repeats the reading silently.

Dr. Hennessy is optimistic, despite some troubling lab results. Lungs are still clear. The blood when I cough, as well as the dizziness, is likely due to low platelet count. My blood work supports this theory. I'll need a blood transfusion.

I nod, put it in my mental queue of things to deal with. I might not even have time to work through it--she's working me in for it this afternoon. Maybe it's better that way.

I don't process anything else she says after that. Dr. Hennessy takes extra care with me, doesn't rush me out, but I tell her I'm fine and wish her a good afternoon. I take my time, use the restroom, splash cold water on my face, and breathe.

I thought for sure my mother would ambush me upon my exit to the waiting room, but there aren't any signs of her or any recognition on the faces of those in the waiting room that they witnessed what occurred in the lobby a half hour earlier.

A young man with dark unruly hair is sitting in the sunlight of the window, leaning forward with his elbows resting on his knees, chin resting in his hands. Color has returned to his skin, even a tan, since he had a clear PET scan a month ago. When he catches my eye, he stands, moves toward me.

I stop short. "I'm going to be fine," I conclude.

This clearly results in more questions than answers.

"Can we go outside?"

He nods and I take his hand, lead him to the elevator, an awkwardly silent ride, and move toward the exit. When I find us standing in a shady spot distanced a bit from the building entrance, I turn. "We have enough memories in hospitals," I say and walk into his embrace, squeeze my arms around his neck.

"Are you OK?"

"From the showdown at the OK Corral or my visit with Dr. Hennessy?"

"Start with the appointment."

I explain to the best of my memory what came from the appointment. I've remembered that I am to check in at 12:15.

"Now the OK Corral?"

I shrug, but I'm sure he can feel my tears seeping through his shirt. I have no words to express the contradictory emotions I'm feeling about it—sadness, overwhelming relief, guilt, validation.

With the wind whirling in the trees and the thumping of my heart in my ears, I don't hear him at first, but as my heart eases, I find he's singing softly in my ear. He continues *The Rainbow Connection* as I find tears streaming from my eyes. A sadness fills me, a longing for something I never really had, but desperately needed, something I will never have. I suddenly feel that gaping hole I felt the day the state trooper showed up at our door, the regret that I didn't run down the stairs and give my dad one last hug, the loneliness I felt in the days, weeks, years that followed; all the things I wasn't allowed to feel.

One day a boy in a vintage Beach Boys concert tee shirt stepped into my world and told me what I felt mattered. He didn't save me; I would have found a way to survive. What that eight year old boy did was show me that life could be good again. I could fake the appearance of happy, but he actually helped me feel happy. I didn't love him because of what he did--it was because of what he did that I was able to love him.

I gaze over his shoulder at the overcast day, the clouds drifting by, the sun peeking through.

18
i love sleep. my life has the tendency to fall apart when i'm awake, you know?

"G ermany was really pretty at Christmas."

Will turns at the sudden statement. My eyes feel heavy, my entire body like a lead weight. I have no idea how I'm going to stand when it's over. I had hoped I wouldn't need to repeat a transfusion, but Dr. Hennessy thought it was best. She also thought it was best not to waste any time, which is why she sent me immediately over to AIC to have it done. We didn't have a chance to have lunch and my hollow stomach is making a fuss about it.

"Remember the Christmas market?"

"I do. You bought an ornament there."

"I did. A glass one. I may have smashed it into the hotel trash can. I've never cried so hard over a Christmas ornament."

His face is regretful.

"That's a lie. I had the Christmas Story leg lamp one—limited edition—dropped it." I press my lips together in a mock pout. "Sometimes I still cry myself to sleep thinking about it."

He exhales deeply.

"The leg lamp," I clarify. "I went back there on Christmas Eve. To the market. If I hadn't been so incredibly sad, it would have been one of the most magical sights I'd ever seen." I settle into the pillow on the hospital bed, breathing deeply and surveying Will in the dimly lit room. "I didn't bring it up to make you feel guilty. I'm trying to think about places that are preferable to the inside of a hospital and it popped into my head. It was really pretty." I sigh. "I do love Christmas. Against all odds."

He seemed to wince a little at that.

"I just mean--" My mind is empty, having abandoned the thought without warning. "I'm talking a lot. I feel a little punchdrunk."

"You look a little *rum* drunk, Reeves."

"My body feels like it weighs a thousand pounds." I inhale and exhale deeply. "Sorry. I shouldn't have brought up Germany."

Will runs his fingertips across my forehead, traces the short hair. "No topic is off limits with me. Nothing you say can change how I feel about you."

"I didn't vote in the last election."

His jaw drops. "You *monster*."

"I think I've lost my tolerance for sitting through medical procedures." I frown. "I feel—anxious."

"What can I do to help?"

"Help me think of other places?"

He leans toward me. "I've got one. Okay, you're lying on your back on a cushion of fresh leaves in the middle of the forest floor. Overhead are great, towering trees that reach for the crisp, blue sky, creating an almost tunnel like view. The leaves, backlit by the sun, are a rich, vibrant shade of green."

"Is it warm?"

"You've been hiking in the sun so you're sweaty and gross from the climb—" he pauses to smile at my questioning glance, "—but now you're in the shade and there's a refreshing breeze."

"That's nice, but the hike *was* a little exhausting."

"OK, well then let's move somewhere tropical." He's thoughtful a moment. "You're swimming gently through the cool, turquoise water at the base of a waterfall."

"No piranhas?"

He smiles. "No piranhas."

"No freshwater dwelling sharks?"

He describes a dozen other places, some we visited together, others from his childhood. I picture rolling mountains, green lush pastures and horses galloping freely over the hillsides, snow capped mountains, fields of wildflowers, of pineapples, I see waves crashing against lava rock.

I feel like a child hearing a bedtime story.

"The piano is nice," I say, hearing the echo of the piano in the lobby. "We aren't usually this close to it."

He furrows his brow. "Is this the song from *Twilight?*"

I smile widely. "*Wow*, are you Team Edward or Jacob?"

He smirks. "Shut it."

"That's not nice. I'm being transfused here. When did you watch *Twilight?*" It all comes out like one long run-on sentence.

"Qatar."

I try very hard not to laugh. "Were you under the covers watching this or are a lot of our military into sparkly vampires?"

"I was alone and I was curious what the fuss was about--"

I snort.

"Out of context that sounds bad."

"Yes. *Out* of context."

"It was just the one time."

"That's what they all say. Go on. You were alone and curious--"

"Evan had uploaded all of his movies to my laptop."

"Evan had it?"

"He had like 200 movies on there."

"Still. Team Edward or Jacob?"

"You can't be Team Jacob. He ends up with Bella's daughter."

I snort again. It quickly morphs into suppressed giggling.

"What?"

"That's in the last movie. Of five. You watched them all?"

He frowns unhappily at first then once he sees me laughing to the point my vocal chords are failing to project noise, he grins. "It's *that* funny?"

"Oh my cheeks hurt. Yes, it's that funny," I answer. I try to keep a straight face, but start giggling again.

The technician pops her head in to make sure all is well and that's enough to sober me a bit.

"You know, that song was playing that day in the cafeteria, just before you literally bumped into me."

"Before you slapped me, you mean?"

"I was angry and you have a very solid face." I pause. "Nothing like Edward, of course. He's some sort of marble isn't he?"

He chuckles to himself. "You know what? I'll take the mockery if it brings you even a little happiness."

"Oh it does." I'm still grinning widely, but I no longer have the energy to laugh.

He strokes my cheek, studying my smile.

"How much longer do you think? Maybe 10-15 minutes at most?"

"They said it should take 4-5 hours."

"And it's been like 4?"

"It's been 19 minutes."

"Oh cheese and sprinkles," I grumble.

"*Language.*"

"I'm probably going to fall asleep--you don't have to stay. I'd like you to, but I'd understand if you go stuff your face with--was it a French Dip sandwich special?"

"Philly Cheesesteak."

"Cheese Whiz or Sauce?"

"Both."

"*Jerks.*" I'm suddenly captivated by how healthy he looks. "You should eat. I'm being silly."

"I'm with you, Reeves. I will even wipe the drool off your cheek while you sleep without judgement. I will leave the judgement to my Instagram followers."

"You don't even know how to hashtag."

He shrugs. "I *still* think you should come back to my place tonight."

My body tenses. "Not yet."

"I know I said I'd wait and I will, but you don't even like that house, Reeves."

"I really really don't."

"Then why do you want to go back there instead of my place?"

"I need closure."

"You don't want to end things with Nathan by phone."

Just tell him. I sigh, intending for the words to spill out of my mouth, but instead, I make some remark about his fingers running through my short hair. My body tingles at his touch and my eyelids slowly close.

I vaguely remember finishing with the transfusion. I remember him explaining that I would not want to be placed in a wheelchair. I remember the technician scowling as Will hoisted me into his arms, carried me out to his truck, which he must have pulled up front at some point. I remember him lifting me into the passenger seat, climbing in the driver's side and gently repositioning my head.

And then I remember having the dream--of having to deliver the babies. It wasn't even accurate to how it happened, but the dream isn't about the babies. Not really. The doctor kept narrating things, kept telling me how well I was doing. They brought in another nurse to console me since I had no family there. When they swept the babies over to the small exam table, usually meant for first measurements, the nurse had me lay on my side. I could see them working to keep the babies alive. There wasn't a point to the effort, but they tried anyway.

As I watched the medical team's backs, I noticed that the hospital room was not private. The curtain was mostly drawn, but behind it was Will in his camo fatigues, his eyes glassy as he lay sprawled on a gurney soaked with blood.

I screamed for help, but the nurse wiped my forehead with a washcloth and told me that he could wait. They needed to tend to my dead babies first. She kept telling me I was doing so well.

His blood seeped through the sheets and started to pool on the floor. His skin was drained of color, turning a dull gray.

I begged them to help him, but I was ignored. I screamed at them that my babies were dead, to help Will. I tried to get off the bed again, as I found I could finally move, but the rails were immediately clicked in place and my wrists and ankles were restrained. Will's hand went limp, the blood trickling down his palm and fingers.

I had lost them all.

When Will wakes me, I'm still in the truck, slumped awkwardly on his thigh, seat belt digging into my hip. It's nearly dark outside. My head is throbbing and rather than being relieved that the man I just watched die in my dream is sitting beside me, I feel anxious. And guilty.

I scramble to sit up, look outside at the dimly lit street. My street. My driveway. My house. And not any of those things, all at the same time.

His eyes are fixed on the house and the real estate sign out front. "I think I need some context, Reeves. That wasn't there this morning."

The logical thing was to just stay at Will's house, but seeing as he presumed we were having an affair until Nathan came back long enough for me to end things "officially," I had insisted on staying at the house, the rocking boat too much for my dizziness. Actually, the logical thing would have been to tell Will I ended things with Nathan long ago, that we weren't actually having an affair.

I do not recall why I chose that particular course of action. Not when I'm this tired.

I dig for my cell phone, thinking that surely Nathan would have texted me.

"*Hey Maggie. Tried calling. Left voicemail. Sorry for lack of notice, but John got house prepped for staging. Didn't want him to surprise you.*" Text 2: "*Still can't reach you.*

Apparently he had ALL our furniture removed. Staging isn't until tomorrow. Trying to figure this out. Call me."

My phone starts ringing as I'm finishing reading his text message.

Nathan repeats the information from his texts, apologizing repeatedly.

"Gosh I guess I *could* pitch a tent."

He explains how this isn't a good idea because of marking up the carpet. Also, we don't own a tent. Also, I still wouldn't have a bed. "I'm sorry. He didn't tell me this was what was going to happen. I tried calling you earlier. I figured you were at the hospital. Did you have treatment today?"

"Doctor appointment and transfusion." I yawn involuntarily.

"Transfusion—another one? I know that really wiped you out last time."

"Yep." Another yawn. "He's lucky I'm too tired to draw a handlebar mustache on his snazzy realtor photo."

Will peers over at the sign and John's ambitious smile. It's one distinguishing feature from Nathan, who never likes to show teeth when he smiles. Will frowns a little.

"Yeah let's not do that. Those signs are expensive."

"I don't even have a Sharpie, Nathan." I release an exhausted breath. "I knew your family didn't like me, but John took it to a whole new level."

"With John, it's not you, trust me."

"I'll take your word for it." *Did he fold all my underwear and pack it up nicely for me?"*

"In the garage."

No censor. "Well that's not invasive at all."

"I think they just use an inflatable mattress for staging—"

"Comfy." Yawn.

"Yeah I know. They're supposed to come by tomorrow. I told him to put in an actual mattress."

"Thanks, Nathan. I was almost cleared out anyway. Don't worry about it."

"Are you sure?"

"Yes."

"You're doing okay? After the transfusion?"

"Yeah," I say, rubbing at my eyes roughly. "Fine. "

We say good night. My brain vaguely understands that I have a few months of omissions, a few days in particular, to answer for. I try to think of how to resolve the situation, but I can hardly stay sitting upright.

"Reeves."

My eyes pop open. I didn't realize I had fallen asleep.

Will retrieves a blanket from the second row. "It might have a little dog fur," he says apologetically. He folds it up and lays it against his upper leg, then pats it.

"Oh you sweet, sweet man." I collapse onto his leg.

He shifts the truck roughly into reverse, peering over his shoulder.

"Where are we going?"

"My place has furniture."

"But my clothes live here," I say sleepily. "*Actually most live on the boat.*"

"We can go to the boat tomorrow. I have some of your clothes at my house."

"Some of my clothes live at your house?"

"They were mixed in with my things."

The flannel blanket feels far more lofty than it is with how tired I am, but my mouth won't stop running. "Gosh I hope the clothes are still fashionable. I went through a plaid button-down phase."

"Sleep, Reeves," he says, placing his hand on my head.

I think I fall asleep as I'm nodding.

19
born on the fourth of july

My twenty-third birthday fell on a Friday. There was a lot of excitement about it among medical staff at the hospital—mainly because that meant everyone had a full weekend to recuperate from the festivities. The excitement would be centered around it being a major national holiday, not the anniversary of my birth.

I didn't have the same grateful patriotism that I normally do. Actually this year and last I've been all in all unenthusiastic about most things. Last year I still went and put flags out at the Veterans Memorial Cemetery. This year I was replaced by Boy Scouts. Which was fine. I offered my services to two cemeteries and was told something about solicitation and propaganda not being permitted. I wasn't in the best frame of mind when I received the voicemails. I may have used the term "snowflake" a bit too many times during my return calls and I think I quoted Lincoln, the Pledge of Allegiance and perhaps Lee Greenwood lyrics.

When Nathan got home from work the Tuesday prior, I was sitting on the floor leaning against the bed, staring out into the backyard. Calling it a backyard is generous. The block fence was probably six feet from the small patio area. He prefers low maintenance gravel to grass. There was a collection of drought tolerant cacti in one corner. It definitely didn't look like a yard prepared to handle kids or dogs.

It made me feel caged in and claustrophobic. Prison inmates get more space.

When he came into the bedroom, he didn't see me right away. I was staring blankly out the French doors at the aforementioned block wall fence.

After Nathan's heart recovered from his apparent, dramatized surprise to find me there, he suggested we get some fresh air.

He drove us to a farmer's market. I was wearing my charcoal gray lounge pants and a well-worn navy t-shirt with a row of palm trees across the chest under the worn-in men's sweater with the suede elbow patches. It was about five sizes too large. He hated when I wore that sweater. He had asked about it once, I believe referring to it as my Mr. Rogers sweater, a passive aggressive attempt to discourage me from wearing it.

Nathan bartered on the price of strawberries as I sniffed fresh flowers, touching the rubbery leaves of succulents that didn't quite look real. It was pure coincidence the market was situated on that particular lot across from Target. It was where Will, Evan and I had come when there was a Christmas tree lot in its place.

In my mind, the summer set up transformed into a wintery wonderland. You'll remember my community pool outing? Admittedly that wasn't the first time that week I tried opioids as a means of emotional escape.

I thought of Christmas, still a half year away. I wanted a wreath for the front door. I wanted a giant tree.

"Can I help you find anything?"

I got a nervous chill, which I shrugged off and exhaled deeply. "No, just browsing."

It wasn't the first time I had pictured Will somewhere he wasn't, but the opioids made it a much more immersive experience. He was back in a beanie and wearing his sporty red and black North Face jacket. He had worn it in Ramstein and was self-conscious that it was too casual when we went out to the theatre. He had a shadow of facial stubble. He nudged me with his water resistant sleeve. "Hey Knobby Knees. Aren't you cold?"

"It's summer. If you weren't a figment of my imagination, you'd be burning up in that coat."

He looked past me to Nathan, who was paying with a large bill. "He seems like a decent guy." His face was as close to neutral as he could manage. "Doesn't like Christmas, does he?"

"Assuming this were actually Christmas? No. He doesn't. Too messy. Too much clutter. Too many cartoon woodland creatures. Santa is promoting obesity and diabetes. Separation of church and state." I immediately looked away at the rows of blue spruce and douglas firs, pick at the imaginary sap on my fingers.

"Reeves, what's going on here?" his voice had turned serious.

I could so clearly see him standing before me. "I chose to experiment with narcotics and am experiencing one of those uncommon side effects the commercials jabber on about. Hallucinations, not death, fortunately."

"Not what I meant, but that's a sunny outlook."

"I'd prefer not to die. I just wish the living weren't so painful."

"I want you to be happy, Reeves."

I sighed, closed my eyes, tried to recall the feeling of his hand on my cheek. "Me too, Mercer."

"Remember our Christmas at the apartment?"

Christmas. Two and a half years earlier. Just me, Will, and Evan enthusiastically making their apartment feel festive. We ended up with a tree that took up the whole of the living room forcing the flat screen to be relocated. Evan tried to be crafty and cut out snowflakes, the apartment glowed with the warm cast of colored bulbs. I remember making us all hot chocolate, using enamel camping mugs because they were the only clean mugs available. Will had been up at 4 running drills at the base so he fell asleep first, as we piled on the leather couch to watch *Christmas Vacation*. He had his arm around my ribcage in somewhat of a spooning position. Evan got up just as the credits started to roll, placing the remote in reach for me. He grinned at his brother snoring quietly behind me then bent down and kissed me on the top of my head. As he trudged to bed, I remember letting the moment envelop me in its simplicity. I belonged exactly where I was. The feeling was sweet and satisfying.

Will got deployment orders the following week. By the next Christmas he had just broken our engagement. The Christmas after that I had two dead babies and a cancer diagnosis.

I opened my eyes upon being sprayed by misters. Despite the vision being broken, the water was intensely refreshing against the heat of the late July afternoon.

"I wondered where you went," Nathan said.

Even the Griswold tree was gone.

"They said there's a booth down here that has eggplant. We could do a vegetarian dinner—how does that sound?"

I suddenly craved a cheeseburger.

There were no signs of Will's red and black jacket and I didn't see his pickup in the parking lot. *You were hallucinating, Reeves.* Nathan's face showed no sign I had been wandering around chattering to myself and the other patrons seemed completely unaware I existed. *It was all in your head.*

"You know what? I'll get them for tomorrow. We can do takeout tonight." He readjusts his canvas bags on his shoulder. "That was probably enough of an outing for you."

I pictured the newly repurposed nursery, now storage for CDs and obsolete electronics as I had discovered that afternoon.

That's not my home. I turned from where I had last seen phantom Will and found Nathan with an indistinguishable look on his face. At first it seemed to display anger, then it softened. I didn't realize I was crying until the wind hit my cheeks.

"We're going to have that conversation again, aren't we?"

I nodded.

The next day, I had felt so dizzy and nauseous from not sleeping that Nathan had concluded that he would drive me to treatment. He did so with a bit of novelty probably in knowing he would never be obligated to do so again. After picking me up, he had flown off a few days early to Silicon Valley.

Then came the pool outing.

The day *after that* I turned twenty-three. I woke after sleeping a solid 18 hours to a sunrise creeping through the windows from where Will had tucked me in on the couch. I went to the garage, the orange sunlight flooding the space around my Jeep, the only thing besides clothes at that house that truly belonged to me. I went to the grocery store in the early hours to stock the small pantry and icebox on the boat, canceling my chemo while fetching a cart. That day I deep cleaned the boat, inside and out, and that night, I sat up top, fireworks exploding in the sky nearby. That night I fully appreciated my birthday falling on the 4th of July. I felt freedom for the first time in a long time. Nice to have a grand spectacular to mark the occasion.

***

I wake up at 11:18, according to the clock in Will's bedroom. His bed is far more comfortable than the bench seat of his old truck, memory foam of some kind. I feel the temptation to sink into it and sleep away the foreseeable future, but I sense some explanations are in order.

I switch on his bedside lamp. The room isn't huge, but the ceilings are vaulted and give the illusion of space. The walls appear to be painted a neutral grey. His bed is made except for the right side where I was sleeping, my usual side. There's a stack of books on the table and I run my finger along the bindings. At the bottom of the stack is a book about the stages of grief and dying put in a cancer treatment context. I own it and I'm pretty much sure it's recommended to every cancer patient, but I hate that it's here. I'm not sure what to think of the fact that it's at the bottom of the stack and looks like it's never been opened. I move on. *Killing Lincoln. The Hitchhiker's Guide to the Galaxy*: his favorite book from high school. A travel guide for Italy, filled with dog-eared corners, a faded cover, wrinkled, moisture warped pages.

I yawn, pushing myself to my feet and quietly shuffle toward the bathroom.

His closet, accessed through the bathroom is tidy and seems to be organized by dress code. I sift through each hanger indulgently, feel the fabrics, dive my nose into the collar of a sweatshirt I recognize.

My eyes find a shoebox with the lid ajar sitting on an otherwise orderly shelf to my left. I walk in front of it, trying to peer inside inconspicuously. This leads to no further knowledge except that Will evidently owns a pair of clog slippers. I decide to peek and immediately regret the decision. Right on top is a photo of him with a blonde girl, very lean and fit, hand on her hip, posed like a model who knows how to get photographed at her best angle. She looks like a pilates instructor--a pilates instructor with caked on makeup imitating a perfect complexion. They're wearing Happy New Year hats and I'm not sure, but it looks like the Vegas Strip in the background. *Who the hell is this woman?*

The one time I was in Vegas, I was pregnant and getting married and trying not to look miserable about it.

I'm not sure what I expected. He wasn't going to pine away forever. He's never had too hard of a time charming women.

My fingers automatically go to my scalp, find my little boy cowlicks throwing my short hair in unpredictable directions.

I take a step back, feel that urge to flee, to disappear. Not because I'm embarrassed, but because I feel a familiar feeling: An inferiority complex ingrained from childhood. Abandonment.

But I look again and I suddenly see the box for what it is: Trash. This is proven by the presence of used Breathe-Right wrappers and tissues and cotton swabs, that thankfully appear very lightly used, behind and under the photo.

I go back to searching his closet. I'm about to the end of casualwear and start to turn back to the dresser since I really just came in here for my rogue clothes, but I see a flash of red in the back corner of formalwear. I know what it is immediately and I highly doubt he has much use for it (unless he's had a change in lifestyle that he hadn't made known): A dress. *My* dress. My red tea-length, wispy dress that made me want to twirl right there in the fitting room when I first put it on, perfectly preserved inside dry cleaner plastic.

I remember reluctantly hanging it in the shadows of my closet after graduation. Part of me wanted to rip it to shreds. A few years later, Will discovered the dress had still claimed a hanger in my small dorm closet. His deployment fell right at the end of the spring semester when I was preparing to move. The building was being refurbished and they wanted everyone out as soon as the last final was taken. He was helping me move in with Evan until the end of the year. They shared an apartment and it just made sense. I had practically been living there full-time anyway.

"I guess I probably need to get rid of some things," I had said, trying to retrieve it from his hold, but he pulled the hanger away.

"You'd get rid of this dress?"

"It's not the best memory attached to it."

"The memory of me being a total ass?"

"Let's go with that." I made another attempt to grab the hanger. The flood of emotions I felt that night started to fill my chest. Admittedly, there was quite a bit of emotion knowing he was being deployed, which I was likely attaching to a less distressing memory. "Not really. The memory of not belonging."

He examined the dress, looked up at me. "Not belonging?"

"With you."

Will had done an appreciative double take when he first saw me wearing it, beaming. There was something about the way he reacted when I entered the room--like I was suddenly in the spotlight and the only thing he saw. The contrast to the look he had on his face by the end of the night--regretful--was painful and jarring. There was a span of time during the graduation ceremony that something drastic changed, which was difficult to grasp, since nothing had changed for me except my upper legs were a little sore from the uncomfortable chairs.

I had finally received clarification on his comments a little over a year later when he was put on the spot by Katie's soon-to-be-husband, Tim, at their small rehearsal dinner. Little did I know, he had been in contact with Katie (and she had issued the last minute invite) so Tim already knew the explanation. He was prompting a public declaration for my benefit. (People gave Katie a hard time for marrying so young, but she really did well.) Will had turned beet red, but graciously accepted the roasting. He explained: "A little over a year ago, I stupidly told Reeves--Well, you all know her as Mags or Maggie. Anyway, I stupidly told her that she wasn't 'girlfriend material.'" There were some collective boos from Tim and his best man. Katie smacked them both. "I took some terrible advice and I'm not going to make excuses for it. Some people have to, and should, go through 'girlfriend material' to make them more certain about who they wind up with. My mistake was not realizing that I was entirely certain already. I stand by my statement that Reeves was not and is not girlfriend material. I've known that since I was eight years old. You date 'girlfriend material.' You don't marry them."

So some time after that rehearsal dinner, packing up my closet to move, I had mixed feelings about the dress. "Fine, I'll keep it. It's a good fancy dinner dress."

"No," he said, grabbing the hanger. "This dress shouldn't go to the apartment."

I thought he was going to make a symbolic gesture and throw it in the trash, but instead he removed it from its hanger, folded it neatly, and placed it on the built in dresser on top of his keys and phone.

"I hate that you have those feelings, Reeves. I wish I didn't put them there in the first place, but I did."

"Where's it going?"

"With me. To show you that you always belong with me."

He took it to the desert and here it is—pristine, preserved and waiting.

Figuring his top dresser drawer is underwear, I try the second drawer first and discover a small stack of my clothes, including the NASA shirt I used to wear frequently. There's a clean pair of lacy red panties in the stack I thankfully recognize as my own. There are no shorts or pants so I take a pair of his boxers, exit to his bathroom, which is very recently remodeled with beveled subway tile with a mosaic trim in the shower, wood tile floors, a bleached wood double vanity.

I find a plush navy blue towel on the open shelving and hang it outside the walk-in shower. As the water starts crashing down from the waterfall showerhead, I peel off the sweatpants and t-shirt that have become my hospital appointment staple.

I wasn't sure before if he was awake, but the aromas coming from the kitchen when I creep out into the hallway are intoxicating. Italian food, I suspect. There's a scurrying on the tile floor and I suddenly find myself being circled and sniffed by a white dog the size of a miniature horse.

Will pops his head around the corner from the kitchen. "Hi." His face is charmingly upbeat given the late hour.

"Hi."

He turns on the hallway light. "Reeves, meet Bruce."

"Well, hello--Bruce?" I coo, scratching his enormous head. His fur is entirely white except for a mask around his eyes and around both ears, which is brindle. *And you thought Bruce was his son.*

"I originally named him Batman, but I felt a little silly calling him that. I was concerned already with PTS, I didn't want to add any questions about my sanity. 'I'm going for a run with Batman' tends to raise a few eyebrows."

I rest my head upside down on Bruce's neck as he tries licking the air near my face. "Well you are very sweet, Bruce. You could have gone with Gotham, as in 'I can't stay. Gotham needs me.'"

"Oh that would have been much better," he says, smiling. "Would be a shame to confuse him now though. He's not the brightest crayon in the box."

Bruce frantically sniffs me, whimpers, bounces into me, whimpers again.

"Dude, you've got 50 pounds on her. Take it easy."

"He's okay."

More sniffing and whimpering. "Sorry, he's not usually this excitable."

I kiss Bruce again, scratch his soft ears.

"I've got to check on dinner," Will says, disappearing back into the kitchen. "Come on in."

Bruce corrals me toward the kitchen.

"I usually try to eat healthier, but dinner will be a departure from that. Hopefully it meets your standards."

"My standard right now is cheeseburgers and nachos."

"Then you might be disappointed."

I run my hand along the concrete countertops. "Your kitchen looks like it fell out of a magazine, Will."

"Thanks, it fought back--electrical and some pipe issues--but I'm pretty happy with it now."

Bruce trots confidently to his food bowl and Will tosses some scraps into it. The American Bulldog quickly returns to my side, nudges under my hand.

Will looks up from the stove and tries to suppress a smile.

"What?"

He furrows his eyebrows. "I made the right choice to make pasta. Bulk you up. Get you solidly in the underweight range." He finishes plating dinner.

"I'm solidly in triple digits now. Watch out."

"Yes, attack of the 5'11" string bean."

I drop my shoulders. "I will torture you with my visible ribcage. Don't think I won't."

His face is frozen in a smile. "Have a seat, Weirdo."

"You keep calling me Weirdo and after I eat all this excellent restaurant quality food, I have half a mind to storm right out of here," I say, dramatically inhaling the air. "Oh sweet baby Jesus, is that homemade garlic bread?"

He slices the loaf, his eyebrows raised. "So what's the story with the NASA t-shirt?"

"You tell me. Seems like a funny one to steal."

"You left it in the dryer. Evan thought it was mine for some reason."

I take a seat on the side with the smaller helping. Will quickly swaps the plates. "I was third runner up in a competition sponsored by NASA in 9th grade."

"Seriously? What was the competition?"

"Designing a habitat for astronauts on Mars, accounting for the hazards and weather conditions. Apparently their scientists were desperate for ideas."

"That's impressive. How did I not know about you being so into space exploration?"

"We weren't really running in the same circles then." I glance down at the shirt that probably shouldn't fit quite so loosely.

"No wonder you love that book," he says.

"Which one?"

"*The Martian.*"

"Oh yeah. Did you read it?"

"I did." He grins. It was one I had loaded on his tablet for deployment. "What's so funny?"

He seems a bit caught up in something. "You look good in this house, Reeves." He places the plates at the table and gestures to me to eat.

Once my belly is full and adequately distended for Will's piece of mind, he pours two glasses of wine.

"Don't get too excited, it's the bottle the realtor gave me when I bought the place."

"Your parents live in Italian wine country and you serve supermarket wine? What the heck, Mercer?"

He nods. "I think she got it at Trader Joes." He examines the label. "The wine my parents brought over didn't last. Who knew Easter was such a drinking holiday?"

"Well there is the whole thing about 'this is the body, this is the blood'— given the events leading up to Easter, I kind of get it."

"Plus Evan had given up beer for Lent and Leigh had given up wine...so they were making up for lost time."

I shrug. "I probably shouldn't have too much anyway," I say.

"Darn right, Crazy Head. Those are both for me." He takes a sip, analyzing the wine and decides it's acceptable. "I'm kidding. Just sip, real slow and sophisticated-like."

I don't intend to laugh so hard, but my belly starts aching. I clutch my stomach, my cheeks tight. Will smiles at the sight of me trying to suppress my laughs so unsuccessfully.

When I've regained enough composure to speak, I thank him for dinner.

He takes a slow sip, then clears his throat. "So a couple days seems pretty quick to end a marriage, list a house for sale, and be on good speaking terms. Am I correct in assuming this has been going on for awhile, Reeves?"

"I think I was going to tell you."

"You *think* you were?"

"Best I can say truthfully."

He nods. "How long since you ended your marriage to the so-called 'robot'?"

"I'd prefer if you forgot I called him that."

"Can I savor the remark for a second?"

"Do you honestly get that much satisfaction from it at this point, Will?"

"I won't call him that again."

I take a swig. "This isn't half bad."

"How long?"

"July."

He pretends to choke on his wine. "July?"

Bruce whines by the back door. "Dog door is the next project, Bud." Will says and stands. "Let's sit outside."

I follow him toward a pitch black backyard. As soon as he flips the switch the pool lights up, the lush palm trees are spotlighted and they are just the beginning.

"Having some trouble with the electrical out here," he explains, taking a seat on the outdoor sectional.

"You designed this?"

"Are you changing the subject?"

"I'm not. If I wanted to change the subject you know I could."

"You're too tired for that kind of exertion."

I point toward him to retort, but wave off the gesture. "Yeah, you're right," I sigh. "It looks amazing though."

"Thank you." He raises his eyebrows.

"I had been asking him for a divorce for 10 months."

I see him working out the math. I had asked for a divorce since October when we were married in August.

"*11* months," I correct. *September.*

"What does 'asking' for a divorce look like exactly?"

"I suppose it's not asking at all. It's saying what you want and having the other person disregard it completely—and not having enough gumption to follow through."

"Did he need authorization from the Pope?"

"Nathan's family are mostly Atheists."

He ponders that and the satisfied arch of his eyebrow tells me he's keeping some commentary to himself.

"Put down the wine glass, you're getting rude."

"I didn't say anything."

I wave my fingers in front of his face as though describing an abstract art piece. "I can see the snark. You're far less snarky when you're sober."

He places his glass on the coffee table, sits back in the corner and pats the cushion beside him. "So *July*."

I sit, but I don't lean into him as he seems to have expected. "July."

"It's October, you know."

"I know."

"I'm not going to bite. Sit back here with me," he says and gets me to settle into the nook of his arm.

"It was after you started chemo."

He nods.

"I ended it Tuesday night. Nathan still drove me to treatment the next day."

"Big of him." His voice is flat. "He drove you home, too, as I recall."

"He seems to feel a lot of guilt to do the right thing, despite not being Catholic."

"I thought he seemed—less patient than he should have."

"Well, our marriage *had* just ended."

"Even so." His arm reflexively reaches toward his glass, but he catches himself and settles back.

"He decided to leave early for his work trip so he could process things-- which was exactly what it sounds like. By Sunday, I had a task list and a zip file of documents to sign and have notarized."

"Efficient."

"I had completed the forms before. It was really a matter of filing. Luckily neither one of us have been looking to drag anything out. He said I could live at the house for a while, which worked out when rocking back and forth wasn't mixing too well with medications."

"What made you finally decide to go through with it?"

"Nathan is a good man and had good intentions, but he treated me like a child and we were entirely incompatible."

He grunts in acknowledgment. "What's that smirk?"

"Something Walt told me. I visited him before I went up to stay with Katie."

He clears his throat. "What did Walt say?"

"I attempted to justify that I'd tried to make it work and he stopped me short and said: 'You can't shine a turd, sweetheart.'"

"I knew I liked Walt."

"He's on hospice now." I frown, shake the thought. "My life was being controlled by everyone but me." The realization that this is no longer the case sweeps through me like a gentle breeze, halted only by an ache in my stomach. *I have to tell him.* "Nathan had made a major medical decision when I was under anesthesia that was not in my best interest. I was not going to allow that to happen again." My glass is now empty so I lean forward and finish his.

He watches me, his eyes glazed over from the wine and the late hour. "This was during the surgery after we ran into each other?"

"It was. As I told you in hysterical sobs, I was supposed to have a hysterectomy and bilateral salpingo-oophorectomy, I think it's called." I'm impressed by my pronunciation, but continue, as it's evident he's not going to compliment me on it. "They remove everything. All detectable cancer cells were limited to those areas, only made sense. Well the surgeon was switched last minute, after I was under anesthesia. He took a look at my chart and approached Nathan about only doing a unilateral and scrapping the hysterectomy. That way I could do some hormone therapy and do an egg retrieval. Then we could freeze embryos and eventually use a surrogate to have kids."

"Had you talked about doing that?"

"Never. Actually when I made the decision to have the original surgery, I told him I didn't want to pass on my cancer genes. Ovarian cancer at 22? Come on."

"So--" he begins, sitting up straighter. "He decided on his own that you would a) have biological children, b) use a surrogate."

"C) go through really grueling chemo in order to make A & B possible, yes. Whilst giving the cancer cells the opportunity to find a way somewhere else in my body."

He didn't seem fond of Nathan before. Now he looks like he's suppressing profanities.

"Dr. Hennessy was out of town, but when she checked in, she was angry as hell about it." I can still see her pinched, yet apologetic face when I had my next appointment. She even swore a bit.

He takes a deep breath. "So what about doing the surgery now?"

"I had the surgery."

"When?"

"July. As soon as I was medically cleared to have another major surgery."

He nods. "That's why you stopped treatment."

"It seemed ridiculous to do the treatment when surgery was still the best chance of remission."

"Smart girl." There's a slight upturn of his mouth. "That's why you went to stay with Katie."

"I had the surgery there. Wasn't great timing for Tim. Katie was like 34 weeks pregnant and health but that she is, somehow ended up with preeclampsia. The doctor had her on bed rest. I was recovering and was supposed to stay in bed, too. Originally it was supposed to be laparoscopic so I figured my recovery would be easier and I could help out with Katie, but then they decided it was better to do a traditional abdominal surgery.

"Katie and I had some good bonding time though. Circumstances were a little unusual--her out of commission because she was having a baby, me out of commission from a surgery that would ensure I'd never have a baby." I had thought the situation was a bit comical for some reason. Now I don't. I allow the sadness and silently remind myself that it was a life-saving surgery. I settle under his arm.

When he speaks, his voice is nearly a whisper. "I wish you had told me. I wish I had been there for you…"

"I thought it would create a really weird dynamic—Since you were still going along with the story that you were married, after all." I peer over at him. "Why was that, by the way?"

He winces, knowing he should have seen this coming.

"A year and a half, Will. Longer than that actually."

"My reasoning sounds pretty weak in hindsight."

"Yeah. Kind of does, Mercer."

Bruce suddenly jumps up on my lap, big heavy paws digging into my legs.

"Batman, off!" Will says firmly, and Bruce hops down, cantering off into the dimly lit yard. The interruption seems to have reset our conversation. Or it seems as though Will is hoping it might have, readjusting in his seat. "Do you remember when I came into your backyard after your Homecoming dance?"

I murmur an acknowledgment.

"You went with that lanky guy."

"Chris. He's a pastor now."

"He couldn't have you so he turned to the church?"

"Hardly and he's a pastor, not a priest. He's allowed to marry. I've actually been in touch with him over the years. For spiritual guidance, " I clarify. "Starting with your deployment."

"You didn't tell me."

"You had enough to worry about. Then I 'ran into him' one day last September."

"Why the air quotes?"

"Katie. She meddles, but he's tried to help me deal with things." I shrug. "It's getting better, but I was a little at odds with God for a while."

"I'd say so. You married an Atheist."

I close my eyes briefly, shake my head, laughing. "Well played."

He pulls me more firmly into his arms.

We're both quiet for a few minutes. "I worried about what you might think of me--when you got back from Germany."

He sighed. "It doesn't matter."

"I want to know."

He sighs. "It wasn't like you. I wasn't really in a place to deal with things though, to be able to see that, to question it. I was angry."

"You hated me."

"I was angry, but I really didn't have a right to be. I ended things. I didn't respond to your letters, emails."

"That's right. I almost forgot I wrote to you." *I tortured myself interpreting your silence.* "Months of obsessively checking for a response. I took every blocked call thinking it could be you. So many scams and telemarketers. It's a wonder my identity wasn't stolen."

He shifts uncomfortably.

"I'm joking, Will."

"No, you're making light of what you felt."

Glancing up at him, I reluctantly admit defeat. "I was devastated."

"I got back in June. I started throwing myself into hobbies, I got very into exercising. Evan called it 'obsessive.' I had a mean temper. Everyone commented on it and had different suggestions, mainly to see a shrink. I kept refusing.

"I had to see you. I knew you would always help put flags on the headstones at the veterans cemetery for 4th of July. I figured if you were there, I'd get to see you. If you weren't, it somehow meant you were an awful person, which I decided would somehow make me feel better." He exhales deeply. "I knew you'd be there. I was counting on it."

I nod. My belly was big already. 16 weeks. The image of the babies flashes in my mind.

"You were just finishing up and I was—mesmerized."

"Mesmerized is a strong word."

"Then I chose well." He swallows hard. "I watched you place a bouquet at Ben's grave."

Hydrangeas.

"I wondered about the significance of them? You were talking to him, but I couldn't hear."

"I think I apologized because the bouquet wasn't going to last. I refused to bring him fake flowers though and the cemetery didn't allow plants. He had told me once--I think when we went to that county fair--they had blue hydrangeas everywhere at his childhood home in South Carolina and that when he saw them, it felt like a piece of home."

Will takes a deep breath.

"I always liked that accent of his," I say with a small smile. "He used to call me Magnolia."

It had been a beautiful, unseasonably mild day. I remember needing a light jacket that morning and the material hugged my expanding belly. The cemetery is a breathtaking place set on a hill with sweeping ocean views. The rows of white grave markers are humbling and moving. The lines of small American flags alongside them make it even more magnificent.

The babies were dead 7 weeks later. I shudder involuntarily.

I remember there were several people at the cemetery. One in particular in a dark gray hoodie had caught my attention. There had been something familiar about how he stood, shifting his weight.

"I found it impossible to even pretend to be angry with you after that," he said softly.

For a moment I allow myself to wonder what would have happened had I gone up to him or vice versa.

"You weren't married yet," he says, reading my thoughts.

We both seem to consider the babies at the same time and break eye contact.

"It wouldn't have stopped things from happening."

The babies. The cancer.

I consider this. "I haven't been a good person to be around. I've had my moments--my sense of humor has gone a little dark at times, but my lows have been really low." I roll my eyes. "I owe Nathan a really well-worded thank you card. Maybe a smiling chimpanzee would bring a feel-good, light-hearted vibe to the gesture?"

"If you're going to say it, why not say it with a chimp."

"Right?" I yawn. "Sorry."

"Well if only you had a good excuse like having several pints of blood pumped into you. Or that I essentially had you carb load pasta."

I m lift my shirt to reveal my firm stomach. "Look, still distended." I didn't mean to expose the newest surgical scar, but there it is--a slightly jagged vertical line up to my belly button. Its presence reminds me of the repercussions of Nathan's decision. "Of course, *regarding* Nathan, he did make a decision that resulted in a second surgery with a painful recovery."

Will tightens his arm around me, kisses my temple.

"He had good intentions," I concluded, covering my belly. "Well, mostly good, subconsciously selfish." I yawn again, fading quickly.

"We can go in?"

I shake my head. "So I'm going out on a limb here. I thought maybe it was the sedative they gave me that had me hallucinating, but--when you said you came to the hospital after the babies were born, but I was being discharged--"

"Yes?"

"You meant you came *back* to the hospital. Right?"

He's silent.

"You *were* there." He had been wearing a dark gray henley shirt and jeans. It was a very similar look to what he wore the day he proposed. It seemed like something my masochistic brain would hallucinate, but I was impressed with how it managed to properly light him in the setting--the harsh glare of the overhead lights on his shoulders, how it made the hair on top of his head look far lighter than it actually was. "I saw you in the hallway when they moved me out of delivery."

"I should have--"

"That's not why I brought it up, Will." I pause, building my endurance to ask the question that's been reeling in my head for over a year. "Did you see them?"

He squeezes me gently. "Is it OK that I did?"

I feel the tears drop from my cheeks onto his arm. Besides hospital staff, only the two of us saw them. I settle more snugly against his side. "I'm actually really glad you did."

"They were beautiful."

I nod, close my eyes. We're quiet for a few minutes. I had been sedated before they assigned me to a room, but his face had been clear to me. My body seemed to be instinctively fighting the medication so I drifted in and out, but I remember pleading with my eyes to stay open as I tried to maintain what I had determined must be a hallucination.

Nathan had gone home, having been told I would just be sleeping and didn't return until well after the nurse at 7am introduced herself and asked if my husband had just left. I had been confused by the thought of Nathan coming back and sleeping at the hospital. He valued his sleep quality too much.

She had told me how kind he seemed, how attentive, and I had nodded along. It was later, when Nathan arrived and she introduced herself to him and he had introduced himself as my husband, that she stammered a bit before awkwardly excusing herself.

I focus on the feel of Will's arms around me. For too long, I've felt like I've been floating in space, surrounded by a hollow void, unsupported by any gravitational force. Now with him, I feel grounded in something real. The knowledge that he had been present in some way all along calms my soul. Those moments suddenly feel less isolated because he was there, feeling the emotions with me, waiting for me, the whole time. "I could feel you there. With me."

He exhales deeply and I'm caught up in the fact that I can feel his breath near my ear, the spectacular closeness I'm now allowed.

He murmurs a response I don't quite hear as I drift off to sleep.

When I wake, I'm back in his bedroom, clinging onto him like a koala bear. I take a less codependent position in the bed as he continues to sleep. Based on the orange tint of the light pouring through the bathroom window, it's sunrise. Bruce perks up on his bed, wagging his tail anxiously, but settles obediently when I wave a hand at him.

It's clear that I'm not going to be able to fall back to sleep, but not wanting to cause a raucous with the behemoth of a dog, I settle in, my back to Will, gazing out at the backyard. The sprinklers have just started.

I had very low expectations for myself today, but resisting the urge to gaze at him while he sleeps (which I really, really want to do), I run through the few items I had hoped to accomplish: at least a small batch of groceries, bills, and now I probably need to claim the last of my belongings from the house. Honestly, if he suggests lying in bed all day, the rest is moot.

I feel movement on the silky cotton sheets and soon I'm being spooned. He kisses his way from my shoulder to my cheek before I turn onto my back to look at him.

"I love that you're here," he says, studying my face with a look of admiration that, for a time, I never thought I'd see again outside of my dreams.

I take a deep breath, smiling up at him. "You must be weight training if you managed to carry me through the house a second time."

"Not saying much. Even with a pasta dinner in you." He runs his fingers along my arm, which I have draped across my stomach. His eyes pause over my NASA shirt and he grins.

"What--you don't like my shirt? You had years to toss it, Mercer. I'm afraid now you'll simply have to deal with it."

"Just the opposite. Everything about this moment is perfect. *Including* that shirt."

My stomach takes the opportunity to growl loudly. I cringe. "Perfection is a tough thing to live up to."

"Depends on what you consider perfect," he says, leaning in close and kissing me.

My stomach groans again.

"Okay, now you're just being rude."

I laugh--until he tugs up my shirt. I know what he sees is far from perfection--several rough surgical scars, one only a couple months healed, making a tic tac toe looking gameboard around my belly button.

I'm about to confirm aloud about the state of my abdomen when he leans down and kisses my newest scar, running his fingers over the line. He kisses the other scars, though with more brevity as he moves up the length of my body to kiss my lips.

Another growl.

"Oh fine then," he says firmly to my stomach. "Let's feed you." His expression softens into a smile immediately upon making eye contact with me. "Breakfast."

I change into a pair of my running shorts I missed last night and an aqua blue v-neck t-shirt. I used to wear it for its curve-hugging quality, but now hangs off me sloppily. We go out to his truck where the plaid blanket is still on the bench seat.

"Wow, it was only like 15 hours ago I fell asleep in here, right? I didn't go into a short coma?"

He tosses the blanket to the back seat, smirking.

"What's that face?"

"You talk in your sleep." He backs out of the garage and starts driving west.

"Yeah? Well come on. Out with it."

"You told me I smell like laundry and Christmas trees." He smiles. "I took that as a compliment," he adds.

"It was." I sigh. His neighborhood has an abundance of sycamores that give the illusion that we're much further outside the city than we actually are. I observe a couple out for a walk in the brisk morning with a pair of enthusiastic Goldendoodles. "What else did I say?"

"You liked my bed. You said something about there not being clouds softer than the pillows in all the kingdoms, not even in Narnia."

"I loved those books."

"Apparently. Then you said some sort of war chant, seeking out soft pillows 'for Narnia and for Aslan!'" He flails his arm out dramatically.

"Now you're just making stuff up."

He shook his head. "Scout's honor. I may have added the gesture. I feel like I'm missing out. I can only imagine all the funny things you think and don't say."

"A lot of useless literary and movie references up there. Science and math trivia."

"You can't manage to be dull, can you Mercer? Not even when you're sleeping."

The restaurant he chose is situated at the end of a strip mall and features pretty little sunflower stems situated in mason jars and chalkboard surface tables.

"This does not look like your type of place," I whisper to him at the outdoor hostess stand.

"I ate here with my parents when they came to town. My mom's friend raved about it."

"So it's good then."

"Mhmm," he murmurs.

The young hostess introduces herself as our server and Will requests a table on the outside porch. As we walk the short distance, he reaches for my hand, squeezes gently. He helps me with my chair and takes his own seat.

She's watching me a little closer than I'd expect as she hands us our menus. "You know, I'm not sure I'd ever be brave enough to go so short with my hair."

It takes me a second to realize she means me. I still have the habit of wearing a hat, but it didn't occur to me to wear one this morning. My hand flies up to assess the level of bedhead.

"I have a couple friends with pixies. Yours is super short, but it's so cute. You have a good face for it. Some girls--it just *does not* work. They just look--" She glances around, then whispers: "*butch*. I know that's not PC, but you know what I mean. You totally pull it off. You've got soft, pretty features."

I feel my cheeks flush. "Thank you, Tarryn."

Will is grinning at me over his menu. "Yes, thank you, Tarryn."

"Have you always kept your hair short?"

"No, up until last year I always had long hair."

"No *way*. I bet that was an adjustment."

"A bit."

She turns to Will. "Did you two know each other when her hair was long?"

"We did."

"And what'd you think when she went short? My boyfriend is totally against me chopping mine short."

Will makes eye contact with me, a little flabbergasted by her enthusiasm about hair. "I thought she still looked like the girl I love."

Tarryn waves her hand out as though dismissing the conversation. "I'm sorry. I just have a hair fixation right now. Did you two want coffee? Juice? Water?"

"You have the full coffee bar, right?" he asks.

"We sure do."

"May I get an iced latte?"

"For you, Miss?"

"Blended mocha, no whip please."

"Oh I really recommend the whip. We make it fresh here. I made them up myself this morning. One is vanilla, the other is hazelnut. It's amazing."

"Reeves, I think I'm going to have to insist you get a sizable whipped cream dollop."

"Fine. I'll take whip on mine."

"Sounds good. I'll be back with those in a few. Oh, we do have a couple specials this morning: SoCal Eggs Benedict--traditional Benedict, but spinach replaces the ham and it's topped with avocado slices. Comes with hashbrowns. And cinnamon swirl pancakes served with your choice of bacon, sausage or tofu-bacon."

Will thanks her and she departs. He peers over at me and smiles. "I can't tell you how nice it was to wake up to your soft, pretty features this morning, Reeves."

I roll my eyes, but my cheeks are tight. I run my hand over my short hair, which does feel considerably less stubbly from the last time I took notice.

He folds his menu conclusively. "So I do need to tell you something--I'm supposed to go to Portland tonight."

"*Oh*--what's in Portland?"

"A hiking/camping trip with some military guys. We met through the PTS group. They plan something like it a couple times per year."

"That's pretty neat."

"I had the plans made in January, before we got back in touch. Before—"

"Everything else."

He frowns.

"What?"

"Well I wouldn't sum it up like that."

"How would you put it then?"

He takes a breath, gazing across the parking lot. "*Everything*."

"You realize that's literally one word less than what I said."

He smiles. "Yes. Words are not my strong suit. One day I will put the life affirming feeling of having you in my life into words."

"*That* was pretty good."

His playful eyes study me. "I'll do better."

"So, how long are you away?"

"Until next weekend."

A week without him holding me. A week without seeing his dimpled smile. I shake off the sadness, but he's seen it.

"I'll stay."

"No. You should definitely go. It sounds like a great trip. Are you going to have time to visit *Twilight* filming locations?" I start rearranging the sugars to give myself something to do.

He raises his eyebrows.

"I'm fine." I peruse the menu with more determination. "I'm good." I bug out my eyes. "Wow, I went codependent really quick. That's a new sensation for me."

"Of all the words I'd pick to describe you, 'codependent' isn't one of them."

"That's comforting. You were asleep when I woke up wrapped around you like a pretzel."

"Sorry I missed that. You can feel free to demonstrate that technique again. Soon, I hope."

I start scanning the menu again, but he grabs a piece of chalk, starts sketching something on the chalkboard table.

Tarryn returns with our coffee drinks, peering over Will's shoulder at his drawing. "Are you ready to order?"

They both look to me. I order the Pacific Benedict, rubbing my bare arms to warm up. Will glances to find the description--smoked salmon on an english muffin topped with poached eggs, hollandaise and avocado with a side of hashbrowns. He seems to approve and orders himself a steak and veggie omelet.

"I'll be right back," he says once she leaves. He walks out to his truck and returns quickly with his North Face jacket. It's slightly overshooting the current weather situation, but still a considerable improvement.

"Thank you, Will."

As he sits, he grabs a couple different pieces of colored chalk. "You didn't peek, did you?"

"No, I was taking in the surroundings."

He glances up at me a few times as he sketches.

I take a sip of my coffee. "Oh my. This is amazing."

He nods. "Told ya."

I take another swig. "Who are you having take care of Batman?"

He smirks slightly.

"Yeah, I see what you're saying. *Bruce*."

"He has a pet sitter."

"Did you want me to just watch him? Think he'd like the boat?"

"I think he'd love it, but I'd have to pay her anyway canceling this late. Plus I'm sure you had plans for the week, Reeves."

Get my things from the house, grocery shop, work on getting my career back on track, laundry, and I really could use some downtime. If I get any surplus energy, I'd love to go for a paddle. Where would he poop and pee anyway? I'd have to haul his food out to the boat. Unless I stayed at his house, but that seems oddly too soon. We were engaged before so what's the starting point here? It's not like square one dating.

"No need to get the hamster wheel turning so fast. Thank you for offering." He smudges something on the drawing, then sets the chalk down. "I borrowed one of your coping mechanisms."

"Oh you did?"

"You're far better, but I still feel like I get a therapeutic benefit from it."

I crane my neck and see a very intricate sketch of my face. He's put a hibiscus covering my ear (explaining that he struggles drawing ears), offset by short, pokey hair. I'm pretty sure my eyes don't have quite that much glint to them and my lips aren't quite as full, but he is remarkably talented. "That's incredible. Could you always draw that well?"

"I never tried drawing people when I was younger. Except for stick figures. Most of those were doing something violent, or otherwise inappropriate."

"You never realized how well you draw?"

"Don't get too impressed--I'm not that great at drawing most people. In my first attempts you looked like some sort of alien species. At this point, I've had quite a bit of practice." He smiles kindly. "You could say I've experienced a little codependence of my own."

"Well that--" I frown because Tarryn has placed the ketchup on top of my sketched face. "*Was* amazing."

"Bon appetit," Tarryn says, putting our plates before us.

He moves the ketchup bottle to the left, satisfied that it didn't destroy the drawing. "What did you have planned for today?"

"Grocery shopping."

"Well, I'm in."

"Seriously? I can put it off until tomorrow."

"My flight's at 4. We can eat, go get groceries, have lunch at the marina. It'll be a food-centered day."

"I can drive you to the airport if you'd like--"

"One of the other guys is swinging by to pick me up. He has a commuter pass for parking."

I nod slowly.

"Tell me."

I feel my breathing get more shallow, but I try to casually cut into breakfast. "Try this. I've added it to my top five breakfasts of all time."

He indulges me in taking a bite after I insistently put my fork in front of his face. "Definitely top five."

I charge forth in conversation and breakfast indulgence and he doesn't question my earlier hesitation.

Before I know it, he's dropping me off next to John's real estate sign at the house [not my preference]. I realized once we got to the marina with the groceries that I had left my Jeep there before the transfusion. I even suggested I get an Uber just to avoid having him take me there himself.

John is at the house, his silver, German-made sedan parked in the driveway, which puts me further on edge and eliminates any chance of resolving the awkwardness of breakfast. Will shifts into Park. "Is that *Nathan?*"

"John, the evil twin."

"I'll go in with you."

"No, that won't go over well. Plus you have a plane to catch, Mountain Man."

"Will he lift the boxes for you?"

"I'll be fine. It's not that much to get."

"OK, *alternatives*: you drop me off then you can take the truck and come back when he's not here."

Tempting. "I'm a big girl. I can deal with John. Just kiss me, go on your wilderness explorer trip, be safe, and miss me a lot."

"I can handle that." He leans across the cab, gazing intently in my eyes before kissing me. His hands brace the sides of my face. "I love you."

I smile lightly. "I love you, too."

I drop out of the truck and wait for him to pull away. As soon as he does, John emerges from the open garage door, where my Jeep is staged like a hostage, blocked by his car. I walk the length of the driveway, trying to seem confident, while also realizing I never put on a hat. Fortunately, this fact seems to be disarming him.

"Hi John. I like the shirt," I say as I reach the garage. Actually I do. His wife tends to force him to wear metrosexual colors like salmon and peach. Today he's wearing a tame neutral blue.

"Maggie. Thanks for coming over. Nathan said you had a procedure yesterday so I would have understood if you couldn't."

"Didn't want to hold things up."

"What did you have--uh--*done?*"

"Butt implants."

I step by him and see I've successfully flustered him.

"I'm kidding." I let him release a laugh, then continue being obnoxious: "That's next week. But Nate said you got familiar with my panties so we're close now, John."

"Sorry--that was probably crossing a line. I didn't--I mean, I just put them in a box."

"Yesterday was a blood transfusion."

"Oh. What is that?"

"They remove several pints of my blood and replace it with donor blood."

"Really? Wow. Can your body reject it, like an organ?"

"I suppose so. So far so good." I find a couple stacked boxes with my name written in Sharpie on the side. "This should be it then?"

"Yeah. You didn't seem to have much left."

"No, not really."

"But you've been staying here?"

"Off and on."

His eyes motion to the empty street.

"My boat," I clarify. "I was doing some work on it and I was up in Monterey while my friend had a baby."

He nods. "Was that--"

"Will."

"Right. *Will.*"

"Crossing a line again, John."

"It just figures."

"This will be fascinating. *What* figures?"

"Nathan really tried to make it work, but you were fixated on the one that got away."

He's walking back into the house so I have to chase him down. "Is that the story Nathan is going with?"

"Seems pretty true to me."

"You know, here I thought Nathan was taking some sort of high road, but since he's playing the martyr, have you met a woman named Tori yet?"

His expression confirms my suspicion.

"When did they start dating again?"

"August."

Yeah, try again. "March." *That's when she started at the company and that's when he started up a weird little techie relationship with her. Just before my surgery.* "I tried, John. You know I haven't been in the best of places, but I tried to keep him at least *satisfied.*" I pause for effect. "I didn't even cross paths with Will until summer. I was committed to Nathan, despite the fact that neither one of us loved the other. For reasons I'm not going into, at the point Will reappeared, up until a couple weeks ago, I thought *he* was married and therefore, off limits. But seeing him did jarr my senses and I realized I wasn't going to be with someone who doesn't love me. So I told Nathan we were getting divorced. I didn't leave him for Will. I left him for myself." I've winded myself.

John seems riveted.

"Oh and I met Nathan roughly 9 *hours* before I wound up pregnant."

"That is *not* what he told the family."

"Noticing a theme here. Well *I* don't have a reason to lie to you, John. I couldn't care less what you or your parents or your uppity sister think of me. As for Nathan's new girlfriend, I suspected he had cheated, but honestly I had been so depressed that I didn't care. He claims nothing happened in those 4 months, but check her Instagram and judge for yourself."

He frowns.

"I allowed myself a bit too much curiosity there. Ignorance would have been better." He was spending 'business trips' at her apartment. He was telling her he loved her, writing her poetry I didn't quite understand because I'm not into fantasy fiction/gaming references. She was taking photos of his writings and posting them. "She uses far too many emojis for my taste, but to each their own."

He shakes his head. "What a shithead."

"Yeah I think I referenced him in that way when I saw Instagram."

"Not him. *Me.* I'm sorry for being an ass to you."

"That's a bit harsh."

"You've been through a lot."

I shrug. "Whatever do you mean?"

He smirks, picking up on my sarcasm.

"I've got nothing but love for you, John. You're a good person. Your *sister*, on the other hand--" I raise an eyebrow.

"Say no more. If it makes you feel better, the new baby? Jaxson? Not Trey's."

"See, in my head I just called him Mr. Jenna."

"Yeah."

"Who's the dad?"

"A personal trainer at the gym."

I slump my shoulders. "That just makes me sad for the kids."

He smiles kindly, though somewhat unusually at me.

"Well I think we've made some excellent progress today, John," I say with faux propriety.

"Yeah, we established that my siblings are cheaters."

"Hey, I'm the last one who's going to judge someone based on their family. Truth be told, the claim that I was pining for the one who got away *was* an accurate statement." I sigh. "It was--not going to work. With Nathan. It wasn't ever going to work—especially after the babies died."

He winces at my choice of words.

"I probably shouldn't have aired his dirty laundry. It doesn't help anyone."

His focused expression makes me a bit uneasy. It also doesn't help that he's Nathan's twin, though he wears contacts and his hair is volumized and styled, which helps my brain differentiate. Nathan keeps his hair short and appears to have drawn the short genetic straw for premature hair loss.

"Well I should get going," I conclude.

He helps me load the boxes of clothes that are still a couple sizes too big and follows me around to the driver's door. "I guess we'll cross paths at close of escrow."

"No."

"No? Oh that's right, you're not listed on the house. Is he just going to wire you your half of the profits? We'll want to make sure the paperwork has that detail."

"We already resolved the financials. Nathan gets whatever the profit is from the house. We only had it a little over a year."

"Maggie, house values skyrocketed. He's looking to make a $50,000 profit. Easily."

I shrug. "Good for Nathan then." I wonder if Nathan lied to him about that part, too, but it doesn't really matter.

"This is strange, Maggie. I have to say goodbye, but it feels like I'm just meeting you."

I shrug. "While I don't care what you think of me--and I don't mean any offense by that whatsoever--it does feel a bit better that you don't think I'm a horrible person."

He laughs lightly. "I never thought you were a horrible person, Maggie." He smiles toward something in the distance.

"Well *that* was a lie."

"No *really*, Maggie. I never thought that about you." He looks sincere--and a bit sad. "Will--he's a lucky man."

I drive to the coast feeling blissful contentment intertwined with conflicting, but deeply-rooted anxiety. It's a grueling emotional battle. When I park at the marina, I find a text from Will. First an old photo, one I'd never seen before. His mother must have taken it one day when we walked home together. I was maybe 7--I had chopped my bangs in rebellion just before my birthday and they were just growing in--and he was 9. He was holding my hand, but bowing, as though to royalty. Clearly in goofball Will fashion. Meanwhile, I was laughing and just very much enjoying the moment. The photo was followed by a message: "'*Once upon a time there was a boy who loved a girl, and her laughter was a question he wanted to spend his whole life answering.*'"

My shoulders drop in a surrenderous wonder. I gaze at the photo, my cheeks beaming.

Thanks to cloud storage, I start scrolling through old photos. I find one from the Halloween a few years back when we dressed up as Carl and Elle as kids from *Up* and write back: "*Whatever our souls are made of, his and mine are the same.*"

I smile, imagining his reaction. Assuming he's probably not going to respond right away, I slide out of the Jeep, take in the sight of the quiet marina. The clothes don't fit anyway so I leave them in the back, start down to the boat.

There's a delay, but a photo appears on my phone. It's another candid. Katie's wedding. Probably one captured by the photographer. It's the bouquet toss. I had been dragged out to the dance floor under the globe lights and palm trees. Despite some very eager middle aged aunts, I easily caught the bouquet one handed. The photo captured the moment that followed. I'm smiling, but clearly distraught from being thrust in the spotlight. It looks like the guys around Will are razzing him, but his eyes are on me and he has, dare I say, a mesmerized expression as I walked toward him. *Does he always look at me like that?*

"*You must allow me to tell you how ardently I admire and love you.*"

Soon after there is another photo of the setting sun through an airplane window, followed by a selfie of Will and another man, Josh I assume, intimately nudging their heads together pretending to sleep. I can just make out the shadow of Will's dimple.

I walk down to the boat, savoring the feeling of belonging. I belong here, a quirky and extraordinary place to live. I belong on that boat with a simple, indulgent yet healthy poke bowl dinner with stacks of books surrounding me. I knew the day I left Nathan that I had made the right decision. When I came back here for the first time--even with the mess of redoing the interior, I still didn't prefer to be anywhere else. I would have been satisfied with that arrangement, but my heart is invigorated thinking dreamily of Will again. Being able to think of him this way.

I belong in my life again.

The weight of a sudden thought hits me so hard I almost drop to my knees: *I belong in my life again, but what if I don't have a place in his anymore?* I feel such a separation from him in his life. It hasn't been that long, but so much has happened. He went through PTS, *is* going through PTS, and I have no knowledge of it whatsoever. He bought a house and is redoing it, all on his own. I always thought we'd go fix up a place together. We've spent time together, but it's not like I exist in his life in any other capacity anymore. I don't know his current friends, not even the man he's taking silly selfies with on the airplane. I missed so much. Will I be endlessly playing catch up or not understand references from the nearly 2 year gaping hole?

He's been a ghost in my life, observing its happenings, but anything new in that time is gone now. I don't have a new roster of friends for him to meet, a new side of myself to present. I'm literally just me.

I make my way to the boat, but I'm desperately trying to manage a deep, cleansing breath. The silence is deafening and the rocking sensation is dizzying. I feel alone. This living arrangement suddenly makes me feel ridiculous.

Breathe.

It's only a matter of time before Will realizes he hyped me up too much in his mind.

Breathe.

We weren't together all that much before the last deployment. He just didn't have enough time to realize he didn't actually love me.

I try Katie's number, but I get voicemail. Twice.

Probably sick of me.

She's married, gorgeous house, beautiful kids.

She's outgrown me.

I'm the only one who hasn't figured things out.

She's better off without me.

The pathetic friend who lives on a boat,

Because it's actually a practical, frugal, simplistic choice.

doesn't have a job,

There's no way you would have managed treatments, symptoms, surgeries and hold down that job. You're fortunate to have been able to do that, but you've been through so much. You will have a job.

doesn't take good enough care of herself.

You've been battling cancer. Take it easy on yourself. You will get healthy. You will get strong again.

It's your fault the babies died.

I clutch the countertop, attempt to gulp down air, but end up coughing.

It was the cancer. There was nothing you could do and no way you could have known.

You know the happiness you feel is temporary, right? You don't know how to be happy. You'll mess it up. You always do.

My phone buzzes in my hand. *"Reeves? My Spidey senses are tingling."*

If I even had a response in mind, my fingers are shaking like nothing I've ever seen. I'd never be able to type a message. I force a deep breath. I think of sitting up top, but the thought occurs to me that, the way I'm feeling, I could faint. Probably not a good idea to perch myself over water.

"Are you OK?"

I stare at his message.

Go to bed. Just lie down, close your eyes and force all thoughts from your head. Listen to the water.

I cross the living space and practically lunge for the cozy sleeping area. I crawl up to the pillows and it's obvious immediately that I'm not going to be able to sleep.

They're on the shelf. Go ahead. Two is prescribed. Take three. You need it.

I dump three sleeping pills into my hand and toss them into my throat. There's a stale, thankfully lidded cup of water and I cringe as I force the pills down.

15-45 minutes. Probably closer to 15. You'll only feel this way for a quarter of an hour. Breathe.

I lie back and focus on breathing. My phone buzzes to remind me I had gotten a text, then Will is calling.

I silence it, stumble through texting back: *"Looks like you're having a good time already. Enjoy the tri*p."

"Answer your phone, please."

It might be a placebo effect because it hasn't been long enough for it to work (although I'm a lightweight and I did take a dose and a half), or pressure to sound normal, but I've slowed my breathing. "Shouldn't you have taken off already?" My voice is constricted.

"There's a lineup on the runway."

"Oh okay."

"There's nothing going on with Josh, I assure you. He's not my type."

I nod. Pills are definitely kicking in already. I know he's joking. Ordinarily I'd have something witty to say in response.

Someone says something about airplane mode. "Reeves? They're making me store my phone. Are you OK? I had a very weird feeling all of a sudden before."

The porthole is blurring. "I'm OK. Just tired."

"I love you."

I think I say it back before hanging up.

Katie tries calling soon after and when I don't answer, texts: "Sorry I missed you. How are you?"

"I'll call in AM. Took sleep aid. Really working. Love you." There may have been some spelling errors.

My eyes flutter shut before I have a chance to set the phone down. The last thing I hear is the lapping of water against the side of the boat.

19

and I asked myself about the present: how wide it was, how deep it was, how much was mine to keep

When Katie answers, she's clearly having a battle of willpower with a toddler over whether he needs to wear clothes when they leave the house. Her greeting to me comes out: "Hey Mag—You need to put your underwear on this minute, young man."

"Bad day?"

"Just a typical morning," she sighs and I can see her dropping to one of the couches, a full laundry basket at her feet. "Thank God I still have a couple hours to pack."

"Where are you going?"

"Disneyland, but only if Trevor wears *clothes*." I hear a shrill "NO!" followed by a door slam. I knew they were going, but my memory has been unreliable lately.

"Do you need me to let you go?"

"Are you kidding? My mom has the babies, Trevor's pouting in his room. I have two minutes of peace and quiet. How are you?"

I picture three-year-old Trevor pulling all his books off the shelves.

"Mags?"

"Um, I'm not sure."

"Are you feeling okay? I'm sorry I haven't checked in this week—"

"Katie, I know about Will."

The quality of her voice tells me she's stood up. "What about him?" *Well that confirms that he didn't call her last night.*

"Everything. I think. Not married, no kid, my mother lied. The whole basis for me having a night of promiscuity was based on a lie. If I had waited it out, he would have been back."

"I didn't know what to do. Should I have told you when I found out? It was too late anyway--it seemed--mean? It would have been a lot to put on you."

"Maybe. I'm also getting divorced. I hadn't gotten to tell you yet." It all comes out as a pile up of words.

There's silence as she plays catch up. "You're getting divorced? When did this happen?"

"Filed in July. So actually the court-mandated 'cooling off period' is probably over. It might be finalized. Mazzeltov to me."

"Nathan is Jewish?"

I chuckle to myself. "No."

"You didn't have a chance to tell me in over 3 months that you were getting divorced? You were recovering from surgery at my house. We were laid up together for weeks."

"You're a meddler. You would have told Will. It would have been a weird dynamic, especially since he was 'married'." I frown. "I'm air quoting."

She sighs.

"Of course if I had you could have been able to tell me he wasn't married."

"Please don't be mad at me. It was really complicated circumstances."

"'I'm not mad. 'I'm just disappointed,'" I say in a proper, parental sounding voice.

"So does that mean--"

"No." I answered automatically and the response surprises me.

Silence again. "Is he dating someone?" She sounds annoyed with him.

"No," I say, but I don't like the pain it sparks in me. "Yes, we kind of--we're--_"

"Together?" Her voice goes up a few octaves.

"Calm down. I had an anxiety attack last night about this so let's not start monogramming towels."

"A tragedy leads to a misunderstanding. The two of you went on with your separate lives, always pining for the other, only to be reunited when the two of you both got diagnosed with cancer and were placed in the same treatment group. You thought he was married with a kid, but that was a lie built by your crazy mother. Now you both are available. Miraculously."

"Good recap."

"This is totally a Nicholas Sparks novel waiting to happen."

"He kills off a lot of characters, Katie."

"_The Notebook_ was sad when she had Alzheimer's, but they lived a long life together."

"OK that's true."

"I was upset at how detached their children were of her when they were old. They seemed ungrateful. Raise these kids and they just ditch you in a sad nursing home because you can't remember anything?"

"Katie? Focus."

"Have you confronted your mom yet? Does she know you're getting divorced? Or is it official by now?"

"Could be. I think Nathan would have emailed me the finalized documents 'for my files.'" I fall face down on the bed, forgetting about the hardcover book I left in the covers after waking at 4am. I nearly break my nose. "Katie?" I say, my hand cupped over my throbbing septum.

"I'm here. Wait, were you serious about having an anxiety attack?"

"Yes. Full blown. It's when I called you."

"What did you do? Did you call Will? Was he there?"

"He's camping."

"He's *camping*?" She sounds annoyed with him again. "Why--So you two are really back together if you know--"

"Katie?"

"Focus, OK."

"I talked myself down with things you probably would have said, if you were more reliable."

"I'm sorry--"

"I was kidding. I tried breathing. Finally I just decided to pharmaceutically knock myself out." I can't cry, though my eyes are tearing up from the stinging in my nose. I need my friend. I need her words, her presence. I need her opinions. In person. "Katie, I need you."

"How do you feel about Mickey Mouse?"

"I can't crash your family vacation."

"Yes. Yes you can. Please come. It's a flreunion with all of Tim's family. Of course you can."

"How many Norrises will there be?"

"53."

"So you're going to sell me as a second cousin no one remembers?"

"There are matching shirts. You'll blend."

"What color?"

"Neon green—as to be gender inclusive."

"Flattering."

"You can stay with us. We have a family suite, plenty of beds. It's at the California Grand--whatever-- hotel."

"But I'm collecting points at Best Western."

"For someone supposedly recovering from an anxiety attack, you are surprisingly quick-witted."

"That's a swanky place."

"I know, right?" She does and she doesn't. She doesn't come from money, but she's grown accustomed to Tim's corporate attorney salary plus bonuses. "Please come. You can come for the whole week. Please. We never get to spend time together. You can spend time with your Godson and your niece."

I feel guilty I can't reciprocate with a "niece" or "nephew" for her. When she got married and pregnant right away (or perhaps preemptively), I think she felt alone, moving to that stage long before anyone else our age. Then when Will and I got engaged, she suddenly burst out with her hopes and dreams (for our friendship), that we (Will and I) could move to Monterey and when we had kids, we could raise them with their kids, we could do play dates, vacations, and maybe our kids would be best friends. She was thrilled when I got pregnant, not exactly with the situation--She questioned me about my lingering feelings about Will a lot, checking in, making sure she shouldn't hide the sharp objects—but she couldn't hide her excitement about the prospect of raising our kids together. Nathan was well off, which meant I could have the flexibility not to work, come visit her and she could visit me.

I got the feeling Tim might have said something to her to drop the kids talk after I lost the babies. She took it to the extreme and stopped mentioning her kids at all. When Trevor broke his arm, I heard about it from my mother, who saw on Facebook that he had just gotten his cast off. Reading the ignorance of the incident on my face, she had remarked about me being a hermit and not having any friends.

This resulted in the only argument I ever remember having with Katie.

"Are you still there?"

"Yeah, sorry."

"Oh I thought I lost you. Reception is horrible in the house. So will you come?"

I'll probably have to get my bedtime in check if I was sharing a room with a three-year-old. "Are you sure it's okay with Tim?"

I hear dialing in my ear.

"Katie?"

"Please hold."

"Honey, I'm in a conference call at the moment, can I call you back?" Tim's gruff voice says in his gentle way.

"Tim, Maggie's in crisis and she's afraid to crash Disneyland without your approval."

"Hi, Tim."

"Hi, Mags. Are you okay?"

"Of course she's not okay; that's why she needs a vacation."

"Tim, I'm kind of in a bad place emotionally. I could use some time with your wife. Nothing kinky. Talking and sobbing uncontrollably mainly."

Silence. Then: "That's not an acceptable resolution."

"The sobbing should be temporary."

"Sorry about that, CEO went rogue. Yeah, the more the merrier. We'd love to see you. Three months, 24/7 was not nearly enough."

"*Tim.*"

"Maggie, you are a joy. Please come along."

"See, Maggie?"

"Was that all you needed from me?" *Poor Tim.*

"Yes, that's all. See you later. Trevor's still refusing to wear clothes."

"I'm fine if he wants to run around naked, just as long as he doesn't start wearing dresses."

"I am limiting him to traditional gender role clothing."

"Excellent. Gotta go. Love you."

"Love you."

"Love you," I add, just so I don't feel left out.

Click.

"So it's settled. We're getting there tonight around 5. We're just going to get settled, go to one of the parks at night for a parade or fireworks."

***

The Grand Californian Resort & Spa is way too rich for most people, particularly someone without a job. I'm going into debt against my own trust account, accessible for any type of expenses when I turn 25. I do wonder if I could qualify this trip as mental health related and make a withdrawal. I feel rather out of place and inferior rolling in there with my scuffed up luggage (the scuffs carrying the memories of those flights to see Will overseas), despite the presence of fanny packs and mouse ear hats.

In the center lounge area, there are about three dozen neon green shirts. I search them for my dear, sweet, short friend, but the color of the shirts and the contrast with the black text, as well as the vastness of the lobby, is having a disorienting effect.

"Auntie Mags!" Trevor shouts, barreling down the ramp from the guestroom corridor. Tim is casually following behind with Savannah perched on his shoulders.

I crouch down and Trevor crashes into me.

With the familiar voice, Katie quickly separates from the crowd and rushes over, clasping a tiny baby to her chest.

"Oh I'm so happy you're here!" She says, tugging Trevor away and passing me Zoe in one fluid motion. "You know what I mean."

While I'm a little thrown off by the maneuver, I feel my blood pressure drop as soon as I inhale her soft, fuzz covered head. "It's a wonder they don't market a fragrance called 'new baby smell'."

"I swear my nasal passages are tainted from poopy diapers. Once you get to baby 3, you just don't soak in as much."

I frown, cradle Zoe a little tighter. "You smell just as sweet as your brother and sister did," I whisper, kissing her head, while Katie passes something to Tim's sister.

Tim wraps one arm around me. "You look like you've put on weight even since we saw you last," he remarks.

"Tim!" Katie shrieks.

"What? She needs to. It's a compliment."

Katie examines my face. "Yeah, actually your face doesn't have the hollow look it had when you stayed with us."

I shrug, kiss Zoe on the cheek. "I have a linebacker's appetite sometimes. That helps."

"Then you should definitely come to the character breakfast we have on Sunday. At least you'll get your money's worth."

"*Timothy.*"

"Unlike 'I'll have a Greek yogurt, berries, and some egg whites' over here." He motions to Katie.

"I probably should mix in some Katie eating habits. You don't get her abs from eating waffles."

"6 weeks postpartum." Katie flashes a small part of her stomach and I whistle at her.

"She sneaks Reese's."

"Still?" I whisper back. "I thought that was a pregnancy thing."

He furrowed his brow purposefully down at me, his arm around me. "You're on your way to being healthy, second wife. Now we just have to get you to being happy."

I savor the bond with Tim for a moment, smile tightly at him. "You really are a catch, Timothy."

He crooks an eyebrow, doubtfully.

"You're going to be OK watching the kids?" Katie asks suddenly.

"You're going to introduce us first, right?" Tim replies, releasing me. "Wait, what's *your* name again?" He says, shaking Trevor's arm. "Cody? No, Rex. That's it!"

"Very funny. I'll go get the diaper bag," Katie says, crossing the lobby to get the plaid bag from one of the couches.

As we wait, he puts his arm around my shoulder again, pulls me into a sideways hug. "You deserve to be happy, you know."

"It's that easy? Just be happy?"

"Yeah. Pretty much. You love him? *Yeah* you do."

I look over at him out the corner of my eye.

"Can I give you some stolen advice?"

"By all means."

"The warden's coming back so I'll be quick. Thoughts are like waves. You can't keep them from coming, but you can choose which ones to surf."

"That was deep."

"Stolen advice. Do *not* quote me as the originator of that quote. Just go be happy. Or move by us and be happy. Don't tell the wife this, but when you're around, she's way nicer to me."

"Oh God, Tim. I had no idea it had gotten so bad."

He grins. "Be happy, Maggie O. We love you," he concludes, kissing my temple.

***

Tim has taken the kids to watch a parade so Katie and I can talk. We're sitting at a bistro table on the patio in Downtown Disney. It's in-between lunch and dinner and the waiter is a little peeved that he's having to stay in the dining area just to refill our water glasses. I decide it must be a non-Disney owned restaurant. Cast members are far better at masking their contempt for guests. I catch him before he leaves the table and order spinach dip without knowing if there's spinach dip on the menu and this perks him up. He offers to bring a drink menu, a bit more optimistic that his potential tip will be worth the effort.

Katie looks concerned, but I'm not sure if it's because she disapproves of my appetizer choice, dietary restrictions and all. "I don't want to bring up a bad subject, but I think you should know something." She runs her finger along her glass, wipes off a column of condensation. "When you and Will came to visit us before he got deployed, he and I had a talk."

"What kind of talk?"

"Well your family can't be relied on for such things so I filled in for the 'If you hurt her, I'll hunt you down and make it look like an accident' talk."

I laugh, thinking of little Katie laying down the law for Will. Pregnant. Actually, that might be intimidating, but considering her slight frame and the fact that she stands just over five feet and Will's six-two, the image is comical. "What did you say to him?"

"I told him that you're family. You might not share our blood, but you're a part of us. We think the world of you."

"What did he say?"

"Nothing I didn't already know, but I wanted to hear the words come from him. The part I was getting to was—" she pauses, watching a family of 6, including 4 little boys passes by below.

"Do you think they just keep trying for a girl?" I ask.

She laughs awkwardly, shakes herself from her thought. "Maybe." She frowns. "I really want to try for another boy."

I smile since this is not a secret like her reddened cheeks would suggest. She had shared this plan with me months ago and Tim had mentioned her plan almost immediately upon bringing home Zoe. "Pretty sure Tim will do anything to make you happy."

She looked up at me, a smile slowly creeping across her lips. "Will would do anything for you, too."

I sigh, rub at my face roughly. "You were telling me something. You were giving him the 'if you hurt her' speech."

"Yeah yeah. I wanted to see what he would say in response."

There's a pause as our ice waters are refilled and we're once again asked if we'd like a specialty cocktail.

"He said how in awe he is of you. I remember this part—he described an apocalyptic movie where basically everything is rubble."

I laugh. "Is that a compliment? My life is rubble? Wait--am I the rubble?"

"No. You're the flower poking through the rubble." She pauses to take a sip of water and a supplement of some kind.

"He said that?"

"He did. 'The good and the beauty that should never have survived.'"

A guitarist is getting situated for an evening performance across the courtyard. I gaze in his direction as he tunes the strings, one leg extended out, drawing my attention to his cowboy boot.

"He loved me, didn't he?"

"*Loves*. He *loves* you. Present tense. Good Lord, woman. What does the man have to do to prove that to you?"

I laugh and wipe at my eyes.

She shrugs. "Actually, when you first told me about him back in high school, I had my doubts. But it took about 10 seconds of seeing the two of you together to know. I could feel it." She takes another sip of her drink. "Of course then he majorly screwed up."

"He did."

"But he really swept you off your feet when he came back in the picture."

"Yeah, you were supposed to be preoccupied being Bridezilla--not playing matchmaker."

She smirks. "I knew you hadn't gotten over him and when he called me out of the blue to get your number, it just felt right."

"You just *had* to invite my mother."

"She RSVP'd regrets."

"Well that's rude."

She shrugs. "She didn't end up coming so no harm done." Katie freezes. "Except for—"

I wave her off.

"Oh my God, I am Bridezilla. Was I really bad?"

I grin. "You still managed to play matchmaker—so, no. Is that why you kept me from going to the spa with you?"

She winces.

"Wow."

"I'm sorry. I felt so bad, but you needed a chance to run into each other."

I process this. "Actually that does make me feel better."

"So your mom just showed up, saw the two of you and left?"

"After smacking me across the face."

"Oh that's right."

I picture the scene. The bubble surrounding Will and me felt peaceful and happy and content. I looked up and it was like a wave of red rage approaching. "I still remember the look in her eyes when she saw me with him."

"What made her dislike him so much? You two were friends growing up, right?"

"She didn't realize how much time we spent together. He'd stay over without her knowing."

"Oh *really?*"

"When we were kids. It was when she and Ray were having their fights—it wasn't every fight since they happened so often, but some."

"So did she find out? Is that why she hated him?"

"No. And she didn't hate *him*. It was me she hated."

"No, Maggie. Your mom does a lot of things to make it seem that way, but she does love you."

"She tried to have an affair with Will's dad."

"Wait, *what?* When?"

"Before I met you."

"Why?" She doesn't seem certain it's the right question.

"She was under the impression she would have had a long marriage if my dad hadn't died. She clinged to that idea and she hated anyone who had a longer marriage."

"So why *him?* Did they even know each other that well?"

"No. She always made sure to keep their conversations short."

"So then why?"

"Because she thought I preferred Will's mom to her. She either a) thought she'd break up their marriage and maybe my friendship so she wouldn't have to deal with these feelings of inadequacy, or b) she thought he'd go through with it and it would prove--something about her being better than Will's mom. Or c) misery loves company and she couldn't stand the idea of me being happy."

"You've put some thought into this."

"I'd like to take full credit, but some of the analysis is courtesy of a licensed mental health professional."

"Oh. I didn't know you were seeing someone?"

"I haven't. Just my spiritual counselor slash pastor. Courtesy of you."

She laughs lightly. "I'm glad he's helping."

"I'm a challenge for him. I brought up that song *Jesus Take the Wheel?*"

"*Yes.* Such a good song."

"I joked that if I said that, Jesus would take a look at my life and go: 'Giiiiirl, you're on your own.'"

"You know that's not how it works with our Lord and Savior."

"Yes, I know that, Katie."

"So how did you find out? About Will's dad?"

"Ray. He used it as ammunition in one of their fights and told me about it."

"When was this?"

"When I found out? I was 12." The night I ran to his house, crashed into his chest, not caring what his parents thought of me, not even considering that his dad was standing right there. All I could think of was losing his friendship, losing him. I remember the heartache I felt as he wrapped his arms around me and whispered: *You're not alone.* It struck something deep within me, knowing how genuine he was in what he said, but tremendous sadness knowing it would be inevitable that a wedge would be driven between us. That I would lose him. That'd I'd be alone.

"That's sick."

I nod, distracted by reeling thoughts. *I drove the wedge between Will and me. My mother's actions were wrong, but his parents didn't treat me differently and Will didn't know. I distanced myself on purpose. Because I didn't deserve him. I didn't deserve to be happy.* "Ray told me she blamed me for—my dad."

Katie appears to be silently using expletives. "Excuse me?"

I shake my head. "I know I'm not—" I can't finish the sentence. "I know I'm not," I reaffirm.

"You do?" Her eyebrows are raised, ready to convince me.

"Yes."

Her shoulders relax a bit.

I'm pondering if it's worth telling her that I drove the wedge during our childhood when she asks:

"Does Will know? About her trying to—" Her face pinches in disgust.

"If he does, he hasn't told me. I got the scholarship after that and switched schools so we saw less of each other, but I think subconsciously I distanced myself."

"Did she say anything?"

"When you and I became friends, she would say how glad she was that I was spending time with 'real friends.'"

"So she was *really* not happy when you two started seeing each other again."

"Which time?"

"Oh that's true. You two have had your starts and stops."

"I'd say between the two, she was probably more upset at your wedding."

"What set her off?"

"We were feeding each other bites of breakfast."

"Okay?"

"After a really blissful night of making love?"

"Were you advertising this in some way?"

"Oh we were really, *really* obnoxious in our happiness."

Katie smiles.

I'm momentarily distracted by how my body responded to his touch that night. How he had kissed every part of my body. How he had held my face in his hands and gazed into my eyes after.

The scene is snapped away by another--by a fiery anger in my mother's emerald eyes, the resolved determination in her gait as she rushed toward me, the pain that surged through my cheek as she smacked me. "She told me that I wasn't her daughter."

Her mouth fell slightly ajar. "That's a terrible thing to say."

I thought I saw a shimmer of regret in my mother's eyes as she said those words, like she knew this time she might actually live to regret them. "Oh she used that one all the time."

"Talk about instilling feelings of conditional love and abandonment."

I raise an eyebrow.

"I minor'd in Psych."

There hadn't been much else to the incident. She saw us. She barreled toward me and slapped me across the face. Due to the blast, I had put an elbow in my plate and the food had dumped in my lap. This had distracted me long enough for Will to stand and put himself between us, saying nothing. I couldn't see Will's face, but she had immediately taken two steps backward, glaring at him. She had told me I wasn't her daughter, biting words said through gritted teeth, and she had walked away. Ray waited in shock on the outside of the restaurant patio.

Will waited until he saw them enter the back entrance of the hotel lobby before turning to me. He lightly touched my cheekbone.

I tried to speak, but the words kept getting suctioned into my erratic gulps of air. And then his arms were around me, not caring that the food grease that had ruined my outfit was now also ruining his. He spoke to the waiter behind me, asking him to charge to his room number. The waiter had waved him off, told him to just take care of me.

I was trembling, I remember, as he led me out to the grassy hill that overlooked the pool area and the vast ocean beyond. He had given me space to breathe, but continued to hold my hand. I stared out at the gleaming horizon and steadied my breathing. From where we stood, I could see the area of the pool near the bar where he found me the day before. I smiled reflectively. The breeze tossed my hair as I looked back to the ocean and watched a catamaran floating a hundred yards off shore. I had glanced over my shoulder at him then, taking in the patient affection in his eyes, and I felt an incredible sense of peace.

My heart writhed a bit remembering how my mother seemed to thrive when I suffered, how she seemed validated in a way. I wince. "Her other favorite phrase was: 'Just wait until—'" I look up at Katie "--just wait until you have kids who do this.' 'You just wait. Wait until *you* have a husband who dies. Just wait. See how you handle it.'"

Katie's jaw slowly fell open. "What the fu--?"

That's when our spinach dip arrives and server quickly departs.

"Was she wishing it upon you? I mean, come on. You lost your dad. Isn't that enough?"

I shrug.

"Listen, you need to erase anything your mother ever told you from your mind. Please don't base any decision or opinion on a threat from her. She was wrong. She was wrong on so many levels. More than even I knew."

I'm on a roll; I decide to air everything.

"I had a younger sister. Well, I don't know if she actually knew if it was a boy or girl, but she always said it was a sister."

"What? Maggie, I have known you *how long?*"

I really do feel like an episode of Maury. "My mom was pregnant when my dad died. She had a miscarriage at 12 weeks." I swallow.

"My God, you were 6. And she told you this?"

"A few years later she did. She said maybe her second daughter wouldn't have been so defiant. Maybe she would have respected her. I back-talked her, told her it wasn't fair to make me compete." I pause to take a gulp so I can get the rest out. "'Wait until you have a baby that dies,' she said. 'Then you can talk to me about what's fair and what's not.'"

I stare at the table, at the spinach dip uneaten in the blue ceramic dish surrounded by heaps of tri-color tortilla chips. There's a cloud of steady heat seeping out of the top. "I guess I have a say about fairness now. Times two."

She exhales. "You know what my thoughts are about her *without* knowing all this—would you like to change the subject?"

"Yes, please," I say without looking up.

"How did you find out that Will isn't married?"

I find myself smiling, despite having tears streaming from my eyes. I see him peering across the table from me at breakfast, carefully sketching my portrait. *Will.*

The beach serenade. The fact that Will does everything with a purpose. His choice of words so that he never actually contributed to the lie. "It never sat well with me. I guess I started to figure it out as soon as I spent some time with him. I kept telling myself I was in denial or something. Then I ran into Cadence."

She gulps. "Say what now?"

"The aquarium. She was there. She didn't know it was me, but I recognized her. She was on the phone talking to Evan--I connected the dots."

"You didn't let on. To us."

"I had a new niece to meet. She was more important."

"You amaze me, Mags."

"Why?"

"All things considered, you are incredibly well-adjusted."

"I had a panic attack last night."

"Overdue."

I raise my eyebrows in reluctant agreement. "Why did I believe the lie so easily? I should have known better."

"I think your mom knew what buttons to press. She set the land mines so she knew how to trigger them." She pauses to devour a chip. "Tim says she's an emotional terrorist."

I snort in my water glass and this makes her smile. "I adore Tim, I really do."

"That's before knowing all this other stuff. He reads people really well. He should have been a prosecutor." She wipes her mouth firmly with her napkin. "Your mother did a total number on you your entire life. She went through a lot with losing your dad, but she should have gotten counseling. Instead she did more damage to herself and especially to you. It's a wonder you can even function." She raises her eyebrows. "'The flower poking through the rubble.'

I feel tears stinging my eyes and look away, back to the musician setting up. "I think I expected him to leave--one way or another. Or to be taken away."

"It makes sense, you thinking that way. There was your dad, then the first step-dad—" John. Nice, hard-working All-American sort of guy. Not really the intellectual-type, but he taught me to fish and we watched a lot of sports together. Then poof, gone as soon as my mom decided she didn't need him. "Then Will went MIA the first time. Then your grandpa when he got sick--Then Will again."

I wish she'd stop.

"Then there was that loser guy from your first job—"

My stomach twists. Jerry. Eased the pain slightly after Will told me I didn't qualify for girlfriend status with office pranks and sexually-charged flirtations. I preferred the harmless antics, but the innuendos didn't seem optional, nor did the nickname "Jailbait." Never mind the fact that he was eleven years older and had nothing in common with a teenager, except for the discovery that he was engaged to one. She was nineteen, lived cross-country and they met online. This hadn't stopped him from having me to his townhouse when I was revved up about Ray calling me to report on my mother's most recent antics. According to Ray, she was suicidal and he didn't know what to do with her. He told me I needed to reach out to her. If something happened essentially it was on me. I had tried to reach her and she had gone on about how she thought he was having an affair, but had dismissed any concern about her as nonsense.

I didn't share the details, but I was clearly upset about it. Jerry made light of it. Actually, he seemed to care very little about it. As I recall, he brushed it off as "family drama," like it was common and uninteresting, then started talking about his own. He never did like to be outdone.

He served me a shot of a mystery liquor to "calm my nerves." The liquid scorched my throat to the point of making me gag. This entertained him. He had me chase them with sips of another drink that didn't taste any better--like mouthwash. As my senses rapidly faded and I told him I wasn't feeling well, he pushed his index finger against my lips to quiet me. My heart was pounding, inflated in my chest, and my brain felt shaken and disoriented. I could not piece together the actions it would take to even stand up. My last thought before I blacked out was that I felt like I was going to die.

"You didn't do anything with that guy, did you?"

She had never met him. I had been embarrassed when I had started talking with him outside of work because he was so much older and I thought she'd think he was creepy. She would have been right--so she had never met him and I had never told her about that night.

I've only told one person about it.

It wasn't long after Katie's wedding when I had woken from a nightmare and Will was there. The nightmare was essentially just reliving the flashes of consciousness I had that night at the townhouse. Finding I had been tied to the bed. My body flopping around like a rag doll. Jerry hissing in my ear: "At least I got to go somewhere Will hasn't." Because we had waited. Because Will knew I wasn't ready.

When I woke the next day, my wrists were sore and I found my body had been washed with ocean breeze soap, something I would never have used. I later discovered bruises where his hands had gripped my breasts, my arms. My fingernails felt raw and sore--two nails had been bent backwards.

He was dressed and on his computer in his bedroom when I woke. He immediately pressured me to leave, saying he had a meeting. He acted judgmental of my "behavior" as though I had initiated it and he had no choice but to participate. He wondered aloud what he would tell his fiancee. I shamefully got dressed and left.

Will had listened to me telling him how I never meant to do anything. I had thought we were friends of some kind, I was insecure and wanted someone to talk to. I thought we were just hanging out together. We were going to watch a movie. I didn't know how alcohol would affect me. I didn't want to let myself off the hook so I had told him I was naive to be so trusting, but Will stopped me. He was gentle in his words as he told me that it wasn't my fault, but I could sense the tension in his body growing. I didn't mean to tell him what Jerry had said about him, but the words escaped and he retracted suddenly. "He said *what?*" he had asked as calmly as he could manage.

"I wish we had," I said, my stomach clenched and tears streaming from my eyes. With a pained expression, he pulled me to him, held me long after I fell asleep.

After I've told Katie, she's speechless for a moment. "You never told me that," she says quietly.

"I was embarrassed."

"Why were you embarrassed?"

"I was *so* stupid."

"Maggie, why didn't you turn him in?" She sits up straighter, her eyes wide. "He probably drugged you. You were only 17--"

"He claimed I begged for it. He said no one would believe me."

She shakes her head. "He *washed* you?"

"No evidence," I point out. "I could have been with anyone."

"That sick son of a--"

The patio door flings open, but it's just wait staff bringing around candles and salt and pepper dispensers for the tables.

"Was he your--I mean, you hadn't with Will--"

I nod, trying not to process that too deeply. During the time Will and I dated, we had found ourselves in the thrall of passion and I had the sense he wanted to go further, but he would reel himself back, tell me he wanted us to wait. He wanted it to be right for me. For us. Back then I sort of interpreted this as something being wrong with me, something that made me easier to resist...as opposed to him respecting me.

She takes a breath. "No wonder Will put him in the hospital."

"What?" My chest is tight.

"Will. He told me not to tell you. I'm sorry. I just thought it was a jealousy thing with his anger."

"He beat him up?"

"Uh *yeah.*"

"When was this?"

"After he got back. Summertime. Last July, I think? It was just before Trevor turned two. Will tracked Jerry down at a bar, beat the hell out of him."

After the cemetery. "He could have gone to jail for that."

"Just a night. The officer was sympathetic--Tim told him he has just come back from a war zone, he had PTS, which was true. He had already been in a program so that made for an easier defense."

"Tim was there?"

"He flew down after he was arrested. He was his defense lawyer. He did well--Will took a plea deal, charges were reduced, he got community service. Jerry tried to drop all charges when he found out who attacked him, but the prosecutor had to proceed considering what he did to that guy."

"It was that bad?"

"Concussion, broken jaw, and I'm pretty sure his penis is just ornamental now."

I don't want to think of Jerry and his pointed features, wire rectangular glasses, permanent smirk, but the image alters and I can see him sprawled on the ground, face beaten to a pulp. "And Will just got community service?"

"Tim's really good. Plus Will truly did have PTS. Luckily a pilot friend of his got him into some support groups and he started dealing with things more constructively. That also didn't hurt his case."

The guitarist has started his set so I have an excuse to gaze off in the distance.

"That's how he got his dog." Katie runs her fingers through her wavy brown hair, which has been its natural darker color since she got pregnant with Trevor. "For community service, he worked with a group that helps match dogs with returning soldiers to help them adapt to civilian life."

I shake my head. "I should have been there for him."

"You can't change the past."

"I'm an idiot."

"Hey—" Katie says, and in one long movement, she's at my side. She wraps her arms around me, squeezes. "I love you, Maggie. *So* much and I am so sorry for all of it."

"Katie, I don't deserve him," I blurt out. "I mean, I can't give him what he deserves. I can't have children. No adoption agency is going to consider me."

"I don't want to tell you what to do about Will," she says, taking her seat. "But?"

"But it broke my heart the first time around when things ended and it's going to break it again if you don't at least try to be with him now."

"I know you're just looking out for me--"

"And for another thing," she says, fired up again. "No woman knows if she can actually have kids until she starts trying. If he wound up with someone else, they might never be able to have kids, either. I could have been infertile, but Tim didn't know that. He took a risk."

"But Katie, what if you knew going in that you couldn't have children and adoption was out because of, say, your drinking problem."

"I don't have a drinking problem, per say, but –" She gives it some thought. "I wouldn't dump him because of it. It would be up to him to decide if it's something he could live with—or without."

"And if he said he was okay with it at the time? What's to stop him from changing his mind later and completely resenting you for it for the rest of your lives?" I'm mentally drained as we let the sound of the guitar fill the space between us. "So do we have the character breakfast tomorrow or the next day?"

"Is that your hint that you don't want to talk anymore?"

"You're perceptive."

She exhaled, taking a sip of her water. "You're afraid. I don't blame you considering what you've been through. Your mother taught you that people lie. People leave. You can't believe Will would love you if you can't be perfect because your mother rejected you as her daughter and denied you her love if you did anything wrong or that she disagreed with. You were taught that love is conditional."

I swallow hard, nod abruptly.

"And *another* thing--you're making Will's decision for him. You're acting like he has this amazing girl just waiting in the wings who is guaranteed to bear children *and* you're presuming that's what he wants. Let *him* decide what he wants and what will really make him happy. Spoiler: it's you. But *you?* You need to do some soul searching and figure out what you want. What will make *you* happy."

I'm about to croak out a response, but she's on a roll:

"You're not perfect. No one is. But imperfect Maggie is one of the best people I know. Will had his shortcomings early on. He didn't trust himself not to screw things up so he went ahead and screwed them up. He had good intentions, but it just—he screwed up. Big time."

I clear my throat.

"Will loves you."

"I'm so afraid of something bad happening if I'm happy."

"Bad things have happened when you're unhappy, too," she points out.

Jerry. The babies. Cancer.

I frown, my brain's theory blown to bits.

She wants to make a stronger case, but stops short, grabs a tortilla chip, ponders consuming it. She can't bring herself to eat it, though.

I try to think of something to say. Something positive. Some weak commentary about a silver lining. "Leave it to us to have the most depressing therapy session at the happiest frickin' place on Earth."

"I love you, Maggie," she says with an arched eyebrow. She plunges the chip into the dip and I follow suit. I have the chip at maximum dip capacity when I sense her staring at me. "I mean it, I love you."

I tap our chips together. "I know. I love you, too."

***

I opted to get my own room, rather than bunking with the preschooler, figuring I'll need the rest. I thought of going across the street and saving a few hundred per night, but my body was so tired, my brain so drained, that I was desperate to take as few steps as possible. Katie had gone off to catch the late fireworks show and I left my suitcase by the bathroom in favor of pulling back the comforter and burrowing into the cool mattress.

Thinking of that night at Jerry's has cast a cloud over me. I tried calling Will, but they're probably out of range. It went straight to voicemail and I didn't want to leave a message. The loneliness I felt the morning after in that cold townhouse starts to gain traction on my thoughts. I could let it consume me. Instead I start combatting it. Every time I hear the echo of Jerry's words in my head, I tell myself that he was weak. I am stronger. My mother's voice takes over and I can see the look of disgust on her face. I push her voice away and try replacing her presence with the image of my dad, calm, patient, and free-spirited.

This doesn't work for long.

I take a deep breath and I visualize sailing. The vast horizon. The cool breeze. The open sky. The water lapping against the boat.

I can't hear her. I can't see her. Only ocean.

I stand at the helm with the wind whipping my hair in a gloriously disheveled way. My skin is tan and warm in the brilliant mid-morning sun. I am free.

The voices, in all their different variations, are silent.

It's just me and the sea.

***

My phone rings some time later and as I go to answer it, I see it's only slightly after eight and I've already slept for an hour. It feels like 10.

"Well if it isn't my rugged outdoorsman."

"Should I grow a beard?"

"I don't know. Actually, no, not if it means it'll hide that dimple of yours."

I can hear him smile. "Are you OK? I've been worried about you—I tried calling earlier."

"Yeah, I forgot my phone earlier. I had a rough night."

"What happened?"

"I think I had an anxiety attack. I took sleeping pills to calm myself down just before you called so I wasn't exactly with it. They helped though."

"I should have stayed, Reeves," he sighs. "You've been doing better today?"

"Better. I was still a little iffy this morning, but I'm better now."

"Well that's good. Those aren't easy to deal with."

Something eases in me—because he knows. Because he understands.

"Talking to Katie helped, too. She said I was overdue for a panic attack so she's not at all concerned."

"I wish one of us could be there with you in person."

"Oh—well—I'm in Anaheim. Tim's family is having a reunion and Katie invited me up." I subconsciously cringe, bracing for judgement. *He's not Nathan.*

"Oh please tell me you got a Minnie ears headband to wear. With your pixie cut and soft features, it would be such an adorable combination."

I grin. "Not yet. Just got here this afternoon."

"Ah. Well tomorrow then."

"How's your trip?"

"Too soon to tell."

"Did you get to hike much today?"

"In a manner of speaking."

"I feel like you're being deliberately vague."

"Well there will probably be three mountains to tackle tomorrow."

"Ambitious."

"Unless one is being refurbished."

"Refurbished? What--" *Space, Splash, Thunder.* "William Harrison Mercer."

"Yes?" He says loudly so his voice bellows against the thick door.

I march over and peek through the peephole before opening the door. He's standing there with a playful smile. I pause, taking deep breaths, then open it slowly. "You're supposed to be in Oregon. Mat Kearney sings obsessively about it--there must be a reason."

"Maybe I'll go on the next trip. I'd rather be with you." He furrows his eyebrows and suppresses a laugh.

"What?"

"Your hair is long enough for you to have bed head."

I roll my eyes, but if I look half as disheveled as I feel, it's probably pretty comical. "I took a power nap in preparation for bedtime, thank you."

"You sure you're alright?" He asks, stepping into my personal bubble, his fingers on my cheek.

I push up on my tiptoes to kiss him. "I'm fine."

"Good," he says conclusively, "because we need to gear up."

"Come again?"

He steps covertly past me, lowers his voice. "Katie's story can be that she happened to run into us. I saw some people in those alien green shirts downstairs--not sure we want to be flagged down by them regularly--or confused for being related to them."

He's right about the relatives. I rode down in the elevator with a couple wearing said shirts.

"Let's get some Mouse gear that's a bit more our style, shall we?"

The night air is chilly and smells rich with aromas from nearby restaurants. Will's warm hand clutches mine gently, the heat spreading into my arm. I yawn involuntarily as we near the super sized souvenir shop.

"Sorry, I'm hoping my energy surge kicks in tomorrow."

"I'll make it a short outing."

"No. I would love to stay out all night--"

"Easy, Reeves. Disneyland is a marathon, not a sprint."

The store isn't too full since the night shows haven't started yet. Most people are either still in the parks or lined up outside trying to get a view over the buildings and trees. We browse hats first. He quickly finds the plush Minnie ears headband he had been picturing for me, complete with red and white bow. After a little deliberation, he winds up with a distressed, collegiate Disneyland baseball cap.

I move in close to him. "But if you wear that, I can't do this," I say, combing my fingers through his thick, short hair. It's come in darker and with a bit of a wave to it since ending chemo.

He closes his eyes, smiling indulgently and leaning into my fingers. "Oh this I enjoy. How could I have forgotten *this*?"

"You had a buzz cut--a little more difficult to run my fingers through."

His eyes open and he gazes at me momentarily before resuming shopping. Suddenly, I'm struck by the information Katie shared earlier. To think of what he went through a year ago, knowing it's been nearly two years since Ramstein, and now we're shopping together at Disneyland? It's all very surreal. So against the odds.

He glances up a couple of times as he searches for his size in a rack of raglan shirts. He holds it up and raises an eyebrow. "How do I look?" He asks in a deep smooth voice I suspect is a character from a movie I don't know.

"You make that look good, Mercer."

He grins, placing it in the shopping bag. "Well alright, alright."

I don't want to think of all the bad memories, not in this setting, but I can't help it. Jerry dehumanized me and I was haunted by that demon. Will essentially castrated him. I want to thank him for, as much as he could, standing guard. For loving me through it all. For waiting. For being here now.

"Here's one for you," he says and looks up, but I'm already moving toward him. He immediately drops the shopping bag and shirt he was holding so he can accommodate me in his arms. He wraps both arms securely around me, exhaling deeply.

"I love you, Will."

He squeezes gently, breathing deeply into my hair. "'You have bewitched me body and soul, and I love, I love, I love you.'"

"You're whispering Jane Austen quotes to me in the middle of World of Disney?"

He pulls back slightly. "I am."

"You're speaking my language, Mercer."

Will smiles. "So tell me, Reeves," he begins in a soft voice, "do you think it will be strange if I call you by your maiden name after I marry you?"

Breathe. "Well I was hoping 'Your Majesty' would catch on."

He laughs. "What about 'Supreme Leader'?"

"You can't go from Mr. Darcy quotes to calling me Supreme Leader, Mercer."

He sighs, leaning close to my ear. "Marry me?"

There's a solid few seconds of silence and then fireworks start booming outside and he leans just far enough so he can see my face, the tears streaming from my eyes.

"Oh don't make me hum the *Twilight* song to cheer you up."

I laugh, trying to slow my breathing. "No, I'm happy. These are happy tears."

He smiles knowingly.

"OK, this quote is from the Academy Award winning screenplay and not an actual literary reference—" He clears his throat and when he speaks again, he has a remarkably believable British accent: "I-I've come here with no expectations, only to profess, now that I am at liberty to do so, that my heart is, and always will be, yours."

I lift my chin to look at him, sure my face is blotchy and puffy at best.

"Marry me?"

"Yes." I smile wider and he mirrors my expression, his hands gently holding my face. "Yes, yes, yes—" And I kiss him.

***

"And then we went to checkout," I conclude, standing in the entrance line the following morning, waiting for the park to open. Katie had been smothering

Trevor's face with sunblock when Tim spotted the ring on my finger. Now Trevor is finding entertainment value in the planter, trying to balance on the railing, his face unevenly smeared white.

"Well we shopped a little more," Will corrects.

"Yeah we found a few more shirts and then we checked out."

"The sales clerks didn't notice there was a marriage proposal in the middle of the store?"

"The fireworks were going on so everyone was distracted." It was almost comical how oblivious the rest of the world seemed to be to our moment.

"What timing with the fireworks—very romantic," Katie offers.

"I honestly didn't pay much attention," I say.

Her shoulders sink.

"Are you disappointed in our proposal story, Katie?" Will teases. "You always have our airport one to fall back on."

"Don't say that," I say, frowning. "I love our story. We had our own little moment in the middle of chaos. It was perfect."

"'Perfect' is a tough word to live up to," he says with a grin.

"It's the right one."

He kisses the back of my fingers.

"Gates are opening," Tim points out. "Should we get Trevor loaded in the stroller?"

Katie peels Trevor off the railing and Will takes the opportunity to nudge me. "Did you not like Heathrow?"

"I loved it."

"But it wasn't private. People applauded."

"In that situation—the anticipation to see you, the dramatic build up—it was 'very cinematic and emotionally satisfying to have had that moment.'"

He raises an eyebrow as we move forward in line at Katie's insistence. The woman is serious about line efficiency and based on the expression on her face, she does not trust the party behind us not to try to cut ahead.

"Heathrow was perfect *then*."

"And last night?"

"There are children present, William."

"The proposal," he says, smirking.

"Well *you* proposed. Why did *you* choose that moment?"

"It felt like you and me."

"Exactly."

"I suppose the retail location was a little unconventional."

"It didn't matter. We could have been standing at the Eiffel Tower, or in a country you don't dislike so intensely, and it wouldn't have made it any better. It was us. I love us."

He hands me my ticket to give to the cast member, who has me pose for an ID photo. She is very cheery and helpful, making sure we have all the maps and showtime schedules. I can feel this raising Katie's blood pressure.

"She's stressed about my family," Tim explains as he makes it through the turnstile. He hands her a coffee tumbler. "Sip your coffee, Dear."

"Do you know where everyone is going first?" She mumbles something about "disarray" as she stuffs the diaper bag under the stroller. "How on earth do you coordinate 60 people with Fastpasses, showtimes, nap schedules?"

"Sip your coffee."

"Fine, here I'll take a sip—" she begins, then stops short. "*Ohhh*, this is nice."

"Say 'Thank you, Husband.'"

"Thank you, Husband."

Tim smirks as he pushes the stroller forward. "I made her coffee heavy on the Irish."

Katie suddenly seems much more relaxed, nursing her coffee as we stroll down Main Street. "Oh I didn't get a good look at the ring," she says as we reach a standstill at the end of Main Street waiting for rope drop.

One detail I'll always remember about our post-engagement evening is that we held hands—back through the hotel, exchanging disbelieving looks, making love in the crisp white sheets that had been re-done and turned down while we were out—our fingers were almost always entwined. Finally, Will got up to use the bathroom and I nestled into the pillows. Despite the excitement, I found it impossible to stay awake. I was sleeping by the time he returned.

This morning, greeted by the sun through the sheer curtains, I found we were turned sideways toward one another, our hands clasped again, his face positioned where it looked as though he had just kissed my knuckles.

His eyes opened and seemed to smile at me. "So my proposal wasn't official."

My brain was having a challenge interpreting this, wondering if this was a cruel takeback?

"Seems it's customary for the man to give his future bride a ring."

"Is that right?" My heart flipped thinking of seeing my old solitaire engagement ring, if it might drudge up the feeling I had when I left it for him at the Ramstein base, but what he revealed was something unexpected.

"I took the diamond from your old ring and had it re-set."

The new setting was a vintage ring with a shimmery band of intricate scrolls and encased the cushion cut solitaire in a halo of diamonds. He explained how he thought I might like the band with tiny aquamarine stones mixed with the diamonds, that it reminded him of the ocean. Gazing at it, I had felt the calm that rushes over me when I take the boat out, standing at the helm, the wind in my face, the sun on my shoulders.

Katie immediately looked up at me when she saw the ring. "That is gorgeous," she says, choking a bit on her coffee. "It's very you.." She holds my hand up for Tim, who smiles politely, uninterested in jewelry, then continues chatting with another dad. "You did well, Will."

He nods, eyeing me.

"When did you have it made?" Katie asks, her voice deliberate.

I straighten up a bit. *Good question.*

Will squints at her and she sips her coffee, grinning sweetly. She knows.

"Two weeks ago."

"After the ER visit?" I ask.

He smiles slightly.

"You thought I was--"

Katie clears her throat.

"You knew?" I demand of him.

"I know *you*."

He knows my expressions. He knows I would never have let him kiss me, would have never gone back to the boat with him if I was still married.

"That's just when you picked up the ring though, wasn't it?"

I look back and forth between them. Katie looks slightly amused. Will looks neutral, but perhaps a little unnerved by her outing him.

"I told them to stop conspiring," Tim chimes in.

I turn directly to Will, putting my back to Katie. "*When*? When did you know?"

He sighs. "When you went 'home.'"

"When I went home," I repeat slowly. *The boat. When I moved out to the boat. In July.*

The crowd starts moving toward the castle so I face forward again, flow with traffic.

"Peter Pan," Katie calls over to us. "Straight through the castle."

We don't say anything as we speed walk through the park, random people cutting across the path in front of us. By the time we reach the attraction, there's a short line, but Katie and Tim manage to sweep both kids from the stroller and veer it blindly toward a planter. We practically walk right on. Will helps me into our own pirate ship and as they lower the waist bar, he kisses the side of my head.

"'Get out of my head, Will Mercer,'" I say, in the same tone as that day back in July, but I'm suppressing a smile.

He sees it. "I love you, too, Reeves."

"Yeah, okay," I say and kiss him back.

And we're off to NeverLand.

20
farewell, hello, farewell, hello

There's a small bakery near home that makes a fantastic chocolate croissant. In just the past few weeks, it's become a once or twice a week ritual, an incentive to get out and get a bit of exercise. Although I'm fairly certain the hollow nutritional contents cancel out much of the good of the walking, it's a pleasant outing for Bruce and me. There's a cozy, modernly small town feel to the place. Everything is fresh. They have stacks of board games available for use. The music is approachable. Dogs are welcome, inside or out.

I hope this encounter with my mother doesn't forever spoil the place.

Bruce senses the tension in how I carry the leash, the stiffness in our walk, and nudges my arm as we step inside.

She's sitting at the very first table and tries not to act surprised or intimidated when she sees the large dog at my side. "You brought a friend."

Having resolved to be tactful, I resist the urge to respond with a snippy remark. I instead motion to the registers. "I'm going to go grab a drink before I sit down," I say calmly. I order one of their smoothies and return to the table. I choose the seat across from her, situate Bruce beside me, and neatly fold the receipt.

"You look pretty with your hair grown in."

I perk my eyebrows a bit. "Thanks. You, too."

She frowns, confused by the statement. "So. You're doing okay then?"

"Yes."

"Health-wise? Is everything--"

"Clear for now."

Her face lights up. "See? Now you can still live a normal life."

My smoothie arrives. I jab a biodegradable straw into the lid, the paper straws the only fault I can find in the place, and take a long swig. "Normal?"

"Well, you know—marriage, kids." She eyes the ring on my hand. I'm not one for showy jewelry, but in the moment, I'm glad it's as impressive looking as it is.

"You know, some people live a 'normal' life without either of those things."

"Oh, I know, I know. But at least you have the chance—for kids, I mean. I know it didn't work out with Nathan, but I'm so glad he decided on the more conservative surgery."

I sip my drink to fill the silence.

"I know you've always wanted children," she further clarifies. "At least now you'll have the chance. Ray and I convinced him it was the best option."

And there we have it. "You and Ray convinced him."

"Someone had to advocate your best interests."

"To be able to have children."

"Yes. And now you can." She looks intolerably pleased with herself, prepared to be showered with gratitude.

"How *is* Ray?"

She's startled by the question. "He's good. He would have come, but I thought it should just be us today."

I nod. "So you two worked things out then."

She waves her hand. "Oh of course."

She sheepishly straightens her unused napkin. I observe her with emotional neutrality. "He cares so much for you. He's been such a good dad."

I ponder her statement. "In what way do you think he's shined the most—as a dad?"

She narrows her eyes. "Well, he was there for school functions, graduation, dinners."

I nod again, scratch Bruce behind the ears. He leans into my hand, tipping onto his side.

"I'm surprised a restaurant lets dogs inside."

"His name is Bruce."

"Pardon?"

"My dog. His name is Bruce."

"Ah. He's what? A pitbull?"

"Common misconception," I say, casually, indulging Bruce in a tummy scratch. "He's an American Bulldog, pulled from a shelter as a puppy. There's a group that trains shelter dogs to be companion animals for Veterans with PTS."

She eyes Bruce, increasingly offended by his presence. "Don't you mean PTSD?"

"No. PTS is not a mental disorder. It's an injury resulting from the experience of war. President Bush gave an interview about it."

"Potato, po-ta-toe."

"No, not really."

"So Will has PTS?"

I don't answer. Bruce has stood up and I kiss the top of his head.

"People with that can be violent."

I shrug. "Having your friends blown up by a roadside bomb isn't something you just get over."

"So you're with Will again." She sounds disgusted, like it's a bad habit I just can't seem to break.

"I am," I answer, picking up my smoothie cup. It's then her freshly brewed tea is delivered. We sit in silence—me with my muddy-colored smoothie and her with iced raspberry tea.

She scowls at my drink. "That doesn't seem like something you'd get."

She has a point, but I don't like the implication she's making. "I thought you'd be pleased that I get my fruits and vegetables. All my recommended servings in one cup."

"Of course now you'll eat them. Will's influence?"

I take a breath, scan the windows and the nearly cloudless sky. "Gosh it's a beautiful day outside."

"I came to tell you that I was in an accident," she blurts out. She pauses, as though to let me process. "Nothing serious, but the first thing that came to mind when I thought I was going to die was you. I feel terrible about what happened, that things became so bad between us."

That explains the wrist brace. I thought you were going bowling. "I'm glad you're okay."

Her eyes brighten by a shade.

"So what do *you* think happened? What made things so bad?"

She waves off the question. I make a mental note to decrease my frequency of using that gesture. "I know you and I had a sticky moment at the doctor's office but I do want to be a part of your life."

Sticky. Moment.

"I mishandled things."

No, you handled things.

"All I've ever wanted is to protect you."

I lift my chin. "I'll accept that you think that's true."

"It is true. But when I see my daughter driving *off a cliff,*" she says, hand flailing with nondescript gestures that lead my eyes dramatically to the floor, "how can you expect me, as your mother, not to do anything?"

"Define 'cliff'."

"A mistake."

"Define 'mistake'."

She's getting frustrated. I'm not easy to herd like I was in the past. "I know you think you loved him."

I rake my fingers through my short, cropped hair. I'm still not used to the presence of hair. Most times I expect to feel one of several soft, knit beanies hugging my scalp.

"Fine, *love* him. We can agree to disagree that he's right for you. He's never looked out for you. He's always been so selfish."

I tilt my head to the side. "Agree to disagree. Why are you here?"

She sighs, stirs Splenda (which she brought along with her) into her tea, which I believe is already sweetened with good old-fashioned sugar, and replaces her lid. I anticipate that when she takes a sip, she'll be disgusted. "I want a relationship with my daughter."

"And what does that look like to you?"

Yes, she hates both her pre-sweetened tea and the fact that I'm not buckling. That I'm challenging her. "We spend time together, we talk on the phone—it's not right that we don't speak. I'm your mother for heaven's sake."

I nod. "If you had died instead of Dad--"

"What if *I* had died? Is that what you wish had happened? You wish your own mother dead?"

"Actually I wish my own dad alive." I let those words sink in, take a swig of smoothie. It's one of the best I've had and for a moment, I ponder what they've done differently. It's icy and thick and just the right combination of fruit, but the paper straw they've provided is now starting to disintegrate. Luckily I know to grab extras so I swap out for a new one. This calmness confuses her and she's silently stunned watching me examine my cup. I sit straighter. " 'If you had died instead of Dad,' how would you have wanted him to raise me? Would it have been okay if he had pretended most of the time like you never existed and forbid me from so much as displaying your picture?"

She glances around at our surroundings.

"Would you have wanted him to force new moms upon me? Would you have wanted him to go break up a marriage? Would you have wanted him to control me, try to make me cower to him?"

She looks older to me than the last time I saw her. I see the crow's feet around her eyes, the thin lines of her lips, her teased, colored hair, which serves to hide the fact that her hair is thinning. Her age seems particularly bizarre in this moment because she's scowling like a teenager who got caught with cigarettes in her purse.

"You loved him, didn't you? My dad?"

"Yes," she spits, sixteen and bitter.

"That's a big deal, to lose the man you love. Especially when you have a child."

She frowns.

"You never dealt with it—losing him."

Probably assessing that she's being let off the hook, she shrugs. "Probably not."

I nod. My phone vibrates in my back pocket.

"I just wanted everything to be perfect for you."

I try that explanation on for size. "I'd like to believe that's true, but I don't. The fact is that you lost your husband. Well, I lost my dad. You may not have wanted to talk about him or think of him, but I did. I needed to. You were my mother, it was your job to be okay for me, no matter what that took. It was your job to get me through living without him. It was your job to tell me about him."

"I'll tell you anything you want to know."

"No, I don't want to hear about him from you. What reason have you given me to believe a word you say?

It looks like I've smacked her. "You're right, I'm a bad mother--"

I shake my head, but not because I disagree with what she's just said. I pull my cell phone from my back pocket, read the text that's just come through: "*People ask me why I walk around looking like this:*" There's a photo beneath of a chimpanzee with a huge gaping smile. "*I tell them it's because you're in my world.*" Then: "*That said, they'd like formal apologies. Apparently my happiness is 'obnoxious.'*"

She's curious about my text. "Well I'm sure you'll be a much better mother than me. Thanks to me, you still have a chance to *have* children."

"Thanks to you," I repeat softly, then sigh, wanting to get my words right. "When my dad died, Will made me smile again. He told me it was OK to not be OK.

"When my mom and stepdad got into drunken screaming matches, Will was there, in my room, holding me, hearing what I heard."

Her cheeks redden.

"When I woke after re-living the night I was raped and confessed for the first time what happened, Will was there to tell me it wasn't my fault.

"In the midst of dealing with the trauma of watching his friend die, Will found out I had believed the most mean-spirited lie about him, that I was with someone else, pregnant with another man's children. He should have been angry with me, moved on, but what did this 'selfish' man do? He tracked down the man who raped me and beat him to a pulp." I shrug. "He shouldn't have done that, but I can't honestly say that it didn't bring me some closure."

Her eyes are wide, disbelieving.

"When my babies died, he went to see them. *Nathan* refused to even look at them and told me they weren't human. *Will* told me they were beautiful.

"And when I collapsed in fear and sadness and terror that I might actually die at 22 from cancer, Will was there."

She purses her lips, assesses the placement of her napkin and her drink cup.

"My happiest moments are with Will. I feel free when I'm with Will."

She narrows her eyes.

I take a deep breath, glance once to Bruce, then let my eyes shift over to the ring on my left hand. "I forgive you, Mom."

And then, silence. I don't move. She doesn't move. Even Bruce seems unsure of what to make of the scene. A young mother walks inside with a baby sleeping in a wrap. She kisses the soft dark fuzz atop the baby's head, her hands braced around the infant's body. I smile kindly to her then return my attention to my mother, who is sitting relentlessly rigid across the table.

There's a methodical, calm way to how she gathers up her handbag, cup, and napkin, walks toward the door, and passes through it.

***

It really is a beautiful day outside. It's unseasonably warm for November, the sky a deep blue, the leaves rich and vibrant. Our trees don't experience seasons, but the leaves seem to be darker this time of year. Bruce and I had stopped by a hamburger lunch spot, where I treated him to a plain cheeseburger, eaten in two chomps, so he's in an especially cheerful mood. The road home has a couple of challenging hills so I take them slowly since I haven't built up my endurance yet, taking in the sights and sounds of the nearby park. There's a mom's fitness group making laps with their double-wide jogging strollers. The playground is occupied by a few younger children, not yet school age. There's a dog park at the far end, which occasionally gets Bruce's attention. He whimpers lightly and I assure him that we'll visit tonight after Will gets home, or sometime tomorrow. I continue on, telling him about going out to the marina over the weekend if it isn't terribly cold. Then I cover the afternoon's events--I have paperwork and bills to do so he can nap, I share my plans to make coffee, to do some pilates--and oh, wouldn't the backyard be lovely for that?

At the neighborhood entrance, the retired firefighter who owns the end house, is out on the ladder putting up Christmas lights. The neighborhood is filled with midcentury ranch style houses at varying levels of remodel. He just finished painting the entire exterior white and installed industrial looking light fixtures, but I gathered the roof would be after the new year, as he was attaching lights to the faded brown shingles. He waves at me.

"Can you believe this weather?" he calls.

"I love it. I hope it sticks around. Front door looks great!" The fresh red paint gleams in the sunshine.

"Festive huh? Have a good one!"

The simplicity of the moment fills me with a calm I haven't experienced for a long time, if ever. I'm experiencing everything with such intensity, but through a new filter—the colors are more saturated, the sounds kinder to my ears, the smells comforting. It amazes me how quickly I acclimated to this new life, this new reality.

As we near the house, Bruce starts to tug a bit more. I see the garage door is open and the sight of Will's old truck parked beside my old Jeep is a sweet, sweet sight to behold. He steps from the storage shed, just to the left of the house, carrying a large green storage tote. He smiles immediately upon seeing us, places the bin on a stack just inside the garage.

I release Bruce from the leash and he takes off running toward Will, but continues on through the garage and into the house, probably to check to see if someone refilled his food bowl while we were away.

"What'cha doing?" I say casually.

"It's only 5 weeks until Christmas--time to decorate." He steps toward me and gently kisses me. He pauses after our lips part, taking in the details of my face. Something in my expression satisfies him enough to take a step back, motioning to the storage totes. "I'm afraid the contents of these bins will not create the winter wonderland I've envisioned."

I lean my head into his chest, hugging him sideways. "We should watch *Christmas Vacation* tonight."

"I think that's an excellent plan, but first, care to join me for a romantic outing to Home Depot?" His eyebrows jump flirtatiously. "I'll buy us amazing takeout on the way home."

"Ask me in Italian."

He squints as he speaks. "Amore mio, ti piacerebbe unirti a me in un viaggio a Home Depot?"

I take a deep breath, inhaling the words. "Now again. In that American character."

21
everything else

I check the time and groan, resettling in bed. I partially bury my face in an unfamiliar down pillow. Across the room is the outline of a lovely flowing chiffon gown hanging in the doorway. The lightly jeweled lace top has a particularly magical shimmer in the glow of a 4 am moon. I smile at the thought of what the day will bring and readjust in the silky hotel sheets.

I had fallen back to sleep for what seemed like 90 seconds when a tiny human comes flying through the air and crashes onto the bed. "Auntie Mags, I'm going to be your ring bear today!"

"Trevor, *what* did I tell you?" Katie lectures through clenched teeth, her arms full of various shopping bags.

Trevor climbs on my back and peers down at my strained face. "Hi, Auntie Mags."

"Hi, Trevor."

"Get off the bed!" Katie exclaims, throwing her hands out. "You're going to get the bed dirty."

"Housekeeping will come by, it's not a big deal." Free from the 29 pounds on my back, I sit up on the edge of the bed.

"I'm surprised you're still asleep," Katie says, settling a few tote bags in the sitting area. She crosses the room and places her hands on either side of my face. "I am *so* excited for today." There are tears in her eyes.

"Oh don't go sappy on me so early in the day."

"I'm going to be a blubbering idiot during my toast."

"It's not a full reception. It's dinner. You don't have to do a toast."

"I am doing a toast and people will cry," she declares, moving to open the curtains.

"Well okay then."

"We brought breakfast. Tim is coming to claim your human alarm clock soon. After that I have us booked for massages and we can have a spa lunch—"

"'Spa lunch' sounds like it would involve kale and exclude meat products."

"Probably. We can go in the steam room, shower...we'll go for hair and makeup around 2:30/3, then it's *wedding* time." She says wedding in a sing-song voice several octaves above her normal pitch.

I stare. "You're being weird."

Trevor starts pressing his face against the patio sliding door, giggling wildly as he leaves blobby marks on the glass. There's a knock at the door. Apparently Tim knows better than to mess with his wife's schedule today.

"Oh thank God. Time to go torture Daddy, Trevor.'"

I wave sleepily at Tim, walking lightly toward the bathroom. "How was guys night?"

"Well, we're all either about to get married or married with kids. Nothing crazy. The stripper scene is ruined entirely when your brain starts thinking in terms of all the girls being someone's daughter."

"That's sweet, Tim," I say, splashing water on my face.

"We went and watched the hockey game at a sports bar on the beach, they had cornhole and ping pong there, we drank some beer and were in bed by 10:30. We are officially the oldest 20-something year olds on the planet."

"Please tell me Will had a good time."

"I let him win at cornhole."

"I hope he slept off *that* adrenaline rush," I chide.

"Right?"

"They're doing a koi fish feeding at 11," Katie instructs pointedly, handing Tim a tote bag.

"He's potty trained. Why do we still have a diaper bag?"

"It has activities for him. A snack. A cup. How is Zoe? Did you check on her?"

"She's fine. My mom was going to make banana nut pancakes with a pineapple strawberry fruit cup."

"Tim! Those are high allergen foods. I packed her food. Why must she deviate? She knows she can't have nuts."

"You're a little nuts," he says under his breath.

"*Tim.*"

"I'm kidding. She's following your written instructions to the letter. Zoe doesn't even know you're gone." He does a silent dramatized laugh.

"That's mean, Timothy," I say sternly.

"She misses you desperately, but she's managing."

"I'm sure they have her journaling as a coping mechanism," I add and Tim low fives me behind his back.

"Tim, koi fish. Did you hear me?"

"Trev, should we go feed the koi fish?"

"It's not for two and a half hours."

"Trev, do you want to wander around aimlessly for two and a half hours so we can feed fat goldfish?"

Trevor squeals his answer and runs for the door.

When they've gone, Katie sighs. "You could have done a kid-free wedding, but no, you wanted everyone to feel included."

"I'm a *monster.*"

***

"Don't give out on me now, Katie," I said, watching Katie's reflection as she clasps a locket onto the twine of my bouquet. It was a wedding gift from Will and contains my grandparents wedding portrait, as well as a photo of my dad giving me a ride on his shoulders in the pool when I was 5. Katie doesn't look up, but attempts to sniffle her tears away as she stores the bouquet back in the mini fridge. "I'm just so happy for the two of you."

"Tim chooses *not* to bring you spiked coffee today of all days."

Katie laughs, which only makes the crying worse.

"You'll make your mascara run."

"No this stuff is waterproof. I've been testing them."

I glance at my own reflection in the mirror. The stylist had embraced the carefree waves of my hair, and threaded tiny white orchids through the strands, creating a subtle crown.

My makeup is not overdone. A half hour of airbrushing had me concerned. I look like myself only less tired and without visible skin imperfections, and much more defining eyelashes. My thick eyebrows have filled in as well. They had disappeared with the rest of my hair and had left my expressions looking incomplete. I tried drawing them in, but they always looked cartoonish. I raise an eyebrow at myself for my own weird amusement.

Katie smiles, catching me.

"So I do have to tell you something-" I begin.

Her eyes light up. I can almost hear her instinctively say "You're pregnant!" but I also see when reality sets in that it isn't even a possibility.

"You're my family, Katie. You, your husband, your kids. You're my family—" I look up and away briefly, tears forming in my eyes. "And I have the best family in the world. So *thank you*--" My voice catches. "I've always been able to count on you--and I'll never be able to express to you how much it means to me to have you in my life." I can feel my nose burning and the tears streaming down my cheeks.

Katie's jaw drops and she dramatically waves her freshly manicured hand at her face. "Oh here we go again."

I stand up, hug her snugly.

Katie can't speak but squeezes me tighter. When we finally separate, she makes a dash for the tissue box. "I'm definitely emotional about all this, but I'm also weaning Zoe so my hormones are wacky right now."

I look at her, incredulously. "Imagine my delight. Pull yourself together, woman."

She laughs, swats at me. "Like you should talk."

I blot at my eyes, then hand her a fresh tissue. "Here, wipe your nose." I turn to give her some privacy and notice an envelope on the carpet by the door.

I'd recognize his writing on the hotel stationary, with its tall, narrow letters, anywhere.

"*My dear, sweet Reeves,*

I wasn't a religious person growing up, despite going to church most weeks. I felt like relying too much on something I couldn't see made me weak, left me vulnerable. Now, more than ever, I'm convinced that God has a plan for me. That's the "everything else" I promised to define better. God's plan and God's hand. When I veered off course, He started shaping me to be a better man, a stronger man...and He guided me to where I'm supposed to be—right next to you.

You are the sunshine that makes my world come alive and I thank God everyday for you.

Come take a walk with me.

With all my love,
Will"

"Don't get sappy so early in the day," Katie chimes, then sees my lip quivering.

"He's not coming."

"What?"

I turn away, shielding my face. "He *left*," I gasp.

"I cannot believe—God dammit, Will—"

"He said—" I stutter. "He said—" I spin back to her, smiling. "Oh I can't pull that off."

She stares at me. "You're joking."

"Yes." I hand her the letter and she clutches her chest, relieved. When she's done reading, she's fanning her eyes. Then she surveys me. "How are you not crying at this?"

I pull my bouquet from the mini fridge, roll my shoulders, and take a definitive stance aiming toward the door, like a sprinter waiting for the gunshot. "I'm ready."

"The wedding's not for twenty-five minutes."

I trudge to an arm chair and plop down in it, releasing a sigh. "*Oh*, I would like that back please," I say, reaching for the paper.

"*HOW ARE YOU NOT CRYING?*"

I fold the letter gently and tuck it back in the navy envelope. "Because I know all this. I feel it. Will proposed four and a half years ago, Katie. As far as

I'm concerned, it's about friggin' time we tie the knot. I love him. He loves me. Let's *do this*." I sit upright in my seat, click my tongue. "Is it time now?"

She grins. "Twenty-four minutes. Want me to fix your makeup?"

"Why, is the Queen here?"

Katie rolls her eyes at me.

"Actually, yes. Yes, I'd very much appreciate if I don't look like a raccoon."

24 minutes later...

I wanted simple.

Let me tell you—"simple" is a highly underrated thing. Simple can be absolutely extraordinary.

There are only eighteen people in attendance. The procession is Katie and Evan, matron of honor and best man, trailing behind Trevor and Dylan, each carrying a ring pillow, and Savannah, who is dumping the basket of orchids in heaping handfuls. From my vantage point behind the privacy hedge, meant to keep me hidden, I see Evan's son is all business, while Trevor high-fives Tim when he reaches the end of the aisle.

I carefully stroll down the grassy hillside behind the privacy hedge, following the direction of the hotel's wedding coordinator. The music is slowing and I hear a small bit of laughter—due to Trevor, I imagine. I glance down at the ground as I walk, catching peekaboo looks at my bare feet, all dressed up with a French pedicure and a pretty anklet beneath the light chiffon skirt. It was the first gown I tried on and I immediately fell in love with the lace cap sleeves, v-neck, deep plunging back.

I inhale the sweet aroma of the orchid bouquet, still cold from the refrigerator, tied at the stems with twine. The locket taps gently against my fingertips as I walk.

I remember telling Will once how I think it's a shame everyone looks at the bride when she makes her grand entrance.

He had teased: "Well some brides starve themselves for who knows how long in order to get in the gown. It just seems polite."

"True. But they're missing out. I like to look up at the groom. Seeing his reaction in that moment is more telling about the relationship."

"What if he looks terrified?"

My whispered response had been (we were sitting through the processional at his cousin's wedding): "If either has an inclination to run away, they probably shouldn't be getting married."

He raised an eyebrow. "What kind of look would you want to see? Tears? A smile? Statuesque like a palace guard?"

"Genuine," I had replied, an answer that seemed to mystify him.

The string quartet, friends of Katie, close their version of 'Can't Help Falling in Love." My cue to emerge will be the start of the next song. Since I told Will to choose the music, it's with anticipation, and a bit of anxiety that I wait for it to begin. He had teased about having them do a rendition of everything from AC/DC to Inferno.

"Here we go—" The coordinator, a young woman with red hair pulled neatly into a bun, says, disappearing behind me to straighten my dress.

The song begins. It's a solo guitarist in place of the quartet. I step forward and everything comes into view, but out of focus at the exact time. Everything except Will, twenty yards away, waiting for me at the start of the aisle. His hair is fresh and tousled. His linen suit with white button down shirt is pressed and the physique beneath it draws an appreciative look from me. His thick eyebrows jump as he watches me approach him. He mouths the lyrics: *Here comes the sun.*

He seems to be breathing in a very concentrated way. There are tears in his eyes, but there's no sadness in them.

In the next moment he takes a breath and smiles the broadest smile that his facial muscles can manage.

I stop inches from him, mirroring his expression.

"It's about friggin' time, Reeves," he says softly, grinning.

"That's what I said!" I practically shout, then clasp my hand over my mouth. I attempt to hide from our wedding guests behind his shoulder.

"They can still see you," he says toward my ear, laughing.

I take a step back. "You smell good," I say; my cheeks are impossibly tight.

Will entwines our fingers, raises my right hand to his lips and kisses my knuckles. He takes his place beside me and we continue onward, my feet grazing over the soft, velvety flowers, the cool, thick grass. The guitarist repeats the chorus as we walk the short length of the aisle.

The scene—lush tropical foliage and a distant ocean horizon, a simple wood arch, folding chairs, orchids lining the aisle, comes into focus. Savannah is disinterested and playing with her pony. Trevor is twirling his pillow. Zoe is sleeping in her carseat. Katie is ugly crying and Tim is offering his handkerchief. Chris, our pastor, my homecoming dance date, spiritual advisor extraordinaire, is standing at the end of the aisle grinning at us. He's grown a full beard since I last saw him, but has given up on growing his hair out for a man bun and has a fresh haircut. Will's dad stands tall and broad-shouldered and he smiles kindly when our eyes meet. He looks like an older version of Evan, his blonde curls tinted whiter. Will's mom is blotting at her bloodshot eyes, her neck strained trying to hold in her cries. She clasps one hand to her chest as we pass by her. Cadence is bouncing newborn daughter, Adeline Reeves Mercer, on her shoulder, lulling her back to sleep. Evan gazes at us, a look of what seems like relief on his face. At first he's watching Will—well, glaring at him, more like. Then he shifts to me and winks.

The guitar fades as we reach the altar. Chris looks back and forth between us. "Well you two couldn't be any cuter if you tried, could you?"

There's collective laughter around us.

"Maggie and Will. You stand together today to commit your lives to each other as husband and wife."

Will squeezes my hand, eyeing me.

Chris sighs. "You really want to kiss your bride, don't you?"

"I do."

"Oh, now you've gone and said 'I do' already. I mean, why am I *even here?*" He snaps the Bible shut, crosses his arms.

Trevor prompts chuckling with a three year old giggle.

"I'm kidding, go ahead." Chris reopens his Bible, looking pointedly toward me.

Will smiles, turns to face me, and starts to lean in.

"Have you lost your mind, man?" Chris exclaims and Will jolts back to place. "Get back over there!"

There's an uproar of laughter.

Chris smiles at me, then at Will, then returns to the marked page in his Bible. ""First Corinthians, chapter 13, verse 4. 'Love is patient, love is kind. It does not envy, it does not boast, it is not proud. It does not dishonor others, it is not self-seeking, it is not easily angered, it keeps no record of wrongs. Love does not delight in evil but rejoices with the truth." He slows his pace. "It always protects, always trusts, always hopes--" He pauses. "*always perseveres.*""

Will's hand tightens around mine, our arms nudged together.

"Maggie, Will—please turn and face each other."

Katie is at my side, retrieving my bouquet. I had forgotten I would be without it for this portion, but now find it difficult to be without the locket, having been advised that keeping my neck/chest free of jewelry was a better look. I gaze at the locket hanging from the twine, thinking of the photos within.

"Katie--" Will says suddenly as she starts to back away with it. He lets go of my hands and takes the bouquet, unties the locket, and clasps it around my neck, his fingers tickling my skin.

I reach up and run the locket between my fingers as he returns to his place across from me. The anxiety I had felt fades away, a peacefulness filling me. Will takes both of my hands in his.

Chris waits patiently, smiling when we finally give him our attention again. ""And now these three remain: faith, hope and love. But the greatest of these is love.""

I take a deep breath, meet Will's eyes again, my body relaxing, as though floating on a calm ocean.

"Will. Please repeat after me--I, William Harrison Mercer, take you, Meagan Olivia Reeves, to be my wedded wife."

"I, William Harrison Mercer, take you, Meagan Olivia--*Reeves*--" his voice is disbelieving, "to be my wedded wife.

To have and to hold from this day forward.

For better, for worse, for richer, for poorer-

In sickness and in health, to love and to cherish all the days of my life." He ends by roughly wiping the tears away from his eye with his thumb, then smiling broadly again.

As I say my vows, I take in the sight of Will, his broad shoulders beneath his linen suit, orchid boutonniere. I gaze at his square jaw, his single dimpled cheek, his dark hair and thick eyebrows--I gaze into his kind, brown eyes that seem to brighten whenever they see me. *Every. Single. Day.* I hear Walt say. My eyes momentarily blink over to where Walt sits in the second row of chairs with his wife. I feel my words catch in my throat, take a breath and continue: "--to love and to cherish all the days of my life."

"Where are those little men with the rings?" Chris asks, finding that Tim is making the delivery since the boys have decided to wander away to play.

I laugh, sniffle a bit. Will takes the opportunity to lean in and whisper "I love you."

When Chris returns to his centered position before us, he glares distrustfully at Will.

"I didn't kiss her yet," Will says defensively.

Chris nods, holds his open Bible with the two rings on top. They are simple bands with a subtle matching wave pattern. "Will, please take Maggie's ring and as you place it on her finger, repeat after me--'With this ring, I thee wed.' "

"With this ring, I thee wed," Will says softly, gently slipping the platinum band on my finger.

I do the same with Will's ring, enamored by the shine of the band against his tan hands.

"What God has joined, let no one separate. Maggie, *Will*, I am honored to say that by the power vested in me, I now pronounce you husband and wife. You may. Now." He does a fake out. "You may now kiss your bride."

Will moves in slower than expected, studying my face. He places a hand on either cheek and kisses me gently. Somewhere in the distance, there is music and applause. I feel tears streaming from my eyes as our lips separate. It's then that my ears pick up on the melody of his choice of recessional song:

I squint at him, questioningly, my cheeks tight.

His eyebrows jump suggestively, daring me to tease him.

"Dork," I mutter, kissing him quickly.

"Family, friends--Mr. and Mrs. Will and Maggie Mercer."

Will twirls me out, presenting me, bowing, channeling his goofy childhood self. Katie hands off my bouquet and I manage one quick glance to Will and his wide smile before I find myself being lifted and hoisted over his shoulder, laughing so hard it hurts as he takes off back up the aisle.

22
people aren't supposed to look back. i'm certainly not going to do it anymore.

F ive years later...
   She wasn't sleeping much anymore. Not at socially accepted times of day anyway. As she was becoming increasingly nocturnal, it wasn't a tremendous surprise when Will found her gently swaying the porch swing at 2am. From where he stood he could just see her bare feet propped up on the outdoor coffee table, her canine stalker, Bruce, under her legs. She was singing softly and he strained over the fountain noise to hear. It wasn't until he was just behind her that he identified the song as "Can't Help Falling in Love." The dreamy scene was illuminated by strings of globe lights, which he dimmed.

"You're going to spoil him."

"Not possible," she whispered.

He still hadn't gotten used to the image of her holding an infant. Even in the early, challenging days, there was a look of joy and contentment in her eyes, mixed with a protective edge.

They first met Abraham when he was 18 minutes old. He was small and angry, having been born addicted to heroin. He calmed when Maggie held him, but after 2 days, he screamed in agony as his tiny body was hit with withdrawal symptoms. Maggie stayed with him throughout it all and by the time he was released from the hospital, that baby was infatuated with her, hypnotized by her face, her voice.

Of course it wasn't ideal. Regular adoption was unlikely due to medical history, but fostering could be a path to adoption, especially since many couples would pass up a drug addicted baby with two older siblings who would probably be joining him. Their case worker was doubtful the mother, only 20 would fight giving up custody since she hadn't been concerned about her 5 year old and 3 year old, but she had to be given yet another chance to go through rehab. The other two were in the same foster care group home until the situation was resolved.

Abraham was nestled into Maggie's shoulder. He was becoming chunkier since starting solids. He had a section of her long dark hair clasped in his fist, while his other rested over her heart.

"You should get some sleep for tomorrow, too," Will murmured, sitting down in one of the armchairs.

"I don't think I can," she replied, her eyes filled with worry.

"What worries you the most?"

"Scenario one: we go to make the adoption official and Holly shows up. She's still clearly messed up, but demands custody of Abe."

"Won't happen."

Maggie shrugged doubtfully. "It's possible."

"This is a formality. That's what Allyson said, right?"

"That *is* what she said."

"Scenario two?"

"Tomorrow we go from a family of 3 to a family of 5 with 3 under 5."

"Are we stocked up on alcohol?"

"Will."

"Asking for a friend."

"Will--"

"At least some wine?" He waved his hand at her. "I have to go to Costco to pick up some diapers and dog food, I'll just grab a box there."

"We're going to be parents to three kids tomorrow and we haven't even met two of them. I mean, it won't be official yet for Chastity and Edward, but since we'll be official for Abe, chances are--" She processed his earlier remark and grinned. "Sparing no expense on the wine?"

"Only the best, baby." He tilted his head. "Can we talk briefly about the name 'Chastity'?"

"We can't rename her. She's not a puppy."

"I'm sure she's a dear sweet girl, but that's a *terrible* name--"

"I know."

"The irony—"

"She didn't know what the word meant. Apparently she thought it was pretty."

"That poor child."

"I think the drug addiction was worse to inflict on her baby."

"The name is forever."

"Well you have something in common with Holly." She perked her eyebrows.

"If you say we're both *Twilight* fans—"

"Oh you're right, that makes more sense for where Edward's name came from. I was thinking Edward Faris, as in *Sense & Sensibility*. You quoted him to me, you know."

"That's probably a better name association."

"Nope. I can only see a sparkly vampire now."

"At least they let us name Abe."

"People probably think it's old fashioned."

"Who cares? It's for your dad. I happen to like the name Abraham."

Maggie sighed. "Maybe Chastity likes her middle name."

"What *is* her middle name?"

"Grace."

He nodded. "*Much* better."

"What is Edward's?"

She smirked.

"*Not* the werewolf."

"No she seemed to have a Robert Pattinson crush. Cedric. Like Cedric Diggory."

He looked confused.

"*Harry Potter and the Goblet of Fire*."

"Edward works."

Her eyes were shadowed by dark circles. Abe's shrieking fits had been happening less frequently, but he was often struck with night terrors, something with addict babies having a hard time with sleep cycles. Last night had been a solid 45 minutes of him flailing around screaming with his eyes open, unable to focus on anything. The doctor said to just make sure his environment was safe for him, but not to try to wake him. It was a tough thing to experience. Maggie had tears in her eyes as she helplessly watched. Finally she started listing his favorite things. She said Bruce's name and he looked straight at her.

"What does Bruce say, Abe?" She asked. "Woof woof?"

Abe gazed at her with his doe-like brown eyes, laid his head down abruptly and fell asleep.

"These kids are so lucky to have you for their mom," Will said, leaning toward her, resting his elbows on his knees.

As was always the case, she ignored the compliment, but he could see her internalizing it, a small smile appearing on her lips. "I worry it'll be different with Chastity and Edward. We've had Abe since he was born, we named him..."

"It'll probably take a little time."

"Edward is almost 5. Chastity is 3," she said, thoughtfully.

"By 3 they're out of diapers, right?"

"Pull-Ups, maybe?" She rubbed Abe's back as he resettled. "I should put him in his crib."

"Oh he's going to wind up in the cosleeper. Just skip the unnecessary step."

"Do you think it's desperate to try to win them over by taking them to Disneyland?"

"They say it's a good bonding experience. There's plenty of entertainment, it's low pressure, as long as we don't over-do it and wind up with meltdowns--"

"And as long as they aren't terrified of the characters. I checked the crowd calendars--the busiest day is only like a 3 out of 10."

He smiled. "Of course you checked the crowd calendar."

"Allyson said Chastity loves Tinkerbell and Edward likes the *Cars* guys. Do you think their rooms are OK? I want them to be able to pick things out--they aren't too plain, are they?"

"Bed."

"Should I have done Tinkerbell for her bed? She has the flower one, which is cute, but--"

"Time for bed."

It was disconcerting when they arrived at the courthouse and Holly was waiting for them. Will saw Maggie's optimistic face morph into devastation she couldn't mask.

"You're Will and Maggie, right?" Holly asked, descending upon them immediately as they came through Security. She had dark hair with orangey red roots, freckles, protruding brown eyes, Abe's same small round nose.

Will placed his hand on Maggie's back. Abraham was in his wrap, peering across the corridor at kids playing at the drinking fountain. The little boy was trying to splash the girl, her fiery red curls bouncing as she giggled and skipped away. She tempted him to try it again, taking one step forward, then running away. "Yes. How are you, Holly?"

She sighed, nodding. "I've been going to church with my cousin and they're getting me into an addiction rehab program--I don't know--out in the woods somewhere." She glanced away and Will took in the silver stud in her nose. Her face was otherwise freshly washed. She looked more like 15, rather than 20. "I always hated that religious shit--" Her voice echoed more than she intended and she looked back at the pair of kids. "*Sorry*. This church is nice though. Normal people. They don't try to seem all goody two-shoe, holier than thou, know what I mean?"

Will nodded slowly.

Holly flinched and seemed to reset herself. "So you're all here to sign the papers, right?" She said this casually.

"That's the plan," Will said, with a slight edge of questioning.

Her face turned serious and she fidgeted with her thumb ring.

Will glanced to Maggie, who was frozen where she stood. She didn't seem to be inhaling or exhaling. He imagined Abe being pried from her arms, complicated by the design of the wrap, her unable to hold back the sobs.

"I just signed my part," she said, swallowing hard. "It was tougher than I would have thought--before."

Maggie's knees buckled slightly as she released the tension in her body and took a breath.

Holly frowned. "I guess it's not--*protocol* or whatever--to have me here. I've read your story, I know today means a lot to you. I just--I guess I needed the closure. To see you both, to see--you named him Abraham, right?"

Maggie was struggling to speak. She nodded.

"We named him Abraham, after Maggie's dad."

Holly pressed her lips together, peering in at him. Abe moved his hand more firmly onto Maggie's chest. There was something in feeling her heartbeat that soothed him. He didn't appear too certain of this new face, his eyes wide, eyebrow frowning. She tilted her head, reached through the side, touched his arm. "You love your momma, don't you?"

It wasn't clear who she was referring. Will rubbed Maggie's back, which had stiffened again.

Holly stood upright and smiled politely. "He really does love you. You can tell."

"He does," Will replied.

"I definitely don't have your maternal instincts. I'm not sure I ever will. I considered have an abortion with the first one." She said this nonchalantly, then peered over her shoulder again, lowered her voice. "I went into the clinic to have it done and I just couldn't—do you know what equipment they use? The tools and suction?"

Maggie shuddered involuntarily.

Will shook his head. "We're really glad you changed your mind."

"Well, no more pregnancies for me. I had an IUD put in. I wasn't exactly consistent about taking the pill. It's crazy--some people can have children, but would make terrible parents--some people who can't have children of their own would make the best parents." She looked back and forth between them. "Like the two of you."

Maggie suddenly stepped forward, wrapped one arm around the young woman. "Thank you for choosing us."

Holly sniffled, but seemed generally uncomfortable with hugging.

"You can visit them, once you feel--" Maggie's voice trailed off as she felt Holly shaking her head.

Holly shook her head. "No, I'm good with this. This is something I know I need to do. For them. For me. If they feel like they need to know me, okay, but--"

"If you change your mind, or want to be in contact, I can send photos--"

Will wasn't sure how he felt about this woman visiting or staying in contact.

"Photos would be nice, thanks. The social worker lady should have my email address." She took a step back. "I haven't been in contact with the older two. They wouldn't recognize me. I think it's best that it stays that way, for everyone."

Maggie swallowed hard. Her cheeks were soaked with tears.

"I do love them," Holly said, defensively. "Will you make sure they know that?"

"We will," they said in unison.

She smiled lightly at Abe. "Amazing how different they each look," she observed.

"I guess we'll see for ourselves soon," Will remarked. "They hadn't done updated photos for their files."

Holly furrowed her forehead, tilted her head toward the two kids that had been playing at the drinking fountain, then walked away.

Chastity sat on one of the benches that lined the corridor at the direction of the case worker sitting with her. She had her knees pulled up to her chest, her pale pink floral sundress stretched around her knees. She entertained herself by allowing her wild red curls to fall in her pale freckled face then forcefully blowing them away again. She giggled silently when something caught her eye across the hall. She crossed her eyes and puffed out her cheeks.

On the opposite site of the hallway, on another bench, Edward sat alone. His dark hair was long and choppy, his skin beige and smooth. He wore a plaid red button down shirt over a dinosaur t-shirt, worn in jeans, and was making glasses out of his fingers, sticking his tongue out at his sister.

All sound seemed to be vacuumed out of that hallway except their suppressed laughter.

Then came the moment when all went quiet, when they noticed the couple watching them.

Will knew Maggie had been sending them notes and photos of their brother. She had also included photos of the two of them, of Bruce.

Edward's face turned serious and uncertain. Chastity seemed more curious, craning her neck to try to see into the baby carrier before standing and slowly approaching. Maggie knelt down on the carpet instinctively.

"Is this my brother?" Chastity asked, her voice high and sweet.

"Yes. This is Abraham. We call him Abe."

She frowned, wrinkling her nose at the name, but then she looked at his face, placed a chubby hand on his soft almond skin, touched his curly hair, a dark version of her own, and smiled widely. "Abe is cute," she concluded, glancing at Edward, waving him over. Then she studied Maggie a little more closely. She reached out and touched her cheek. "You look like Princess Belle."

"She certainly reads a lot like Princess Belle," Will added, smiling kindly as he dropped to one knee, placing his hand on Maggie's back.

"And you look like Prince Eric," Chastity said suspiciously, then leaned in close to whisper: "Does Ariel know?"

"I'm more worried about *Beast*," Will whispered back, widening his eyes dramatically.

Chastity burst out in giggles. This prompted Edward to rise off the bench and start toward them. His sister retrieved him, pushing him forward. "Eddie, this is Abe."

Edward's face softened considerably upon seeing his brother. His dark eyes were large and round, his eyelashes thick. He kept them lowered, focused on Abe, who had reached out a hand toward his siblings.

Meanwhile, Chastity stood back watching everyone, tilting her head inquisitively. "So you're our Mommy and Daddy now?"

Maggie smiled. "If that's okay with you."

Chastity's face broke into a smile, one cheek shadowed by a single, prominent dimple.